DYING CONFESSION

TAKING HIS SECRETS TO THE GRAVE

DYING CONFESSION

TAKING HIS SECRETS TO THE GRAVE

PHILIP OAKLEY

PALMETTO
PUBLISHING
Charleston, SC
www.PalmettoPublishing.com

Copyright © 2024 by Philip Oakley

All rights reserved
No portion of this book may be reproduced, stored in a retrieval system, or transmitted in any form by any means–electronic, mechanical, photocopy, recording, or other–except for brief quotations in printed reviews, without prior permission of the author.

Hardcover ISBN: 979-8-8229-5294-2
Paperback ISBN: 979-8-8229-4559-3
eBook ISBN: 979-8-8229-4560-9

FORWARD

By LTG (R) Ray Palumbo
US Army (Retired)

There are few human relationships that compare to the relationship formed between people who have served their country in uniform, particularly if they served in combat. This book is the story of two "battle buddies" who, after becoming fast friends in basic training, encounter several years of life-changing experiences on and off the battlefield that cement their loyalty to one another.

Above all else, this is a story about trust and the deep love between best friends. That said, don't be fooled that this is a serious-as-a-heart-attack story about the nature of war or what happens when life circumstances go awry. Our battle buddies, Anthony and Scott, are keenly adept at taking virtually nothing seriously, even as they encounter sadistic drill sergeants, terrifying battle situations, the uncertainty of pursuing their dreams, and the fear of losing one's liberty when, in an instant, everything goes wrong. These boys have an unnerving ability to get in trouble – often – as you shall see, but they are gifted at viewing life through a comedic lens. Their "smart ass" and oh-so-competitive natures, which frequently get them into tense situations, are not only the source of their close friendship, but also a vehicle for winning over their brothers in arms and perhaps more significantly, those who attempt to lead them.

Anthony and Scott put their money where their mouths are. They are hard workers, they seek to be the best at what they do, and they have the confidence of young men with nothing to lose and everything to gain. We see them grow from reckless kids to driven young men, and we see them fall in love and strive to continue to serve their communities as police officers. One of them teaches us a lesson about trusting God to see him through the most difficult challenge of his life.

Author Phil Oakley covers a lot of human territory in this book about friendship. We've been business colleagues and close friends for over 10 years, and his witty intellect, sense of humor, compassion for others, and deep sense of friendship is reflected in every page of this book. The plot has twists and turns that keep you wondering what will come next. That's Phil in real life! There is intrigue, especially in a surprise ending, that will leave you wanting more. And while there is so much about this book that is serious, it shows us that our attitudes matter as we struggle with and celebrate all that life presents to us. I am reminded of a quote by Joseph Campbell that I love for its irreverence and real-life flavor: "As you proceed through life, following your own path, birds will shit on you. Don't bother to brush it off. Getting a comedic view of your situation gives you spiritual distance. Having a sense of humor saves you." Phil does a remarkable job of capturing this sentiment in his story. Enjoy!

CONTENTS

FORWARD	*V*
CHAPTER 1: Chance Meeting	*1*
CHAPTER 2: Gulf War, 1991	*30*
CHAPTER 3: Finishing Basic Training and AIT, May 1985	*57*
CHAPTER 4: Fort Sheridan, Illinois, June 1986	*71*
CHAPTER 5: Fort Wainwright Alaska and Bertchesgaden (Germany), August 1987	*108*
CHAPTER 6: Fort Bragg, March 1988	*124*
CHAPTER 7: Back to Iraq after losing his battle buddy, Anthony is in a fog	*156*
CHAPTER 8: Rhode Island Police Academy, December 1991	*189*
CHAPTER 9: A Hero's Day	*231*
CHAPTER 10: Surrendering	*263*
CHAPTER 11: Everyone Knows Now	*284*
CHAPTER 12: Impatiently Waiting	*309*
CHAPTER 13: Pleading Guilty	*315*
CHAPTER 14: Food, Friends, and Alcohol	*335*
CHAPTER 15	*349*
ACKNOWLEDGMENTS	*354*
PICTURE GALLERY	

CHAPTER 1

CHANCE MEETING

How do two men from vastly different parts of the Northeast manage to not only cross paths, but create their own path together?

Easy.

First, both must have screwed up enough to find themselves on an MD-11 flying to Fort McClellan, Alabama. Then, to their surprise, they must have formed a bond unbreakable even through blood, sweat, tears, and dying confessions.

Some questions never need to be asked when it's true friendship, but you ask anyway.

Would you cover for me?

Do you have my back?

Would you risk your life for me?

And lastly, and maybe the most important of all: Would you take my secrets to the grave?

In a perfect world, none of us would need these answered. But we don't live in a perfect world.

It's widely known that a brotherhood formed in combat is a brotherhood that will last forever. It is a mantra that has rung through soldiers' barracks for years. Such soldiers live by the "battle buddies" creed. No question, you are best friends. When soldiers mention their "battle buddies," they are referring to people with whom they've built unbreakable bonds, backed by promises and principles. Each would die for the other, and each knows the other would, too. Maybe both will make it out alive, and maybe they won't. But it is a certainty that if at any given moment one's life is in danger, the other's is, too.

***

After spending my entire life in the small village of Manville in Lincoln Rhode Island, I enlisted in the Army in the mid-1980s with the intent of becoming a military police officer. When I made this decision, I had no way of knowing Christopher Scott was making the same decision in his little town in upstate New York. Had either of us flown out a few days earlier or later, our paths might have never crossed. The decision to become MPs on that exact day proved to be one of the most life-changing decisions either of us would ever make—and not all those changes were for the better.

Scott and I became buddies early on in our military careers, but our bond was cemented during combat operations in the First Gulf War. Scott often talked about how aggravated he'd been with me when we first met. I, on the other hand, was pumped up. I had spent a lot of that day running through thoughts in my head. I vividly remember driving to the Military Enlisted Processing Station, or MEPS, with my closest friends from back home: Debbie, Tom, and Cheryl. MEPS was where enlistees gathered before flights to Fort McClellan and other training centers. Many turned out before I started my journey to McClellan. They stuck around with me as I waited for the departure clock to run out.

We'd been joking on the drive down, trading high school memories. They'd been poking fun, making bets on whether I'd even be able to graduate MP school, given my propensity to run my big mouth. Cheryl and Debbie got teary-eyed, which was nothing new, they were more emotional, like me. But even Tom was welling up—although he would deny it to this day. Sure, I was touched. It made me wonder if maybe I'd been more important to Tom than I had thought all that time. Maybe to others, too.

Most of my life to that point had been spent cracking jokes, never taking things too seriously. For the first time, I saw how important those jokes had become to some people. Even stoic Tom.

Once I got on the plane, my memories slowed down, and I began to take in the reality around me. Finding myself on this tiny cropduster of an aircraft with a stewardess asking, "Would you like something to drink?"

"Sure," I said. "A Coke please."

After guzzling the first plastic cup of Coke she'd handed me, I asked, "Can I have another please?"

She wasn't quick to accommodate my request. "As soon as I serve everyone else, I'll be more than happy to get you a refill," she said, loud enough for half the plane to hear.

Christopher Scott and I didn't even speak on that plane. I didn't even know he existed until I took the bottom bunk at the in-processing station at McClellan. Scott, however, had apparently formed an opinion of me quickly.

"You know, Anthony, back then, I thought you were a bit of an asshole," he later said, with that shit-eating grin of his. "But then I got to know you, and I realized you're an even bigger asshole than I imagined."

I was not shy, that's for sure. Credit for that goes to two women—my grandmother Phyliss and my mom, Sandra. Because of this, Scott liked to poke fun at my "feminine side," wondering out loud if I was cut out to wear a uniform. In the '80s, young men rarely talked about their emotions. I was different than most. When I needed to make important decisions, the facts rarely mattered as much as the feelings—a way of thinking that has gotten me into my fair share of trouble. Since then, I've learned that sometimes thinking things through is better than going with a hunch or a fleeting emotion.

Scott was the polar opposite, always slower, more methodical. He kept to himself when he needed to, and when a decision had to be made, he'd take a few days to get back to you. That asshole had to weigh every option to protect his back—which, ironically, became my job down the road. Scott was an extrovert like me, he was just better at turning it off at the right time. The differences in our ways of thinking quickly became a staple of our friendship. Good cop/bad cop.

When most young people join the military, it's not their first choice. Normally, it's their last option, a means to an end. A way to get to where they want to be without a long list of prerequisites or a fancy college education. That's how it was for Scott and me. It wasn't going to be a career for either of us—or at least we didn't think so at the time.

***

These days, Fort McClellan exists only as a reserve training base, with a couple of other government agencies occupying some of the older buildings. In the eighties, however, the base was home to the US Army Military Police School and the US Army Chemical School. It is located in Alabama, just north of Interstate 10 and just west of the border with Georgia, in the middle of nowhere, covered in thick woodland. People who have been there call it "crazy hot" and "too humid for humans." Soldiers used to joke about how if you were to look up "nowhere" in the dictionary, you'd see a picture of Fort McClellan.

We had some real characters. Private Centers was a tall, very fit guy from upstate New York. He was in his mid-20s, much older than most of the crew—a no-nonsense, "Let's get the shit done" kind of guy who seemed annoyed by the slightest juvenile antics. This was bad news for both Scott and me. Centers was not our biggest fan at first, but he tolerated our behavior. Centers wore glasses with thick black frames, like Clark Kent used to wear, although Centers was no Clark Kent. We called them BCDs, for "birth control devices," because of the way they drove women away.

John Roy was a tall, skinny kid from Kentucky. Must have only been 19 or so. He was a quiet kid but in great shape. He practically flew through Basic and Advanced Individual Training, or AIT. He was also more of a toe-the-line, follow-the-rules kind of guy, but he didn't take himself too seriously and seemed to enjoy our energy.

Private Watts was from Pennsylvania and the spitting image of Conan the Barbarian, so much so that all the MPs ended up calling him Conan. Six-foot-one, short brown hair, with a big space between his two front teeth. We were glad to have him in our corner. We needed anyone we could get on our side, seeing how we were about to piss off a lot of people.

Lastly, there was Fishbach, a tall, blond, quiet dude who stayed completely under the radar. He was the calmest guy you ever met, born to be a soldier or a mortuary worker.

There were certainly other soldiers from our unit, Delta 10, but they are lost to memory unless I peek back at the photos—every picture I look at brings a memory with it.

Scott and I shared almost everything with the group over the short four days we were together; the others were not as forthcoming. But once you arrived at your unit, you would only be able to call your family so often, so creating meaningful relationships was the only way to maintain that human connection.

On our first night, Scott, Roy and Fishbach were playing cards. Scott mentioned how crazy it was that guys from New York, Rhode Island, Kentucky, and Minnesota all ended up in the middle of Alabama to be trained in law enforcement. Roy and I chimed in that it was odd for sure, but since we might not ever see each other again once we moved out, we'd better make the most of it.

Day Two was about getting our uniforms and other gear needed for training. On Day Three, we had medical appointments and haircuts and minor paperwork for in-processing. Day Four was mostly free time, which led to a calmness for all of us.

After four days, our time was up at the in-processing station. The dreaded day of departure was upon us. All the new recruits being assigned to Delta Company 10 Battalion, or Delta Ten as we called it, were advised to be ready to leave early in the a.m.

Throughout our stay at the holding center, I was always talking how easy training was going to be and how they weren't allowed to hit you. "All you have to do is keep a low profile and you can get through the program," I said.

The group chuckled, and Scott said, "Anthony, I've known you four days, and that is not going to be remotely possible."

"I will," I said. "Trust me, I got this!"

Everybody smirked as Scott headed off to breakfast. One of the holdover students said, "Enjoy the last supper!"

None of us understood how true this statement was. The next morning was cool, misty, and overcast, rare for Alabama, but Scott and I were not fazed by the chill. The shuttle bus arrived carrying 20 newly minted basic trainees with fresh haircuts and clean-shaved faces, their duffel bags between their knees. One of them shouted, "Hurry up and wait," which was practically the Army's motto.

We climbed aboard and once we were all situated on the bus, we headed for our new home.

"This is not going to be bad at all," said Scott.

"I'm not worried," I replied.

"Agree," said Roy.

But Fishbach shook his head and said, "Hmm, hope so."

The bus went as quiet as a library. After a few more miles of utter silence, we knew our anticipation would end soon.

I said, "Getting close, ladies."

Scott responded, "Is this how cattle feel on their way to the slaughterhouse?"

A few chuckles as we waited for the bus to reach its final stop. I felt like a kid waiting for his father to get home, knowing he was not going to be happy.

The mood was eerily quiet. It caused me to laugh, but a nervous laugh, for sure.

I was alone. Even Scott did not smile as I made eye contact.

The rest of the ride was short and extremely quiet. Then we pulled up to the Delta 10 parking area. A hard left, then a right as the bus came to a slow halt.

Scott had big eyes looking around the bus. So did the rest of the crew, including me. We were greeted by a tall, lanky drill sergeant, who slowly and deliberately stepped on board, surveying the faces looking up at him before quietly introducing himself as Sergeant Frances. You could hear a pin drop as we all expected him to scream at us. Roy allowed his eyebrows to raise a fraction. This was a warm, courteous welcome. Nothing like what we'd been given to expect from a first meeting with a drill sergeant. Nothing like what others had described.

I peered out the window and noticed a couple other drill sergeants standing calmly with hands behind their backs. Scott later said he felt comforted, like he was visiting his grandfather. Sergeant Frances spoke with a reassuring, oh-so-soothing voice that seemed to instantly transform Roy's stress and worry into calm and relaxation.

Scott and I made eye contact again, sharing a look that asked, "Can this really be this calm?"

It simply did not make sense.

Frances said something like, "I would like to welcome you all to our unit, Delta Ten. We are excited to see all of you and hope your stay here is as enjoyable for you as for us."

Then, without warning, he began to scream maniacally, like a crazed demon had entered his body, his face turning beet red and spit flying out of his mouth. "You dipshits have five minutes to get the hell off this bus or I will rip your faces off myself, and four of those five minutes have already gone!"

Pandemonium descended over the bus. Clothes and personal items began flying. Soldiers were grabbing possessions within arm's reach and dragging them off the bus; anything else was left behind.

"Move, move, move!" Frances screamed. "Move your asses right now! Get off my fucking bus right now! What the hell is taking you so long, Private? You don't know what I'm capable of, boy!"

Leaping from our seats and moving quickly, most of us got off the bus with most of our items. Six or seven drill sergeants were waiting outside, ripping into each trainee who exited the bus and got into a disorderly formation. We had no idea where they came from, but later learned they had been hiding under the tree line to the right of the bus, like predators, like alligators at a riverbed waiting for animals to cross. If they latched onto a fellow trainee, you were happy and hoped it meant you'd make it out of the river alive.

Multiple drill sergeants poked their hat brims into soldiers' faces, yelling, "Don't you eyeball me, Trainee!"

Some of the drills also whispered, which seemed to get the biggest reaction.

"I am six months from retiring," one whispered to Scott, "and you are my focus. I will ruin you and get you to drop out, Soldier."

Roy zoned out and calmly waited for the flame-throwing treatment to end while following orders as best he could. He told me it wasn't all that different from being yelled at by his sisters, everyone talking incoherently at the same time and nobody making any sense.

Other trainees were getting rattled, however, and the more rattled they got, the more they were picked on.

Off to the side was one silent drill sergeant, motionless except for the noose he was spinning in his hand, occasionally holding it up near a trainee, like he was sizing him up.

The point seemed to be that the ones who couldn't handle a bit of verbal abuse would learn there and then, on the very first day, they weren't cut out for an MP's life and would turn in their equipment and simply go home.

Suddenly, Watts, the giant trainee we called Conan, went over like a felled tree. He hit the pavement hard, drawing big-eyed looks from Scott and Roy. If they could take out that guy, we were all in trouble. But on a positive note, Watts going down brought the feeding frenzy to a close rather abruptly.

While the drill sergeants were busy attending to the unconscious Watts, I looked around at the ground attack area. It looked like a mini-explosion had gone off. The contents of trainees' duffel bags had been dumped out on the ground for "inspection" and thrown about by the drill sergeants. Evidently, a couple of trainees had been trying to smuggle in cigarettes, chocolate, and other candy. I was willing to guess it was Longview and Collins, two heavyweights at the back with sweat pouring down their brows.

Frances seemed to read my mind, his head swiveling back at them with fresh ammunition for even more torment. "Look at all this damn chocolate," he yelled.

One of the other sergeants yelled out at Longview and Collins, "Surprise, surprise, it's coming out of both you fat boys. You fat boys should not be eating candy!"

This kind of verbal abuse would never be allowed in today's Army. They ripped on the big guys for a few minutes saying, "Look at this shit...You disgust me, Soldier...Did your mama let you eat like this?"

Then Frances gave Longview one Snickers bar and Collins another, and said with an almost evil tone, "Eat it, boys!"

Longview without hesitation started chewing. At first, Collins said no, but then Frances said, "Eat it, fat boy. This is your last chocolate bar for fourteen weeks."

When it was finally over and we were walking away, Scott checked to make sure we weren't close to the drill sergeants, then turned to me. "Can you believe there is almost fifteen more weeks of this shit?!"

This turned out to be our first escape from danger, but not the last. Basic was already feeling like it would take a lifetime.

***

Basic Training is an experience that can't be explained to people outside the military. However, those who have taken part in it all understand when you say it is unreal. Most of the actual training consisted of basic soldier skills, such as marching, running, weapons training, uniform preparation, and simple classroom things like map reading and terrain awareness. However, Advanced Individual Training, or AIT, was all about military police skills and basic law enforcement training. The drill sergeants focused on the Physical Test, or PT, since if you weren't able to get in shape, there was no way you were going to make it as a military police officer. The first seven weeks in the Army was all about conditioning: running, walking, and marching. Push-ups, sit-ups, and the two-mile run were how they determined who could cut the mustard. The ones who could not were encouraged to go back home and, "Eat their mama's cooking!"

When we were training to be MPs, Basic and AIT had recently been combined into One Station Individual Training, or OSIT. This was done so Military Police could transition right from one phase to the next. The Army thought this was a great idea. However, new soldiers certainly felt otherwise. If you were stuck with a bitter, angry drill sergeant in Basic, then that was who you had for almost sixteen weeks instead of eight, as had been the case in years past.

This was case for the Delta 10 Demons of 3rd Platoon and our angry, bitter, and universally unloved Staff Sergeant Scruggs. He was so angry, soldiers joked he could win the lottery and still wouldn't smile. We eventually learned that he was bitter about this being his second tour as drill instructor. The first time around had been during Vietnam, so his understanding of the limits of trainee hazing differed from his colleagues' comparatively kinder, gentler approach.

Scruggs chewed tobacco. It created a bulge out the side of his cheek whenever he yelled, and the smell of it would almost make you gag if he was in your face. He clearly had high blood pressure, because when he got mad, his head turned redder than a lobster fresh from the boiling pot and the vein in the center of his forehead would stick out.

Whenever he asked a question, no matter your answer, his response would be, "Hah?" and you knew, without a doubt, your ass was in a serious bind. Much to my dismay, I heard this phrase more than anyone else in our platoon. To this day, when I smell Copenhagen tobacco, in my head I hear him saying, "Hah?"

It still gives me an uneasy feeling, but it never affected Scott. Back then, he even started chewing it, making Scruggs believe he was the perfect soldier.

Basic Training is life changing. You have to experience it in person to fully appreciate the verbal and emotional abuse soldiers endure. Oddly, if you ask any soldier, no matter when they served, they will tell you that Basic Training was an emotional and electrifying experience they will never forget. But while they all think back on it fondly, nobody would ever want to return.

Like any unique experience in life, people are the key ingredient. We had a great platoon, with people from all over the country who were without question some of the most fascinating and unusual people I have ever met.

This was also the first place I ever heard the term "Yankee!" Early on, one of the drill sergeants said, "Oh, listen to his accent! We got us a Yankee from way up North in our company."

The next day, Allen John Patrick, who hailed from Alabama, asked Scott, "You a Yankee or a Damn Yankee?"

He went on to explain that a Yankee comes to the South for a visit, then goes back home up North. A Damn Yankee is one that comes to the South and stays.

After we stopped laughing, Scott and I had reassured Allen that we were just Yankees, because who the hell would want to come to the shit hole that was the South and stay there?

Scott and I realized then that we were cut from the same cloth.

Allen was a hardcore redneck; he would say crazy racial things. His most radical statement was that his lifetime hero was John Wilkes Booth.

Scott and I got a kick out of provoking him and the others, and they'd always rise to the bait. More likely than not, that's how our friendship was formed.

David P. Longview, one of the big boys who ate the candy bars, was a good ole boy from Baton Rouge, Louisiana. The Snickers-eating phenom stood six-foot-five and weighed 295 pounds. He was on what was affectionately called "the fat boy program," which limited the amount of food trainees could eat in the hopes they would lose weight and graduate. He was a happy guy who had all these funny statements about life that the group would crack up to every night while shining shoes near the sand pit, where the drill sergeants would abuse you, hoping to get you to drop out. After one night of abuse, Longview said, "I think my mama would not be happy if she knew they were so mean to me. Do think I should let them know?"

Every night after evening chow was mail call, when soldiers received their love letters, letters of encouragement, and, most importantly, treats. During the first week, soldiers learned the hard way that when packages were sent from home, you had to share all the sweets with the entire platoon. If the fat boys got cookies, they could have only one, and they had to give the rest to their platoon mates. The sad looks on their faces is stamped in my mind to this day. It was like you had robbed them of ten thousand dollars.

The thought of sharing food with everyone did not sit well with me, either. Scott and I developed a foolproof plan. We gathered eight of our buddies and established what would later be called the Greedy Club. The members arranged for family sending them treats to hide them under clothes, so none of the other trainees would be any the wiser when we Greeds received our packages. We'd hide the cookies and brownies in the ceiling of the laundry room and wait until midnight or personal time, when we'd gather and eat all the goodies.

We had a little ritual: Before we ate the food, we would put our hands to our faces, wiggle our fingers, and say, "Better me than you!" This worked as planned right from the start. It kind of felt like sneaking things into a prison. You knew you would get in holy shit if you got caught, but the crime was worth the time...well, so we thought anyway.

The Greedy Club bond got us through some of the more miserable moments in Basic. We knew we had each other's backs. If you happened to be the one getting abuse—or, as the drill sergeants called it, "getting your mind and body conditioned"—you'd look over and your Greedy Club partners would be rolling their fingers and mouthing, "Better you than me." It became something of a rallying cry for the club when things got particularly tough.

The only real pleasure you had in Basic Training was chow. Being a food lover, one thing I hated more than anything was standing in line for up to 45 minutes, moving from parade rest to standing to attention the whole way to get your food, and then being hurried to finish it and get out as soon as you got it. "No need to chew! Swallow it, and your stomach will do the rest." That's what we were told.

I also hated when people cut the line. Most of the soldiers were RA (Regular Army), but if you were Army Reserve or National Guard, you could go to the front of the line. Two kids from North Dakota would always yell, "Make way! National Guard!" One of them was a fun guy who would share farm stories with the Greedy Club. The other, Wolf, was only five-foot-seven but had a yell that sounded like a drill sergeant. You'd jump back, only to see this little guy cutting in front of you.

Our group loved to mess with him about his height. Sometimes, we would sing, "We're Off to See the Wizard." Other times, we would ask him whether he was a full-grown wolf or just a wolf cub. He was clearly annoyed with us, but that only fueled us to mess with him more. This behavior was not seen as hazing back then, as it was equally given out, but Scott and I were good at it, so most times we were giving, not receiving, the verbal assaults.

There are moments in Basic that define you. One afternoon, I had perhaps one of my most defining moments. It was chow time, and I was ravenous, as usual. As I got the main meal item, I looked and there were two coconut cream pies winking at me from the dessert table. Shit, I grabbed them both, licking my lips while putting them on my tray, knowing this was going to be the highlight of my day. Walking slowly toward my seat, I noticed Sergeant Scruggs following the tray with his eyes.

"What the hell is that?" Scruggs asked, his voice dangerously quiet.

"My lunch?" thinking it was pretty obvious.

"Hah?"

"Oh, sorry. My lunch, Sergeant."

"No, hero." He pointed to the offending pies.

"They're coconut cream pies—I mean, Sergeant. They're my favorite!" I now realize I should have taken only one of them.

There is a term we learned in Basic —tea-kettling. Just before the pot starts to whistle, you can hear the steam bursting through the steam hole. It was abundantly clear to me that all was not well.

Scruggs looked like he was about to blow his stack, his face turning his famed boiled-lobster red. You could almost hear the telltale whistling.

Then, *boom!* "Put your fucking tray away and meet me at the Pit. You think you're the only one who wants a goddamn slice of pie?!"

Every head in the chow hall looked down at their food, hoping they would not get caught in the crossfire.

"There's still plenty pies left," I said, as if Scruggs cared one bit about the remaining pies.

Only later realizing how stupid it had been to try to get in the last word, I quickly took the food back to the tray area, frustrated, angry, and starving, to boot. Two beautiful-looking pies had cost me my lunch. Not even a chance to take one measly bite. In a moment of stupidity, I decided, hell, if he's going to smoke my ass anyway, I'm eating one.

Cramming an entire pie into my mouth, I ran out the door and rounded the corner, straight into SSG Scruggs, who was standing stock still, hand up, waiting for me.

Scruggs was now eerily calm. "Now chew that shit slowly. Don't choke on it, Boy. I certainly do not want to give you mouth to mouth, nor will I."

"Yes, Sergeant!" I said, pie covering half my face.

"Now take your ass to the Pit and run in place until I get there."

The Pit had now taken on an almost mythical quality among the new recruits. Composed of very compressed sand slightly less coarse than gravel, it was the setting for feats of endurance that turned boys into men. Or broke them. It was where many trainees discovered their limits, and I was about to become one of them.

Once Scruggs arrived, he screamed at me, "High crawl!" Then after a minute, he yelled, "Low crawl!"

Scruggs was a stickler for doing low crawl right. You had to put your face in the sand, so you got full-on scratches on your face and scalp. This was to simulate getting below the enemy firing at you, but the only thing firing at me was Scruggs.

After a good ten minutes, Scruggs shouted. "Back to the high crawl!" Then, "Low crawl!"

Twenty minutes in, my body was starting to really feel the burn. After thirty, I was starting to shake.

Scruggs was clearly enjoying himself. I was feeling nauseous.

"Okay," Scruggs shouted, "leg lifts, up, open them, close them, open them, close them, down."

After ten minutes of this, I could taste the pie at the back of my throat and was starting to regret eating it. Which, I figured, had probably been his point. I didn't know how much longer I could keep going and began to question whether Army life was for me.

Scruggs was winning this battle.

I don't need this shit!

Another round of low crawls was followed by Scruggs screaming again, "On your back! High speed!" He used this term in a sarcastic way.

Leg raises. "How's that fucking pie tasting now?"

After an hour of pure torture, I was about ready to give up. I'd reached my breaking point. I'd had enough and did not need this bullshit one minute longer. I resigned myself to saying, "You win." However, as that thought started to crystallize, I noticed movement in the windows to the barracks just above the Pit, where the entire

Greedy Club was pressing their faces to the glass, all grinning broadly, wiggling their fingers at me, and mouthing, "Better you than me." That was a defining moment. Knowing my buddies were up there, watching and had my back—much as it might not have looked like that to an outside observer—was the boost I desperately needed to rally my last remaining reserves of strength. I wasn't quitting today.

Fuck this, and fuck him.

However, at the sight of my Greedy Club members, a slight smile crept across my face.

"You find this fucking funny, Anthony?" Scruggs was outraged and jumped onto the ground and into my face, yelling obscenities, and showering me with spit and pieces of Copenhagen. He was almost on top of me, and I believed he was about to inflict physical pain, like he had lost his mind.

But then an unlikely guardian angel appeared at the edge of the Pit—Senior Drill Sergeant Frances.

"Scruggsy," he said, "I need you in the office. You almost finished there?"

Scruggs shot me a furious glance, and as he trudged reluctantly away, he put a finger in my chest and said, "This isn't over, jackass."

Frances knew Scruggs was crossing the line and did not want this to end badly. I lay on my back in the gravel Pit, breathing heavily, thanking my lucky stars. Of all people, it was Frances who'd come to rescue me.

I looked up at the windows, at the Greedy Club members still flicking their fingers, and I flipped a finger of my own. When I finally managed to raise myself off the ground and limp back to the platoon area, I was raucously greeted by the club, still laughing their asses off.

"Holy shit," Scott said, "I thought you were going to die. That was unbelievable. How the hell did you not quit, man?"

Scott then asked point-blank, "Why the hell does he hate you so much?"

I shrugged. "Because I ate his fucking pies."

"He fucking smoked you," Fishburn said. "That was bad."

"Looked painful," said Scott.

Longview said, "Yeah, my mama would not like that at all."

We all laughed again loudly.

"You weren't the only one who thought I was a goner," I said. "He lost his shit when I started smiling after seeing you jackasses up here."

"Yeah," Fishburn said, "that was Scott's idea."

"I have to tell you assholes. That was the only thing that got me through that shit." I shook my head. "The guy's a fucking psycho."

They all agreed, but I realized, psycho or not, I had to find a way to get on Scruggs' good side if I wanted to live until graduation.

***

I decided to wait in the long line again to call home. Fortunately for me, I had all these calling cards Marty Gaughan's dad had given me before I left—although I had used half of them already, so I wasn't sure I'd have enough to make it to graduation. Every night after mail and phone calls, there would be a gathering at the Pit where we'd all shine our boots. Scott and I would mess with everyone there, including members of the other platoons. Nobody was off limits. In our platoon, there were two Mormon MPs, Haines and Gary, and they were the target of our (mostly) good-natured banter.

"I heard you guys gotta stay virgins till you're married," I said, kicking off the evening's roasting.

Not to be outdone, Scott joined in on the ball-busting. "I hear you get your own planet when you die."

As Basic progressed, we were becoming something of a tag team, and we were in rare form that night.

"And you can't have coffee, tea, or alcohol, either, that right?" I asked, all straight-faced innocence.

"Well, that one doesn't get followed as closely as the others," Haines said defensively. "But if someone drinks it, they might be called a 'Jack Mormon.'"

"And you can't lie, right?" Scott said, gearing up for something, I could tell.

"That's right. We must always tell the truth," said Haines earnestly.

Scott thought for a moment. "And, from what I understand, you're not supposed to masturbate either?"

Both guys shook their heads silently, suddenly engrossed in their boots.

"Well, then. Let me ask you this," Scott said leaning forward. "Have you ever masturbated?"

"Now remember, before you answer, guys," I said, with a subtle warning tone in my voice. "You can't lie."

Gary shot up like he'd been lit on fire, grabbed his things in a huff, and stalked away.

Some of the other guys disapproved. "You're so crude. Why would you ask that?" and "Come on, man."

Haines whined, "I can't believe you would ask that. That's offensive, man. You guys never stop."

I looked at Scott, both of us shaking our heads in a "disappointed father" way, then, at the same time, we both said, "Yup. They masturbate."

The MPs fell over laughing for several minutes.

As the Pit rebounded from their laughter, Scott cast his eyes round the circle of MPs shining away. "What do you guys miss the most about being away from home?"

I responded first. "Oh, man, I miss driving in my car and listening to the radio. All we do here is walk all over the fucking place and hear the psycho drills sing their horrible jodies."

Jodies were the songs they sang when they marched you around the base.

Longview's eyes took on a sheen. "I miss my mama's cooking." The big guy looked dangerously close to crying. Mind you, the poor guy had eaten only boiled eggs for breakfast and salads for dinner for four weeks in a bid to lose enough weight to stay in the unit. He'd been pretty successful, too, but still had some way to go.

"Your mama can cook?" Scott asked, looking up.

Longview smiled. "You taste my mama's cooking, you go back home and slap your mama!"

The group chuckled, and now my interest was piqued.

"What does she make that tastes so good?" I asked.

Longview licked his lips and swallowed a few times, and his Adam's apple bounced a couple of times before breathing, "My mama's étouffée is delicious. You got the shrimps, potatoes, Creole sauce, bugs, and sausage."

"Wait, bugs? Who the hell puts bugs in a stew?" I asked.

"It's like dem lobsters up in your state but much smaller!"

"Oh, crawdads," I said.

"Yup," he said licking his lips.

"So, it's good?"

He looked at me sternly and said, "Boy, what you talking 'bout! My mama's étouffée so good, you have a bowl, you will go take a shit just to lick your ass to get the taste back in yo mouth!"

The group erupted in laughter. We all agreed that at some point we needed to visit Longview and his mama and try that dish. I made sure they knew I was game as long as I didn't have to lick anyone's ass.

***

Another night, sitting around the Pit, shining our boots, the group got to talking about where we came from. Wilks and Peters started talking about North Dakota, and what it had been like to grow up on farms and how much farmers loved sheep.

Peters then went on to tell our motley crew about how they performed the act. He said on his farm, they'd put on their "waders," get themselves one of the "good-looking female sheep," take her up to the top deck in the barn, put her back legs in their boots, then put their junk inside her. The group laughed at first, but then most seemed to think he was telling the truth and got squeamish, especially as Peters went on to elaborate how they'd walk the sheep close to the edge of the top of the barn but leave about six inches.

Standing up now, demonstrating, he said, "You would then push her forward and she'd back into you."

Scott and I started laughing, thinking it was BS, but in the back of my mind I wondered if it were true. It was such a detailed account, and his face was unsmiling, calm, and matter of fact. I hoped for the sheep's wellbeing he was only joking, but it was a revelation that I've never forgotten, that's for sure.

Another memorable revelation came a little while later, when we found out from another trainee that the ceiling speakers in our barracks had built-in microphones, and that Scruggs and the other drill sergeants would gather around the dayroom office and listen to us all talking and joking.

Of course, I was the one doing most of the chatting, and they heard me talking shit about all of them. One thing I used to do constantly that surely pissed Scruggs off was my trademark impersonation of him. It never failed to get all the soldiers fired up and laughing hysterically. My portrayal was perfect: his walk, talk, and mannerisms. But being such a smart ass was going to come back to bite me in the ass sooner than I thought.

One evening after chow, the drills waited until all the MPs were gathered round and Sergeants Frances and Rowe asked the platoon who could do the best imitation of the other drill sergeants. Those guys knew exactly what they were doing. Obviously, I didn't volunteer myself. I'm not stupid. But of all people, Fishburn, the guy who never said a word, yelled out, "Anthony, Sergeant." What a little tattletale!

I knew nothing good was going to come of this.

"Get up here, Anthony," DS Rowe yelled out. Rowe, mind you, was about five-foot-three, and that guy loved to double-team you with DS Frances. They'd both be saying, "Look at me when I'm talking to you, Private." Frances was six-foot-six, so up and down went your head trying to look them both in the eye. You'd look like one of those nodding dogs in the back of the old cars.

So, there I am doing my imitation of Scruggs across the quad area and squawking out his trademark "Hah?" The drills and all the trainees are cracking up. Well, that only encouraged me. I started with all Scruggs' favorite sayings, including, "I will rip out your heart and eat it right in front of you." I had Rowe keeling over.

Like an idiot, I believed them when they told me they wouldn't tell Scruggs. But one thing you could never trust was for a drill sergeant to keep a secret from another drill sergeant. You'd spill your guts to these guys, like telling them the love of your life broke up with you, and the next day you'd hear another drill sergeant singing a jody making fun of your pain. "This goes out to Private Smith, whose girlfriend ran off with somebody else. Jody is the name given the guy who steals your hometown girlfriend when you left for the Army. Jody is not your friend, and he's mighty strong, but now he's got your girl and gone. Sound off, 'She ain't your girl no more.'"

The next night, Scruggs requested that I come to the front of the platoon. With a poker face and deadpan delivery, he reassured me that he found it flattering that I imitated him. Oh, shit, was all I could think. Then he said he wanted to see the impersonation for himself. Naturally, I gave a less enthusiastic performance than the previous night. Scruggs gave me the look, the "I would like to punch you in the face" look.

But he didn't want to give me the satisfaction of letting me know right then and there that I'd gotten to him, so he just told me to get back into formation. I thought I'd gotten off lightly. No siree.

The next few days, all I heard was some variation of, "Hey, Mr. Impersonator. Maybe you should work on shining your damn boots rather than imitating me. Drop for twenty push-ups." Or, "Maybe you should give more attention to your bunk instead of imitating me." Or, my personal favorite, "Your uniform looks like shit. I hope for your sake you're not imitating me right now, because that would be a damn insult. Drop for more push-ups!"

Scruggs continued screwing with me nonstop. Toward the end of the eight-week Basic Training, most of the trainees were not being messed with at all. However, I was still on the receiving end of Scruggs' wrath for anything and everything. Even the rest of the Greedy Club started to feel bad for me.

Around Week Seven or Eight, the troops got their first on-post wet pass. This was when soldiers could have a couple drinks on post. Most went to the PX or to drink and dance at the Pistol Palace, a dive of a dance club on Fort McClellan. Like most military installations in the '80s, the Pistol Palace was a grungy-looking place with cheap beer and a jukebox—yeah, they still had them back then.

In Week Nine, things were a bit more relaxed—for everybody *else*, that is. AIT was set up to be less stressful than Basic, and the MP trainees would all head over to the Pistol Palace every weekend to get a few beers and cut up. The song "Billie Jean" had been popular long before we ever arrived at Basic and AIT in 1985. It was still a favorite, playing just about every hour on the jukebox. And whenever it did, Scott would always hit the dance floor with a female trainee named Esposito, cutting up in battle dress uniforms and black combat boots.

The other MPs would clear space for Scott and Esposito to strut their stuff, and it would always pump up the other MP trainees.

Whenever Scott and I walked in, the crew would say, "Here they come, looks like 'Billie Jean' is going to start playing over and over again." Probably not what Michael Jackson envisioned when he wrote the song. I decided to make more time to call home again, and thank God Marty Sr. had hooked me up. When you were in Basic, the call home was the one link you had to keep you from getting extremely depressed about being without family and friends.

Somewhere midway through AIT, Sergeant Frances gathered all the soldiers together and asked how we felt about our time at Fort McClellan. Many soldiers talked about how much they felt they had grown and what they had gotten out of their training. A few kiss-asses started talking about how they would never forget how good their drills were and how fortunate they were to be in D-10. Frances laughed at that and told one of them to drop for being an ass kisser. One trainee raised up and profoundly said, "I have made friendships here like I've never made in my life, and there is no way I will ever forget this experience. I am not sure I will ever have a closer friend than my buddy," and he pointed over to his platoon mate. Another trainee then yelled out, "Coming out party!" This caused a huge laugh from the unit.

Meanwhile, Frances sat motionless, staring quietly in deep thought, nodding his head slowly up and down. He somberly asked the group, "So, you all think these are going to be your greatest friendships?"

The group remained mostly quiet, waiting for what he was about to say next. A few responded, "Yes, Sergeant."

Frances said, "Jimmy Simmons." Nothing else, just the name.

Then Fishburn asked, "Who is Jimmy Simmons, Sergeant?"

Frances sighed and began to tell the story of a good ole boy from

Mobile, Alabama, who loved his mama, loved food, loved God and country, and most of all, loved Alabama football.

"I used to harass him nonstop, because he was from the South, and I would call him 'Roll Tide.' I hail from Philadelphia, so he would call me 'Philly.'"

They had met when Frances arrived in Vietnam, four months after Jimmy. The more experienced soldier, Jimmy did not talk much, he just pulled up near the rear in the patrols carrying an M60 machine gun.

"Toward the very end of his tour, we were on patrol, moving about in a relaxed but methodical manner, when from out of nowhere we were ambushed from the wood line to my left."

Frances' eyes welled up as he was reliving it in detail, staring straight ahead like he could still see it happening.

"It was an intense firefight. Our patrol was getting hit hard, when Jimmy, without fear, ran up the hill, showing no regard for his safety, and began firing his machine gun toward the tree line where enemy fire was coming from. I quickly moved up to help him reload his M60. I knew that machine gun was the only way we were getting out of that shit alive." He paused briefly. "Unfortunately, so did Charlie. I was bent over trying to get another ammo belt when a grenade rolled up next to me and I froze. I fucking froze!"

Not a word for a good 30 seconds. Nothing but silence, 185 future MPs hanging on his every word. The regret was clear in his eyes as they began to water even more. He swallowed a couple times, then looked away to regain his composure before continuing.

"You see," Frances said, his voice quivering, "I'm sitting here today for one reason, because if Jimmy didn't jump on the grenade and at the same time push me off to the side, I am not here."

He took a breath and let it out. "After the blast, I rushed back to his side, and he was in bad shape. His stomach was destroyed. Blood was pouring out of him. I tried to treat his wounds, but it was clear he was not going to make it. He told me so immediately. He made me promise to do two things. He said, 'First, tell my dad I was a good soldier. But most of all, tell my mama I'm sorry I didn't make it back; I promised her I would. Oh, and one last thing—you better start loving my football team.' He half smirked up at me, then said, 'Roll Tide.' He last words were 'Roll Tide!'"

The entire group sat quietly for a few minutes while Frances gathered himself.

"When I returned from Nam, I kept my promise. His dad said, 'That's my boy,' and his mama just cried and said, 'Thank you.'" He paused again, looking around the formation, and said, "If you find yourself in combat, be like Jimmy. Roll Tide."

CHAPTER 2

GULF WAR, 1991

Much has shipped since Sergeant First Class Frances' speech in Basic. Both Scott and I went on our grist duty station to Fort Sheridan for a year, and we completed our overseas assignments. Scott went to Alaska, and I went to Germany. Now, we both decided to reenlist to be stationed at Fort Bragg, North Carolina. Scott got divorced after leaving Alaska, and I had found new love, or should I say old love made new. The reason for choosing Fort Bragg was to implement our new plan: to leave the military and join a police force. "Soldiers make plans and the Army laughs," said the NCOIC. Selecting Fort Bragg was only supposed to be a steppingstone to the next challenge. Some stones—including steppingstones—are better left unturned.

Scott and I had always been practical jokers, and you'd be mistaken if you assumed combat would change that. Not so. Not one bit. We never took life seriously. But there was one thing we didn't joke about. One thing that would go on to change our entire military experience and our friendship: roadside bombs or land mines, later called Improvised Explosive Devices (IEDs). The enemy's use of IEDs forever changed the way the US forces trained and prepared for conflict in Iraq. As a country, we were woefully unprepared for the enemy's use of IEDs, and everyone was learning on the fly during the First Gulf War and to a much greater extent in the next Iraq event.

In May 1991, immediately following the cease-fire in the First Gulf War, Scott and I were on driving patrol in the standard MP Humvee. Normally, we would have been traveling on a Main Supply Route (MSR in military terminology), but throughout the day there had been intelligence that the Iraqis had been laying new land mines. MPs were to pay attention to activity by locals, specifically digging on or near the roads. Given the limited number of MPs in the combat zone, we'd been given specific sectors to patrol both on foot and in vehicles to prevent Iraqis from placing these explosive devices.

Around 12:15 p.m., we pulled over in downtown Bagdad. I was hungry, and it was hot as hell on the ground—the start of Iraq's long, hot, dry summer. One of the NCOs yelled, "It's hotter than the ass cheeks of a sumo wrestler locked in a 125-degree sauna."

Scott said, "Yeah, with no water to pour on the hot rocks to add steam, no door to walk out after ten minutes, and no shower to jump into."

It was a dry heat, too, so damn dry you if you rubbed your nose, it would start bleeding. Nobody on the US side was happy about it.

Scott and I were doing snot rockets to pass the time while the other MPs milled around nearby. Bouford and Grand, two MP buddies from Bragg, were standing a short distance away, laughing at us. Combat was down to near zero, so seeing soldiers standing around blowing dry boogers out of their noses was not a surprise.

To effectively launch a snot rocket, you had to hold a finger on one side of your nose, tilt your head away from your body, take a deep breath, then blow out very quickly while keeping your mouth closed to ensure the sand and dried-up snot were projected far.. Scott had set a snot rocket distance record the day before, counting 15 steps, toe to heel. I was feeling competitive and not wanting to be outdone. It was a bit windy, and I was positioning myself to have the wind at my back.

"It won't matter," Scott said. "Just accept defeat."

Most soldiers in the area were milling about, but Scott seemed more tense than normal.

"Dude, why are you so worked up?" I asked. "You that worried about me beating you?"

He seemed agitated, like a sixth sense was telling him something was wrong as he surveyed the area, focusing on a small group of Iraqi men off in the distance.

I cocked my head back and told him I was getting ready to launch a real doozy, a belter that would have him falling out of the lead. Then suddenly, he threw me to the ground and took off running. I scrambled up, my arm aching from the heavy fall, as shots rang out around us. A "skinny"—that's a name given to some of the Iraqis because they were so skinny compared to the US soldiers—had snuck up behind us, crouched behind some boxes some fifty feet away, firing a handgun haphazardly in our direction. Without hesitation, Scott, Bouford, and Grand unloaded their 9mms at him. It was over in an instant. I was bent over, hands on my knees, slowly shaking my head. My heart was beating in my ears as adrenaline coursed through my veins.

"Holy shit!" I said. "You guys fucking saved my ass. That was way too close."

Scott glanced over at me, not amused.

"How did I miss this, Scott?" I said. "I owe you one for sure."

"Yeah," he said. "That's why I'm here. To save your ass and get you home safely. Hopefully, we'll be leaving soon, given your lack of focus, ass bag."

"Well, bud, you're lucky. That snot rocket was going to be the best you ever saw. I had a strong wind at my back and—" I couldn't tell if he was annoyed with me or if something else was bothering him, but he was not himself at all.

I stopped talking as Sergeant Hankel strode toward us, looking even more fired up than usual. Grand and Bouford quickly moved away from us, keenly aware that Hankel was going to rip into our asses and not wanting to get in the way.

"What the fuck is going on with you two idiots now?" Hankel said.

Scott explained, a bit annoyed. "Anthony was not paying attention, but we took the guy out. All is okay, Sergeant Hankel."

"I'm tired of you two ass clowns," Hankel said. "You're going to get each other killed. Why do I have to keep warning you idiots that you have to be alert at all times? You fuck around and play your snot rocket shit back on the FOB," he said, referring to the Forward Operating Base. "Or do you want to leave here on a MEDEVAC bird?"

"No, Sergeant," we said at the same time.

"I'm not telling you ass bags again. Wake the fuck up and pay attention. You princesses aren't in Rhode Island anymore."

Hankel was a big guy from Washington state whose family was of German descent. Standing at six-foot-four, he towered above everyone else and walked like Arnie in *Terminator*. Hankel had the pastiest white skin you ever saw and a big, crooked nose that he said he'd got "from breaking up bar fights in Korea!" His feet were huge, size fifteen. When Hank walked into a room, everyone knew he was there. He was in great physical shape and could run two miles in less than twelve minutes, but the younger soldiers called him Grandpa because he looked way older than he actually was.

We didn't know it on that deployment, but while he talked a big game, he was a big-ass softie.

Sometimes he'd share stories of the '70s and early '80s in Korea with the juicy girls, regaling us with detailed accounts of their "steam and creams," massages with oil and how they'd "rub" you down, with predictable results for the nooky-starved soldiers. When he was feeling less good-humored, he'd yell phrases he'd picked up in Korea like, *"ISHI BAALI MA!"* which made no sense to us. To this day, I still don't know what that hell that means.

Back at the FOB a few days after the incident with the skinny, Hankel stopped over to commend me and Scott. Well, it was more like, "Hey, shit stains, it's been three days and no more close calls. Glad to see you're staying focused. That'll keep you alive."

For him, that was high praise. Then he warned us that the Hajis were getting more and more sophisticated, and that we'd recently lost two of our MP brothers to a roadside bomb. That warning turned out to be prescient.

But Hankel was so conditioned to military life, he was oblivious to how these land mines, of which there seemed to be more and more, had shaken us all. During a casual conversation, he suggested we consider being lifers. We all laughed out loud at his suggestion.

Bouford said, "There is no way I'm staying past this tour. I'm going to be a state trooper in PA."

Scott and I later debated this crazy idea anyway. After all, it would only have meant working 14 more years, then we'd have a paycheck for life. And I was always on the lookout for how to swing the best deal with the least amount of effort. But in the end, we knew a life in the military wasn't for us. For one thing, we couldn't deal with the politics.

We were still laughing at Hankel's suggestion when Grand walked in with a guitar.

"How the hell did you get that?" I asked.

"Traded four MREs with some Iraqi dude."

"Can you play?"

"Yeah," he said, "mostly country or soft rock."

"Well, bitch, play something!"

Grand made some adjustments to the guitar and started strumming. He played a few Bread songs I didn't really know, then something more familiar.

"Wait, I know this," I said. It was "Danny's Song," by Loggins and Messina, and I started singing.

The whole group joined in—rather horribly.

Hankel walked back in, singing, and holy crap, he could *sing*.

He and I sang the rest of the song as a duet, and it sounded so good, all the MPs screamed in joy and surprise.

When we finished, Grand yelled, "Only Loggins and Messina did it better."

"Yeah, the desert heat has your ears messed up, Grand, AKA Kimchi Boy," another nickname from Hankel.

Most every night, when we settled back in the FOB break area, Grand would try to teach me how to play this song. My fat fingers made it difficult, but I was nonstop persistent, every night picking that one song, over and over.

Eventually, Scott yelled at me, "Stop playing that fucking song!"

"Dude," I said, "not till I get it right."

He rolled his eyes. "We don't have two years for you to learn that shit."

"Watch, I'll get it," I said. "One day when I have a son, I'm gonna sing it to you."

Scott looked to the heavens. "Please God, only give him daughters."

When we were not singing, we mostly talked about how we were all ready to leave Iraq. Very few people had been here as long as we had, and we all just wanted to get the hell out of this shit hole, and fast. After I put the guitar down, in walked Specialist Scalici.

He was a reservist and an MP dog handler who was also a New Jersey state trooper. By his side was his dog, a tiny beagle named Peete.

Scott yelled over, "I hope we don't need this little guy to save us."

Scalici smiled. "He's a bomb-detection dog."

"Thank God," I said. "I thought the Reserves were operating on a limited budget."

We talked with him for a while about being a real police officer. Scott and I were completely focused on our plan to join the Police Academy back in Rhode Island after our ETS, or End Tour of Station. I was planning on making some extra cash while I climbed the ladder. We had learned the police department paid for new recruits to take college classes, so I had a plan to go back to college after I passed the Police Academy course. Obviously, I assumed I'd get through with flying colors.

One night in May at the FOB, I told Scott, "Dude, I am going to be drawing a police salary and getting paid to take college classes."

He laughed and said, "Keep your eyes on the prize instead of looking to get promoted before you've even got the job."

"Nah," I said. "I got it all figured out."

Scott wasn't like that though. He just wanted to give whatever job he was working on in that moment his full attention and focus.

Grand, Bouford, Scott, and I were all in the chow hall one day, talking about stuff going on back home—St. Louis for Grand and Pittsburgh for Bouford, who was a diehard Steelers fan and never shy about sharing that with others. Although he was the most reserved of the crew, he was the best fit and the most consummate soldier.

Grand was a bit on the wild side and had no issue letting others know it, either. He was food-crazy like me, and the two of us talked about food all the time. Grand was not happy with the chow hall food, but his breakfast routine was to order an omelet with everything in it. He would cut it in half and eat it in two bites. His mom was Korean—which is why Hankel called him Kimchi—and she owned a Chinese restaurant that he promised to take us to when we went home on leave.

As the four of us headed out of the chow hall after breakfast, we were informed we would be on foot patrol that day.

In town, we saw a few boys around 10 to 13 years old playing soccer. Grand and I handed our M16s to Scott and Bouford and proceeded to join in the game. At first, the young boys were surprised and stopped playing, but I yelled out, "Okay, US versus Iraq! Winners get candy bars."

One of the kids, a boy named Mo, short for Mohammad, happened to speak English, and the game was on. We played for a good ten minutes, but they outnumbered us, eight to two. We called out to Bouford and Scott for help, but Scott said, "Hell, no! You're going to lose!"

And we did, 7-1.

"At least we scored," I said after the game. Then Grant and I made Bouford and Scott give up their chocolate, so we'd have enough for all the boys.

The kids all gathered around us laughing and eating the chocolate like it was the best in the world. They all had traces of chocolate around their lips as they joked around in their native language.

"What is he saying?" Grand asked Mo.

Mo said, "Your legs look funny, like you rode a camel all day."

Grand joked, "We'd be six-for-two if I wasn't bowlegged. Now, I am a camel jockey!"

Everyone laughed at that.

We were still winded and sweaty when Hankel showed up and said, "What are you idiots doing now?"

"Just building relations with the locals," I said.

Hankel sighed and said, "Pay attention, ass bags." As he was leaving, he yelled back, "And no more fucking soccer!"

Mo turned to Grand. "We call it football here!"

More laughter from all.

A few days later, we were on foot patrol again, and the young boys wanted another game. Grand and I wanted to, but Bouford, the voice of reason, reminded us that Hankel would for sure lose his shit if he saw us messing around again.

"Just a quick one," I said. "We'll play to five, but you or Scott have to be the goalie."

Bouford shook his head. "Hell, no."

But Scott stepped up and agreed to play, although he was not very enthusiastic about it.

The game was close, 4-3, and the Iraqi boys were only one goal from winning. Meanwhile, Grand and I were playing like this was for the Olympic gold medal.

"Woo! I thought I was competitive!" Scott yelled.

"Fuck these little shits," Grand yelled, going for the ball a bit too aggressively and knocking down one of the smaller boys.

"Chill out!" Bouford yelled. "You're too fucking competitive. They're only kids, you idiot."

"Well, they shouldn't be talking shit!" Grand yelled. "Call me a camel jockey."

We refused to let up, but unfortunately, it was yet another loss for us. Afterward, the boys gathered around to get their winning chocolates. Bouford shook his head and acted like he was angry having to give up his candy, but he willingly handed it over to the boys.

As I took his chocolate away, I said, "If they like us, they may keep us safe, so just give it up. And you don't need it, you big-headed fucker."

"Your head's almost as big as mine, and at least mine has a brain inside of it," Bouford shot back.

Grand called over to Mo, the young boy who was translating, "We'll be back in a few days."

One of the older ones said something in his native language, and Mo said, "You better bring more chocolate!"

Grand scowled as the boys all laughed.

"Bye-bye, Camel Boy," said Mo.

"Damn, he's talking shit already," I said. "Looks like we're having an effect here after all." I turned to Mo and said, "Next time, you won't be winning any chocolate!"

The boys all laughed again, and Mo grinned. "Okay, but bring more chocolate just in case."

"Bullshit," Grand said. "They are not winning next time, I will lay a few of them fuckers out before we lose again."

The group erupted in laughter, knowing Grand would do exactly what he said.

Over the course of several days, Scott seemed to be growing more and more reserved. Time seemed to drag for all of us there. The heat was certainly a factor, but everyone wanted to head back to Fort Bragg. It was mid-May, and our time there should have ended by July, but nobody ever knew for sure when they were leaving.

I asked Scott what was going on, but each time, his reply was, "Nothing."

It wasn't like him to be so out of it, so I pressed him about why he was so down and so quiet.

"Hello!" he snapped. "We're in the fucking desert, people here hate us, there's no guaranteed timetable for us returning, and you ask me why I am pissy?"

"Come on, Dog Jaw," I said, "you can't let this place get you down. Remember how shitty it was in Alabama?"

"I'm fine, just in a combat zone, in case you forgot."

"I get it, but you can't let this shit weigh you down," I said. "Besides, we should be leaving soon, just a couple months."

"Not soon enough," he said. "I've been ready to leave this shit hole for months."

***

Iraq was truly a third-world country for most of the population. Saddam took care of the elite and left the less fortunate to live in poverty and despair. They all professed to hate him, and at first, we thought it was a game, but these people had been neglected for years. It was amazing what giving the slightest thing to the locals could do for their spirits.

There was a great money-making opportunity there, but I told Scott I had no desire to ever go back, regardless of how much money I could make.

"Wow, you're finally willing to pass up a money-making endeavor," he said. "We'll all be happy to be out of here soon. I want to get started on the next chapter of my life."

On foot patrol, the MPs would take turns eating, and I always ate last, because they knew I would have some kind of concoction.

One day, a few MPs were relaxing off to the side, talking with Grand and Bouford in the shade of a building that had been mostly destroyed by US munitions. The MPs were on break from patrol, eating their MREs, packages of ready-to-eat food that was mostly dehydrated. The brown plastic bags came complete with a main meal, a snack, and a dessert. MREs had so many preservatives, people said, that if you fed them to a rat, it would live forever. They also constipated you pretty badly.

There were normally plenty of Iraqis milling about, but that day there was almost nobody other than US soldiers. The soldiers were sitting on their Kevlars on top of a few old wooden cases, eating and watching me make that day's masterpiece.

For most people, eating freeze-dried foods was a simple "open the pack and eat whatever they put in there." But I liked to turn my lunchtime meal into a project—slowly crumbling the dried beef patty into pieces, mixing them into my canteen cup with hot water, then adding the beef packet and, lastly, the cheese sauce.

Once again, I noticed that Scott seemed to be distant, uncharacteristically quiet. "You okay, Scott?" I asked.

"Yup!"

"Yup?"

"Yeah, I'm good. Just thinking about shit from home."

"Ahh, you miss your mommy again," I said, and the group all laughed it off.

"No, I'm thinking about your wife," he said. "Lisa must be enjoying being away from you. Hell, I'm with you half the time, and you annoy the shit out of me."

The group liked Scott's joke and laughed even louder.

Turning my attention back to my hamburger stew lunch, I continued my commentary. "You have to get the water extremely hot before you put the cheese into it."

"Nobody cares!" said Scott.

"...And you need to get the salt and pepper in there early, as well."

I could see that Scott was only half-listening. He'd heard it all before, blah, blah, blah, and again seemed distant. Then he shook his head, mimicking me, "'Food has to taste good, even in this shit hole.' Yeah, between Basic and over here, I've seen you make that pot of shit twenty times, so spare me the constant babbling."

"Somebody is in a bad mood today," I said.

"You're just annoying sometimes."

"Wooo, you're on your period!"

When the food was finally ready to eat, I began lowering myself into a "kimchi squat," something I had learned from Hankel. But just as I started bringing the plastic spoon to my lips, I was violently knocked to the ground. Scott screamed, "Heads up!"

An explosion ricocheted through the dusty space just off from the play area where the soccer games were held. Lying flat on my back, I watched as Scott grabbed a hand grenade from the exact spot where I'd just been crouching. Without hesitation, he tossed it toward a beat-up car parked about 15 feet away, then he dove to the ground, shielding my body as an explosion roared out from under the hooptie.

There were no injuries, apart from a thousand pin-needle beads of sand spraying our faces and the exposed skin on our hands and forearms. With the blast still echoing in our heads, we all looked around trying to make sense of the moment. Dust and smoke and a sulfur smell hung in the air, and there was almost complete silence for a good two minutes as Bouford and Grand took off after the Iraqi who had appeared out of nowhere to toss the grenade.

I turned to Scott. "What the hell?! You knocked over my beef stew. I was ready to eat that, ass clown."

"Yeah, I did."

"Shit, now I'll have to start the whole process all over again."

"You're an idiot," said Scott.

"Do you have any more beef packets?"

"You almost fucking died again, and you're worried about your hamburger stew?"

"Well, you know that shit is tasty as fuck," I said. "And since it could have been my last meal, I had to make it perfect."

Relieved laughter rang out from some soldiers as they got to their feet, but a few minutes later, the grim reaper came heading toward us in the form of Sergeant Hankel.

"What the hell are you limp dicks doing now? Anyone hurt?"

"No, Sergeant!" we all exclaimed.

"Did you get the bastard that rolled this shit in?"

"Grand and Bouford took off after them, sir," I said, "but you know those two knuckleheads couldn't find their way out of a one-way alley."

Grand, Buford, Scott, and I patrolled together because we were some of Hankel's best MPs, and we all knew it. Other MPs referred to us as the Golden Boys, and Hankel did not care.

"How the hell does this shit happen twice in the last five days?" he said, turning to Scott and me. "I'm seriously thinking about splitting you dipshits up before you both get killed."

"Come on, Sarge," I said. "We were just getting some chow."

"I'm not joking."

"You should blame the new guys, Smith and Johnson," Scott said. "They had overwatch."

"What?"

Smith and Johnson were new in country, and Hankel was not happy we were being so reckless, in his mind, even with the new soldiers there.

"That's who almost got us killed," I said.

"I'm done with you two screwing off out here. If you dick wads have one more close call, I'm separating you."

"What?" Scott and I said simultaneously.

"I am dead serious. You're both way too relaxed, and I need you way more focused. We are not here for a Field Training Exercise. This is the real deal."

"Yes, Sergeant!"

"You do realize who sends the commander all the info to send home to your family if one of you idiots gets killed?"

Now even louder and more firmly, "Yes, Sergeant."

I nodded and gave him a focused look that I reserved for special circumstances and saw Scott doing the same.

Hankel was not amused. He stormed off, telling his driver, "Let's go."

The next few days, foot patrol was mostly quiet, with the exception of the scheduled soccer rematch. It was up to ten-plus kids wanting to play, and I was trying to gather enough candy bars. I was also trying to get more MPs to play.

"We can't let them win next time!" I said, drawing a look from Scott. "I'm serious!"

Scott shook his head and walked away.

The next day started like any other, with Scott shirtless, bragging about his abs as he flexed. He loved reminding me that he'd never get fat because he didn't like food the way I did. After PT, we showered and headed to the chow hall for breakfast. Scott had opted for his standard, an omelet with ham and cheese, and sat down to eat. He wasn't picky and liked getting his food quickly.

Scott took a few steps then stopped to wait for me. The mess cook, Staff Sergeant Robert Jones, loved me but didn't show it to others. By this point, he was already acting annoyed with me and my requests. He turned to me, warily. "What the hell are you gonna order today, pain-in-my-ass Anthony?"

"Okay, Cookie, here's what I want today," I began, feigning obliviousness. "First off, put some of that cooked bacon on the grill. Then mix in some oil and bacon grease on the grill. Let it get hot, then crack three eggs on the grill and spread out the whites, but don't crack the yolk. Let 'em crisp up, then flip 'em over to another spot on the grill where you have a little more oil."

"Anything else?" he said, rolling his eyes and shaking his head, giving me that look people give when they just want you to stop talking so they can leave.

"Well, they'll crisp up quick, and the yolks will stay runny," I said. "Then when you're finished, put some shredded cheese on the crispy whites of the eggs, pretty please?"

Jones looked at Scott, and they both shook their heads.

"Do you get your wife to cook like this for you?" Jones asked.

"Hell, no," I said. "My wife says, 'Make it yourself, you're too friggin' picky!'"

"Maybe I should tell you that, too!"

"Come on, Sarge," I said. "You love my special requests. It allows you to be a real cook."

"I *am* a real cook!"

"Bullshit. You used to be a military intelligence NCO but got two DUIs, so they made you a cook."

"Who told you that shit?"

"Not sure, but it's true, right?"

"Nope," he shouted sarcastically, "it was three fucking DUIs. Commander wanted me in Leavenworth for the last one."

This got a small chuckle from the group, as they weren't sure if he was pissed or laughing about it.

I was too busy adjusting the timer on the toaster, making sure it was just so, because they burned the toast around there.

By now the eggs were up, bacon slid onto the plate, toast done to perfection. I made my way over to the table and dropped into my seat just as Scott was finishing his meal. Grand showed up with the usual omelet with extra bacon on the side, while Bouford had two eggs over easy with bacon and toast.

Looking at me, Scott pointed to everyone else's plate, "Why can't you be like everyone else and just eat what the hell people make for you?"

Grand said, "You would love my mom's cooking. She owns a Chinese restaurant in Saint Louis."

"I love Chinese food," I said.

Scott, Grand, and Bouford all responded at the same time, "Yeah, we know."

"Okay, High Speed," Scott said, in the same sarcastic tone SSG Scruggs used, "we gotta get rolling soon."

"Got it!" I said.

Scott leaned closer. "See SFC Hankel over there? He's giving us the hairy eyeball."

"Yeah, I see him."

"We need to get out of here."

"Hankel can chill the fuck out," I said. "His big ass loves food as much as I do. He won't bother us."

Scott shook his head and sat in quiet amazement as I ate the bacon first—leaving the fatty pieces behind—then dipped the toast into the yolk, scattering the bacon fat pieces over the yolk-covered toast, then seasoned the eggs, before combining the whole lot into a sandwich and taking that first glorious bite.

Scott shook his head. "Okay. We gotta go, like now!"

"Why are you in such a rush, Scott?"

He got to his feet. "I'm heading over to the vehicle. See you there."

Holding my last piece of toast, I looked up at Grand and said, "Can't a guy take a few minutes to eat?" Then I shoved the entire thing into my mouth and stood up with my tray.

It was only later, on patrol in the Humvee with the other MPs, that I realized Scott had been uncharacteristically quiet all day, even more than the last couple times.

"What the hell is going on with you today?" I asked, shifting closer to him.

"Nothing."

"Doesn't seem like nothing."

"Just a bunch of shit on my mind from back home. No big deal."

"You're not with it at all, like you're in some sort of fog or some shit," I said, then shifted into an imitation of Hankel's deep bark, "Stay awake! Stay alive!"

Scott barely reacted.

"How's everything with your mom and brother?" I said.

"They're all fine."

"If it's your mom, dude, you can talk about it."

"No, she's okay. It's just some other crap I was dealing with before I left, you know, stateside crap."

"Well, I haven't seen you this quiet since you walked in on Peggy and Buster." I knew the deal. In a big ass family, someone was always bitching about something. Somebody pissed off someone else. It never ended. With my sisters, half the time, I never even knew why they were mad at me.

"Yeah," he said, "I just have to figure it out."

"Maybe you want to talk about it?"

"I'm going to deal with it at some point," he said. "But not now."

I nodded, like I understood, quiet for a moment. But not used to having anything withheld from me, I blurted out, "Well, what the hell is it, man?"

"I just said I don't want to fucking talk about it right now! You never fucking stop!"

"Okay, okay, whatever!"

He let out a sigh. "Maybe one day, but not today. Can't you ever just accept an answer and not dissect it?"

"Oh, okay, so you're still on your period!"

This elicited a small smirk from Scott, then he looked over at me, his expression closed, wordlessly telling me to let it go.

"Alright," I said. "I'm done asking!"

Without warning, the entire world moved sideways in slow motion as a massive explosion erupted. I could feel it in my flesh and my bones as it ripped through the air. The Humvee flipped onto its side like a toy. The engine compartment, which took most of the blast, separated from the passenger compartment. I felt totally disoriented but knew exactly what it was. *A land mine!*

I squeezed my eyes shut as my body bounced around, waiting for the earth and the vehicle to stop tumbling. There was a stillness combined with the deafening sound. Confused, still inside the vehicle, I surveyed the chaos through the thick smoke. Fortunately, I'd been wearing my seatbelt—not something I always did. Dazed, with a loud humming ringing in my ears, it dawned on me that we were still being fired upon. My training took over, as I twisted around from where I'd been pinned in my seat and fired back toward the source of the rounds.

In the seconds between hails of bullets, I glanced around. Where was Scott? He'd been thrown from the vehicle. In front of us, the lead MP vehicle was attempting to turn around and make its way back, but it was taking fire from another area. Just above my wrist I had a large gash that was oozing blood. I could feel lacerations on my cheeks, and my hands, wrist, and face were covered in tiny blood spots where the sand had embedded into my flesh.

I yelled hoarsely over the sound of bullets, "Scott! Scott! Hello, Scott, answer me!" Firing my weapon as I looked around, then screaming, "Scott, you okay?"

Contorting my body painfully, I maneuvered myself out of the vehicle, firing the last round as I changed the magazine on my M16. I could hear more firing off in the same direction where the first rounds had come from.

The engine compartment was burning hot, causing a thick black smoke that concealed Scott's location and mine from the enemy.

In a crouch, I quickly ran away from the vehicle. Off to the side of the road, I finally caught sight of Scott lying on the ground a short distance behind the overturned Humvee. Without thinking, I rushed over to him. He was lying on his stomach, unconscious, and I rolled him onto his back and pulled him farther away from the wreckage.

His uniform was drenched in blood from the waist down, and my stomach nearly dropped when I saw his bloody legs. His right leg was badly mangled, and his left leg was almost totally severed at the knee. His foot was loosely attached by some small ligaments, flopping around while I dragged him to safety. Flesh and bone were exposed on both legs, blood pouring out from them. I had never seen an injury like that before.

Mercifully, he was unconscious, because he was in ghastly shape.

A couple of shots rang out, but none of that mattered. Both legs were pumping out blood at an uncontrollable rate. I was horrified, but I knew I had to shake it off and stay focused. I didn't have much time. I tried dressing the wounds, screaming, "Medic! Medic! I need a fucking medic now!"

Scott's eyes fluttered, then opened wide as he peered down at his disfigured legs. "Holy shit, this is fucked!" he screamed. "God is punishing me."

"Stay with me," I said, frantically trying to stop the bleeding.

In a pissed-off tone, he yelled, clearly disoriented, "Dude, I'm not gonna make it. This shit, this is not ending well for me."

"Shut the hell up," I said. "Just stay with me, let me dress the wounds. You're gonna be fine." But even as I uttered the words, I knew I was lying.

He passed out again, and again I screamed, "Medic! Fuck! Medic! Where the fuck is the medic?!"

No more shots were being fired, but I barely noticed, my attention laser-focused on stopping the bleeding. I ripped off my belt and wrapped it just above the knee on Scott's nearly severed leg to create a makeshift tourniquet. Next, I grabbed Scott's belt and wrapped it around the other leg.

As I tied it tight, Scott came to again. His voice husky, he whispered, "I think we know one thing for certain."

"What's that?"

His face twisted into a half-smile. "After all these years, you might finally be able to beat me in a race."

Determined to keep it light, I said, "If I put any kind of effort into training, you know I'd smoke your ass. I just don't, because I know how much you like to win."

"Yeah, right!"

"I let you win."

"Well, we don't have to worry about me running any more, do we?"

I was choking up. Although it had only been four or five minutes, frustration was setting in. Full of rage, I spun around. "Where the hell is the fucking medic?"

The combat medic had been traveling close. What was taking him so long?

Time slowed. The smoke from the burning vehicle was still screening us, and I was pretty sure Grand and Bouford had taken out the shooter. But Scott was fading in and out of consciousness, and I knew that unless we got him out of there, got him some blood and fast, he was done.

Without warning, Scott's eyes flew open again. "Anthony. I have to tell you something. It's important," he said, his voice urgent and his face pained.

All I could think about was keeping him calm, keeping him alive until help arrived.

Mustering a sarcastic tone, I replied, "Yeah, you love me, I know. Relax and stay with me. I love you too, fuck face."

"I'm serious," Scott said, his voice firm. "I'm not going to make it, and I need to tell you something important."

"Stop it, man, you're gonna make it. You've got to stay positive. 'Stay awake! Stay alive!' remember?" I leaned in to wipe the sweat and blood off his face.

"Anthony. Dude. Can you stop talking for just two minutes and fucking listen to me? I am not gonna make it, for Christ's sake, and I have to tell you something."

"What the fuck is so important right here, right now?"

"Listen to me. When we were home on leave before we came over..."

"Yeah, I remember. What about it?"

"Remember that girl I told you I hooked up with a couple times?"

"Yeah? What, you want to marry her, or you knocked her up? Or is it something else?"

I was barely listening, just hoping to keep him distracted as I tried to dress the wounds. The bleeding had stopped on the left leg, but I was still trying to stop the right one and having only marginal success.

"No, dude, just listen to me please. Or I won't be able to get it out. The night you went out with your family, I met her at a bar."

"Okay," I said, allowing myself an instant of relief as the medic finally pulled up in a Humvee.

"She's d-dead!" Scott said, his voice drenched in sorrow and remorse.

I quickly pulled my hands back, in shock. Scott had my attention now. "What?"

In the most sad, somber, shameful way, he said, "I think I killed her!"

I sat back, stunned, just staring at him, trying to understand what he had said. "What are you talking about?"

"I can't explain it, it just happened," he said quietly. "I'm not even sure. I was wasted and woke up next to her and she was dead."

"Who was dead?"

"It doesn't matter, dude, I just needed to tell you. God has punished me for it. Don't feel bad for me, feel bad for her."

"Who?" I said. "For who? Who was she?"

Instead of replying, he shook his head in shame and said, "I'm sorry, man."

Then his eyes closed, and he stopped breathing.

"Scott!" I screamed. "Wake up, Scott!" Then, even louder, "Scott, wake up! Stay with me!"

I frantically started CPR, but seconds later the medic pulled me off and took over with a firm, "I got it."

I crouched motionless a few feet away, eyes on the medic as he continued CPR. Scott's last words replayed in my head, tangled with the dawning realization that I was watching my best friend die. I was in complete disbelief about Scott's passing, and also about what he had just told me, about some girl I'd never met and knew absolutely nothing about. How could Scott, one of the most decent guys I'd ever met, kill some girl? Who was she? What had happened? What the fuck just happened?!

The surrounding chaos dissolved in the wake of Scott's confession. I don't know how long I sat there in appalled silence. Time seemed to have stopped.

Sergeant Hankel's bark drifted into my consciousness. "Anthony. Anthony. Hey! Anthony! You need a medic, too."

I just sat there, unresponsive, watching the medics secure Scott onto a gurney and carry him quickly toward the MEDEVAC helicopter that had landed forty or fifty feet away. My best friend, the best man at my wedding, my battle buddy and future Police Academy partner, had just confessed to killing a girl, then died in my arms.

This can't be real. This is a dream, a nightmare. There's no way this happened.

Still in a fog, I somehow made my way to Hankel's Humvee, and we headed back to the FOB. I asked for water, but apart from that, no words were exchanged during the 15-minute ride, which was unheard of for Hankel and me. But there were no words that could make the horrific situation go away.

Arriving on the FOB, we were met by MP Company Commander Captain Brian Fester. As we disembarked, without ceremony or warning, Fester walked over and silently embraced me—no words, just an embrace. Dimly aware of the rarity of such displays of compassion from my commander, I made no effort to reciprocate. Blood still dripped from my arm, but the cuts on my face had stopped bleeding.

As he pulled away, Captain Fester muttered into my ear, "I promise you. We will get the motherfuckers who did this. You have my word."

Hankel tapped me on the shoulder. "Gotta go see the medic."

In a trance, I went to get checked out by the medics. Hankel stood nearby, watching in silence as they dressed the wounds on my arm, then worked on my head wounds, relatively minor given the magnitude of the explosion. I have absolutely no memory of the next hour or so I spent in the medic tent. Still stupefied, I made my way back to the makeshift barracks—alone, as Hankel had gone his own way by now.

The sight of Scott's empty cot conjured a swell of despair. I looked at it, replaying our banter from the morning. Mindlessly, I picked up Scott's camera, remembering Scott's irritating habit of pointing and shooting while yelling, "Smile! You're on Candid Camera!" I allowed myself one small drop of mirth before I tossed the camera onto his bunk then flopped down onto my own. My sole focus was his dying confession. Who was she? How did it happen? When did it happen? He would never kill anyone, and he can't be dead, he *can't* be dead!

My emotions were overwhelming me, and I thought I would never fall asleep, that my head would never empty of thoughts of the side of the road, But somehow, still fully clothed, I drifted off to sleep, my last thought that Scott would shit himself if he knew that Hankel had called him "soldier."

I woke up later, thinking to myself about how we had gotten there, my mind drifting back to the speech SFC Francis had made about the bonds of friendship, about how watching your battle buddy die has no equal. He was so right. I was transported back in time to the face that Francis was making as he talked about the loss of Roll Tide, his Bama buddy.

I now understood why Francis had gone quiet. There were no words to ease the pain.

I remembered, after he'd told that story, I walked back upstairs to our barracks, telling the group this was a solemn night in Basic with no joking, just appreciation that a fellow soldier had died protecting his battle buddy. Now, I wondered how I had ended up in the same situation. I needed to go back in time and figure out when this could have happened— and, more importantly, who Scott could have killed.

CHAPTER 3

FINISHING BASIC TRAINING AND AIT, MAY 1985

For most trainees, AIT was a lot more enjoyable than Basic. But not for me. Scruggs tormented me right up until Week Thirteen, five weeks into AIT. With less than three weeks until graduation, Scruggs decided I needed another talking to. He was baiting me, trying to get me to demonstrate a bad attitude so he could recycle me back to Week Nine, the start of AIT. Unfortunately for him, my PT score was near the top, my common task training score was the second highest in the entire company, and my marksmanship was excellent. There was absolutely no legitimate reason that I should be recycled—well, except for attitude. But if a drill sergeant had it out for you, he would almost always win the battle. He just needed me to fail in a couple areas.

Most trainees had no idea that there needed to be a comprehensive record of poor performance in writing before a soldier could be tossed. That said, in Basic and AIT, the Army still wanted to cut its losses early and weed out the poor performers.

I realized I needed to do something drastic to change Scruggs' mind, but the guy hated my guts.

Remembering the movie *An Officer and a Gentleman*, my inspiration to join the Army, a flash of brilliance went off. The ending of the movie jumped into my mind, inspiring me once again. I realized that to change his mind, I needed to let Scruggs think he was breaking me down, just like Richard Gere let Louis Gossett, Jr. think. He had to win.

This was just after I had learned that the speakers in our barracks were two-way. My plan included using this information to my benefit.

Returning to the barracks after a particularly thorough chewing out in Scruggs' office, I changed my tune. Rather than talking about the Army's college fund money or making fun of Scruggs, I talked to some of the guys about how I couldn't take much more of this, that I felt broken and picked on. Scruggs had grilled me in the office, I said, and he had told me I wasn't making progress and that I was going to be recycled, that he would send his request to the commander.

That was the easy part. The second portion of the plan would require the performance of a lifetime. I needed to get myself so worked up that I could make myself cry in front of Scruggs.

I knew it wouldn't be long before he called me into his office again, given how much the guy had it in for me. I had a whole speech prepared: The Army was everything to me, and I was still trying to be better. I wasn't prepared to quit. This was my last chance. I didn't make it in college, and my parents needed me to send money home to support the rest of the family, I had eight brothers and sisters.

My performance had to be just like the character Mayonnaise from the movie, or Scruggs would stay on me until he could recycle me back to Week Nine. I even used the exact line about having nowhere else to go. But to seal the deal, I still needed to cry. And conjuring memories of my dog dying when I was eight years old, I actually managed to squeeze out a few tears.

At last, Scruggs seemed satisfied that he'd finally broken this smart-ass down and made him cry. Then, just like in the scene from *How the Grinch Stole Christmas!*, Scruggs' heart seemed to grow three times its normal size. He seemed uncomfortable with my tears, almost as if he had gone too far abusing me. After all, I was just running my mouth keeping the rest of the platoon amused, but it was clear from his reaction that he was finally showing some care and concern.

"Anthony," he said.

I replied, "Yes, Sergeant!"

"Stop crying, Anthony."

"Yes, Sergeant." I knew I had him hooked.

"Listen, I'm not one hundred percent sure you're going to do this," he said. "But I need to see you improve. This is your last chance. If not, you're gone!"

"Yes, Sergeant," I said, tears flowing from both eyes.

"Okay, stop crying already," he said, somewhat choked up himself.

He quickly dismissed me, and I went back to the rest of my platoon mates in the barracks. They all asked how I was doing, and I made sure to keep playing for the crowd, all sad and humble. I said I had to keep trying to do my best. But when we got to the break area—away from the microphones—Scott said, "I can't believe he bought it! How did you make yourself cry?"

"Remember my dog Ginger?" I said.

"Not really."

"She got hit by a car."

"Well, I never thought you would pull that shit off! Maybe the tears were real!"

We both laughed, knowing I had totally convinced Scruggs that I was a beaten man.

Scott would later ham it up, "Can you believe this pussy was crying? Mr. 'I don't care what they say to me.'"

Scott knew I was going to do this, but he joked with me, saying, "Now, they all think you're a crybaby." He called BS and insisted that Scruggs made me cry like a baby for real. Funny thing, the others thought he was heartless for busting my balls about it.

My Oscar-worthy performance worked like a charm. By the next weekend, I had Scruggs complimenting me. The rest of the platoon's jaws were practically on the floor. The bastard even called me up to the front and said that in the last two weeks I'd made a 360-degree turn. I thought better than to correct his math.

Even though Scruggs had been on my case for most of Basic and AIT, those months out in McClellan were some of the best of my life. There was that indefinable spirit of camaraderie that came from marching and singing and camouflaging up together. We felt like a championship high school football team. When you have no music, singing becomes sacred. One of the platoon's favorite cadences was "The Early Morning Rain," which SSG Scruggs loved to sing the whole time.

In the early morning rain,
In the early morning rain.
In the early morning rain,
In the early morning raaaaiiiiin.
See the MP dressed in black,

No, he's never coming back.
See the MP dressed in black,
No he's never coming baaaaaaaack.
Mama, Mama can't you see?
What the Army's done to me.
Mama, Mama can't you see?
What the Army's done to me.

When Scruggs sang that song, the platoon got so pumped up that it was no effort to march around for miles on Fort McClellan.

The inventive ways the drill sergeants came up with to punish us were painful back then, but when I look back now, I have to laugh.

In Basic, the only extra break you got was if you wanted a smoke. DS Kelly was normally kind of a reasonable drill, but he was a hard ass about granting permission for a smoke break. But, if you wanted to take a smoke break, you damn sure had to ask.

Once, one of the trainees decided he was going to light up without permission. Kelly lost his mind.

"Who the hell are you to light up without being told? Are you a damn drill sergeant now, Private?"

"No, Sergeant!"

"How many cigarettes you have in there?"

The trainee was terrified, now unsure what to say. "Almost a full pack, Sergeant."

"Great," Kelly said. "Now, you can smoke them all. You got ten minutes. Smoke 'em, Private. Don't let me see any left over."

Then Kelly walked away—given his hatred of cigarettes, he did not want to smell the smoke.

Eight minutes later, the trainee had only smoked five. Some of the other troops wanted to help, including Scott. Looking over at me, he mouthed, "Hey! Free smokes!"

But that was not going to happen, Kelly would have lost his shit.

With two minutes to go, the trainee still had four to five left.

"Smoke'em," Kelly said. "You're running out of time."

When time ran out, there were still a few butts left. Kelly took them—even though he wasn't even a smoker. The trainee, looking four new shades of yellow, walked over to the Pit and gagged for nearly ten minutes straight while the drill sergeants stood off to the side and laughed. That kid never smoked again. I'm sure later in life he would have thanked Kelly, if he ever saw him.

I look back with particular fondness on the part of our training where we had to live in tents together in a field. Not because I'm big on camping—to this day I hate camping, except in my RV.

The field training exercises in both Basic and AIT were a combination of misery and fun. While I was consistently messed with, Scott seemed to be the drill sergeants' favorite. He did well on PT, his uniform always looked great, and he seemed to never say the wrong thing.

On one occasion, Scruggs even said to me, "Why can't you be more like Scott?"

In the field, it was no different. Scott always seemed to be ready and excelled at all aspects of field training. During field training, you got very little sleep and chow was terrible. The eggs arrived in green metal containers, and there was a green color to the outside area of the eggs. Gags me to this day, how bad the food was.

Away from the drills, even Scott was not happy being in the field, for a variety of reasons. The way the drills all loved him, that might have been the first time in the whole of training that Scott experienced any kind of adversity, lucky bastard.

Back in the 1980s, soldiers had to share a small two-man tent, with each soldier having half the equipment to put up the tent. Scott had a tent mate in Basic called Ghetts, who seemed to be allergic to deodorant. And in Alabama in April and May, it got very hot.

Soldiers' uniforms back then were very heavy material. Ghetts' BO wouldn't usually have been that big of a deal, but when you're camping in a field for a week at a time, sharing a tent, with no shower, it becomes a problem. After a few days, Scott, ever resourceful, jokingly decided to sleep with his protective mask on due to the BO, but did not keep it on at all times.

While you were doing Nuclear Biological Chemical (NBC) training, all soldiers had to keep their protective masks on. Ghetts was outside the tent with no mask on when the company commander showed up and said, "Where the hell is your mask?"

Ghetts responded, "Who the fuck are you?"

"I am your fucking commander, Soldier!"

"Holy shit," said Scott, and while the commander ripped into Ghetts, Scott quickly put on his mask, once again looking like he was following the rules, something he was very good at and that constantly earned him praise as a good example for others to follow.

On the fun side of going to the field was driving the jeeps around the training areas. Back then, MPs were still training in the old World War II jeeps with M60s mounted on the back. During the night patrols, Scott and I would talk to each other over the radio but not use our names, in case the drill sergeants wanted to know who was talking.

I would tease Scott, "Your teeth are so spaced apart, it looks like you have a dog jaw."

Scott would respond saying, "Your teeth are so bunched on the bottom, you look like an inbred dog yourself."

From this came the call signs, Dog Jaw One and Dog Jaw Two.

We drove our jeeps recklessly all over the training areas of Fort McClellan —I almost rolled mine one night, which could have ended my Army career right there.

When we got back to the main area, where the soldiers would sleep at night, Scott announced that our Dog Jaw days needed to end before we got tossed out of the course.

He laid into me, telling me I had to just play along, that's why they liked him so much more than me.

He was right, and we knocked it off, but we later used the Dog Jaw call signs a couple times in Iraq, to pass the time or reduce tensions. It always brought a smile.

Another miserable field training experience was the gas chamber. For most, the gas chamber would have been considered adversity. It was an old cement-block structure made to keep 2-chlorobenzalmalononitrile gas, or CS gas, from leaving the building. It was a dark and dreary place that evoked fear in trainees, who knew they were going to have to take their masks off inside the building. But—and this might just be the good old rose-tinted specs speaking—even then, when we were suffering together, it didn't seem all that bad. We were comrades. We had each other's backs. We all knew what the other was going through. There was a bond being formed. We knew that. We sensed it even then.

At the end of AIT, there was a second FTX to help prepare MPs for war. Part of that preparation was the gas chamber, where soldiers performed exercises to learn how well our protective masks worked. This was a real-life concern dealing with Saddam Hussain and Iraqi forces, but it was also another BS way for the drill sergeants to mess with young soldiers.

While we were in the chamber, we were required to take off our masks and breathe in the CS gas, demonstrating the ability if it ever happened in the real world. At least, that was what was meant to happen. The gas would make you gag and make your eyes water. Most could only stand a minute in the chamber.

One of the female MP trainees was so nervous, she started holding her breath as soon as the gas started being pumped into the chamber. By the time she needed to breathe again, the air was thick with gas. She freaked out and took off out the back door, eyes closed, running full speed into a big tree, which knocked her out cold. Stress caused people to react differently, and she was clearly overwhelmed by the chamber. For some reason, Scott and I were unfazed by the chamber.

Chow in the field was truly horrible back then, when we were soldiers. They put the food in these green metal containers called Marmite cans. When your eggs arrived, they were like soup and almost always had a greenish tint to them. Somehow, I grew to like them slimy like that, and to this day, I still only eat my eggs cooked slimy, but not at this point in my life. The portions were always small, and after scooping them from the Marmite can onto paper plates, you ate what they gave you. More often than not, it was raining like hell as you moved through the chow line, and you'd have your poncho on, trying to get a portion of those slimy eggs and a sausage patty.

Somehow, they never mentioned this in the recruiting videos. These were the times I thought of quitting, but I could never have faced my grandfather if I did.

One silver lining of chow was Scott turning me on to grits. He's the one who told me that the only way to eat them was to add sugar and your jelly pack.

The boys from North Dakota and Alabama said we were disrespecting our grits, that they looked disgusting, but that didn't stop us from eating them every day in the field. Once you found something you liked that you could look forward to every day, you held on to it, through hell or high water, no matter what anyone said. I still eat grits that way.

Speaking of things, we liked (which we surely couldn't get every day, week, or even month), when you had been locked away for 12 weeks, only seeing women marching in battle dress uniforms, and you got your first weekend pass, it was every man for himself. A lot of the boys went hell-for-leather on the liquor, too. But the rules were very clear: If you messed up and got arrested, you were getting kicked out of MP school. But many troops got to the twelve-week mark, with just three weeks left to go, and fell at this final hurdle. Maybe the timing made it some kind of test.

On our long-awaited weekend off, Scott, Watts, Ray, and me combined to share rooms off base, and while the drill sergeants had one rule, we came up with another, even more important one: If you happened to link up with someone, you hung a sock over the door handle and the other guys had to wait outside. It was no secret the female soldiers missed us just as much as we missed them.

I'd been dancing all night with this tiny little dark-haired trainee, buying her drinks and romancing her as if my life depended on it. I really liked her. I took care of the taxi ride back to the hotel where she was staying and offered to walk her to her room. She agreed. After being cooped up for eight weeks, I thought I was finally in for some love and affection. Did she invite me in to meet her roommates before we went to the bedroom? Hell, no. She stopped at her door, looked up at me all innocent, and said, "I had a great night. Thank you so much."

Say what, now?

"How about I come in for another beer?" I asked, hopeful she was just playing hard to get at the final moment.

"No, my friends are here, and that wouldn't be okay."

Pushing my luck now, I tried one last time. "How about we go to my room? My roommates won't be there."

"It's kind of late. Sorry." Then she kissed me on the cheek and disappeared inside. I was so disappointed, but I respected her wishes. I was so blind, oblivious to the fact that she was not interested in me that way.

But at least one of us had gotten lucky. When I got back to our room at the Holiday Inn, the sock was on the door, and Watts and Ray were sitting on the floor outside our room, looking like they needed their beds soon. Scott's partner had a particularly shrill voice, I noticed. It only took five minutes, and I hoped for Scott's sake I'd arrived in the final act of the production. His female friend slipped out the door quietly and down the hall, and we all found our way to bed.

The rest of the weekend, there were no more socks on the doors, just lots of beer drinking and storytelling.

Weeks Eleven to Thirteen were when soldiers were notified of their next assignments. I got Fort Sheridan, Illinois; Scott got 8th MP Brigade Korea; Ray got Korea; Collins got Fort Campbell, Kentucky;

Walters, Fort Lee, New Jersey; and Centers got Fort Drum, New York. Ghetts had been assigned to Fort Sheridan, but for reasons we never learned, he wanted to go to Korea instead. Korea was a terrible assignment, literally the worst place to be assigned as an MP. The hours were long, and the barracks life was terrible. Maybe Ghetts heard it was a good place to find his future bride. Whatever the reason, he agreed to swap with Scott, so Scott came to Sheridan with me while Ghetts went to Korea.

Maybe later in life, Ghetts realized he had made a bad trade, but Scott and I were thrilled to be going to the same duty station, where we could hang out together for another year or so.

In exchange for the swap, Scott did whatever Ghetts wanted, buying him beer every weekend that we had a pass, and lots of shit from the Post Exchange.

Unlike me, Scott had a ball in both Basic and AIT. Not running his mouth was the biggest difference between us. Even before we knew about the two-way speakers, he made sure that no matter what he did or where he was, he put the Army first. I ranked that third, with food being Number One and everything else Number Two.

One thing Scott dealt with that I did not was a long-distance love affair with his high school girlfriend, Peggy. Knowing that his Army future was going to include her given our new duty station, he felt things were finally falling into place. He was ready to start life as an MP, which was just a steppingstone for him to get to a destination. He did not know where that was, but he knew it was starting here in Alabama.

By the end of AIT, everyone was in amazing shape. Even one the good ole fat boys were fit, ready, and trained, except for our Cajun boy, David P. Longview, who went back home to Louisiana to eat his mama's cooking.

But his spirit stayed on in one way. From then on, whenever we ate something delicious, David's description was the barometer against which everything was measured: "You need to go home and slap your mama," which I still use almost 40 years later.

The bonds we established in Basic and AIT were unforgettable. These were only to be trumped by combat, just like Frances said, but at this point we did not understand this. No matter how much time passed, whenever we saw each other again—which we often did over the following decades—we would immediately be transported back to the good old training days in McClellan, reminiscing and laughing about our shared misery and retelling all the old stories into the early hours.

And whenever I ate coconut cream pie, I flashed back to that moment. I still love it, even with the bad taste Scruggs put in my mouth.

When graduation day arrived, our dress green uniforms and spit-shined dress shoes showed a level of commitment we did not have 14 weeks prior. The entire unit formed up to march over to the parade field. Even Scruggs had a smile on his face. I said to him, "It took fourteen weeks to see you smile. Now, I understand why you never smiled, Drill Sergeant."

"What are you talking about, Anthony?"

"The tobacco-chewing has done a number on those teeth, Sergeant!"

"Drop, Anthony!" he said in his old angry tone, which caused everyone to laugh.

But I just jumped to the ground and yelled, "Yes, Drill Sergeant." Then I jumped up and said, "Just like old times."

Scruggs smirked at me, although I'm not sure if he wanted to punch me or congratulate me.

After that, the unit moved out to the parade field, with Scruggs singing our favorite song, "In the Early Morning Rain."

We all arrived safely on the parade field, looking like the finest trained military unit in the world. Well, at least that's how we felt. After numerous long-winded speeches and a few soldiers passing out from standing at attention and locking their legs up, we were finally announced as graduates.

As we cleared the parade field and greeted our families, we rejoiced that this chapter in our lives was over. Scott's girlfriend was a knock-out, and all the MPs commented on how attractive she was. Even I had to agree. My mother and grandmother were there, as well as my brother Michael. It was a joyous day for both Scott and me, and we knew we would be seeing each other again soon. Both our families shared their appreciation that we had become friends and would hopefully stay in touch.

My grandmother said, "You guys are close to Niagara Falls." Then she turned to my mom. "Hey, Sandra, now we have friends we can stay with on our trip to New York."

Scott's family laughed, but I knew they were getting a visit for sure, as Niagara Falls was on my mother's list of places to visit.

After a quick pack-out of our clothes and uniforms, we were on our way. Goodbye, Fort McClellan, and off to Fort Sheridan.

CHAPTER 4

FORT SHERIDAN, ILLINOIS, JUNE 1986

Scott's girlfriend, Peggy, flew in from his hometown to celebrate his graduation, then they went back to New York. I had no girlfriend, but I was happy that some of my family was there. After graduation, I flew with them back to Rhode Island to visit more family and see some friends. It was strange being apart from Scott. I don't know if I would have made it through Basic and AIT without him. I was glad we'd be together again at our first duty station.

My dad was waiting to pick us up at the airport with my pal Phil Gold. Phil had joined the Army National Guard a year earlier. He was a reserve MP, too, not active duty, but he was also a Lincoln police officer, which was my goal.

"What a great surprise!" I said.

Gold grinned, looking sharp in his dress police uniform. "Well, I needed to be sure you graduated."

I exchanged hugs and firm handshakes with them both.

My dad said, "Proud of you, Son."

"Thanks, Dad."

Gold offered to drive me home, and my dad said, "We got a full car, go ahead. We will see you at the house."

As we drove, I talked about how easy everything had been, and about my new battle buddy, Scott. There was very little mention about Scruggs and the nightmare he had put me through; perhaps that memory was already fading.

Gold told me he had enlisted as a means to get into the Lincoln Police Department, and said I should consider doing the same thing.

"Sounds like you found a great bud in the Army," Gold said, "but hopefully we can all work together if my National Guard unit gets activated."

"Maybe," I said. "But if we ever get activated, that means we're going to war. I didn't join to do that."

Gold shook his head. "Highly unlikely. We haven't had a real war since Vietnam."

"Let's keep it that way. I'm too pretty to go to war."

Gold cracked up. "You're a lot of things, but pretty is not one of them." Then he turned the conversation serious. "Ant, for real, becoming a police officer is the best choice I ever made. I really think you should consider doing this when you finish your first tour."

"No, I think I am going back to school, do something in the business world."

"Well, think about it. You could get in here easy. Not many will have the experience you will after three years."

"Yeah, maybe," I said, changing the subject to my college fund. "Dude, I get over twenty-k, and they pay it directly to me—can you believe that?"

"Wow, that's a lot of money."

Gold dropped me off at 1179 Old River Road, a Colonial home with faded white-slate siding—the house I'd grown up in. For the next ten days, that's where I would be hanging out. I pulled out my duffel bag, and Gold appeared to drive off. In the moment of quiet that followed, I looked around, surprised at how little had changed.

The quiet ended when I went inside to find all seven of my brothers and sisters, my cousins Deena and Rhonda, a couple aunts, and a few of my old buddies, including Tom and Cheryl, Dave Long, Bob Wall, and Marty Gaughan.

My dad again let everyone else talk to me first, and then he simply walked over to me and extended his hand. "Son, like I said, I am damn proud of you. I never thought you would join the Army, but I am sure you'll do well."

I shook his hand. "Thank you, Dad. And I know, me either."

My dad was a no-nonsense, say-it-like-it-is kind of guy. If you ever needed an honest opinion, there was no better person than my dad, and I had always gone to him with my most difficult dilemmas.

And all my siblings talked about how calm and relaxed he always was. Like at the airport, he stepped back to let Gold drive me home even though he wanted some time with me as well.

None of us referred to him as our stepdad—he was always Dad. The only dad we ever knew. No better man of character than my dad, or maybe a close second after my Grampa Walter. The demons dad had slayed as a recovering alcoholic gave him the ability to remain calm. Our family was lucky to have him—who adopts six kids? We say, "No wonder he became an alcoholic!" He was a great provider, too, something we needed or we all would have gone in different directions.

The next day, I decided to call Scott to see how he was doing and to make sure we were on track for our arrival at Fort Sheridan.

"Hey, Dog Jaw," I said. "How is it being back home with your lady?"

"Well, I already proposed and obviously she said yes. We're getting married in a small ceremony next year while I am assigned to Fort Sheridan."

"Wow! That's pretty soon for a wedding date."

"Yeah, it's so Peggy can stay in school here in New York while I'm in Chicago."

"You have this all figured out, I see."

Scott's mom was in the room, and I could hear her blurt out, "A little too soon, if you ask me."

Clearly, she was not happy he was getting married; she wanted him to see the world first before he settled down. Scott seemed to be pretending not to hear her.

I changed the topic. "How is it in upstate New York?"

"It's like other country areas in the US," Scott explained. "Just because it's New York doesn't mean it's the big city."

"Well, maybe I'll swing through and see in about a week."

"The days seem to going by extremely quick, dude, soon I will be separated from Peggy again. I suggested we get married sooner, but she said no. She's on summer break from college, and I think she likes her freedom."

"How did you propose?"

"Last night, we went to the restaurant where we had our first date, and I said, 'We need to get married before I go to my next duty station so you can join me there.' She agreed and said she looks forward to becoming Mrs. Scott before the unknown next duty station, which would more than likely be overseas."

"That doesn't sound too romantic. But she said yes?"

"Yeah," he laughed. "It's me, brother."

The next night, my friends and I went to a local bar called Brooksies. There was nothing planned, but several of my high school buddies heard we were there and showed up and started asking the big question: "How the fuck did you keep quiet, man?"

I also saw Lisa Misiaszek, whom I used to play hide and seek with when we were kids. I'd heard that her brother Al was a navigator in the Navy.

"Congratulations on becoming an MP," she said, sounding almost surprised. "There's quite a few things I thought you might do, but the Army? And a policeman in the Army?"

"Why not?"

She laughed in a flirtatious kind of way. "Well, you were crazy in high school. How are you going to follow the rules in the Army when you never did in high school?"

I grinned. "Easy. I get paid to do it now."

"Maybe they should have paid you in high school." She smiled again in her sweet, subtly flirtatious way.

"Tell your brother congrats on his new job in the Navy. I wish him well."

"You got it. Keep in touch, it was nice seeing you," she said, flashing a big smile my way as she walked away. I reached out and touched her on her shoulder, and I could tell by her reaction she liked it.

It was kind of strange seeing her there. She was still as cute as ever, but I heard she had a boyfriend. *Oh well, maybe next time,* I thought, watching as she walked away. When she got to the end of the bar, she turned around one more time to see me smiling at her, and she smiled back. I knew she would look back; I had a sense she wanted one more smile.

Just then, Marty Gaughan walked through the door, joining Dave Long and Bob Wall. The three of us were the most out-of-control guys at Lincoln High School. All crazy guys for sure, but the thing about Marty and his family was the respect and honor they had for those who served. Marty's dad, Martin Senior, was a Vietnam War veteran and, as I mentioned earlier, a huge help to me during Basic and AIT.

We were all taking turns hugging, and after I hugged Marty, I said, "Hey, brother, tell your dad thank you for sending me those calling cards."

"No problem, he does that for everyone who leaves for the military."

"Really? I thought I was special."

"Yeah, you are," he said, rolling his eyes and making everyone laugh. He was cute, the smart ass. "He gets folks to donate, nothing more important than calling home when you join the service, Pops says."

"Oh, man, they saved my ass for sure," I said. My eyes were pulled away again as I noticed Lisa headed for the door with Linda Kay and Susan Strange, her friends from high school. "Man, she was always so pretty in high school. I think she's even better looking now."

"Yeah, dude," Marty said. "Everyone else thinks so, too."

Dave Long laughed and yelled, "Including me!"

Lisa paused at the door and looked over at us. "Good night, boys."

Strange coincidence, I thought to myself, smiling at her one more time as she, Susan, and Linda headed out the door.

"I can't believe you made it through Basic," said Dave. "Seriously, how the hell did you keep your mouth shut?"

"It was easy."

"Bullshit, it was. I know you."

Marty laughed. "There's no fucking way you shut up. No shot, dude."

"Well, I got my ass ripped for the first thirteen weeks, but then I figured it out."

Just then, the volume went up five decibels as four of my old football buddies showed up, all shouting, *"ANNNNNTHONNNY!!"*

The rest of the night was filled with lots of shots and talk of old parties on Dexter Rock Road, old girlfriends, and who was doing what. Gold showed up later, and it was a good thing, because I was in no shape to drive home.

"Gimme your keys, Soldier," he said. "Let's go, I'll drive you home."

I unlocked the car then tossed him the keys. "Man, things seem so different now, even though everyone's doing the same shit."

"Yeah, my thoughts exactly when I got home from the Army. It changes you in ways you never understand."

"But I pride myself in being me. I can't let it change me."

"Well, I'm back here working as an officer in my hometown, but things are so different for me now as well. I'm not putting the place down, but it seems like most of the people are stuck in this part of their lives, and they're missing so much more by not getting away from here."

"They haven't changed one bit. You have."

"Yeah," he said. "I guess you're right about that."

I woke up the next morning with a huge hangover, my first in years. I went to see my grandmother and grandfather the next day, and we went to lunch at one of his favorites, Chelo's, at the initial location in Cumberland near the Boys Club. They had a great menu at reasonable prices. My favorite meal was either the roast beef sandwich or the fish and chips. Grampa always ordered just the fish and ate my fries or Granma's. She yelled at him to get his own damn fries, but he said, "We never finish them all, so why pay for them?" (Apple and try came to mind, but this was only years after reflection on these moments.) Grampa told me he was proud of me, and that I should consider becoming an SP in the Navy. He faked grabbing the check, but I took it from him quickly and paid.

Granma said, "You know you weren't going to pick that up, Walter!"

The day before I left for New York to pick up Scott to head to Chicago, I decided I had to hit all my favorite places to eat, including Pawtucket House of Pizza, Asia Grill, Wiener Genie, Kay's, Stanley's, and the Lodge. I missed them all, and it was going to be some time before I'd return to Rhode Island.

On arriving in Scott's hometown in upstate New York, I thought, *No kidding, this place is the country. It feels like Alabama!* We went to Peggy's dad's house, and I saw his planes and more broken-down vehicles than running ones. What a great guy, though. I could see why Scott loved him. He had an infectious optimism about him. Scott broke the news to me that he was going to stay one more day with Peg so he could have more fiancée sex. He would take the train to Chicago.

The next morning, I said goodbye to Scott and Peggy and drove in my blue 1975 Chevy Vega to Fort Sheridan, Illinois, although now I was Chicago-bound first, to pick up Scott. With both our Class A uniforms hanging behind the driver's seat, I arrived in downtown Chicago. I parked outside the train station, and for once I was on time.

If you had never been to the train station in Chicago, it was quite an interesting place, especially on a Sunday morning. There was very little action but numerous people walked around begging and asking for change to get a coffee or food. Being a soldier, I probably looked like an easy mark—too bad I was too cheap to give them any money.

Scott's train arrived on time, and we went down to the bathroom in the basement of the train station to get dressed. It was old and dirty, with black and white tile, ancient fixtures, and a thick layer of grime.

"This is the darkest, dingiest bathroom I've ever seen," I said.

Scott nodded. "Clearly, these wall tiles have been around since Al Capone's day. The sinks, too."

"I agree."

"Kind of smells like someone died down here."

"Well, let's get out quick before we end up dead, too."

We were both nervous being in the big city and afraid of being robbed, so we decided to take turns shaving while the other stood watch.

I went first and found that the water coming out of the taps was ice cold. Trying to get a close shave without hot water was extremely painful, but I managed to do it. Scott had much thicker facial hair, so it was worse for him, and he ended up with ten or twelve bloody pieces of toilet paper all over his face.

"What the hell?" I said. "You look like you shaved with a machete."

"It was torture," he replied, as one of the pieces of paper fell away from his face and fluttered to the floor.

We put on our Class A uniforms and headed out from the train station to our first duty station.

Funny thing, when you first joined the Army, you had a general idea of what things were going to be like. But once you were in uniform, nothing you had learned could prepare you. Getting yelled at day in and day out by drill sergeants made you believe the rest of your time in the Army would be just as painful—even after you heard otherwise from people who had served. Once you arrived at your first assignment, you too came to realize it was nothing like Basic Training, and you understood that Basic was precious.

As we pulled into the main gate of Fort Sheridan, still wearing our Class A uniforms, we were met by Specialist Charlie Parasails, the MP pulling gate duty.

I lowered my window and said, "Good afternoon, Specialist. We have assignment orders here. Can you help us find the Military Police Company?"

Parasails screwed up his face. "Why the hell are you two idiots in your Class As?"

I glanced at Scott, then said, "Because we're reporting for duty here and need to be in our dress uniforms."

Parasails burst out laughing and picked up the phone to call his patrol supervisor, Mark Peters. "Hey, come over and see this."

Peters arrived a few moments later in a green 1976 Ford Maverick. He walked over and leaned into our car, taking a moment to study us. "Can you explain to me why the hell you two are wearing Class As?"

"We're reporting for duty," I said.

He shook his head. "Never mind, follow me. I'll call Top and tell him to meet you at the MP Company."

DYING CONFESSION

He got back in his car, and we followed him. Scott and I wondered out loud, what the hell was going on and why were these guys razzing us about wearing our Class As?

The building was old, circa World War I, made of brick with large concrete decks on the two levels. It must have been an office building before it became barracks. We waited patiently for the first sergeant's arrival. We were kind of nervous, as the highest-ranking enlisted soldier we had ever spoken with prior to this was Senior Drill Sergeant Frances.

First Sergeant Carl Krieger arrived and greeted us warmly. We stood at parade rest while he spoke to us. He looked at us funny and said, "You're not in Basic Training anymore. No need to stand like that."

"Yes, First Sergeant," we said in unison.

Chuckling a bit, Krieger said, "Relax, boys. Basic is over."

We were assigned to the MP barracks, which was directly above the company headquarters, where the first sergeant, commander, the training NCOs, and support staff worked from 8 to 5 daily. Our first assignments as military police had finally arrived, and we were filled with excitement and anticipation. We were both assigned as patrolmen, but in different squads. Scott was assigned to SSG Meehan's squad, and I was assigned to SGT Rodriguez's squad.

It turned out they were both great NCOs to have if you were a new soldier, and Scott and I excelled early and were recognized as outgoing yet squared-away soldiers. We quickly realized that for MPs, as in Basic Training, appearance was the most important thing for being successful. Highly shined boots should glisten every day, haircuts should be crisp, and the uniforms should always be cleaned and pressed. The first sergeant, whom everyone referred to as Top,

81

said, "Appearance is seventy-five percent of your job. If you look like you know what you're talking about, it will get you past most any problem you face at this hole in the wall."

From Day One, Top pushed his "Army for Life" agenda. He insisted that we should consider the Army as a career. The only reason either of us was there was to get money for college via the Veterans' Education Assistance Program (VEAP), but we were smart enough not to admit it to Top.

We settled in nicely and really enjoyed being stationed at Fort Sheridan. After our first day on patrol, we talked about how cool it was being MPs and riding along with more senior MPs. I patrolled with a guy named Sgt. Smith, while Scott was on patrol with Sgt. Brock.

After our second day, Scott was beside himself. He told me Brock had driven them out to the firing range area and then sparked up a freshly rolled joint and smoked it in the patrol vehicle.

I was shocked. "What the hell did you do?"

"Nothing, I just got out of the car and walked around while he smoked his doobie." He shook his head. "I'm confused. What am I supposed to do?"

"Don't put up with that shit," I said. "Tell him if he smokes again, you're going to turn him in. If you put up with someone doing something wrong, it will eat at you. If you know it's wrong, then speak up, you're an MP now."

Scott confronted him and was shocked: Brock never fired up a joint in front of him again.

I had problems of a different sort with Smith.

Everyone called the First Sergeant Top, but I never did. Finally, one day Top pulled me aside and said, "You can call me Top. No need to keep calling me First Sergeant all the time."

"No, First Sergeant," I said. "I would never disrespect you like that."

"What the heck do you mean by that?"

"Well, I was talking with Smith, and he said they call you Top because your head has an odd, somewhat funny shape to it."

Shaking his head, Top chuckled a bit and said, "You've been had, Anthony...and what the heck is wrong with my head?"

"Nothing, Top! For the rest of my life, I'll call you Top!"

After a few months of patrol, we were regulars and more new MPs arrived at the unit, so we were the more-senior privates. To seasoned soldiers, that might not mean a thing, but to us it meant there were now MPs in the unit whom we outranked.

I came into the Army as an E-3 and Scott was an E-2, but as I mentioned, we took great pride in our uniforms and appearance and wanted to rise quickly in the ranks.

Another key factor for being a successful MP was taking college classes to obtain promotion points, so we both signed up for classes as soon as we arrived. After less than six months, Scott was selected to be the provost marshal's driver. The provost marshal, Lieutenant Colonel Denny, was the senior military police officer on the installation. He loved having Scott as his driver and liked to talk about all the young women Scott and I seemed to be around all the time. Many times, Scott was confronted about his single life and how the young ladies at the club were easy prey. The colonel liked to reminisce with Scott about his college days and how he had been a ladies' man.

After a few months on patrol, I was overjoyed to be selected to work in the AWOL apprehension branch. This job required that I travel in and around a five-state area looking for soldiers who had gone absent without leave. I could not have been more excited. This was a great job, working with all E-4s and above.

I started training with Timothy "Tim" Boggs, a Southerner who didn't just love country music, he lived it. Unfortunately, I couldn't stand country music and hated it whenever Boggs put a cassette tape in our boom box, which was always, making rides in the AWOL apprehension van painful.

"I simply can't understand, why don't you like country music?" Boggs would say.

"I prefer disco and soul music," I'd explain.

"Trust me, one day you'll grow to love country music."

And I'd say, "Not a chance in hell."

But I did, in fact, come to love country and western night at the club on Fort Sheridan. It happened every Wednesday evening, and Scott and I never missed the sounds of Kenny Rogers and Dolly Parton singing "Islands in the Stream," a host of Alabama songs, and even Hank Williams. It seemed all the good-looking soldiers would attend the club, which was in the basement of the officers club and would be packed every night of the week. So, it was farmer jeans on Wednesdays and tuxedo shirts and bow ties on Friday and Saturday nights.

We could be found there almost every night, unless we were working, or we'd at least start the night off there. If it was country night, we'd be two-stepping with the ladies, sporting our jeans and cowboy boots. If it was soul night, we'd be mashed together in a disco train, bumping and grinding with all the sisters who went to the club. Most times, we'd be there in our tuxedo shirts and bow ties, dancing all night.

On soul music nights, we might be the only white guys in the club. This never mattered to us, because we stood out no matter who was in the club. If it were soul or rock night, DJ Ross was back there spinning records.

To this day, everyone still calls him DJ Ross—we never knew his real name. At some point in the evening, Ross would say over the microphone something like, "This is going out to my main man Anthony, and I'm talking about Scott, too." Then he'd play the song "White Horse."

He would then challenge all the ladies in the club. "Okay, ladies I got my two white horses out there, so get out there and take them for a ride! Yeah, baby!" DJ Ross had a way of making everyone in the club feel welcome and always had some pretty young lady sitting by him at the DJ booth. Whether he was playing "White Horse," "Somebody Else's Guy," or "No Parking on the Dance Floor," people were always engaged. He had very little inventory of rock or country music, and would play at best three songs per hour, but he was the kind of guy that always made you feel special. Years later, I still talk to him.

But life wasn't all dancing at the club. Part of working as an AWOL apprehension officer meant you had to take control of military prisoners from civilian detention centers. Some of these AWOL soldiers had been accused of violent crimes and had no desire to return to military duty. I was instructed by Boggs to make the prisoners fearful or intimidated when I first picked them up, so they'd know I meant business.

"You need an intimidating speech that gets their attention,"

Boggs told me. "Regardless of your rank, they need to know you mean business!"

I became a master at my speech, and whenever we picked up prisoners from various jails near Fort Sheridan, I was ready to give them "The Speech." The clear purpose for the speech was to intimidate AWOLs. With a loud and stern voice, it went something like this: "I am PFC Anthony, and I am a military policeman from Fort Sheridan. My partner and I have been assigned to pick you up from jail. When you address me, you will call me PFC Anthony. When I walk, you walk; I stop, you stop. You don't talk unless I give you permission to talk. When you answer, your response is 'Yes, PFC Anthony,' or 'No, PFC Anthony.' When you walk, you keep your head and eyes facing forward, and you do not talk to me or anybody else unless you request permission to speak. We will not stop to let you use the facilities, so if you must go, you need to go when we tell you to use to the bathroom."

Boggs got a kick out of the speech, as I tended to ham it up like I was a drill sergeant. He thought it was kind of funny, higher-ranking prisoners getting dressed down by a PFC Anthony.

After a while, the police officers in detention centers across Iowa and Illinois wanted to hear the speech. This only made me ham it up even more.

A couple months after I got there, Boggs left Fort Sheridan for Anchorage, Alaska, and I was assigned a new partner, Specialist Anthony Jones, a.k.a. Tony Rome. He said the ladies gave him that name, but we all suspected he made it up—although it was too cool, for sure.

On a trip to Des Moines, Iowa, with my new partner, I was getting ready to show off my speech skills. Tony Jones, who outranked me but was new to AWOL apprehension, had been told by more experienced MPs the importance of the speech, but he just gave his trademark Tony shoulder shrug and said, "Whatever, cuz!"

As we prepared to walk into the cell, one of the local police officers asked to stand in and listen to "The Speech." I greeted the AWOL prisoner and immediately started to go hard and firm into my speech: "My name is PFC Anthony…"

But in the cell just off to the right, two Marines wearing impeccable dress uniforms were there to pick up a Marine who had gone AWOL.

They simply walked up and asked, "Are you Private Tanner of the United States Marine Corps?"

The prisoner responded with a firm, "Yes, Sergeant."

The Marines then grabbed a black bag with gold rope on it and put it over his head, fixed the rope, and simply stated, "You are an embarrassment to the Marine Corps," and they pulled the string tight.

Talk about taking the steam out of my speech. I never gave it with the same level of passion again.

One of the prisoners I picked up had gone AWOL from Fort Ord, in Monterey, California. This soldier was a self-surrender, which meant he had turned himself in. If it was a cool place to visit, we would escort prisoners back to their units. Places we liked to go were Germany, Hawaii, and California. Places we did not like to go to included Korea, Fort Drum, NY, and Fort Hood, Texas. After landing in San Francisco, I secured a rental car and drove the prisoner to Fort Ord over two hours away. I brought the soldier to the MP station, and once they signed for him, my work there was done. My good buddy

Bob Walters from back home in Rhode Island was stationed at Fort Ord, and we met up that afternoon at the PX.

After joking around about life in the Army, Bob turned serious and said, "I'm done after my first enlistment. Headed to be a state trooper, if I can pull it off."

"No way," I said. "I'm going into some type of business, not sure about being a cop."

His face brightened, and he said, "Dude, tonight is male stripper night at the club! We gotta go there!"

"Whoa! What happened to you in California, Bob? You into dudes now?"

"No, idiot, the male dancers perform until 10 p.m., then they let the guys in."

"Okay?" I said, unsure where he was going.

"Trust me, Ant, the room is full of starving ladies, and we're the buffet. If you can't find a lady there, your skills are horrible."

"Okay, whatever. I just want to have some fun."

I picked Bob up in my rental car, a white 1984 Buick Century with red velour seats.

He got in and said, "Did you ask for the pimp mobile when you rented the car?"

We arrived at the club and waited at the door. After ten minutes, they let us in.

We were like cattle, as all the women stared at us walking through the door.

Bob smiled and shook his head. "See what I mean?"

It was crazy. Ten to one, women to men. Sporting my Calvin Klein jeans and a dress shirt, I got on the dance floor to show off my skills, and within minutes I had my pick of several very attractive ladies. I settled on a good dancer with a pretty smile (whose name I am leaving out on purpose). We danced for a couple hours. She seemed to have gotten her appetite before I arrived, but I was okay with that.

We dropped Bob off at the barracks then headed to her house. She lived in a duplex, and I parked in the long driveway. We made it into the home, where a small puppy was waiting.

I took my shoes off, and we had a drink in the living room. She told me she was a student in her senior year studying to be an accountant.

Things ramped up quickly, and after our clothes fell off in the living room, we made our way to the bedroom.

At the exact same time we started to take things to the next level, the neighbors in the apartment next door decided they wanted the whole world to hear them making love.

My partner started to match the neighbor's volume and excitement.

This was completely baffling—it wasn't me making her scream, "Oh yeah, give it to me, yeah, yeah, you're the best." I had just started our session, so it wasn't all that. I was thinking, *I can't wait to tell Scott.*

She barked out a command, then proceeded to roll over on all fours, like the "stop, drop, and roll commercial."

How the hell did she do that? I thought to myself.

With each thrust, there was a loud, "Yes, again, yes, yeah, like that."

I was looking around for a camera, because this simply was not real. I'm not that good, and I'm okay with that. Then, from out of nowhere, I felt this warm, wet sensation under my asshole. *What the hell was that?* I was in the throes of it, so I kept pumping, then I felt it again. I turned quickly, and there's the little golden retriever licking just behind my ball sack.

Holy shit! What is going here? Somebody rescue me, now!

I jumped up, grabbed the dog and took him out of the bedroom then closed the door.

My partner and I swapped positions, and we continued the session.

I was almost at the finish line when little Lassie snuck back in and started licking my toes, but I was on the bottom. It was a little too freaky, but we both finished. Shortly afterward, I took Lassie out of the room and grabbed a Miller Lite from the fridge, then went back to bed. I fell asleep quickly and woke up thirty minutes before the alarm was set to go off.

I decided to leave her a note and try to leave quietly rather than the complicated goodbye. One sock was missing the toe section, completely eaten by the dog. I slid it on with my all my toes poking through the hole.

What the hell? I thought. *Lassie, you got some serious foot issues.* I was glad she hadn't found my underwear.

I tried to exit quietly, but Lassie snuck out the door ahead of me. First, I said the heck with it, but I didn't want to the dog to get run over, so I chased her.

If you chase a dog, they run, but if you run from them, they chase you. I went to the fridge again—mind you, the girl was still sound asleep—and grabbed some Velveeta cheese. Back outside, I tried to entice Lassie to come home. A quick toss of cheese and she grabbed it. I raced back to the door, and she followed me right into the house. Still trying to be quiet, I was sneaking back out the long driveway when I looked up and saw the girl in the window.

Using my hands, I tried to explain why I had left, sort of circling them, pointing at my chest, then I just gave up. I'm no lip reader, but it was very clear what she was saying: "You fucking asshole!"

Not my best move!

I never saw her again, but Bob told me that every time he saw her out after that, she would say, "Your friend is a fucking asshole!"

***

MPs were like every other soldier in that there were squared-away ones and not so top-notch ones. Scott and I first arrived at Sheridan in the middle of a big investigation. A few MPs had driven their patrol car over a ramp, trying to play *The Dukes of Hazzard*. On one jump, they landed, and the driver lost control and hit a tree dead on. Not something MPs should ever be doing, so they decided to fabricate a huge story. They called in a fake vehicle hot pursuit, saying that the car was headed toward the front gate. After that, they called in that the patrolman had lost control and hit a tree.

When MPs investigated each other, someone always gave in and told the truth. This time, it was the driver—whom the others all tried to cover for—who broke down and told the truth. Kind of strange that the guy who did it ended up rolling over on all the others, who were trying to cover for him. He got a slap on the wrist, but the others all lost rank.

We learned a valuable lesson: tell the truth or say nothing—a lesson that was to have significant impact on us later in life.

As mentioned earlier, most of our free time in Illinois was spent out at the nightclub on base or one right off the installation. For Scott and me, this was especially true when new female MPs arrived. We turned the charm on for any and all who arrived, so much so that First Sergeant Krieger would warn the new female MPs that they should stay away from the "self-proclaimed Casanovas" Anthony and Scott.

All this accomplished was to make them wonder who these guys were, and several would fall for our special charming ways. We would welcome the new soldiers in a way that only the two of us could do. Like most things between us, winning the affections of the new female soldiers became a competition. We had simple rules, like no slow dancing and you didn't ask to go to their rooms, they had to ask you. The rules had to be followed so that the girl would be the one making the call on who she would be with.

One night, an extremely attractive new MP named Beth arrived. Scott and I were circling the water like sharks. We danced with her and others at the club all night, careful not to break any of the rules. However, the competition was on, and neither of us wanted to let the other win. When I left the room, Scott, normally the rule follower, decided he was going to move in for a slow dance.

This was clearly a huge violation, which he denied, and I gave him crap about it. I could tell he was lying just by his actions.

Scott insisted, "Beth asked me to dance!"

This was a bald-faced lie, and we both knew it. Like we were back in Basic Training, he gave his greedy little finger roll and laughed. As the three of us drove back to the barracks, I was fucking pissed. In all honesty, I didn't care about losing the girl, but my buddy had broken the rules to win. He cheated!

The MP barracks were relocated to some WWII-era housing buildings, all the exact same size, lined up, side by side, along the streets.

In this case, the female barracks and male barracks were side by side along the main road. These were very old buildings, and certainly not something people enjoyed living in, even though they had been upgraded just before the MPs moved in. They had old toilets and small rooms, but they did have newer windows in them.

The rest of the soldiers on the installation resided in a newer high-rise building with all the amenities of new construction. The female day room backed onto the male barracks' day room and was easily viewable from the second floor, where I decided I was going to watch.

Scott sat on the couch and slowly put his arm around Beth's shoulder. When I saw this, I ran over to the black military phone on the wall and called over to the female barracks. I knew the number by heart, it was one number away, 457-0039 and we were 457-0038.

I saw Scott get up and answer the phone on the wall, then I heard him. "Hello…? Hello, hello?" But I stayed silent.

Scott hung up and moved back to the couch, but as he started making his move again, I redialed.

Ring…ring…ring.

Scott got up and answered again. "Hello? Hello?"

His voice was angry this time, because he was starting to suspect what was going on. Scott lowered the shade so I couldn't see him making his moves. He didn't realize that the light from the TV cast his silhouette against the window shade. As soon as he moved in again, I got back on the phone.

Ring, ring, ring, your favorite buddy calling over.

"I know it's you, Anthony," Scott said, his voice tight. But I didn't make a sound. He slammed the phone down, and I snickered at his extreme frustration. Apparently, at this point, Beth decided she was going to go to bed—alone. This was too much for her to deal with. She later said Scott was not all that.

I watched Scott storming out of the female barracks. I ran back to our room and got there just before him.

"You're such an asshole," he said when he burst into our room. "You're so fucking childish."

"What are you talking about?" I said, still pissed, but determined not to show it.

"I know it was you on the phone, so stop lying."

"On the phone? What? That's crazy!"

"Bullshit! Admit it!"

"Okay," I said, "as soon as you admit you asked her to slow dance."

"Yeah, I did, so what? She obviously wanted me more than you anyway."

"Yeah, right."

Then, Scott exploded. "You're such a dick!"

For the next four days, we didn't say a word to each other. Complete and utter silence. We literally walked by each other without speaking—and mind you this was all while we were living together in a ten-by-twelve room.

This went on longer than either of us wanted it to, but with our competitive natures, neither of us wanted to give in first.

Finally, after four days, we were sitting there still not speaking to each other, and we looked at each other and just started laughing. That's how the fight ended. No words, other than, "I knew you asked her," followed up with, "Yeah, well you're still a dick." We never talked about it again. However, when I wanted to poke him, I would hum the Kiss song, "Beth."

Besides partying every night, we also played on the Fort Sheridan MP Company volleyball, softball, and football teams. The football team won the base championship that year, and Scott and I both played key roles in the victory.

One of the best athletes on the team, an MP named John Richter, was getting married, and he asked Scott, Tony Jones, and me to be in his wedding. Richter and Jones had been stationed in Germany together and were both from the North Chicago area.

This was going to be a great hometown wedding, with the reception in some basement close to where Richter lived but over an hour from Fort Sheridan. I agreed to be the designated driver and not to drink too much. Having a designated driver was a rule we always followed, as a DUI would ruin our MP careers and any future entry into the police academy. The wedding was a typical military wedding, with soldiers holding up swords for the bride and groom to walk under after they said, "I do." With our Class A uniforms, white shirts, and bow ties, all the soldiers looked super squared-away. As was the case with most military weddings, the party afterward was quite a celebration, with maybe a bit more alcohol than a normal wedding. The bonus with this party was that the bartender was very attractive. I started to work my charm, recycling some of my best one liners.

Scott rolled his eyes but decided not to turn this into another competition.

Before long, I had coaxed her into coming out from behind the bar and dancing with me. This resulted in a de facto open bar. Soldiers having access to free alcohol never worked out well for the people providing the booze. Many years later, Richter told me, "You ruined my wedding reception by stealing my damn bartender."

The small fact that the bar was open with easy access would later come back to haunt Scott. I decided I was going to leave the reception with the bartender. Rick was just shaking his head at the quick departure of his bartender. I figured the event was almost over anyway, so all I did was limit how much alcohol the MPs drank that night—I was doing him a favor. I tossed my keys to Scott and asked, "Hey, you okay to drive? Because I'm not coming home."

Scott just nodded, and I said, "Okay, drive safe. See you tomorrow!"

But he stayed even longer and had a few more cocktails before leaving. He made it close to the military base, but he was, in fact, pulled over. Scott insisted he wasn't too drunk to drive, but more likely the officer cut him some slack. Either way, he dodged a bullet. He still blasted me for almost messing him over in the name of female company.

And things were not calm or simple for me either. It was not a simple night of connection and love making. (I won't go into excruciating detail; this is not that kind of book). But a simplified version would be something like this:

The dancing bartender lived in a mobile home in a wooded area two miles down a gravel road, with the only light coming from a couple other mobile homes in the distance. Upon our arrival, she gave me a big wet kiss, put her hand on my chest and said, "Wait here on the couch."

She ran off to the bedroom and I took off my uniform and hung it up near the closet, in view of the front door, as I eagerly awaited her return. Five minutes later, she opened the flimsy trailer door and posed seductively in a slinky peach negligee, but I couldn't take my eyes off the large stain above her left breast. Apparently, this was not the first time she'd worn this outfit. I was unable to focus on anything but the stain. As she approached, it became even more visible, a creamy, almost coffee-looking stain. I laughed to myself, thinking, *I can't wait to tell Scott this story,* as she rapidly approached, walking like she was on the catwalk, attempting to look sensual.

We kissed passionately for a few moments, and I had two things on my mind: that the desired ending was just moments away in the bedroom she had just exited, and that the first thing I had to do was get rid of that stained peach negligee.

As our romantic actions continued, it became apparent that this young lady was extremely vocal, to say the least, loudly commending my performance. I was trying not to laugh, knowing I was not that good, and thinking, *I wonder if these are the same responses she uses all the time,* and *Shit, I really hope that's a coffee stain.*

At this point, it was around two in the morning and suddenly the phone rang. She picked it up and responded with great hostility, "Yeah! You bet your ass there's someone over here, and he will fuck you up. He's an MP!…Yeah, well if you don't believe me, bring your pussy ass over here!"

Holy shit! I thought, *this is crazy!* I wondered if this was the dude who stained the peach negligee. This development had a decidedly negative impact on the situation, and I found myself unable to concentrate on the one thing I was there to do. My penis shrank like it had been dropped into a bucket of ice water.

Having some guy show up out of nowhere to fight, maybe even naked, was not how this evening was supposed to end. I tried to continue, thinking, ironically, that I was no longer worried about that coffee stain. Every little sound distracted me as I worried that some guy was going to show up from out of nowhere and whack me in the back of the head.

I was like an overactive dog, stopping and listening as my ears picked up on every sound.

Then it happened—*boom, boom, boom*—someone banging at the door. As this was a trailer, you could feel the vibrations all the way in the bedroom.

She jumped up and simply said, "Hold on," then she bounced quickly to the front door, only pausing slightly to throw on her stained peach negligee.

I sprang up and started looking around for something I could use to defend myself. All I could find was a five-inch ceramic egg that looked like it was made somewhere in Asia. So I was standing there behind the bedroom door, naked, with a huge boner, holding this ceramic egg in one hand, waiting to knock the guy out if he came into the bedroom.

The two of them argued for five minutes, then, somehow, she convinced him that this manly guy in her bed was a soldier who would fuck him up if he didn't leave right now. She walked briskly back into the room, ripped off the stained negligee, and grabbed my hand. "Okay," she said, "where were we?"

The ex-boyfriend departed almost as quickly as he showed up, but I didn't sleep a wink, waiting for him to return. Finally, around 8 a.m., she drove me back to the barracks. The ride was rather quiet—clearly neither of us had much to say. It was rather awkward, with a leaned-over embrace before I exited the car. Numbers were exchanged, but we both knew we were never going to talk again.

***

Barracks life started to change in the middle of our time on Sheridan, when we began dating two girls from the medical command. Carleen and Darleen hung out together as much as Scott and I did. The four of us would double date all the time, but one night we decided to get a hotel room for a whopping $35 a night. We partied at Fort Sheridan's NCO club, then went to a Denny's-like restaurant for a late meal.

During the meal, Scott took a sip of my soda, and the girls said in unison, "Oh, that's gross!" It seemed the medical sisters were way more worried about germs than we were.

Scott turned to me. "How was your steak?"

I said, "It's flavorful, but kind of tough. You want to try it?"

"Sure."

I took the steak out of my mouth and handed it to Scott. The girls both cringed in disbelief.

Darleen said, "You guys are disgusting!"

Carleen said, "I can't believe you would do that!"

Scott and I just laughed, and once the girls finally stopped being grossed out, he handed the partially chewed piece of steak back to me.

"Oh, my God, I'm going to be sick!" said Darleen.

"What?" said Scott. "You stick my penis in your mouth, and now you are worried about a little piece of steak?"

As we were headed to the hotel, Carleen told Scott to stop off at a gas station. She ran in for more beer and came out with whipped cream, as well.

"What the heck is that for?" I asked.

The girls shared a look and chuckled—clearly not their first time with a can of whipped cream.

I barely slept that night, constantly waking up to find whipped cream all over my body, including my privates and nipples. As I finally drifted off to sleep, I turned to Carleen and said, "Yeah, and eating that steak twice was the grossest thing you ever saw before."

We were a great group, all about fun and no commitments.

A couple months later, though, I met a new girl named Kathy. We spent a lot of time together in the barracks room I shared with Scott. This room was always a bit of a mess, with bunk beds on one side and across from it, an old couch that had clearly seen lots of activity by the previous owners. The room was extremely small, but it was laid out nicely for entertaining the ladies.

When you are a 20-year-old soldier or college student, the conquest is what you strive for. But sometimes things happen that you don't expect: You fall in love, and that lifestyle ends. This is what happened to me.

Kathy was from a military family at Fort Bragg, North Carolina. She was a blonde-haired, blue-eyed beauty who was fun no matter what was going on. She had a Southern accent that Scott and I made fun of all the time. She wasn't crazy about being the brunt of our jokes, and she let us know it. She was not an MP, but a "71 Lima," or administrative assistant assigned to the garrison command, which had all the support people on the base.

Although Scott and I didn't keep our barracks room clean and up to standards daily, we were always ready for the barracks inspections. Almost always, after inspections, we would be commended for how clean and organized our room was. As we told the other soldiers, "Play the game, fellas."

One day we were getting ready for inspection, and I found an old pair of white underwear lying on the communal bathroom floor with large yellow pee stains on the front and brown shit stains on the back. It appeared as though the owner had been okay for a while with the piss stains, but the newest shit stains caused him to leave the undies behind in the bathroom. My first thought was, *My God, these are disgusting.* Then I had an idea. I grabbed a pen and wrote SCOTT on the elastic waistband. Then, just prior to the barracks inspection, I dropped them on the floor near Scott's locker. During inspections, soldiers all lined up outside the rooms waiting for the chain of command to enter.

Somehow, before LT Clifford and 1SG Krieger inspected the room, Scott had found the nasty drawers and used a black Magic Marker to write ANTHONY on them, totally covering up the SCOTT I had written. Top and the LT were dying laughing.

Top said, "Damn, Anthony, you need to toss those undies in the trash and get some new ones!"

"Bastard!" I muttered as I realized my own joke had backfired on me. I had to figure out a way to get Scott back, and I promised myself it would happen before Scott left Fort Sheridan.

A few days later, there was another surprise inspection, and I scuttled Kathy out the window and down the fire escape just before the inspectors showed up. Soldiers were not allowed to have their girlfriends in the barracks. I tried to hide all her clothing and dress shoes in my locker to avoid the leadership noticing. It seemed to work like a charm, as the LT said the room looked good and told us to keep it up. However, as he was leaving, the LT leaned in and said, "You need more polish on the pumps, and your red dress needs to be worn next time I inspect your room."

We all cracked up after that. I was relieved that the leadership liked us enough to cut us some slack on the little stuff.

That Friday night, we planned to hit the club on the base, as usual. Scott had taken out a loan for $5,000 from the base bank and purchased a small yellow Fiat from SGT Rodrigues. Sporting his temp tags on the vehicle, Scott was going to drive it to Alaska when he PCS'ed because it was supposed to be a good car for the cold. We left the barracks with Scott driving his car and me driving my blue Chevy Vega. I picked up Kathy on the way.

Once we arrived, the night started off with pitchers of Miller Lite, because that was the cheapest. After a couple pitchers, we decided to head off post to a club called Scornovaccos. We drank and partied until after midnight, then it was time to head back to the base.

Scott was driving with another MP named Lori, who was quite frankly plastered and barely able to walk. I realized I'd had too many and asked Kathy to drive my car. We got back to the base and the MP gate guard waved us in, recognizing both our vehicles. He shook his head as we sped past him.

Competition was still a key ingredient in everything Scott and I did, so being the first one back to the barracks became the challenge, without either of us having to explain it.

Scott passed Kathy in a no-passing area and got to the stop sign just before Kathy did. However, she didn't stop, instead just flew through the stop sign, passing Scott and then moving back to the right lane.

The speed increased as we moved toward the back-foot gate, and I yelled for Kathy to slow down, but she was just as competitive as Scott and I were. Scott continued to race toward the corner.

"Slow down!" I yelled again, and I pulled up the e-brake slightly.

Scott was unable to stop and appeared to forget the road made a 90-degree turn to the left. His Fiat ran into the building at full speed, without his even hitting the brakes. The back end of the car came off the ground a good six inches.

"Holy shit!" I yelled.

Kathy started laughing before she realized they had hit the building hard.

I jumped out of the car and ran over to Scott's vehicle in a panic. Scott was bleeding from his forehead, but I was relieved to see he was not dead. Lori was moaning and yelling, "Holy fuck, fuck, fuck, fuck…my chest is killing me!"

They were both hurt, but neither seemed to be seriously injured. Now, I had another issue to deal with. My mind was racing, thinking Scott's career could be ruined by this.

I jumped into action. There were several beer bottles in the car. I was in complete panic mode now, realizing I had to get shit right before the MPs arrived.

"Shit, Scott, when did these get in here, and why the fuck didn't you put them in the trash?" I said, but I knew he never drank in the car, so they must have been from the beach. Fortunately, there was a dumpster not far away, and I ran over and dumped the six or seven empty beer bottles.

The MP arrived quickly, and it was Specialist Smith, a guy we did not like at all.

"Oh, shit, you're fucked," I said to Scott. "Look who it is."

Specialist Smith said, "Well, well, well, if it isn't the pretty boys."

"Fuck you," I shot back at him.

Blood was rushing down Scott's face, but it appeared much worse than it was.

Smith said, "Well, gotta call an ambulance. Anyone else hurt?"

Lori barked out, "My fucking chest is killing me."

Smith radioed the desk sergeant requesting an ambulance, saying that there were injuries and that the incident involved Anthony and Scott.

Whenever MPs were in an incident, the highest levels in the Provost Marshal's Office got involved immediately. There could be no favoritism for MPs, and perceptions were reality, the upper chain of command liked to say.

SFC Rowland arrived just after Scott was taken away, and he called me over.

"Child, listen to me very clearly," he said. He was from Panama and would call all the MPs child. "Don't say a damn word to the MPs."

"What?"

"This could ruin his career if you don't handle it properly."

"How? It's an accident!"

"They will try and railroad you guys, so keep your damn mouth shut."

"Yes, Sergeant."

"You are not an NCO, so you don't have to tell them anything."

"Yes, Sergeant."

Rowland was trying to protect Scott. He did not want me to be forced to admit he had been drinking and driving, that would end

Scott's career. I could honestly say Scott had not been drunk, but this was sage advice. If you were not an NCO, you could not be forced to be a witness. This reminder might have saved Scott's career.

I was checked for potentially drinking and driving by another MP and told to go ahead home without writing a statement. I dropped Kathy off at her room—where she rarely stayed—and then headed to the hospital off post to check on my battle buddy.

Lo and behold, SFC Rowland had left the MP station and beat me to the hospital. This became a very difficult situation, as Scott had been drinking and the hospital was going to ask for his blood, which was protocol after a traffic accident. However, Rowland stepped up and said Scott had worked that day as an MP, which was true, although it was the day shift. But the doctor said, "Okay, no need for a blood alcohol test then."

I was surprised, but Rowland knew Scott was a great soldier and there were no serious injuries, just damage to his personal vehicle. He would still recommend punishment, but not something to ruin Scott's career.

The next morning, however, Criminal Investigation Division (CID) called and told me I was required to testify about what happened. After SFC Rowland's advice, I understood that was not true, that since I was an E-4 and not a sergeant, I was not actually required to testify. The rule allowed younger soldiers to keep some things between peers without the leadership forcing them to tell on each other. The MPs in CID, however, did convince Kathy to testify, but she said she had been sleeping on my shoulder—obviously she did not tell the truth. Now, I found myself in a difficult situation. I had to ensure Kathy did not get in trouble for her false statement, while also making sure I didn't get my best friend in trouble.

Kathy was extremely upset about being dragged into this, so I knew I had to make things right. But how could I make an honest statement without contradicting Kathy's false statement and getting her in trouble? My counsel allowed them to rip up Kathy's statement and let her write a new one. I insisted she be honest in it. The CID team didn't buy the story and continued pressing for information. The interrogation continued for a few days, and my legal team on base supported my position that I did not have to testify. This didn't go over well with the unit, but in my mind, nobody was hurt but Scott. Why ruin his career, or Kathy's for that matter? I ended up making a vague statement without specific details on whether Scott was drunk or not. For example, they asked how many beers we had, and I said two—but this was two *pitchers* of beer, so I did not lie to them, but I was vague enough to keep Scott out of big trouble.

The entire incident eventually blew over. There was no other way to keep Scott and Kathy out of trouble, but not being completely forthright bothers me to this day. Scott and I both got counseling statements in our personal files, negative official statements regarding your actions that could affect promotion if you had multiples. It could have been much worse, and we both agreed we were lucky.

The day we received our statements, SFC Rowland walked us into his office, yelling loud enough for the whole base to hear. "You two embarrassed the MP leadership, and it is going to take a long time to fix this. Anthony and Scott, I'm beyond disappointed in the both of you!"

Mind you, the door was closed, and he was smiling as he yelled at us. "Yes, Sergeant," we replied.

About a month later, Scott changed duty stations and began his move to Fort Wainwright, Alaska. I remained at Sheridan a few more months, and my bond with Kathy continued to grow stronger. But at the end of October, we parted ways, and I flew off to my new assignment in Berchtesgaden, Germany.

CHAPTER 5

FORT WAINWRIGHT ALASKA AND BERTCHESGADEN (GERMANY), AUGUST 1987

Our assignment at Fort Sheridan had lasted a little over a year, and the bond between Scott and me was cemented and, although tested, remained completely unbreakable. Shortly after Scott changed his duty station to Fort Wainwright, Alaska, I got my orders for Berchtesgaden, Germany. Soldiers would say these were the two best assignments in the Army, but Top had once told us, "The two best duty stations for every soldier are the one they just left and the one they are going to." Later in life, I would come to understand how true this was, and that Top was a wise man—even if we thought he was off his rocker with all that "stay in and reenlist" crap.

Scott's plan to drive his yellow Fiat to Alaska ended when it lost a game of tag with that building on Sheridan. So, after saying goodbye to all our other friends, I drove him to the airport in Chicago.

As we were approaching the airport, I reminded Scott that this was the same airport I routinely took Army AWOL prisoners to. "One day, maybe I will be taking you to jail," I said.

He snorted and said, "Yeah, more likely that you'll be the one going to jail."

After a few minutes, I said, "Okay, just don't fall in love in Alaska, I can't see you with little Eskimos."

"Yeah, same goes for you in Germany. I could see you finding Heidi on some mountain top over there."

"Not likely."

The innocent banter was easier than admitting we were going to miss each other or wondering if our friendship would last, given the extreme distances.

When we arrived, Scott got out of my Vega and walked to the terminal—one last wave, then he never looked back.

A few months later, as I was preparing to leave Sheridan, I considered asking Kathy to marry me. But I decided to wait and see how the separation went before making such a leap. She broke up with me after just a few weeks. I learned much later that another MP named Marty had lied to her, saying I had cheated on her, which I did not; we had broken up for a week, and that is when I was with another girl. Otherwise, we might have ended up together. Too bad, she was a fun-spirited girl with a passion for life.

In Frankfurt, Germany, I was assigned to the 21st Replacement Detachment, where all new military arrive in Germany to replace the current military member assigned there. One of the older NCOs told me that as a young E-4 it was key that I be bold and ask for a good job location.

"Most importantly, don't go to one of the nuke sites and be a tower rat," he said. "You'll hate it."

A tower rat is an MP who sits in a tower for ten to twelve hours a day protecting the nuclear missile sites located in Germany to slow the Russian forces' march into Germany if a war were to start. So I was pretty disappointed when I got to the replacement center and was informed that I was, in fact, being assigned to be a tower rat.

I was frantically trying to think of any way out when I heard the receptionist's accent and asked her where she was from.

"I'm from Connecticut," she said.

"No way!" I said. "I'm from Rhode Island, just up the road from you."

Turned out she grew up less than 30 minutes from my hometown of Lincoln. We started talking about Rhode Island and the beaches in Newport.

Then I asked her, "Are there any better jobs than this tower site they're trying to send me to? Can you help me out here, since we practically grew up together?"

"Well, it's too bad you're not an E-5, or you could have gone to Berchtesgaden."

"Where is that?"

"It's the Armed Forces Recreation Center, AFRC, where the soldiers stationed in Germany go for vacations." I could hear the enthusiasm in her voice. "It is simply the dream job for an MP in Germany."

I blurted out, "I am promotable." That meant I had been nominated for promotion and had gone to a military panel and answered questions. "Does that matter?"

Now, this was a bald-faced lie, but it was worth a shot to get a job like that over in Germany.

"Let me ask my NCOIC," she said, referring to her non-commissioned officer in charge. She got up from her desk and disappeared for a few minutes, then came back smiling.

"Okay, I got great news. He said I could send you there."

"Awesome," I said. "You should come visit me when I get there."

She promised she would, but we both knew it was never going to happen.

Everything seemed to be falling into place, but then Staff Sergeant Johnson, the NCOIC, came out of his office and asked me to show him my promotion packet. "It's not in your files, Sergeant?"

"Oh, no," I said, looking through my stuff. "Where is it?"

The sergeant frowned, then started quizzing me to make sure I knew what I was talking about. "When did you go to the board?"

"Last month."

"What was your score?"

"I got a 192!"

"What questions did you miss?"

"Baron Von Stuben, the father of drill and ceremony."

The questions were rapid-fire, and my answers were just as quick, all complete fabrications. I really wanted that job, and at that point in my life, I felt that white lies weren't really lies if they helped you get something you should have been able to get anyway. In this case, my little white lies did the trick.

My assignment was changed from tower rat duty, and I was on

my way to Berchtesgaden. Our higher headquarters was in Garmisch, Germany, which is where I spent ten days getting all my paperwork finalized and some minor training completed. It is also where I saw a German man order bacon, eggs and toast with a tall beer instead of coffee.

On my second day there, I met the senior MP, who asked me, "Why the hell are they sending an E-4 here?"

"I don't know, Sergeant."

"You haven't even gone to the promotion board?"

"Beats me," I said. "They just told me I was coming here and said the NCOs here were top notch!" I figured it couldn't hurt to butter him up.

"Well, a warm body is better than no body," the sergeant said.

A week later, I arrived in Berchtesgaden and gave the same answers to the same questions with the same result.

The MPs assigned to Berchtesgaden worked as desk sergeants and criminal investigators. However, patrolmen who were assigned there were part of the 218th MP Company out of Augsburg, Germany, who would get moved to Berchtesgaden for six-month duty stints.

Berchtesgaden was the most amazing place I had ever been to, nestled in Bavarian mountains that had snowcaps almost year-round. There was plenty of skiing in the winter months, and a short drive over the mountain was Salzburg, Austria. The duty was very light, perhaps even boring compared to real MP duty. My job was to be an MP desk sergeant. For the most part, the MP duty consisted of dealing with traffic accidents by military vacationers and, on occasion, bar fights or drunken soldiers getting out of hand at the hotels. There were three main hotels that were exclusively for military and civilians in Berchtesgaden: the Alpine Inn, the Berchtesgaden Hof, and the General Walker Hotel. All the hotels were former Nazi Party buildings that were converted by the Americans and led by American civil service workers but staffed by German citizens.

My boss and senior MP was SSG Brett, a much older African American MP who had served in Vietnam and was just trying to make it to retirement. Brett was very outgoing and loved to have parties at his home.

He would brag about what a player he was and all the ladies he had there—"I got a bunch of my bitches coming over this weekend"—and unlike many people who bragged in the Army, he was truthful. His most famous quote was, "When I leave here, they're going to bronze my dick!" Back then, this type of talk was acceptable in the military, but a few short years later it would not be tolerated.

Although Scott and I were successful with the females, we were not the type to brag about it, or degrade women, or use the term "bitches." We used our charms to get what we wanted from young ladies, but we never crossed the line.

We had both been raised to treat women with respect, and although I shared some stories here, I didn't include any real names. And apart from that, it was just the conversations between the two battle buddies.

I settled in rather nicely and decided this Germany stuff was surprisingly fun. I got a part-time job as a disc jockey, working nights at the German disco. This perfectly suited my personality and allowed me to use my charms with the young ladies—although I had to learn another language.

While there was no real police duty there in Berchtesgaden, there were a lot of traffic accident investigations, because US soldiers couldn't drive in the snow as well as the Germans. This was especially true for the visiting chaplains, who held their biannual meetings in Berchtesgaden. Every time there was a chaplain gathering, there were accidents.

I once said to the Berchtesgaden chaplain, "I guess God doesn't protect you guys so much when you drive around here."

He replied, "Why do you think there are never injuries to my chaplains?"

The MP duty hours were also amazing. We would work six days on, then have four days off, which worked well for my late-night DJ side hustle. Another great feature was that in the winter, for PT, we would go skiing, both downhill and cross-country. While I had just over a year left before reenlistment, I certainly made the most of my time.

There was one young lady, Sabine, whom one of my MP buddies had pointed out as his challenge. I loved the way she danced, and I tried to talk with her, but she blew me off completely. She was really nice, a nursing assistant at an old folks' home. Her English was not very good, but somehow I learned enough small phrases in German to get our conversations along.

I courted her for two months and offered to buy her a drink if she would not smoke for one hour. I bought her the drink and she walked away without saying another word that night. A while later, I saw her dancing the fox trot and I decided I had to learn how to do that. Eventually, I mastered this dance skill, which I put to very good use during my stay in Germany.

I ultimately wore Sabine down, and before long we were an item. I spent much of my off-duty time with her, and we got pretty serious, but I still planned on getting out of the military and going back to the States.

All my friends told me I would leave Germany with a wife, to which I always said, "Not going to happen. I'm going back to Rhode Island to become a police officer."

***

I had gotten a few letters from Scott over the months, and it seemed like he was doing well.

Having expected snow and igloos everywhere, even in July, he'd been relieved to see that Alaska was thoroughly modern, with black-topped roads and fast-food restaurants like Burger King, McDonald's, and Wendy's.

On his first day there, he passed this little log cabin, the Farthest North Harley Shop, that had a party going on in the parking lot, with a band performing on a trailer and a woman dancing topless. He decided then that he just might like Alaska.

During the summer months, there was very little darkness, maybe an hour or two, which could cause sleeping issues for many, but for Scott it wasn't a problem, probably because of his shift work on Fort Sheridan.

But it wasn't perfect.

"It is cold as shit here in the winter," he wrote, "and I'm starting to think polar bears are sexy, seeing some ladies wear fur up here often. Let's get on a call on the first of February."

I called him from work on the military line, which allowed military units to talk to each other. They called them DSN lines, although I never knew what that meant.

Scott shared how excited he was to be doing real police work. He told me that, unlike Fort Sheridan, he had arrived in Alaska in civilian clothes and was assigned to the 472nd MP Company as a patrolman, or Road MP, for his first few months. Again, easily recognized as a good young soldier, after four short months he was assigned to the Fort Wainwright Military Police Investigations, or MPI. This was a separate branch of military police focused on investigations. These were exciting times for Scott, going on his first undercover duty as a member of a two-person Drug Suppression Team, or DST. His supervisor was a Criminal Investigations Division agent. On Fort Wainwright, the MPI was supervised by the CID special agent in charge, and they all worked in the same office to ensure investigations were well coordinated. Scott was still assigned to the MP Company, but his official duty was with CID and he was supervised by CID.

He worked some significant cases. In one year, they seized over a million dollars' worth of drugs. This was very significant, as Alaska in the eighties didn't have the same drug problems as the rest of the nation, where the "War on Drugs" was raging.

His two-person team often worked with the civilian law enforcement agencies, including the Multi-Agency Drug Team, called Metro. Led by the Alaska State Troopers, or AST, Metro included members from the Airport Police, Army CID, Fairbanks Police, and North Pole Police.

It seemed like the biggest adjustment was the nightlife or time off. At Fort Sheridan, we would dress up nicely almost every night and hit the NCO Club or the local bars. There weren't really any nightclubs in Fairbanks, but he'd met a few soldiers at the replacement center and headed out with them to meet the ladies. He was wearing shiny blue pants, a blue striped shirt, a thin red tie, and dancing shoes, like what he'd wear in Chicago. Feeling confident and thinking he looked pretty good, he walked into a local country-western bar called the Sunset Inn. But his mood changed drastically when he was whistled at by a huge guy in a big ole cowboy hat.

Scott realized his "nightclubbing" days were over. From that point on, he wore strictly jeans and cowboy boots.

He told me stories about working on the Drug Suppression Team, where he'd go undercover to buy drugs.

"I'm really good at it," he said. "Being outgoing is a key ingredient to winning favor with people."

Sometimes, his boss would call him up at night and tell him they had to go to work.

"He might tell me it was going to be a 'Light Night,' which meant we were going to a bar and have a beer," Scott explained. "Well, we would go out and then travel back onto post and try to purchase drugs. We would target a taxi on post, flag it down, and ask the cabbie if he had anything for the 'head.' The cabbie would ask, 'What do you want?' I would order a quarter-ounce of marijuana or more, and the driver would leave the base and return shortly thereafter with the drugs."

Scott and his DST partner would buy it from him and then write up a case for the assistant U.S. attorney. It was shockingly stupid on the cabbie's part, because selling drugs on the military installation was a much bigger deal than outside the gate.

Scott told me about another drug operation with Metro in Delta

Junction, a small town outside Fort Greely near the end—or the beginning, depending on where you start your travel—of the Alaska-Canadian Highway.

His team was targeting soldiers going off base to buy drugs. Much of the time, they would stay at hole-in-the-wall hotels, like C's Motel in Delta Junction, which was targeted because there was information that someone inside the motel was selling drugs to military personnel on Fort Greely.

C's had a bar, and Scott ended up buying "eight balls"—one-eighth of an ounce of coke—from a barmaid named Sissy. After a few buys, Sissy brought Scott to another bar, the Buffalo Lounge, to pick up the cocaine he was going to buy. They went into the women's bathroom, and she put out two lines of cocaine on the sink. Thinking fast, Scott told her that he couldn't because he was probably going to be given a urinalysis in a day or so, but he pretended to taste a small amount, dabbing it with his index finger, but then licking his middle finger instead.

The AST lab confirmed it was cocaine, but there was a boll weevil mixed in with it; apparently, the dealer was cutting his cocaine with flour. A month later, AST had a warrant for Sissy's arrest, but she had already left the state.

Besides drugs, Scott learned about crime scene processing, evidence collecting, photography, interviews and interrogation, report writing, and forensics.

After CID school, he was assigned as a CID special agent, mostly working general crimes—rape, robbery, murder—but sometimes much stranger stuff.

On one occasion, a woman reported that she had answered the

door to her government quarters and found a white male with long hair and a Megadeth leather jacket. She said he pulled her workout shorts down and put a pickle up her vagina. Scott met her at the hospital, where they had removed a small portion of the pickle from her private area. Scott felt this seemed odd, so he interviewed her and then went to her house. He conducted a crime scene search and found a jar of Vlasic Zesty Crunchy Dills in the refrigerator. He said those pickles were huge!

Since the suspect was probably a civilian, he turned the case over to the Fairbanks PD, but after a month without progress, he asked them if he could interview the girl again and they said yes. He told her that the lab had found fingerprints on the pickle by doing spectro analysis—a bald-faced lie, but she didn't know that. Scott had her describe how far down her shorts were when the pickle was put inside her. When she said halfway down her thighs, he suggested she might not have been completely truthful, and that it was better to tell what really happened.

She eventually confessed that she had been masturbating with the pickle and it got stuck inside her. The only thing that would come out was seeds and juice. She was charged with making a false statement but convinced Fairbanks PD to drop the case. Scott vowed to never eat Vlasic Zesty Crunchy Dill pickles again.

On another call, he told me how he had started hunting with the other MPs, and he simply couldn't get enough of it, stalking moose and caribou in the Alaskan wilderness. He even talked about staying in Fairbanks, becoming a police officer there.

He tried to get me to come up. I told him I'd go salmon fishing with him, but that shooting my mouth off was the only shooting I had any desire to do.

"How can you shoot an innocent animal?" I asked him.

"Because I eat them, dip shit," he had said. "I don't just shoot animals. I enjoy the hunt, and more than anything I love eating what I kill."

"Seems harsh to me."

"I know how much you love meat," he said. "You'd be screwed if you had to hunt for your meat. Shit, as bad as you shoot, you might as well become a vegetarian. You might even be able to do some sit-ups."

We decided to talk again in four months, prepping for our decision to get out of the military and perhaps become police officers. Six months prior to your End Tour Station, or ETS, you could start looking for a new duty station. You had the option to reenlist and, believe it or not, Scott and I were thinking of doing just that.

It was not easy to use the DSN lines, but we arranged to get on a call at 6:30 a.m. Germany time, to make sure Scott would be home, as it was 8:30 p.m. in Alaska. Unable to use the DSN lines, I drove out the gate near my duty as an MP desk sergeant to a German pay phone, equipped with ten German five D-Mark coins to make the call. They were the largest of the German coins, but a call to Alaska made the coins go very quickly.

"Hey, bud," I said. "Hope all is well."

"No real crazy MPs like you over here, so other than partying at the club, I don't do much of anything."

"How is Alaska?"

"Lots of hunting. Not much clubbing, really. Had some dudes tell me I was cute because I had a tie on."

The call was rapid fire, and the seconds were ticking down. "Okay," I said, "coins are running out. I need to know what you're going to do on reenlistment. I got an offer to reenlist for Fort Bragg, but I'll only do it if you agree."

"Well, if we did go there, we could put our police academy packets in as soon as we arrive at Bragg."

"Are you in or not?"

Scott said, "Shit, talk about making me decide quickly. If I do reenlist, it's only for three years, and I am for getting out regardless if we go to the police academy or not."

"Fair, I agree," I said. "I'll tell the reenlistment NCO later today. He was holding the slot for me."

"Okay!"

I had mentioned that I needed to call my buddy, Scott, before I would be fully committed.

Reenlistment NCOs would tell you anything to get you to stay in.

He asked if we were married. I said yeah. He said I must be the wife then. WTH, why did everyone say that?

Scott yelled, "Because you are the woman for sure!"

We agreed to call again in three days, once the NCO had it all worked out. The plan was, if there was a problem, I would call Scott's mother and she would be able to reach him.

It was done. We decided we needed to be stateside and have more experience before attending the police academy. Being overseas made it almost impossible to attend all the required written and physical exams. I had first suggested we reenlist for Fort Hood, then get out in Texas, as they were paying $40,000 for police officers. However, the death rate for police officers in Houston was very high, so Scott suggested looking elsewhere. We chose Fort Bragg, North Carolina, which was much closer to Rhode Island, hopefully making for an easier transition to the civilian work force.

There was no way to walk right into the Rhode Island police academy, given all the prerequisites, so since we needed to be stateside to complete all the requirements, Bragg seemed the only other good holdover location. Additionally, another MP bud of mine, Rick Venus, was able to end his term a year early due to the high-paying job as a police officer in Raleigh, so maybe we could try and do the same thing.

So, we signed up for three more years, planning to apply to the police academy in Rhode Island right at the 18-month mark. Scott was still skeptical about getting out early, but he talked to Rick and confirmed that was how he got out of his enlistment.

Within a couple of days, both of us had reenlisted for Fort Bragg. I arrived two months later, and Scott arrived two months after that.

I headed back to Rhode Island and ran into Lisa Misiaszek again. We talked again about her brother, who was somewhere in Arizona. I asked her for his number, and she gave me hers, as well, telling me she had recently broken up with her boyfriend. As the conversation continued, I found her to be the easiest person in the world to talk to. I told her I remembered her smile the last time I saw her, and that she still looked great.

She said I was easy to be around and talk with. She liked that she could simply be who she was and not hold back, having known me for years.

I told her I felt the same. "Why didn't you stay in the pool years ago?" I asked, referring to when we were young and we almost got together.

"You were too immature," she said.

I laughed. "Well, I am always me, but sometimes that pisses people off."

We met for dinner a couple days later at a place called Asia, the best Chinese food in the world.

"I love the beef teriyaki best," I said. "Never had it better."

"I agree," she said. "I order that all the time. But you've been all over the world, and you love this Chinese food the best?"

"That's right. You want to get a scorpion bowl?"

She laughed. "Hell, no. I can't handle liquor like that."

She ordered red wine, and I ordered a Miller Lite.

"So, you signed up for another term," she said. "Are you making a career of it?"

"No, I think I'm going to be a cop, right here in Rhode Island."

"Oh, boy, hopefully not in Lincoln. Chief Strange will never let you in after you bit Nancy's butt back in high school."

"No, he'll like me," I said, laughing. "I'm a changed man these days."

After dinner, we headed over to Brooksies bar. The next night, Kool and the Gang was in town, and we attended our first concert together and discovered a shared love of soul music. Although I was home to see my family, I spent the next eight days with Lisa. I told her about my life, and I learned she had been working as a dental assistant since she left high school. She was a spry, sassy, spunky little lady who would tell it like it is, something I certainly needed in my life.

As I was driving down to Bragg in my new Honda Accord hatchback, I realized how easy it was to find my perfect mate. I only had to look up the hill, where Lisa had been my neighbor growing up.

CHAPTER 6

FORT BRAGG, MARCH 1988

After twelve hours, mostly on I-95 South, I arrived at Bragg and was a bit surprised at the size of the base. I had not been assigned to a tactical unit prior to this, but Scott was in Alaska, so it surprised me much more than it did him. After briefly talking about the new assignment, I told Scott I had fallen in love with Lisa, a girl I had adored since high school. I explained my friendship with her brother Alan and how Lisa was recently available, so we had gone out for dinner. Suddenly, I was no longer interested in finding Lisa's brother, who had now moved to Pensacola at the Naval Air Station, awaiting acceptance into the FBI.

"So, now you are in love with a hometown girl?" Scott said. "I've been to Lincoln, and there's not too many good-looking women there."

"Bullshit, dude. Lots of great-looking women in Lincoln. By the way, my sisters were devastated you got married."

"Well, about that," he said. "Peggy and I just got divorced."

"What? I had no idea."

"She didn't want to leave Alaska, and things hadn't been good for a while, so we called it quits."

"Shit," I said. That blindsided me, for sure.

"I was looking forward to the good ole days, but now you are in love," he said. "Maybe she'll realize you're a pain in the ass sooner and dump you."

I laughed. "Funny, but you know that will never happen. By the way, her brother is looking into the FBI, so if we don't like being cops, that could be our next challenge."

He shook his head. "Anthony, why are always thinking of the next adventure before we even start the one we are preparing for now?"

"Keeping options open," I said. "I think I'm going to marry Lisa. What do you think?"

"Wait," he said, shaking his head. "You've known her your whole life, you played hide and seek at age ten, and now you find yourself in love with her, wanting to marry her?"

"When it's right, you know it's right!" He shook his head as I continued. "I've been all over the world and met lots of women, but she is the most fun, she loves to dance, and she gets me. We fit together perfectly. And she is without a doubt one of the funniest people I have ever known—she might even be funnier than you."

He cocked a dubious eyebrow. "Really?"

"When you see how we are together, you'll get what makes me want to be with her forever. I've never laughed so much with someone in my life."

"I'm shocked," said Scott.

"I know Peggy wasn't the right person, but you're better for it. You'll find true love."

Scott made puking sounds and said, "What the hell happened to you?"

I laughed. "I found my one and only."

Over the next four weeks, Lisa and I spent a lot of time on the phone. At the end of the month, I drove back to see her. She had the right amount of energy and passion for life that I needed.

When we were out one night, I asked her why we never got together in high school.

"It would never have worked," she said. "We were too immature."

I laughed. "Yeah, you would have followed me all over the world."

"Yeah, probably—collecting child support!"

We both laughed.

"You might be right," I said. Then I reminded her that I was still immature.

A month later, she came to visit me at Fort Bragg. On her first night there, she blurted out, "I love you."

I froze. "Wait, what did you say?"

I knew I loved her but was not ready to say it back so quickly. After a short delay, I said, "I am falling in love with you, too." Best I could do, even though I knew I loved her.

She just smiled, knowing I felt the same.

About a month later, we were lying on the couch in my room in the barracks, and I said rather unenthusiastically, "You know I love you, right?"

She said, "Yeah," but didn't say it back.

I was like, "Well, are you going to say it back?"

"Maybe in about a month!"

That May, after I'd been at Bragg for about five months, my family took a road trip to see me, and Lisa came along for a surprise early birthday party. Before the party was when I realized I was finally going to ask her to get married. I guess I simply needed to see her around my family, I don't know for sure, but that was the plan. Maybe there was more incentive, given I learned that married soldiers get paid more than single ones, plus a free house on the military base.

I decided I wanted to propose in a very romantic way. On my last trip home, I went to the telephone pole that was our base when we used to play hide and seek. I found several stones in various colors and took them to a jeweler, who reluctantly agreed to make them into an engagement ring. I had it ready for a couple months, just waiting to make sure the time was right.

I proposed to her on my birthday with all my friends and family present. Funny thing: The birthday party was organized by Lisa, but she had no idea it was going to be her engagement party. I dropped to my knee and held up the ring, explaining that the rocks inside it were from the side of the road where we used to play hide and seek as kids. I pulled out an old picture of her as a kid when we first met and held it up for family and friends. They all knew I was going to do this. She looked around at all the friends and family looking at me, down on one knee, as I said, "I have everything else I need in life except a wife to share it with. I picked these rocks off the side of the road where we first met and wanted to propose to you."

The room burst out in laughter, and one of my sisters said it was yet another cheap way to save some money. Most of the ladies loved the idea, although later when her mother—Lady Dolores, I called her—heard the news, she was not happy that stones on the side of the road were made into a ring.

"That's fine, but when are you getting her a real ring, Mr. Phil?" Dolores said. This was the name she would call me to get my attention.

"At some point, Dolores," I said.

"Well, don't wait too long!"

For the next few months when I would visit, that was all I heard from Lady D. "Mr. Phil, when are you getting my daughter a real ring?"

I decided to make Lisa wait even longer, just to aggravate her mom a bit—something I was getting very good at.

We decided to have a small wedding and celebration two months later, July 23, 1988, at the country club where I had worked as a dishwasher in high school. Most people were unaware that this was also the very place where Lisa and I almost "got together" in high school, before we were interrupted by the Lincoln police.

Scott was there, serving as my best man. As he said to Lisa, "You know, I'm the best man in any wedding I attend."

It was a festive little wedding with very little fanfare, apart from all the screaming and partying by my family and the MPs who were there, including Gary Grand, Rob Buford, Steve Houlihan, Tony Jones, Steve Stefano, and John Richter, to name a few.

At one point, Scott turned to Richter and said, "Too bad there's no bartender to steal from his wedding."

Richter said, "Well, you can take one of his sisters."

Scott laughed. "Then we'd be related! Can't do that."

Lisa looked around, wondering why everyone was laughing so hard, not knowing the story behind the laughter.

After the wedding, there was talk of a future honeymoon, as Scott and I had to head back to Bragg the following morning. Lisa would have to wait for me to secure government housing on the base before she joined me there. The wedding reception was surprisingly low-key, without the traditional drama and craziness that was normal for this crew.

The day after the wedding was spent packing for the trip back to Bragg and thanking the MPs who had driven in for the wedding. I was saying goodbye to all my friends and almost forgot to say goodbye to my wife. I walked back into her apartment yelling, "Wife! Wifeee, oh wife, Mrs. Anthony, where are you?"

"I'm not sure I like the sound of 'Mrs. Anthony'!"

"What, you like the sound of Mrs. Misiaszek?"

"Well, the Anthonys are a crazy bunch, so I don't think that's me!"

"Depends how many glasses of wine you have," I said. "And I'll have a few bottles waiting on you at Fort Bragg, for sure."

She laughed. "Now, I have an incentive to come see you. Good move!" Then she turned tender. "Okay, darling, love you." She looked down at her ring. "I guess we're married now!"

I kissed her and said, "See ya in a few weeks!"

As Scott and I made our way down I-95 in the Accord, we talked about how in a little more than a year and a half we might be getting out and coming right back to RI for the police academy. We had changed our minds three times on which academy we would attend, but we were now certain, maybe, that Rhode Island was the place. Lisa and I were both from Lincoln, and it was a great place to raise a family. After all, now I didn't just have to think about what was best for Scott and me, I had to think about what was best for Lisa and me, as well.

Most soldiers did not reenlist to go to Bragg unless they had been previously assigned there, but our plan was to use Bragg's proximity to RI to help us get into the police academy. Although there were a couple locations closer, Bragg was the only one offered by the reenlistment NCO. So that was it. Fort Bragg was our only choice.

After arriving, we were assigned to the 118th MP Company. I managed to work the system to get Scott assigned to my squad—something Hankel must have regretted every time he yelled at us to be more serious.

Fort Bragg was entirely different from the units we had been in prior. It was a real Army unit with a real-world mission. The 82nd Airborne was the Division Ready Force (DRF), which meant the soldiers assigned to Bragg had to be ready at a moment's notice to deploy anywhere in the world. But apart from that, life there was pretty routine. There were plenty of things to do in Fayetteville, a medium-sized town outside the installations of Fort Bragg and Pope Air Base called "Fayette-Nam" by those stationed there. The businesses near the base catered to things young soldiers might spend their paychecks on: gun shops, massage parlors, strip joints, liquor stores, alteration shops, and auto part stores. Scott and I stayed clear of the strip joints, apart from a couple of bachelor parties or birthday celebrations.

Bragg soldiers were known for being the Airborne Infantry, and, while Scott and I were not airborne-qualified, this assignment meant we could finally go to airborne school, something we'd been trying to do for a long time.

Being married, I got NCO quarters, which, having grown up on welfare, seemed genuinely nice to me. About a month after the wedding, I flew up to Rhode Island to pick up Lisa and packed the car with her things for our new home. I explained it as a nice house, or as nice as military housing could be. The houses were over 50 years old with some minor updates like new kitchen appliances and countertops. The cinderblock walls that made up the exterior gave them an almost low-income housing feel, but our house had covered parking, something I had never had in my life. Lisa was very positive when she first arrived, but I could tell from her body language that she had been expecting something more.

"How long before you get to the police academy?" she asked.

"Only about a year and a half."

"Okay, this will be our first home. We can only go up from here!"

She was a team player and found the positive in most things, so no exception there.

Scott was living in the barracks, where the single soldiers lived, but most days he could be found hanging out at our house. Lisa thought highly of him and liked to comment that he was just as stupid as her husband, but much more polite and respectful.

The first year at Fort Bragg, we saw a few rollouts and alerts, but no real deployments for the MP Company. We were both working patrol duties, which on Bragg meant a lot more police action than our prior assignments. The infantry seemed to get drunk more, get into more fights, and crack up more cars.

This was where we met our platoon sergeant, SFC David L. Hankel, and got a taste of what it was like to be messed with daily.

We enjoyed our banter with Hankel, mostly because he seemed to get us. He confided in me that while assigned in Korea he'd had a buddy like Scott named Pandal and they had ruled Korea in their youth.

As military policemen, we were told in Basic Training and at just about every military base an expression about dealing with officers: "Don't get your rank confused with my authority, sir!" SFC Hankel told a story from when he and Pandal were out patrolling in their M151A2 quarter-ton jeep. They spotted a civilian vehicle on the camp with Status of Forces Agreement plates, driving erratically. They signaled the driver to pull over. Hankel walked to the passenger side, while Pandal approached the driver. They noticed that there were two other occupants besides the driver, one in the front and one in the back.

"Listen up, MPs," said the guy in the back. "We are all field grade officers in this car. I'm Major Henley, the driver is Lieutenant Colonel Bare, and this is Major Jacobsen," pointing to the seriously intoxicated front-seat passenger.

Pandal asked the driver to step out of the vehicle to conduct a field sobriety test, because his breath smelled like a brewery. All three objected, and Bare said, "If you go through with this, Janet will have your asses!"

He was referring to Captain Janet Roland, the military police detachment officer in charge and local camp provost marshal. Hankel decided it was best to contact CPT Roland so she could come to the scene of the incident to see for herself that the three officers were blitzed. Besides LTC Bare, the other passengers were also at risk for apprehension, because public intoxication was a crime under the Uniform Code of Military Justice

When Captain Roland arrived, the three simultaneously started to whine how they had never in their military careers been subjected to such disrespect by two *enlisted* soldiers.

Hankel wasn't sure what she would do, because the officers all outranked her as well, so she was in the same position Hankel and Pandal had been, except she had much more to lose.

"We got our answer quicker than expected," SFC Hankel said with a smile. "She silenced them with a soft-spoken yet powerful voice. 'Don't let your military rank get confused with my MPs' authority to apprehend and throw you in the D-Cell!'"

The next morning, start of the day shift, Hankel and Pandal were summoned to the camp commander's office. Panic set in and both of their hearts sank, mostly in fear of retaliation toward CPT Roland by the post commander. When they arrived at the commander's office, there, standing next to the commander, were the three officers they had apprehended the day before.

Hankel thought, *Here we go, we're about to get our asses handed to us.*

But the next words gave faith to the system. The post commander said, "I've asked you two soldiers to my office so that the three officers you see here may apologize to you both for their behavior yesterday."

Hankel loved telling that story, and it frankly upped all of our morale to see that the system still worked when you did your job the right way. We all loved that phrase, "Don't let your rank get confused with my authority."

When the units were on base police patrol, Hankel would sit in the chow hall and ensure that the MPs got in and out of there so they could all eat when they were on patrol. The chow hall was near the MP station and served decent food, but the best part, for sure, was the cook—Bob Mayors. Bob was nearly deaf and wore hearing aids, having lost his hearing in Vietnam. He was a Medal of Honor winner, which was why he said he had a blue sticker on his vehicle.

133

In the military, officers' cars had blue stickers and enlistees' cars had red. If you saw a blue sticker, you were to salute the vehicle regardless who was driving it, out of respect for the rank of the vehicle owner. Some MPs would get aggravated having to salute the colonel's wife as she drove in and out of the base.

While on patrol, I used to like to eat my chow last, so I didn't have to hurry out, and so I could listen to some of Bob's stories. He would also give me extra chow for free while I stood quietly and listened to him talk about his warrior days.

It was like a movie every time. You never knew what the hell was coming out of his mouth, and most of his stories were so far-fetched there was no way they could be true.

This was one of them:

"When I was in Vietnam, I was airborne and air assault, so once you and Scott get your airborne wings, you'll be like me. One time on a night jump, my parachute got all tangled up and didn't open until I was a hundred feet off the ground. I landed in a seventy-five-foot-tall oak tree. My feet landed on a thick branch, pushing my hips all the way up to my shoulders. I was in extreme pain and a good distance from the drop zone. So, with no help at all, with my hips pushed up to my shoulders, I had to cut myself out of the tree and get away before Charlie could find me. So, I cut the ropes and got myself onto the ground, all while remaining completely silent."

"Wait," said Scott, "how did you get yourself to the ground with your hips in your shoulders?"

"I had to climb down like a monkey, using only my upper body."

"Then how did you get out of the area before Charlie found you?"

"I low-crawled through one hundred yards of tall grass to an area near a fast-moving stream, so my movement would be muffled by the stream noise."

Scott gave me a look that screamed bullshit, but I wanted Bob to keep talking, so I motivated him with a few "Wows" and "Oh, mys."

Another soldier at the table, Steve Houlihan, who was a year or so older than us and had a perpetual smile, completely lost it. "Wait," he said, laughing, "low-crawling one hundred yards with broken legs is fucking impossible."

"It was for sure hard," Bob said, "but my life depended on it, so you do what you have to do."

Houlihan said, "I gotta call bullshit," but I shook my head angrily for Houlihan to stop.

The lower-ranking soldiers would often call Bob out, which would make him stop telling stories. Not me though. I said, "Just let him talk, he's harmless."

LT Alan Mahan, our lieutenant, would get aggravated and call him out every time. Mahan was a prior service officer and constantly encouraged me to go to Officer Candidate School. "Life is much better on the officer side of the house," he liked to say.

One night, Mahan was on the gate when Bob drove through with his blue officer sticker on his windshield.

LT Mahan said, "You were an E-4 in Vietnam. Why do you have a blue officer sticker?"

Without skipping a beat, Bob said, "That's because I am a Medal of Honor winner."

This infuriated LT Mahan, and he embarked on a mission to disprove Bob. This was long before you could look up whatever you wanted on your iPhone, but the lieutenant got on the computer and did his research.

The next day, he was waiting at the gate, and when Bob pulled up, the lieutenant blurted out, "Bob, I checked the list. You are not a Medal of Honor winner!"

Again, without the slightest hesitation Bob said, "Listen, Lieutenant, I was in special operations. My missions were classified, and so is my Medal of Honor citation."

"What?"

"It's so secret only two people know about some of my missions," Bob said with a grin. "Me...and the next guy I tell." Then he drove off, leaving Mahan visibly pissed.

This was potentially serious business. SFC Hankel told us not to question whether Bob was really a Medal of Honor recipient, because a soldier who pretends to have awards that aren't authorized could end up making "little ones out of big ones" at Leavenworth.

Another night in the chow hall, Bob was on a roll, and the stories got even bigger.

"One night, I was deep behind enemy lines, surrounded by Viet Cong," he said. "So I rubbed mud all over my body and hid inside an old tree that had rotted out but not fallen over. There were at least thirty gooks nearby trying to find me 'cause I'd just snuck onto their base and killed their commander while he slept in his cot." Bob paused and made eye contact with each MP at the table.

"Charlie stopped and was getting ready to light a smoke, but I grabbed him by the neck, covered his mouth, stuck my knife up though his throat. After I scrambled his brains, I buried him in the leaves and sticks so Charlie wouldn't find me."

Later that night, Scott said, "Wait! That was a scene from *Rambo!* He is so full of shit!"

DYING CONFESSION

I said, "Don't call him out on it! These stories keep me going at night, for sure."

Sometimes at the end of the night, Bob would come over to the MP table and share even more stories of his glorious service. One night, Hankel, Houlihan, Grand, Bouford, Scott, Ewbank, and I were finishing up our dinner and Bob came over to shoot the shit.

"Hey, Bob," I said, rubbing my belly. "That sandwich was awesome. I think I ate two pounds of meat in there."

"Well, that's no big deal," Bob said. "I eat twenty pounds of meat every day. I have a rare disease where I can lose fifteen pounds a day if I don't eat twenty pounds of meat."

Grand laughed. "What the fuck?"

Houlihan lost his cool again. "Fucking Kimba the Lion does not eat twenty pounds of meat a day, Bob. There's no way you eat twenty pounds a day. I'm calling bullshit."

I gave him the death stare, and mouthed the word *Why?*

Bob stood about six-two, but only weighed about 160 pounds. There was no way he could eat that much meat in a week, let alone a day, but I wanted to hear more stories.

Another cook on Bragg was a guy called Happy Jack, who no kidding weighed 550 pounds. He was so fat, sometimes the MPs would put him in the cab of their pickup truck to drive him to his vehicle in the lot just 200 yards away. He was so heavy, his white XXXL chef's outfit would not cover his belly. Back in the mid-1980s, young girls would show their stomachs off—it was sexy. Happy Jack was not.

It wasn't much of a problem, except for when he was working the grill. He would rest his belly on the edge of the counter, right near the grill. If you looked closely, you could see his burn marks from prior cooking and see his current tummy sizzle.

Rule of thumb was order anything in the second or third row, nothing from the front of the grill, but most of the MPs wouldn't eat anything off the grill.

Not me. I would say, "Cook it up front, where I can watch. You know how picky I am."

Once, Grand was standing next me, and he whispered, "The sweat is dripping off his nose and hitting the hot grill. Watch it."

Just then, Happy Jack's sweat ball splashed down and sizzled on the grill. The other MPs in line grimaced in disgust and walked away without ordering.

Bob Mayors would never tell his stories in front of Happy Jack, because Jack would call him out. Bob loved to tell people he won a Purple Heart in Vietnam, which was true, but it was due to losing his hearing, not from getting shot in combat or anything. Bob would explain how the enemy blew up his jeep and ruptured his eardrums.

Happy Jack would pull them aside later and explain, "That jackass was not special ops. He was a damn cook and lost his hearing due to a kitchen explosion, not the enemy."

Happy Jack was Bob's boss, and when Bob was alone, he was a completely different guy from when the boss was around, full of life and, most importantly, full of stories. He also provided the fuel to keep us awake on night shift. Thank goodness he was alone most nights when we grabbed chow, because I'm not sure I could have stayed awake without his stories.

Between Bob's yarns and all the DUIs and bar fights, our time at Bragg moved quickly. With less than a year left on active duty, Scott and I began our police academy application packets, hoping to attend in December of 1990.

Throughout the summer of 1990, I was in constant coordination with Phil Gold to ensure we met all the deadlines for submissions to the police academy. It was difficult making the preparations from Bragg. Lisa and I decided it would be best to buy a home and get settled before starting the academy. Although she never said it, I think she was not a fan of the hot summers on Fort Bragg. Both our families resided in Lincoln, so we limited our search to our hometown, which would make life easier after we moved. My friend Marty knew a family that was going to sell a small home but one that would work for us. We were excited to find it before it even went on the market.

We timed the trip up to Rhode Island to coincide with academy testing, so we were able get Scott to help move our stuff up North. Our plan was to move before the Fourth of July holiday.

When Scott pulled up at our government quarters to pack up, I already had the U-Haul open and waiting in the driveway.

"Jeez," he said. "You're on time when Lisa is around, that's for sure."

"Nah," I said, "just don't want to take too much of your time."

"You're full of shit, Ant. And why don't you just wait for the military to move you?"

"If I move it myself, I get eighty percent of what they'd pay a moving company, so for every one hundred pounds they pay me eighty bucks."

Scott tilted his head and looked at me funny. "And how much am I getting paid to move you?"

"Lunch and my heartfelt appreciation."

Scott snorted and shook his head. "Starting to wonder if I'm cut out to live in Rhode Island after we leave the military. Plus, not too many good-looking ladies up there." He looked over at Lisa. "No offense."

"No, you're right," she said. "That's why your friend should be even more grateful he found me again."

Scott said, "Wait, why are you bringing your weight set? You haven't use that since before Germany."

"I've never seen him use them," said Lisa.

"Well, these are about four hundred pounds," I said. "So that's three hundred twenty bucks to drive them to Rhode Island."

They both yelled at the same time, "But you won't ever use them again!"

"Maybe not, so I sell them and make fifty bucks for them *plus* three hundred twenty dollars. Who's the idiot now?"

"Still you," said Scott. "And now us for moving it."

Next, I started bringing out my five eighty-pound bags of concrete mix.

"Hell, no!" Lisa shouted. "Throw that shit away, already."

"Oh, my god," I said. "This is over three hundred dollars, and you want me to throw it away?"

Scott pointed to his little car and said, "We can load this if we need more space."

"No, I only get paid for my vehicle and Lisa's on the move, plus we can dump the other shit in her car, and I'll get paid for that, too."

The trip went well except for crossing the George Washington Bridge. I was pulling up to the tollbooth, driving the vehicle with the U-Haul trailer, and Scott was right behind me.

"Hello," said the attendant, a well-aged New Yorker, possibly of Italian descent. "That will be eight dollars."

"Do you guys give a military discount?" I asked. "And I'm paying for my buddy behind me as well."

The attendant shook his head in amazement, and in a very strong New York accent said, "Listen here, buddy. It's a fucking tollbooth. No disrespect to your service, but this is a tollbooth."

I gave him a twenty, and he handed me back my four dollars in change and said, "But you have a nice fucking day already, and clear my damn lane, please."

When Scott pulled up, the guy said, "That cheap fuck paid your way, too."

Four hours later, we arrived at my mom's house in Manville. We left the trailer parked out front, full, because we wouldn't get the house for two more days. The next morning, Scott and I met Gold for breakfast at Frank's, a place in Lincoln known for large portions that always came out quick and hot.

Gold arrived a few minutes after we were seated.

"Hey, nice to see you, Ant," he said. "This must be the famous Scott."

As we stood and shook hands, Scott said, "Oh, that's my last name. It's Chris."

"Nice to finally meet you, Chris," Gold said. "This will be a cakewalk for you two, but do well on the written test tomorrow and the fitness exam in August."

"Not sure I'm gonna like this little town," Scott said.

Gold said with excitement, "It's a great little town."

Scott looked at Gold. "You think Ant can pass the fitness test?"

Gold snorted. "Long as he doesn't eat like a pig the night before, I'm sure he'll be fine."

"I kind of miss Basic," said Scott.

"Fuck that," I said in a pissed-off tone.

"I do."

"If Scruggs hadn't been in my ass for fourteen weeks, maybe I'd miss it, too," I said.

Scott announced he was going to stay in Rhode Island a few more days before heading back. "I want to see some of my future state."

"Crap," I said. "If I'd known I would have driven back instead of buying a ticket."

The next day, we took the exam and had lunch after at Pawtucket House of Pizza again. After finishing our roast beef sandwiches, we went our separate ways. Before I left, I asked Scott where he was staying.

"I'm at the Clover Leaf Hotel."

"What a shit hole!" I said. "Why there?" The Clover Leaf was a terrible place, adjacent to the Rustic Theater, an old drive-in that used to show porn.

"It was cheap and close to everything, and all I do is sleep there."

The next morning, I got up early and headed south. On Highway 146, I passed the Clover Leaf Hotel and saw Scott's vehicle sitting there toward the end of the parking lot. I chuckled to myself, thinking, *Maybe he got lucky at the Clover Leaf.* But then I thought, *Nah, he's only successful if I'm around.*

I got back to Fort Bragg on a Thursday evening and settled into my new room. If you were drawing housing for your spouse, you could live in the barracks again free of charge. One thing about life at Bragg was that there were constant test rollouts, to make sure soldiers were ready to deploy to war if needed. Our unit was on call that weekend, and I was hoping they weren't going to pull that shit while I was trying to get settled in.

On Sunday evening, Scott returned from Rhode Island and seemed a bit off, like he was cranky again or maybe he was simply tired.

"Hey, Scott," I said. "How was the Clover Leaf? You get lucky?"

"No, I just went to Newport and Jamestown," he said. "Those are some old-ass towns."

"Lots of history there for sure, the hotbed for the American Revolution. Did you meet anyone?"

"Yeah, kind of, just some chick at a bar."

"Really?"

"Yeah, a college student. Nothing happened, just talked some."

"Look at that," I said. "You're already in love."

Scott snorted. "Fuck that. We just talked. Surprised to find anyone in Rhode Island that could have a normal conversation."

"Okay, well don't blow it. Like you said, not lots of good-looking women in Lil Rhodes. Although my sisters still got dibs on your ass."

"No shot of me being related to your monkey ass."

A month later, Scott and I had to ask for more leave time to take the fitness test in Rhode Island. We loaded our vehicles again—yes, I made some more DIY move money. After packing my car to the gills, I got it weighed, then moved the items from the front seat into Scott's car again, along with a few other light but bulky items. We decided to drive right through, seven hundred fifty miles, only stopping for gas and to piss.

As we pulled up to the George Washington Bridge tollbooth, I was surprised to see the same guy in the same booth as last time.

"I'm paying for the guy behind me again," I said.

He looked at me and said, "Hey, I remember you! Last month, you asked for a military discount. Told all my boys at the bar, and they bitched me out for calling a veteran a cheap fuck."

"No problem," I said. "I get called that often."

I paid and pulled away. Behind me, Scott pulled up and waved at the guy, who pushed his hand out and gave him a high five, yelling, "Thanks for serving and glad the cheap fuck paid for you again!"

About four hours later, we arrived at the house, where Lisa was now pretty much settled in.

Scott spent the first couple nights with us there, but then said he was going to get a room at the Clover Leaf again.

"Dude," I said, "I know you're just going over to watch porn movies at the Rustic drive-in."

"What the hell are you talking about?"

"That's a porn drive-in next door. We used to go there as kids and rub it in the bushes outside the fence line. One time, Marty Gaughan found an old truck seat and moved it to the spot just outside the fence."

"Whatever," Scott said. "Dude, it's twenty-nine bucks a night—a bargain if it means I don't have to hear you snore from the other bedroom."

Lisa laughed. "Leave him alone and let him do what he wants."

After a few days, we both passed the fitness test. Scott did more sit-ups than me and just beat me in the two-mile run by three seconds. I still couldn't believe he beat me again.

"Dude, I did more push-ups," I said. "You just did more sit-ups and ran three seconds faster. I let you win."

Scott laughed. "You never let anyone win. Nice try."

"I'm serious."

It killed me to lose at anything, especially to Scott, who loved rubbing it in. Wanting to save some more of my leave time so I'd be done before the holidays, I decided to drive back later, on August 3, when there would be less traffic. Scott said he would leave a couple days later, maybe Saturday, again stating that he wanted to see more of his future home state.

I arrived back on Bragg and spent the day moving more stuff into my new room. I was just finishing up, thinking about how much I hadn't missed the place, and how I was for sure going home for Thanksgiving, when SFC Hankel showed up in civilian clothes.

"This can't be good," I said when he walked into my room. We were the MPs on call for DRF again, so if alerted, we'd have to pack all our gear and head to the flight line and potentially deploy. We were on call a week every month, but we had not rolled out since Scott and I arrived. People in the barracks were going about their business like nothing was going on.

"Listen to me, Anthony, I already called your bud and told him to get his ass back here. We have a real-world rollout at 0500 tomorrow. I need you to make sure the idiots in the barracks don't tie one on and are back in the rooms NLT 2200, per their Division Ready Force rollout guidance."

"Yeah, another drill?"

"No," he said, his face showing great concern like I hadn't seen before. "No, this appears to be the real deal."

"What? No way. Where are we going?"

"Can't say, but it's hot. Middle East hot. I told your buddy he better make it back or you will be deploying without him."

"How did you reach him?"

"I did not know you were back, so I called your home number. Your wife told me where he was staying."

"Is he on his way?"

"Yeah," Hankel said. "He told me he had to deal with something up there, but he'd be on the road soon. That was early in the a.m. Keep an eye on him, he seemed a little freaked out about the rollout. Maybe I woke him up or something, but I'm not sure I've heard him sound like that before." Hankel then pointed at me and said, "Get ready." Then he turned and briskly headed out.

That didn't sound like Scott, but it wasn't like we'd ever had a real-world rollout. I figured he was nervous and planned to bust his ass about it when he got here.

Around 2130, Scott showed up at my room. He seemed a bit off, like he was pissed again or maybe he was scared to deploy.

"Hey, what's going on?" I said.

"No fucking idea," he replied. "Hankel said 'real-world rollout' on the phone, so I came right back."

"Yeah, that's all I know too. You doing okay or something going on?"

"Of course, I'm okay," he snapped. "Are *you* okay?" He plopped on my desk chair.

I asked him again, "What's bothering you?"

"Nothing, I just drove seven hundred fifty miles, okay?"

"My bad, you must be hungry, being so sensitive and all." He was almost too reserved, given we were rolling out to a real world and not joking about anything. "You 'hangry?'"

"No, that's you, bitch, I don't get hangry. I'm tired, and you just can't let shit go."

There was a knock on the door, Hankel again.

"Good to see you two homos again in the same room," he said. "Here's the deal—find out who's not in their room and track them down tonight."

"Well, where are we going?" I said. "There was nothing on the news."

"This is not a DRF. The Iraqis invaded Kuwait, and we're headed to Saudi Arabia pending a potential full-scale response. Make sure the other guys are ready. I'm counting on you two!"

He closed the door and left.

"Fuck," I said. "How is this going to affect the police academy if we deploy?"

"Dude, let's just worry about getting there and getting back safe." Scott gave me a strange look. "That's why I rushed back. You can't go to a combat zone without me watching over your stupid ass!"

"Yeah, right," I said, grinning. "You know it's just the opposite."

That got no response from Scott. He just turned and went to his room. A few minutes later, I followed him.

"What is going on with you, skinny dick?" I asked, standing in the doorway.

"Nothing!"

"Come on, what's the deal? Why are you acting all weird and shit?"

"I'm not. Just tired from the trip and glad I made it back!"

"Did you come up empty with the ladies in RI?"

"Yeah, like I ever come up empty."

"Is your mom doing okay?"

He sighed. "Yeah, but she's not getting better." He paused and looked up at me. "I guess that's what's on my mind."

I nodded. "Sorry." Scott was a real mama's boy, and it killed him when she was ill. I knew better than to press him on that. "Do you like the new room?"

"Oh, it's fine for now," he said, seeming relieved to change the subject.

"Just think," I said, "I get Basic Allowance for Quarters for RI, but get to stay here for free."

"But you don't get to be with Lisa!"

"Yeah," I said in an extremely sarcastic tone, "but that means more time with you."

***

It all came suddenly and without warning on August 2, 1990. Even before any news channels were talking about Saddam Hussein's invasion of Kuwait, the 118th had already exercised the alert roster, so soldiers were being notified by phone or pager to come in. The MPs in the barracks of the 118th MP Company were suddenly awakened by SFC Hankel. "Hey, girl scouts, get your lazy asses out of bed! Drop your cocks and grab your socks! Pack your shit, we're going to war."

I was still half-asleep, thinking, *This can't be happening*, even though I had known it was coming.

"Where the fuck are we going now?" someone shouted.

"We're going to the desert, folks," Hankel boomed, "to kick the ass of some camel jockey named Saddam Hussein."

This was a surprise to everyone. No one knew that Iraq was planning this. And this was not a test rollout, it was the real deal. This was really happening!

"Hurry up and wait" was one of the first things you learned about in the military. This alert was no exception. Most of the soldiers in the 118th were disappointed to hear that there would be a few days' delay before hitting the ground in combat.

"Any of you having thoughts of getting your mustard stain over your wings, you can forget about it," Hankel told us. "We're flying to Saudi in a few days, no combat jump."

A yellow star, a.k.a "mustard stain," was awarded to troopers who had participated in actual combat jumps. This hit us all hard because we had been practicing our mission and making airborne jumps every month. Now that the shit was hitting the fan, we were flying in like any other leg unit.

"Shit," I said. "We're still five jump chumps," a reference to airborne-trained soldiers who had only jumped in Airborne School. Scott and I went to Hankel and explained that we were attending the police academy in January.

"How long you think this thing is going to last?" I asked. "Is the entire unit going?"

"Listen, Spanky," he said, a name from *The Little Rascals* that he used on soldiers who didn't seem to get something obvious. "You are a soldier in the United States Army, and the Army doesn't give a flying fuck if you are going to the civilian police academy."

"We just wanted to know."

"Maybe this will motivate you to reenlist," said Hankel with a big belly laugh.

Scott and I both rolled our eyes. "Never happening," said Scott.

For the next couple days, the 82nd was rapidly preparing its equipment for transport to Saudi. The unit then loaded anything not being transported via aircraft to a railhead, where it would be loaded onto a naval vessel headed to the deployment location. Luckily, the 118th didn't have any items of that sort, so our time was spent getting our personal equipment ready, going to the range to requalify, and doing Nuclear Biological and Chemical training. There was real concern that Saddam would use chemical weapons, so all deploying soldiers had to retrain on chemical procedures.

The second day of the alert started out with the 118th going to the gas chamber. This was a time when anyone under the rank of staff sergeant got seriously fucked with by senior NCOs under the guise that this was important to test to see if the Mission Oriented Protective Posture (MOPP) equipment was working. We all knew that the M17 masks worked. Despite this, SFC Hankel still made all his soldiers remove their masks in the chemical mask training chamber and run through the gauntlet of senior NCOs, who were blocking the door and making soldiers recite their first and second general orders.

Outside, the exiting soldiers were walking around a circle holding their recently removed masks, coughing, spitting, and sneezing while the chamber NCOs looked on with huge smiles. The sudden burst of CS gas on the system affected people differently. Scott already had hay fever, and he was bent over coughing with snot hanging out of his nose. It was total torture!

Finally, the time came for the 118th to fly. On the morning of

August 6, four days after the invasion, we all got our uniforms on and grabbed several days' worth of clothing and our alert bags, which consisted of two duffels and a rucksack full of all our essential TA-50, the tactical gear used during war. Then we proceeded downstairs. Soldiers were gathering in the courtyard between the 118th's barracks and the transportation unit across the way.

I snuck a call to Lisa from a pay phone. "I can't say anything, but I'm headed out of the country and don't know when I am getting back."

With obvious panic in her voice, she blurted out, "What the hell? You better find out where you are going!"

"They won't tell us."

"Well, I need to know."

"I can't say anything. Even if I knew, I couldn't say. Just wanted to tell you I love you and I'll see you when I get back."

"I don't like this," she said, her voice sad. "I love you, too. And don't be a hero. I just found you again, and I enjoy having you in my life."

"Aha! Finally, you admit it!"

She laughed a little, but I could tell from the sound of it she'd been crying. "I tell you all the time. It's going to be no fun without you, Mr. Anthony."

"I will be back soon, Mrs. Anthony, no matter where I'm going."

"Promise!"

I did, and after a few more "I love yous, SFC Hankel started yelling, "Time to move, lover boy."

The platoons lined up in formation with our duffels and rucks behind us, then the commander, Captain Brian Fester, addressed the troops.

"Our commander-in-chief, President Bush, has directed the 82nd AB Division to come to the aid of Kuwait, who was suddenly and without warning invaded by Iraq this week...*blah, blah, blah, blah...*" His speech seemed to go on forever.

My stomach growled, and Scott chuckled.

"When the hell is he going stop pontificating so we can eat our last hot meal before deploying?" I whispered out of the corner of my mouth.

After formation, the 118th all drew our assigned weapons and went to chow. It all seemed surreal.

"Is this really happening?" I asked.

"Looks like it," Scott said, still oddly quiet.

I was standing near the grill, kissing Bob's ass for some extra food.

Scott shook his head. "I don't want to hear his stories," he said, and he went to sit on his own.

"Okay," I said, "your loss."

After chow, it was still dark, and we were all lined up in formation in the courtyard when the cattle trucks showed up. These were five-ton trucks, each pulling a trailer big enough for an entire platoon to ride in. SFC Hankel appointed Scott, me, and several others to load the duffels in one of the trucks. The soldiers were told to keep their rucks. After the last duffel was loaded, we all climbed into the cattle trucks and headed to the rally point two miles away on the base.

There we were told to dismount and march to the flight line approximately a mile away. As we got ready to move, SFC Hankel noticed something strange about Sergeant Jackson, a squad leader in one of the other squads.

Hankel went over to him and said, "What the hell is wrong with your feet, SGT Jackson?"

"Well, Sergeant, in the mad rush this morning to pack my gear and get ready to deploy, I packed two left boots at the bottom of my ruck," Jackson said. "I was running late, so I said I'll just wear these. That's why I have two right boots on."

Hankel shook his head. "You must be kidding me, Jackson. What kind of meat head move is this? You are a damn NCO."

"Yes, Sergeant!"

"So, you're going to march over to the center, then fly on an aircraft for almost twenty hours wearing two right boots?"

"I have no choice now. My duffel is already loaded and packed."

Scott and I started snickering, and then the whole unit erupted in laughter.

One of the best times in the Army was marching. Something you despised in Basic became something you loved, and having someone who could call a great cadence made the march even more enjoyable. SFC Hankel could march the unit with vigor and precision, he honed these skills singing karaoke in Korea. He started off the jodies with my favorite song. "See the MP dressed in black, no he is never coming back, see the MP dressed in blaaaaaaackkkk, no he is never coming baaaaccccccckkk!"

After this song, Hankel explained a deviation in the next cadence call. Normally, when the cadence caller said, "Up on your left!" the unit would say, "Your right," as soon as their right feet hit the ground. Hankel explained that most of the platoon members were to say this, as usual, but then he singled out Sergeant Jackson, telling him to respond with, "I'm still on my right," when his left foot hit the ground, because no matter what foot hit the ground, his boot would always be his right boot.

SFC Hankel had a unique way of rallying his military police team, and the pending mission clearly warranted a special approach. The MP unit was so relaxed by this simple act of joking with the NCO, it diffused the fact that we were being sent off to a conflict. When we marched to the flight line, it looked like an old WWII movie. Hundreds of soldiers all carrying rucks and weapons lined up in "chalks," or lines on the tarmac, as the C141 aircraft taxied in the foreground. It seemed like just another training deployment. Little did we know, it would turn into the biggest military deployment since World War II. Then we got on the planes, and the 82nd Airborne was headed to the Middle East.

How and why did the U.S. military—and more importantly the MPs from Fort Bragg—end up in Iraq before the war? Here's a quick summary, for those unaware of what happened.

In August of 1990, the Iraqi military invaded Kuwait to take control of the oil fields. The United States responded by deploying forces to Saudi Arabia. For several months, US and coalition forces moved into Saudi Arabia in preparation for what would be the first Iraq war. Soldiers who were part of the XVIII Airborne Corps had the specific mission during the First Gulf War to protect the flank just off to the east of Iraq. Although the military campaign was over rather quickly, it was two or three months before all of the Iraqi forces surrendered.

The wartime mission resulted in the 82nd Airborne Corps being located post-conflict directly between Iraq and Kuwait. Our unit provided law enforcement support for the XVIII Airborne Corps. Although there were very few MPs performing police duties, the corps thought it best to have us there both before and after. The MPs were there to provide some patrol-like duties and were co-located with our infantry brothers from Fort Bragg.

During the Gulf War, very few MPs performed services or participated in direct tactical ground combat. There were some MPs in the region accompanied by working dogs and used for base security and alerting procedures. Part of the mentality for the XVIII ABN Corps was the belief that MPs would better deal with the local populace than combat soldiers, due to their experience in dealing with the public. This is a long drawn-out way to explain that the military police who served in Iraq were not as prepared for what they encountered as they could have been.

CHAPTER 7

BACK TO IRAQ AFTER LOSING HIS BATTLE BUDDY, ANTHONY IS IN A FOG

In the days that followed the explosion, I didn't know what to do with myself. I packed up Scott's personal effects, ready to ship them back to his family, and was told by the commander to stand down. I could only ride on patrol with limitations. Was I a liability? Maybe the commander knew how pissed I was—he couldn't have soldiers going out unsupervised into the field with personal vendettas.

Then SFC Hankel came up to me and said, "You're riding with me today, Anthony."

"Wait, what?" I said, stunned. "I'm a sergeant. I don't need to ride with you."

"You heard me."

"I am a freakin' NCO! I'm fine!"

"Well, Commander says you're not, so that's how we're going to roll. "

Slowly, we made our way to the Humvee in complete silence, no talk whatsoever.

Hankel started the engine, and a few minutes after we pulled away, he said, "So how are you doing?"

"I'm fine!"

He sighed. "Yeah, that's what I expected. Well, I'm here if you want to talk."

"No shit," I said. "I'm sitting right next to you."

That made him smile.

We spent the entire day driving up on unsuspecting foot patrols, Hankel telling them in no uncertain terms how things should be with his usual dubious charm.

"You really enjoy this shit, don't you, Sarge?" I said.

"Make the most of any shitty situation, Soldier."

Out on patrol, the dry, dusty air brought me back to that dreadful day. Driving into town, the smell of food cooking and seeing the locals brought back more thoughts of Scott that I couldn't seem to shake off. While Hankel laid into each set of troops, my mind wandered again to my battle buddy, and I grew angrier and angrier.

Watching Hankel talk to soldiers, hearing the same shit over and over, that was not new. But watching it without Scott there to smirk at my one-liners when Hankel's back was turned, that was something I'd never experienced and never wanted to.

We drove past the area where Scott had saved my life. The damaged vehicle was still sitting there on the side of the road. I looked over and saw an MP I'd never met, sitting on his Kevlar on the damaged hooptie. He noticed Hankel and immediately strapped it back on, hoping he hadn't been noticed.

I lost my shit for a moment and jumped in his ass. "Hey, dipshit! Pay attention! See that vehicle? Yeah, the one you're sitting on. I almost died right there."

"Yes, Sergeant!" he said, then he nodded back. Meanwhile, everybody else was simply going about their business, like nothing had ever happened. I couldn't help but wonder, if my life had ended there, what would have happened to Scott?

The more I thought of Scott, the more I thought of the last words he had uttered to me. No matter how I tried, I couldn't get them out of my head: "I killed some girl when I was home on leave."

Whatever happened, it had to have been an accident. There was no way he would have killed anyone on purpose, let alone some girl. I had to stop thinking about it or else, I knew, it would drive me crazy.

As the sun was dipping below the horizon, Hankel drove us into the most congested part of Baghdad, where there were reports of activity by a small group of Iraqis who had not surrendered.

"Okay, listen up," Hankel said, leaning in and whispering. "I'm going to go past this one house, and you just need to look over without making a big deal. You see that Iraqi female moving about?"

"Yeah."

"My intel buddies say she is assisting the people we're looking for relating to Scott's land mine. Right there—don't stare!—that's her."

She was in her mid-30s, short, but wearing a hijab and a dark burka that hid her body type. She was moving about in a steady, almost direct manner, like she was heading somewhere specific.

She looked over at the MP Humvee, then quickly dropped her head, so as to not bring attention to herself.

"They think she helped move explosive material for the guy they're tracking in your event. We don't know for sure, but our intel team is watching her. I'm only showing you this so you know we're actively trying to find who was behind it, and we won't stop until we do."

I said nothing to Hankel, but in the back of my mind I was thinking, *We better find all of them.*

At the end of the day, Hankel drove us into the heart of the city to share one more tidbit of information. The buildings had seen significant gunfire and some damage from mortars or tank rounds. People were moving about the area like nothing ever happened here.

"Okay," Hankel said, "remember the bomb maker I told you about?"

"Yeah. What about him?"

"We think he's in one of those bombed-out buildings."

I looked over and saw bullet holes in these adobe hut-like buildings and military debris all over the place. There was no street-cleaning crew, and if the soldiers couldn't use it, they just left it all in place. A painful reminder.

"This guy is supposedly making remote detonation devices," Hankel said. "Including the one in the bomb you guys blew up in."

"The land mine?"

"They're more sophisticated now," he said. "They're calling them improvised explosive devices now, or IEDs."

Hankel leaned in again and said, "We need to head back to the FOB."

"No problem."

"Okay," he said. "I shared all this with you to let you know we have people working on this. They will find Scott's killer, and you need to focus on your mission when you are on patrol going forward."

On our way back to the FOB, his face lacking any emotion, Hankel told me, "I'm sending you out with Private Pool for the next few days. Stay alert. He's a newbie, and we need to make sure you both come back with us stateside."

"Roger."

"Additionally, I don't want to see you butting into the investigation. Just wanted you aware we are actively looking for these bastards."

"Roger."

"And don't talk about this with anyone. The CO will have my ass for even telling you any of this shit. I just wanted you to know our entire team is leaning in on this effort."

"Roger."

The next day couldn't come quickly enough because I wanted to find Scott's killers at all cost. I was greeted by a fresh-faced MP barely out of his teens, keen to fall in line and secure the approval of his superior. I was hoping he'd look the other way while I found these bastards who killed Scott. I was happy he seemed a kind of carefree guy.

"Morning, Sergeant," said Private Pool in a strong Southern twang. "I heard about your buddy, Specialist Scott. I am really sorry about that, Sergeant."

"Thank you," I said. "We've got to make sure nobody else ends up like that, Pool. Just pay attention to your surroundings and stay alert, stay alive." My response may have seemed callous or uncaring, but I refused to give any thought to anything other than finding Scott's killer—that and the fact that, holy shit, I was starting to talk like Hankel.

"Roger that, Sergeant," Pool said.

We made our way around our patrol sector in Baghdad, but after a short while, I drove to a different location, and before long I found what I was looking for, an Iraqi woman crossing the street. Being so new, Pool had no idea we were not in our assigned sector, but easily noticed how hyper-focused I was on this woman.

"Who's that, Sergeant?" he asked.

"Nobody in particular," I said.

We were very close to the area Hankel had specifically told me to stay away from. But I had to know for myself: What was the deal with this lady? I did not approach her at all. I just wanted confirmation that things were going the way I hoped they would.

Pool asked again, "What's up with her?"

"Oh, nothing. She just looks familiar. I couldn't remember where I saw her before."

I stepped on the gas, and we sped back to our area of operations in the other part of town. There, I turned to Pool. "Stay in the Humvee. I'm going to check on the foot patrol."

The street was not very busy, mostly people on foot and occasionally older vehicles. There also did not appear to be a large military presence in the area, but I spotted Steve Scalici, an MP specialist dog handler I'd met a few weeks earlier, on patrol with his bomb-detection beagle, Peetee, and another MP.

I moved up to Scalici, smiling and friendly. "What a cute dog," I said. "How long have you been a dog handler?"

"Hey, Sergeant. Couple of years now. I'm a reservist. We usually work at the airport in Philly. I'm hoping this winds down quickly, so I can get back to the US."

He was a big kid, obviously of Italian descent and with a strong

Jersey accent. We exchanged small talk about the East Coast and getting back home soon. The dog seemed to understand that I was a dog person. He was quite friendly with me.

"Okay, see you around," I said. "Be careful out there."

"I will. The threat level is low right now."

"Well, I said goodbye to my best friend about a week ago."

Scalici looked at me with big eyes.

I made my way back to the Humvee, where Pool was standing, smoking a cigarette.

"Who was that, Sergeant?" Pool asked, drawing out the R, like "Serrrrrgeant."

"A reservist I know. Just saying hello."

"That's an MP dog? Not much protection there."

"No, Pool, he's a bomb dog."

"Oh."

"Damn, Private. You know how much money you're wasting smoking those damn things?"

"I know, Sarge. just can't give 'em up."

"Well, the price of buying them is never going down," I said. "The only thing that will is your life expectancy."

As soon as I said it, I realized I was sounding like Hankel again. *"Man,"* I said to myself, *"I gotta go back home soon."*

We spent the next five days doing basically the same thing every day, in the same area of operations, and each time I told Pool to remain in the vehicle. As I had hoped, he was so new he didn't have a problem with that, he was happy to have the time to get in a smoke or two.

During my last stop of the day, I saw Scalici and Peetee again and, as usual, told Pool to stay in the vehicle as I headed off. When

I returned ten minutes later, I was breathing heavy, like I had just run two miles.

"What's going on, Sarge?" Pool asked. "Why so winded?"

"Oh, I, um, had to run back because I lost track of time."

"Well, you might not be able to run so much in this heat, Sarge."

"Yeah, that's it for sure. I'm not used to the heat."

Pool seemed to accept my answer without concern.

As we drove back to the FOB, I got us up to a high rate of speed. Pool seemed slightly alarmed. "What's the hurry, Sergeant?"

"Nothing big, just wanting some chow."

"You must be hungry."

An instant later, another bomb went off on the other side of the road, pushing us off the road. It was not a direct hit like the last one I'd been in, but I knew to get the hell out of the area. I gathered myself quickly and kept on driving.

Pool's eyes were wide open as he blurted out, "Holy shit, that was close."

"Yeah," I said, keeping my voice steady. "We're lucky it wasn't a direct hit."

"You're so calm."

"The last one was a nightmare. This is nothing compared to that."

Back at the FOB, we reported the incident, explaining it was a low-level bomb with no serious damage to the vehicle or its occupants, then I visited with the medic to get a bandage for a cut and some Tylenol for a suddenly raging headache. They quickly released me back to my quarters, and I hit the rack early that night. The sweat from running was now dry, but I was too tired to take a shower.

The events of the day would rattle me for a long time, I thought, as

I drifted off to sleep with images from both roadside bombs running through my head. I actually rested okay that night, considering I had just survived my second IED event in sixteen days. I should not have been out there. I needed to slow my shit down. Scott's death had changed me, and I was not the same guy who had climbed onto the plane at Fort Bragg nine months earlier.

After what seemed like a two-hour nap, I was alarmed to be awakened by a giant standing over my cot. SFC Hankel.

"Okay, shit-talker, time to get up," he said. "We are sending you to Landstuhl, the military hospital in Germany."

I sat up. "What are you talking about?"

"Next flight out, sad sack."

"What? Not interested," I said. "I'm going back out on patrol. Got to finish what these fuckers started."

"No, ass bag, your time here is done."

"Nope."

"You need to pack your shit up ASAP. You're headed out. You have a concussion, and a very serious one at that."

"No way! I'm fine!" I knew Hankel knew I was, so why was he trying to make like I was concussed? "What the fuck is going on?" I demanded. "Why are you trying to ship my ass out of here?"

Clearly having trouble sticking to his story, Hankel blurted out, almost apologetically, "Dude, I can't say why. Can you just trust me?"

"You are frustrating me, Hankel. What, are you worried again how I am dealing with this shit?"

"Fuck, you are a pain in my ass. Just get ready and then we can talk with the CO."

"I'm fine! I told you, that explosion last night wasn't even close to the one with Scott. I don't need to go anywhere."

"Ass clown, you are leaving today, period," said Hankel, now even more annoyed.

"I'm a fucking NCO! I know what I need to do," I said, my tone growing more aggressive and pushing the line of respect I should have been giving to SFC Hankel.

"Listen, Anthony, sit the fuck down and close your pie hole. We're trying to help you."

"I don't need any fucking help. I need to go find the bastards that took Scott's fucking life."

In a quiet voice that demanded attention, Hankel said, "Sit the fuck down, right now."

I was still fuming, but I sat without hesitation.

Hankel sat next to me, then leaned in and whispered, "Scott's alive."

I was stunned into silence, my eyes wide, staring at Hankel, trying to find words, finally managing, "What?"

"He's alive. They resuscitated him."

"No way," I said, my voice barely a whisper.

"Listen to me, he died on the table last week, several times. But each time, they managed to bring him back."

"What the fuck?" I shook my head. "That can't be. Don't fuck with me, Sergeant!"

"Captain Fester wants your ass there immediately. He hopes you can convince Scott not to give up." Hankel looked around to ensure nobody was listening. "I wasn't supposed to tell you any of this. Fester didn't want you to go through this shit again in the event—in case Scott loses his fight before you arrive."

165

I sat in stunned silence for a moment.

"So, can you do me a solid and pack your shit up and get ready?" he said. "I need you to act like you don't have a clue what is going on if Captain Fester sees you."

My disbelief was quickly replaced with excitement. "Holy shit! I can't believe he's still alive, that little shit!" I started laughing, and for a few moments felt like I couldn't stop. I started cramming my stuff into my duffel. I didn't see it at the time, but as I was packing, Scott's camera fell on the floor.

I was the kind of guy usually able to hide his emotions, but when the commander appeared outside my quarters, he took one look at me and turned to Hankel, "You told him!"

Hankel nodded and shot me a look like, *You couldn't do this simple task.*

Fester just shook his head.

"He needed to know, sir," Hankel said. "This will improve his trip tremendously, if there is still even the slightest hope Scott is alive."

"Now, for the record," Fester said, "I am sending you there for your multiple concussions."

"Yes, sir. As a matter of fact, I have been having lots of headaches. I think I mentioned that."

Fester looked at me and said, "Remember what I told you when we first lost him? We got this!"

"Roger, sir," I said. "I'm beyond grateful. Thank you."

My leadership team pulled strings to get me on the next military flight, arriving in Germany early the next morning. Military flights were nothing glamorous, and this was no exception—a beat-up

C-130 full of soldiers with limited injuries. Shortly after landing in Frankfurt, I was picked up at the airport by a military shuttle bus carrying four other injured soldiers. They were not MPs, and I had never seen them before. The drive took about an hour and a half. There was very little conversation, which suited me just fine—I just wanted to know that my buddy was still alive.

My mind drifted off to the last time I had been in Germany. I had fond memories, especially of the food, and I wondered if I could find a good restaurant close to the hospital.

The driver grabbed my duffel bag but made me wait until a wheelchair arrived to take me inside to get me checked into the hospital. The medical staff took my vitals and quickly processed me into the hospital and put me in an exam room. A male doctor came up to me, he was about 5'7", with close-cropped dark hair and was carrying a stack of charts. I noticed his nametag and the rank on his collar. I said, "Hello, Major Brown."

"Hello," he said. "What's going on with you, Sergeant?"

"They tell me I have a concussion," I said, quickly following with, "sir, I really need to know what is going on with my partner, Specialist Scott. He came in last week. Please tell me he's still alive."

Major Brown waited for me to take a breath, then he held his hand out. "Okay, slow down. I understand you must be the MP who was with him during the explosion."

"Yes, sir!"

"Great. Our team is expecting you. Your commander informed me that you were on your way here. We believe hearing your voice could be helpful to your friend's recovery. I'm happy to see you are in much better shape than he was."

"Roger that, sir."

"All I can say is, my gosh, your friend is a fighter. The fact that he's still with us is a miracle. Right now, he is in the ICU, and it's touch-and-go. He's coded on us repeatedly now, and he lost a ton of blood. Good news, he's stable right now. I am not really supposed to tell you this much, but your commander said you two were like brothers."

"Yes, sir. He is, without question, the best friend I've ever had."

He smiled. "Okay, great. Be patient with this and give our team some space."

"Sir, I need you to listen to me. You've got to do whatever you need to do to keep him alive. I already lost him once. I need you to keep him alive. Please."

"I understand, Sergeant," he said, his eyes welling up. "Trust me, I really do."

"If you need blood, I'll give it. If you need money, I'll give you everything I have, and if it's not enough, I'll rob a fucking bank for the rest."

The major chuckled, but I was completely serious.

"I understand," he said. "We've already been moving heaven and earth for this kid, and we'll continue to do our best, Sergeant. Our entire staff has been working on him nonstop for the last two hundred fifty hours or so, and nobody is complaining or slowing down one bit. We all want what you want, almost as much as you do."

"Thank you."

"Let me check on him again. Be patient." Then he walked away, wiping a tear from his eye.

I sat there in the exam room for thirty minutes, until Major Brown returned and said, "Scott is still stable. Would you like to see him?"

"Hell, yes!"

"Okay, we're going to need you to get completely cleaned up and sterile to go in there. Captain Jones will set you up."

"Got it, sir."

The doctor left, and a few minutes later a woman in medical scrubs came up and introduced herself as Captain Cheryl Jones, the nurse in charge of the ICU. She was African American, approximately 5' 5", and she had her hair pulled back tightly.

"Okay, Sergeant," she said. "I know Sergeant Scott is a good friend of yours, but to say he is in pretty bad shape would be a gross understatement." By her tone, it was obvious that she took her job over-the-top serious, and that her rules were nonnegotiable.

"I know, ma'am, I was there. I put the tourniquet on his missing leg."

"Well, he has lost the other leg, as well. They had to remove it. He has not regained consciousness, and we are not sure he ever will. Follow the rules to a T, and no messing around," she said, giving me a big-eyed *You better be listening to me* look.

"Yes, ma'am," I said.

"There are no second chances; you will not be allowed back in there, do you hear me?"

"Yes, ma'am! Got it. Now, let me get in there, please," I said, wondering if someone warned her I was going to be screwing around or something. She didn't even know me, but thought I was going to be messing with her operations.

"First, I need you to completely scrub up," she said. "This is a very sterile environment."

"Yes, ma'am."

She held out a medical outfit wrapped in plastic. "You will also put on this outfit, including the booties. Stand by the door, here, when you're ready, and I will come retrieve you."

"Yes, ma'am."

I raced into the room to clean up and stripped off my uniform with the kind of enthusiasm that previously only occurred when I was getting ready to have sex. As I put on the medical outfit, I started thinking about what the hell I was going to say. Thoughts raced through my mind—the explosion, seeing Scott bleeding out, the medics taking forever to arrive, and then watching Scott die in my arms. I didn't want to experience any of that again, but it flashed through my mind, along with another memory. Scott's confession.

Holy shit, I can't bring that up. No, no, just have to tell him to keep fighting through it, that I will always have his back.

I went to the door and waited, growing more impatient as two minutes turned into ten, then fifteen. I felt like I was waiting for my baby to be born. *Let's fucking go, already.*

When CPT Jones finally returned, she inspected my hands and coverings. "Do not remove your mask for any reason," she said. "And there is absolutely no touching. You are allowed to talk quietly to him, nothing dramatic. Just let him know you are there, okay?"

"Yes, ma'am," I said.

She led me down a long hallway to the last room on the right, reminding me once again to follow the rules. Then there he was, right in front of me, barely five feet away. I couldn't speak at first, couldn't even feel. I was too shocked at seeing him alive. The last time I saw him, he had died in my arms. How the hell was he alive?

He lay completely motionless, with no legs and a few facial cuts that appeared to be healing. They had removed his mustache to stitch his upper lip. I smiled, thinking, *Man, he is gonna hate that.* Then I remembered, this is what he looked like the first time we met. I felt bad for even smiling for a brief moment about something so trivial as my eyes returned to the bandaged stumps Scott now had for legs.

In a very low voice, I said, "Hey, man, can you hear me?"

There was absolutely no movement, no response at all.

"Scott, I know you're in there. Can you do something to show it?"

Nothing. Not a flicker or a movement, not so much as an eye quiver. Nothing at all.

I was almost never at a loss for words, but in that moment, I had no idea what the heck to say. After a few minutes, I said, "Dude, I know you can hear me. Give me anything, just so I know you know it's me here."

Still nothing. I took a deep breath and then just started talking.

"Okay, well, here's the deal. Right after the explosion, Hankel actually called me 'soldier.' Do you see the humor in that?" I paused, then said, "I know, right?" like we were having an actual conversation. "I'm not sure I can be in an army where they call *me* 'soldier.' And get this, Captain Fester even gave me a hug. What the hell is that all about?" I laughed. "They say I've got some kind of concussion. That's why they sent me here. But shit, I feel fine, so not sure why they sent me all this way, but I'm glad I'm getting a chance to talk to you, to see you're still here."

I lowered my voice and said, "You see, here's the deal: People don't understand we don't like to talk about serious shit, and I'm not sure we ever had a serious conversation in the five years we've known each other. So, this is the only time I am going to say this, and I won't admit it later, but I cannot imagine having to deal with those guys without you around to buffer the professional bullshit that comes out of their mouths. I have never known someone as stupid as you in my entire life. You met my family, you know they're a special kind of disturbed, and you blend with them like you've been with us from Day One. And I'm not about to go looking for a replacement battle buddy, so you just need to get your shit together and pull out of this."

I paused for quite a while, then leaned closer and lowered my voice even more. "And I don't give a rat's ass about what you told me. You're my best friend, and I will never tell a soul."

I noticed then that Captain Jones was standing by the door, her eyes filling with tears as she tried to remain professional.

I dropped to my knees and said, "God, you know I never pray, but this is a simple request. I am begging you, God, with all my heart, don't let him die on me again. No matter what has happened, he is a good man and I need him here on Earth. So, if you could just do me this one favor, I will forever be in service to you and promise to live a more purposeful life."

It had been a long time since I had prayed, and such religious words didn't come easy. "Neither of us would ever hurt an innocent person. Lord, we all have our issues in life, and if you could just find it in your heart to get him past this, I give you my forever promise I will make things right. I say this in your name, Jesus Christ, amen."

I looked over at Scott, hoping my prayer would be answered immediately, but there was no change.

For the next two hours, I sat there, sometimes silent, sometimes chatting away as if Scott and I were having a two-way conversation.

Then Captain Jones came in and said, "Okay, time to get some rest. I'll keep an eye on him. I promise he is a top priority for me, as well."

As I walked out, she said, "Every soldier needs a friend like you."

I paused and glanced back at Scott one more time, hoping to see some kind of sign, but there was nothing. I thanked CPT Jones once more for her efforts and asked her to keep me posted if there was any change at all. I told her that if nobody else was available to watch over him, I would do it, however long they needed.

This routine went on for the next eight days, with Scott unresponsive and me going on about Basic, Fort Sheridan, Fort Bragg, and Iraq, about the girls we had conquered, and how Lisa had changed me. How Scott would find the same kind of love someday.

I also talked about current events.

"Well, I don't miss the shitty food over in Iraq, that's for sure, but this hospital needs some help on the chow side, for sure," I said one day. "The mess cook is already pissed at me for helping him prepare my meals better. Can you believe some people don't want their customers completely happy?" I chuckled to myself and looked over.

Still no response, but I carried on anyway. "Remember in Basic, we thought they put saltpeter in our food, so we wouldn't get boners?"

I laughed again, but all to myself, as I was the only one talking or laughing. I did earn a slight smirk from Captain Jones as she walked past the room.

"Dude," I said, "this nurse captain is a hard ass. She is on me for each and every thing I do. 'Don't touch that.' 'Did you wash your hands?' 'Don't bring food in here.' 'This is not the barracks, so keep things quiet and professional or I am throwing you out.' Fuck, I think she might be Scruggs' sister or Hankel's or something. If she says, 'Stay alert, stay alive,' I'm out of here for sure." I looked over, thinking maybe Scott would laugh at that, but nothing. Nothing to see here but a soldier lying motionless and his best friend hoping and praying that he would wake up and talk to him. But not that day.

After two weeks of this, my visit time was almost used up. Major Brown told me I seemed to have healed well from my concussion, and that I wouldn't have much time left at the hospital. "Hopefully, your battle buddy will wake up soon."

Shit, I can't leave until he wakes up.

Maybe if I fell and banged my head, I could extend my stay. It was a good thought, but probably too obvious. Besides, I had made a promise to God that I would start doing things the right way going forward. No more short cuts.

I went to see my favorite guy at the hospital—you guessed it, the mess cook, SFC White. He was a crusty old African American sergeant, heavyset and always sweating. He kept a white rag on his shoulder to wipe his brow all the time. SFC Smith acted like I annoyed him, but I knew he secretly enjoyed having me there to battle with over food—so secretly, he didn't even know it himself.

"Oh, great," White said in his big, bellowing voice when I walked into the mess hall. "Look who's back for some good old Army cooking!"

"Hey, Sarge!"

"What in the good Lord's name are you going to request from us today?" he said, glaring at me.

"Well, Sarge, that depends. What's on the menu?"

"You know what the hell is on the menu, and you can read the specials board, too. Are you going to order something? I got shit to do and can't play with you all day."

I was excited to see that pastrami sandwiches were one of the day's specials. I ordered one, along with another special food request: "Cook a burger, top with provolone cheese, then put the hot pastrami off the grill on top, but make sure you melt another piece of provolone on top of the pastrami. Add some Thousand Island dressing and some grilled onions."

SFC Smith shook his head in disbelief. "Are you serious?"

"Yes, please," I said. "I'd love that."

SFC Smith made the sandwich per my request, and handed me the plate. "Hopefully, your stay here is ending, so I can get back to cooking for the rest of the soldiers and doctors instead of catering to your special requests every day."

"Yeah, right, you know you love making these special requests. And I know you make them for yourself, too, because you damn sure aren't eating salads all day!"

Smith chuckled as he walked back into the kitchen, shaking his head the whole way. I got that reaction a lot from the people who cooked for me.

I finished my lunch and headed back up to see Scott in the ICU, talking to every person I passed on the way.

I noticed Captain Jones by the elevator. "Hey, Cap, any good news today?"

She shook her head. "Nope. Same as every other day since he got here, but we are all standing by, waiting for his awaking."

I plopped down in my seat next to Scott's bed and started talking about random things. "Dude, this window has not been washed in ten years, not that there's much to see when you look out it."

Then I lowered my voice and checked to make sure we were

alone. "Jones is still pissed at the world.... I think the cook really likes me. He always comes out to talk with me when I pop into the chow hall. They had pastrami today. Remember the pastrami at Beef Barn in Rhode Island? Boy, I could go for that right now, with the melted provolone dripping all over it. SGT White in the chow hall here made me this amazing pastrami burger. I told him, first grill the burger, then top it with provolone, then grill the pastrami and top it with more provolone, then put Thousand Island dressing on the side with grilled onions."

"That does sound good."

"I know, right?" I said. Then my head whipped around as I realized Scott had spoken this.

"Wait, what? What the hell, you're awake!" Scott's eyes were open and staring at me. I screamed, "Nurse Jones! Captain Jones! Nurse, Captain Jones, he's up, he's awake!"

"What's going on?" Scott said, his voice groggy. "Where are we?"

I shouted, "Holy shit, you're awake!"

Jones dashed over to his bedside and shooed me out of the way. "Hello, my name is Captain Jones," she said in a steady voice. "I am the ICU nurse here. You have been here for over six weeks. Do you know your name and how old you are?"

"Yes, I am Christopher Scott," he said, his voice sounding clearer. Then he gave her some personal information to confirm he was aware of who he was.

Major Brown walked in and said, "Well, look at this, will you? It's about time, young man. We have been working on you day and night for a month for this very moment."

Scott tipped his head in my direction and said, "Well, I hope he hasn't been here the whole time. Maybe that's why I didn't wake up sooner."

"Yeah, right!"

"He can be pretty annoying, in case you don't know him well."

Captain Jones rolled her eyes and nodded in agreement, smiling at Scott.

The room began to fill as all the people who had been working on Scott filed in, including the surgical team. Literally 20 beaming people crowded into the room over the next few minutes.

Then Major Peters asked Scott, "What do you remember?"

The room went quiet as Scott said, "I remember driving on the main supply route…and then waking up here in the hospital."

"What is your date of birth?"

Scott looked up at Major Brown. "March 15, 1965." Then he looked down at his missing legs.

The room went quiet.

Brown said quietly, "We're sorry. We did everything we could, but there was no saving them."

Scott was silent for a moment, then he blurted out, "Good news for Anthony over here, he may finally be able to beat me in a race."

My mind flashed back to the side of the road. That was essentially the same joke he made when he was injured. He didn't remember.

Someone chuckled softly, then it spread across the room filled with people who were clearly overjoyed to see Scott awake and responsive, knowing they all had played a part in his recovery. Military medical teams were always extremely invested in the military members they worked on, way beyond the normal doctor-patient relationship.

I reluctantly left the room, allowing the medical staff to do more tests and evaluations. Back in my room, I prayed again, reaffirming my promise to live a more purposeful life going forward, no short cuts, to live my life with honor and purpose.

An hour later, I went back to see Scott. Captain Jones told me he was fast asleep, but that I could see him in the morning. She told me she had been in to check Scott's vitals, and my name had come up.

"How so?" I asked.

"He told me not to tell you, but he said he was glad you were there when he woke up. I told him how long you'd been here, how dang persistent. That I wasn't sure I'd ever seen someone so dedicated to a friend."

I didn't know what to say.

She continued, "I told him there have been several young men who came here from Iraq, but he might have been the most damaged of all. I told him every one of those doctors who came in were truly joyous seeing him awake. Nobody ever talks about all the ones we lose, but there were three soldiers last week alone. I told him you were a heck of a good luck charm, and he agreed."

I was too overcome with emotion to speak, so I just nodded.

She smiled and said, "We also agreed you were a terrible pain in the rear end. And he didn't ask me not to tell you that."

I woke up early the next morning and wolfed down a quick breakfast—there was no sign of SFC Smith, so I settled for a simple two eggs over easy. When I got to Scott's room, I found him wide awake and very alert.

"How's it going?" I asked, maybe feeling a bit wired from the excitement the night before.

"Just getting ready to go for a run," he said with a sarcastic grin. "How about you?"

"Look, man, I get it, I know how much it sucks what happened to your legs, but you're fucking alive. You almost didn't make it. My grandfather lost his leg in WWII, and he had a great life. You'll be okay."

"Oh, yeah, I remember you talking about him. His name is Walter, right?"

"Yeah. When we were kids, I used to chase my sisters around with his fake leg. It would freak them out, so there is always that. Plus, you'll always get a close parking spot."

"Yeah, there's that!"

"Scaring my sisters with his fake leg, to this day they hate me for it. I'll do the same with your legs as well."

"Hey!" Scott exclaimed. "You know what's greatest thing about all this?"

"No. What?"

"Without legs, my penis looks fucking huge!"

We both cracked up at that one.

"No, I mean it," he said, "I looked yesterday. My next job for sure will be as a porn star."

"That's a good job!"

"I'm thinking my porn name will be Tripod."

"You're such and idiot, the ladies will love performing with me," I said. "Yeah, I think the ladies are going to love that name."

I noticed CPT Jones outside the door, listening, but I didn't say anything.

"I'm dead serious," Scott went on. "If I get a hard-on, I'll look just like a freaking tripod!"

"That would have to be a very small tripod."

CPT Jones shook her head and walked away as Scott and I laughed hysterically.

As our laughter died out, Scott turned serious for a moment.

"I know for sure I'm happy to be alive," he said. "But it's weird, I don't remember much about that day."

Biting my bottom lip, I said, "Really? What do you remember?"

"I remember it was hot, and we were headed into town. And then the Humvee blew up."

I was watching him intently, hanging on every word. "That's all you remember?"

"Yeah, that's about it."

"There were rounds flying in after the explosion, with smoke and dust we hadn't seen prior. You were tossed from the Humvee and were on the side of the road."

Scott was listening closely, but I couldn't tell if he was playing me, saying he didn't remember.

After a brief pause, he said, "Then what?"

"Well, the smoke concealed our position, kept you from getting shot as there was a shooter on the other side of the vehicle." His face stayed very still, not showing any emotion whatsoever. "It was fucking crazy, man. One leg was gone, and you were bleeding out. I was just trying to stop the bleeding."

Reliving the event as I explained it to him, I could feel myself getting more and more emotional. "I looked over at your other leg and it was mangled, too, but not bleeding as much."

"Fuck," he said. "You must have been losing it."

"Shit, yeah! I'm screaming, 'For the love of God, where's the medic?'

Screaming at the top of my lungs, 'Medic! Medic!' They took fucking forever. You don't remember any of this?"

He shook his head. "Nope."

"Nothing?"

"Not a single thing. All I can remember is bullshitting in the Humvee, and then a loud *boom*. Nothing else."

I took a deep breath and continued. "After I got a tourniquet on the leg that was mostly gone, I dressed the other leg. I was told afterward they were still firing at us. Glad they shoot like you do, or we'd both be dead. Anyway, then you looked up at me and died."

I let out a breath, and so did he. "Wow," he said. "Intense."

I nodded. "Helicopter showed up, and the medic ran over. And they took you away."

We were quiet for a moment, then I said, "Hey, guess what? The doctor says the tourniquet saved your life, so I guess we're finally even now."

"Hell, no! I saved your ass twice in one week! And don't forget all the times I had to rescue you from bar fights, as well."

"Yeah, well, I didn't need your help in the bar."

"Okay, well when I saved your ass in Iraq, you got to keep both your legs, so I would certainly like my legs back, asshole."

We continued talking about things, but after a while, I asked him again, "You really don't remember any of this?"

"Absolutely nothing," he said. "Not a single thing you've said."

After a short, uncomfortable silence, I said, "After they took you away, I went numb. I don't even know how I got back to the FOB. I think SFC Hankel drove me, but all I remember is walking back to the barracks after the medic checked me out. And then crashing hard."

He shook his head. "Man, I can't imagine."

"The intel bubbas have an idea of who was behind this, and they're trying to roll them up."

"They can all die, if you ask me. Cocksuckers!"

"Agreed."

An angry silence filled the room, both of us wanting vengeance for what happened, but knowing that chapter was closed in our lives.

"I hit another bomb a few weeks later—nowhere near as bad, but they said I had a concussion." I looked around to make sure nobody was listening. "Fester knew I didn't really have a concussion. He sent me here, partly for that, but I believe Fester didn't trust me there without you, thinking I'd be looking for the nasty fuckers who blew you up."

We made eye contact and nodded, agreeing with Fester's decision. Scott was looking tired, and I decided to end the conversation there, not wanting to get into the post-blast life I was living—if he only knew.

They let me stay a couple weeks longer, then I was informed I was going back to Fort Bragg, so I tried to enjoy what little time I had left with Scott. Our unit was leaving Iraq soon anyway, so it was normal to be heading to Bragg. The last few days in Germany passed quickly, packing and preparing for my flight, and knowing that I was going to have one last talk with Scott.

I grabbed a wheelchair and headed to his room. "Okay, brother, I'm heading back to the States tomorrow. Let's go get some chow and push you around this place."

"Leaving so soon?" he said sarcastically. I got him into the wheelchair, and I pushed it into the hallway. On the way to lunch, I wondered if I should hint about his dying confession. I didn't.

We passed CPT Jones in the hallway, and I told her I was headed out. I thanked her and reminded her not to let Scott get away with anything.

She smirked and said, "I got this, Sergeant."

Then, to my surprise, she wrapped me up in a firm hug and said, "You boys are heroes, and we are lucky to have you protecting our freedoms."

Then she pulled back and said something that would stay with me for a long time. "You only need one true friend in life. With the friends you two have in each other, you've got lives many others would envy."

I thanked her, and we finally made our way down to the chow hall. SFC Smith shook his head when he saw us.

"Hey, Sergeant," I said, "this is—"

Smith cut me off. "I know who the hell that is. That's all you been talking about the last eight weeks, when you weren't driving me damn crazy with your special food requests."

"Come on," I said, "I'm not that bad."

Smith looked at Scott and said, "Does he really believe that? Look at what's on the menu today." He pointed over his shoulder with his spatula. There, written clearly on the menu, was ANTHONY BURGER.

Scott just shook his head and said, "You're only making it worse for other cooks! Erase it now, or there will be no living with him."

We all laughed, and Scott and I both ordered the pastrami burger, a.k.a. "the Anthony Burger." It was even better than the first time he made it for me.

As we ate, once again we only exchanged small talk—nothing of any substance, other than what was next after release. Scott was headed to Walter Reed Hospital for rehab, only six hours from Bragg.

I wheeled him back to his room, and we said a final goodbye, never acknowledging why we would miss each other so much, but it would have been clear to anyone who knew. As I looked back, knowing I was leaving Scott's hospital room for the very last time, Captain Jones walked up.

As I turned to leave, Scott said to her, "Finally, some damn peace and quiet around here. Let's have a party to celebrate that big mouth is gone."

***

Heading to the airport, so many thoughts raced through my mind. Still stuck in my head was a word CPT Jones had said. If, like me, she knew what Scott had told me, she certainly would never have called either of us heroes.

I realized I had to stop letting it consume me. He said he didn't remember—maybe it never happened. I remembered something my mom used to say: Don't go looking for pain.

I was processed for the Military Airlift Command (MAC) flight from Germany to Dover, Delaware, after which I would take a commercial flight back to Fort Bragg.

If you have ever ridden on a MAC flight, you would know I wasn't looking forward to this trip. I boarded the aircraft along with two dozen other soldiers, and we all looked for open seats—although you couldn't really call them seats, just mesh netting lined up along the walls of the aircraft, like baskets. Extremely uncomfortable.

In the center of the plane were large pallets of equipment tied down by straps but usually not tied perfectly, so there was the constant worry that a pallet could slide into your seat.

Sitting there, I recalled the last time I had been on a C-130, when I deployed to Saudi Arabia from Fort Bragg with Scott. I smiled as I remembered the stunt we had pulled on our MP brothers.

Before the flight, Scott and I had bought a pack of butter cookies. Before takeoff, we went up to the pilot, Captain Benson, and Scott said, "Hey, sir, you flying this old crappy aircraft?"

"Yeah, I am," he replied. "Are you one of our frequent fliers? Are you in coach or first class?"

"No sir, not at all," I said, "but me and my buddy Scott never ever get air sickness, and it won't matter what you do to us, it won't affect us one bit."

Scott acted unaware, looking at me with big eyes that said, *What the hell are you doing?*

I grabbed a handful of butter cookies, put them in my mouth, and said, "See if you can make me toss these."

Benson and his copilot exchanged a slight grin, and he said, "We will see!"

We climbed aboard quickly, and the C-130 started its high-powered engines, with immense power and handling so it could be used in combat environments.

We were seated next to the crew chief, who managed the back of the aircraft while in flight. We all wore headsets, and I said, "Okay, Captain, what've you got? This thing reminds me of an old crop duster we had on the farm."

I had never set foot on a farm, but I wanted to mess with the captain.

We took off and got to about 3,000 feet, and then sharply banked to the right. The soldiers were swinging around in their nets, their eyes as big as saucers. Then the plane banked to the left and there was some laughter, like this seemed like a fun ride, but a few looked like they were feeling sick.

Over the headset, I said, "Hey, Captain Benson! Everyone back here is laughing at you."

The plane climbed rapidly and then dove immediately back down, and now you could see the fear in the passengers across the plane, on the other side of the pallets.

I started to fake like I was getting sick, and the others started to crack up, seeing the smart ass was getting sick.

"Okay," I said, "I'm done, slow it down. I can't take it anymore."

Benson laughed. "You can't quit yet," he said, and the plane banked again, hard to the left, the cargo shaking a bit.

I grabbed my puke bag and a big sip of water and simulated swallowing the water. The plane banked again, now to the right, and I pretended to throw up in my puke bag. Everyone had that disgusted look on their faces, their Adam's apples dancing as they tried not to join me in throwing up.

Scott started laughing loudly, calling me a pussy and an embarrassment to the MP Corps. Then he looked into my bag, at the wet slimy cookies I had slipped in there before the flight and grimaced. "Yup, he threw up, and it's gross." He reached into the bag, grabbed some of the mess and put it in his mouth, saying, "Oh, and it tastes so gross, too."

The sergeant across from us projectile-vomited into the center of the plane. Another enlisted soldier, who had just finished an orange soda, puked it back up into his bag. You could clearly see it was still orange. A soldier to his right began to barf, and the plane started smelling like holy hell and pure vomit.

The crew chief was pissed off beyond reason, yelling at the pilots to knock it off. "It's horrific back here!"

Scott and I were laughing hysterically, but the smell of puke was so overwhelming we were starting to gag, too. The entire ride smelled like puke, but none of it was ours.

Once we landed in Saudi, the crew chief came up to us, and said, "You two assholes are cleaning all this shit up."

"Sorry, Sergeant," I said sarcastically. "Not my plane, and I did not throw up."

The crew chief was livid. "You two are the biggest assholes I've ever met."

"Oh, we knew that already," said Scott.

"But thanks for recognizing that," I added. "We strive for that title."

"You're really not going to clean this shit up, are you?"

"No, Sergeant, not our mess," I said, and we giggled like teenagers.

To get back at us, he dumped our pallet of equipment off to the side of the runway, far away from the terminal. Now, we had to load all the equipment ourselves.

A few minutes later, we noticed Sergeant Hankel moving quickly in our direction, clearly pissed off. "What the hell have you jackasses done to cause this shit to be dropped here?"

"Nothing, Sergeant," we both said.

One of the other MPs said, "Bullshit! They fake-vomited and got everyone else to throw up."

Hankel just laughed, and before he walked away, he looked at me and said, "Come on, you're a damn NCO now." He later told us he thought it was hilarious as well, but he had to be firm with the younger soldiers around.

Swaying gently in my mesh seat on this C-130, I smiled at that great memory with my battle buddy, who was now alive and mostly well.

I drifted off to sleep, recalling our first meeting on the plane from Atlanta to Anniston, Alabama, and how our lives were forever changed, bound together for life, a meeting that turned into a life-altering friendship.

CHAPTER 8

RHODE ISLAND POLICE ACADEMY, DECEMBER 1991

The big day finally arrived. It was the day Scott and I had dreamed about, talked about, and planned our lives around: first day at the police academy. But it was nothing like we'd dreamed of, nothing like we had talked about or planned for. It was a sad reality about life, but shit got in the way of the best laid plans. As I pulled up to the building—alone—I hoped that the Rhode Island Police Academy would be nothing like Basic.

I got out of the car, and as I approached the entrance, I paused, thinking how different it would be if Scott were walking through the door with me. He had made his way to Rhode Island and planned on going back to school, although for what, he was not sure.

I was wishing again he was with me, but I had accepted that was not happening today. At that moment, I knew, he was at home doing nothing once again, more than likely getting into soap operas. Either way, he would not be joining me today or any workday in the future.

Maybe I'd find a new friend, someone I could bond with, who I could count on, who would always have my back. But I quickly realized no one would ever measure up. Once you had a friendship like I had with Scott, you simply wouldn't settle for less.

I thought about how Scott must have been feeling, not being by my side at the academy. A wave of emotions crept up on me, but I shook my head, clearing it. "Not happening," I said to myself, as I continued into the building.

Prior to attending the police academy, I had learned that it was certified by CALEA, the Commission on Accreditation for Law Enforcement Agencies. That meant recruits attended a 33-week course at the academy prior to responding to their first call for service. This was a much longer and more rigorous program than had been in place back in the 1980s.

The academy was divided into four modules: criminal investigation, legal, patrol, and skills. All recruits had to meet three separate proficiency standards to successfully complete the school. First, you had to attain a minimum cumulative grade average of seventy percent in each of the four modules. Second, you had to successfully meet all state-mandated objectives and criteria. Third, you had to successfully complete all performance-based tests.

The final grades for the modules were based on written examinations, and all performance-based tests were pass/fail. Major components of performance-based training included first aid, CPR, control tactics, firearms training, and driver training. Once you completed your course and graduated from the academy, you were assigned to a field training officer for several more weeks, with weekly evaluations and direct supervision, before you were released for solo duty. The training was long and arduous, both mentally tough and physically challenging.

Inside, the candidates were directed to a large gymnasium and told to line up. There were about forty of us. Looking around at them, I wondered: What was it that made people want to become police officers? There were several prevailing thoughts about why young men or women might decide they wanted to become police officers: action and adventure; carrying a gun; all that cool shit. I knew for a fact that some guys did it because girls would think it was cool, and some did—blue-light-chasers were an interesting breed.

We were waiting to meet our lead instructor, whom I had already heard about. Officer Timothy Dana Yale—or TD, as most people called him—was at the end of his career, and as we waited, I wondered about his reasons for staying at the Police Academy.

Other officers had said that staying friends with cops was what kept Yale in the profession more than anything, their camaraderie and their twisted sense of humor. For many cops, such humor was a coping mechanism for dealing with all the twisted, ugly things they saw. Make fun of it, ideally in a way that was politically incorrect and horrifically inappropriate.

Yale walked in, early sixties, thinning gray hair and a bit of a belly, with a hitch in his step and a gleam in his eyes.

"Students," he began, as he walked down the line. "I understand most of you have no real police experience in this world. Take, for example, Billy DellaCorte. Best experience he may have had is having a few cop friends, maybe from martial arts class. Then he set out to get hired 'Somewhere.' Based on his application, he tried to make himself the most desirable candidate." He stopped in front of one of the students. "Tell me more about yourself, Candidate DellaCorte."

Looking puzzled at first, DellaCorte blurted out, "I volunteered, I trained religiously by video in MMA, a form of martial arts that would be very applicable to law enforcement. I did ride-alongs with law enforcement. All the coffee shop owners knew me by name."

Yale nodded. "Well, on Day One of the academy, as you see the other 39 best-of-the-best applicants who were 'selected' based on all their extensive experience and capabilities, you will quickly realize that many factors may have been at play in the decision-making process."

Now, he addressed the entire group. "Why do you want to be a police officer?"

Rick Walker spoke up first. "My father just retired as a police officer, and I wanted to follow in his footsteps."

Looking around the class, I could see that while maybe ten of the candidates were as fit as I was, several others were not fit at all. I realized that while the law enforcement side might be more challenging than Basic Training, this probably was not going be the Navy SEAL training we were told it would be when we applied.

The introductions continued, and Yale seemed interested in all the students and why they chose to become police officers.

The next student was Kimberly Reed, a former MP from Burrillville, who said she wanted to transition from the military and move forward with her ambitions to serve more. She hoped to finish her degree and maybe one day marry a fellow officer, making family life easier.

Next up was John Smith. The group giggled a bit when he said his name.

"Are you related to the real John Smith?" Yale asked sarcastically.

Smith grinned. "Yeah, he's my daddy!"

Yale chuckled. "Not the guy who befriended the Indians?"

"No, my dad likes the Red Sox. He hates the Indians!"

The group laughed again.

Smith, who from then on would be called Smitty, said, "My uncle was a cop, and I've always wanted to be one."

When he got to me, I said, "I come from Lincoln, Rhode Island, Lincoln High School Class of '83. I wanted to be a police officer as a student at Rhode Island Junior College, but somehow I ended up in the Army as a military policeman."

Another cadet called out in an excited tone, "That's where I know you from! You saved your buddy's life in Iraq, and he saved yours a couple times. You guys are heroes."

"Yes, that was us," I said, "but I wouldn't go that far. We're not heroes,"

Several other students said they'd seen a story about us in the *Providence Journal.* A few of them clapped.

"You're all too kind," I said. Mind you, this was the new Anthony, the modest one. I was a changed man, committed to doing the right thing, and also feeling extremely uncomfortable. Every time someone called Scott or me a hero, my mind flashed back, and Scott's dying confession that he had killed some girl replayed in my head. I couldn't feel like a hero knowing I had never confronted Scott. That title went to people who earned it. Giving my friend first aid on the side of the road should not be considered heroic. I just wanted the group to move on to another candidate and take the attention away from me.

A few other cadets mentioned they had always wanted to be officers, and that this was their dream, as well. By the time we were almost done, I—and I'm pretty sure most of the other cadets—had stopped listening to the reasons why the students wanted to be police officers. Well, until one of the last students spoke, a young Hispanic cadet named José Lima.

"My name is Cadet Lima," he said. "I'm from Woonsocket, Rhode Island. My family are immigrants from El Salvador who came to work in the mills in Woonsocket years ago. As a young man, I had always thought about becoming a police officer. Finally, a little over a year and a half ago, I decided to follow through. That was the day my sister, Jean, was murdered."

He paused and licked his lips, swallowed, and cleared his throat. In a very soft, firm voice, full of conviction, he continued. "She was the kindest, most generous person you could ever know, and someone killed her, for reasons I'll never understand. I have vowed to my parents, my wife, and everyone who knew her that I would find the killer or killers if it's the last thing I do in my life."

I stared intently, my eyes watering as I wondered, *Wow, could it be? I never thought how the family of the girl Scott killed must be feeling. Could it be this girl?* I quickly dismissed the thought. It was just a coincidence. It had to be. I once again remembered sage advice from my crusty old NCO SFC Bryant: There was no such thing as a coincidence.

Lima's story cast a solemn mood over all the cadets, and Yale decided it was time to shake the group up some. "Okay," he yelled. "Let's go! Half the class to my left, and the rest to the right."

I ended up standing next to Lima, who extended his hand. "It's nice to meet you," he said. "I read about you many times."

"Sorry to hear about your sister," I said. "I hope they find her killer."

"I know you have a lot of experience. It would be great to have someone in here I can lean on."

"Sure thing," I said, thinking maybe I had found my new buddy. *Just a coincidence.*

"Okay," Yale's voice boomed. "We need the Police Academy classes to break down into different subgroups: those with no experience, and those who have prior police or security experience." The cadets crossed over into these subgroups, then one by one, the more experienced paired up with the less experienced. Somehow, Lima got stuck with me.

As the learning began with basic law enforcement understanding—which for me was very boring—the cadets began to get a feel for each other and how they matched up to others. The natural and capable leaders began to establish themselves, and the instructors tried to replicate the structure they'd had in the military. It quickly became obvious that two cadets, Bernie and Eric, were going to spend a lot of time screwing off, responding with sarcastic witty answers to every question the trainers provided. No, this was not the military, no matter how hard they tried to make it that way. If it were, they would not be barking off these funny yet inappropriate statements.

One of the main personality types drawn to law enforcement was people who did not function well submitting to authority. Ironically, this was how I felt in Basic Training.

There was a subgroup among the overachievers, the wiseass troublemakers, and Bernie and Eric were both in this subgroup, clearly the new class clowns. They seemed to derive a strange sense of joy from identifying someone's weakness and then poking it. They weren't leaders in the overachiever group, more like outliers who were and always would be very difficult to supervise. Lima and I just stared at them and shook our heads.

I whispered to Lima, "I used to be a jackass like those two. I hope I wasn't that bad when I did my stupid shit." In some small way, I did find them funny, but watching my friend die had made me a different man. I just didn't screw around like that anymore.

"Given what you went through, I'm sure it was justified," Lima said.

Stumbling awkwardly, I replied, "Well, um, losing your sister like you did, that will certainly change you, as well."

"Yeah. Perhaps we are a couple of lost souls?"

I looked over at Lima and nodded.

The next class was weapons training, led by Officer George Stansfield, who was highly respected by students, and was an active police officer on the job.

Stansfield was adamant about proper firearm training and being prepared to shoot someone with extreme accuracy and responsiveness. After a session at the shooting range, he pointed out that the academy would be spending a lot of money on our training. "But you know what else is expensive?" he asked. "Massive civil lawsuits, funerals, training new cops to replace the dead or wounded ones, etc. I mean, it's just a gun, what could go wrong with this plan? It has success written all over it." He gestured to one of the cadets' targets. "Good job, you hit a paper target under ideal conditions at least seventy percent of the time. Next time you do it, it will be under *extreme* stress and your life and the lives of others will hang in the balance… You feel ready for that, right?"

I leaned over to Lima and said, "Okay, I think this is their version of shock treatment."

Perhaps I had been drawn to Lima because he had known death and trauma, just like I had. The other recruits were horsing around, but I couldn't be like that anymore. Part of me had been lost forever. I was a changed man.

The group broke for lunch, and Lima and I found ourselves at the table with Bernie and Eric. It was clear that those two were going to cause a lot of trouble: They were smarter than the instructors, or at least more devious, and they needed to be stimulated, like a smart dog who would chew up your furniture if he got bored. Eric and Bernie would chew up your life.

Stansfield found his way over to our table and began talking about becoming a police officer. "Now, I must preface this by explaining to those of you who don't really understand the police mentality," he said. "Good cops operate in the gray. They have the ability to discern between what is important and what doesn't matter. You have to understand who is a criminal and up to no good and a regular everyday citizen who's just having a bad day. Good cops like to screw around and make light of virtually everything, right up until it's time to go to work, and they know that, when to become the police. Otherwise, they take virtually nothing seriously. Now, we've all dealt with cops who don't know how to operate in this realm, who would write their own mother a speeding ticket, everything is black or white." He paused and looked around, then continued.

"Law enforcement is really a sales job, in that it's far better for everyone involved to convince people it's in their best interest to cooperate, or that you're doing them a favor rather than fighting with everyone. It's easy to escalate, a lot harder to de-escalate. If you spend your career fighting with everyone, you're going to have a rough time of it."

All of this wisdom seemed to be interesting to me, and it struck me how much I was paying attention, given my history of always messing around in class.

Stansfield looked at me and said, "You know, they say, 'Everyone who has been in the military used to be Airborne, Delta Force, or a SEAL—apparently nobody cooked or drove trucks, they're all special forces.' What was your MOS?" He meant Military Occupation Specialty.

"I was an MP, sir," I said. "Nothing special."

"Well, stay humble," he said. "It's a great character trait that I don't see from most military cadets."

The rest of the day went by slowly. During the breaks, I found myself chatting with Lima again about his sister and how it happened, hoping to learn basic information without digging too hard or being too intrusive.

I felt a creeping sense of unease about the correlation between the date of Lima's sister's death and the dates that Scott was in Rhode Island. I didn't ask a lot of questions, just provided comfort and understanding about Lima's loss. I was worried that something was going to come out of my mouth and lead to questions like: When did you guys leave for Iraq? When were you in RI? It was like a bad horror movie, where you know something bad is about to happen, sitting on the edge of your seat. You want to leave, but some sick part of you wants to stay and watch it. Problem was, I couldn't change the channel. This was real life, and I was already way too close to it to drift away.

I had planned to call Scott as soon as I got home after Day One at the academy, but before that I called my brother Michael. He was a FedEx driver in Scott's neighborhood, so I had asked him to check in on Scott now and then when he was in the area.

He picked up, and I said, "Hey, Michael."

"Dragon Balls!" he said, a nickname he—and only he—had been calling me for years. "How was your first day of cop school?"

"Fine," I said. "It was good. Did you get a chance to check in on Scott?"

"Yeah," he said, his voice falling a bit. "I did."

"How did he seem?"

"I don't know, man. Okay, I guess. Bored beyond imagination, he said. He kept checking the clock, but he didn't have anything going on. He was watching game shows, so maybe he was waiting for *Match Game* or whatever to come on. But I think he was thinking of you, what was going on with your first day at the academy and all."

"Yeah," I said quietly. "This was our dream, our plan. This was supposed to be our future. Together." I let out a sigh. "How's he doing with the prosthetics? Getting around?"

"He wasn't getting around much when I was there. He seemed angry at them."

"I guess that's natural."

"Fuck, yeah. I'd be pissed, too. We talked a little about his plans for the future."

"That's a good sign."

"Said he's thinking of becoming a dispatcher or admin support at the police station, something like that. Do some good in the world. You gonna call him?"

"Yeah, soon as I get off with you. Maybe I'll go on over there."

"I bet he'd like that."

"Alright, thanks, Michael."

When I got off with Michael, I took a deep breath, then I called Scott. He picked up on the second ring.

"Hey, dipshit," I said. "What are you doing?"

"Been busy all day planning my future," he said. "Got a couple of ideas, but nothing concrete."

"Well, I know you must be wanting to know how the day went today, right?"

"Why, what happened today?" he asked in a fake breezy tone.

"Shut up asshole, you know I started today!"

"Oh yeah, how did that go?"

"It's okay. How about I come and visit and share how it all went?"

"Oh, that's cool. Sure, come on over. I can put off what I'm doing till tomorrow," he said, although we both knew full well he was not doing a damn thing.

As I walked up to Scott's front door, I heard him shout, "Bid a dollar, you fucking idiot! Everyone is over on the price, you don't need to bid four hundred!" I could also hear the theme music from *The Price is Right*, but it went silent as soon as I knocked.

Scott answered, unsteady on his prosthetics. "Hey, man," he said, not really looking at me. He was back in his chair before I was through the door. I sat on the sofa across from him.

"So?" he said. "How was it?"

"Dude, I wish you'd been there with me."

"Yeah, me too," he said, not too convincingly.

I told him about my day, and after a few minutes I got to Eric and Bernie, the two clowns in class, how annoying they were, fucking around all day.

"Wait, hold up," he said, raising a hand. "You're unhappy there are people screwing around while the instruction is going on?"

"Yeah, and?"

He laughed bitterly. "What the hell happened to you after I left Iraq? You are way too serious now. It's like I don't know who you are."

"Well, let me remind you," I said. "You left in a fucking body bag, so yeah, it certainly changed me a shit ton."

"Wow, my boy is growing up so fast."

"Well, I still think you're a dick, so at least that hasn't changed!"

"Great. I feel the same."

Scott tried to get me to do some celebration shots, but I wanted no part of that. We talked about how the VA had offered to send Scott back to school, and I suggested maybe he should become an attorney. "We could work together again, and school would be completely paid for by the government."

"No, I think I need to do something with the police in some form or fashion, but I'm not sure what that is."

"I was talking with my grandfather, Walter. He asked me how you were doing with losing your legs. I told him I never asked that question, so…how are you doing?"

201

Scott's face darkened, but he said, "I'm good. Just making a few adjustments."

"Well, he said he would like to go to lunch with you."

"Sure, what's his number?"

I gave him the number, and added, "But you know you're gonna have to pay!"

Scott snorted. "Yeah, I remember you talked about him—cheap, just like his grandson!"

"Yeah, right," I said. "Okay, I gotta get home and tell Lisa how the day went."

After a quick handshake and a hug, I was off.

The rest of Week One's training was relatively uneventful other than a few jokes between cadets. But now, I was doing less talking and more listening. I thought about what Scott said: "Man, you've changed." Then I thought, *You're damn right I have.*

My first weekend was spent at home with Lisa, still doing house improvements. She wanted new tile in the bathroom, so I called my bud Rob Turner. He had been doing tile for years. He was almost too good, and I wished he would go faster, but in the end it looked great. Lisa couldn't seem to get past the constant banter about how dumb we both were in high school, and our special education math classes.

When Rob left, she asked how the training was going. I just said, "Okay," but she wanted more detail. I had not mentioned Lima, as I didn't want any questions about him or, more importantly, his sister.

Week Two came around quickly, and that Monday I arrived in the parking lot at the same moment as Lima. We walked together from the parking lot to the classroom, mostly talking about our weekends. But as we approached the classroom area, we were met by a detective wearing an older suit. He looked physically fit, mostly bald, and seemed to be angry.

I said to Lima, "He looks pissed off about something."

The detective looked over at us and said, "Cadet Lima, can I talk to you?"

Lima said, "Sure, Detective Katz." Then he turned to me and said he'd meet me in class.

Fifteen minutes later, Lima came in and took the seat next to me. "Who was that?" I asked.

"That's Detective Katz," Lima said. "He's the lead investigator in my sister's death."

"Oh, sorry," I said. "I didn't mean to poke my nose into your business. He just seemed angry. Most detectives don't seem so angry."

"No big deal. He comes to see me every few weeks or so and goes over anything they've found out on Jean's case. It keeps her memory alive with me, even if it's in a negative way." He shook his head. "I sure am looking forward to the day we find her killer."

"I bet," I said. Then I finally worked up the courage to ask directly, "How did it happen?"

Lima paused for a moment, his eyes glassy, and in a somber tone said, "They found her outside a bar up the road from here, in Smithfield. Bloodied, her clothes ripped open."

"I'm so sorry."

"Not a topic I enjoy talking about. Never gets easier."

"I hope they find whoever did it, too," I said, secretly praying that it wouldn't be Scott. "If I can help in any way, let me know."

That night, Grampa Walter called to tell me he had met with Scott. They'd gotten hot dogs at one of Grampa's favorite spots, Wiener Genie, just off Smithfield Avenue in Lincoln.

Before I could even ask about Scott, Grampa told me about the hot dogs they'd had. "The beef topping is the key, you know, and lots of onions and celery salt. Add a dash of mustard and you will be happy as a pig in you know what." Grampa never swore.

I laughed, then I asked him how Scott seemed to be doing.

"He says he's doing fine, 'as good as one can be losing both legs,' he said."

"And do you believe him?"

"'As good as one can be losing both legs?' Sure, I believe that. Doesn't mean he's doing great. People looking at him and feeling sorry for him. He doesn't want anyone's pity. He just wants to figure out his next steps. He's pissed off, or he's getting there. I told him he should be."

"Angry at who?"

"Everyone. His supervisor, his country, heck, even his battle buddy."

"Me?"

"The whole world shares some responsibility in what happened to him. He needs to tell people that and blow off some steam about it."

"Are you angry?"

"I was at first, sure. I was very upset, but World War II was about saving the world from evil. I don't regret for one day raising my hand up to serve. And I have a great life, a great wife, and great kids I got to come home to and watch grow up, and now my grandkids, too. I'm blessed. But there were times when I didn't see that, when I focused on the bad stuff. But the anger was important. It's natural." Grampa's voice turned gravelly. "I told him if he doesn't accept how he ended up losing his legs and get upset about it, quite frankly he wasn't even close to being recovered. But I also told him that while being angry is good, feeling sorry for himself isn't. There're soldiers in every war that don't get to come home at all. I told him about my friends who didn't come home, John Conklin and Billy Thomas and Jack Brady, who never saw their families again. That's who I feel sad for. I got a second chance, and anyone who has fought in a war and died would trade places with me. Same's true for Scott. I told him, 'Don't ever forget that. You dishonor the dead when you throw this life away.'"

I was getting kind of choked up by then, thinking about Scott hearing all that, and Grampa saying it, what they'd both been through.

After a brief pause, Grampa told me about the rest of their conversation, how they talked about Scott's career options, about Scott talking to a priest.

"He did go on a bit about mistakes he'd made in the past," Grampa said, "mistakes that haunted him."

I felt a chill, suspecting I knew one mistake in particular he was talking about.

"Did he seem depressed about this issue in his past?"

"Sure, it's having a big effect on him."

"Did he say what that was?"

"No, and you never press someone who is struggling. Let him come to you or suggest he get professional advice."

"I'm not a professional?"

"No, you're his link to a previous life that he wishes he was still in. Give him time, he'll find his way."

I laughed at his answer. Then, very softly, like he does when he wants me to pay attention, he said, "I told him, we all make mistakes. When we make them, it's imperative we learn from them." He paused and was quiet for a bit, then chuckled slightly.

"What's so funny, Gramps?"

"I'll tell you something else. Your friend refused to use the handicapped spots, and when I asked why not, he said, 'I'm not handicapped. I'm just hindered a bit!' I enjoyed hearing him say this, I feel the same way."

The next six weeks were uneventful, mostly focused on basic law enforcement things I already knew about from my experiences in the MP Corps or had read about. However, my curiosity was getting the best of me, and more and more I was looking forward to learning about Jean's death, to get a better understanding of it and find the missing pieces that would prove it was not Scott who killed her. Detective Katz showed up every other week to talk with Lima, who would then share the information with me. Around Week Nine, Katz showed up and Lima asked me if I wanted to go to lunch with them.

As we made our way down the road, Katz said, "How about Kay's Sandwich Shop?"

"They have the best steak sandwiches, even better than Philly cheesesteaks," I said. "And for the record, I don't even make one change to the way they cook it."

Lima and Katz looked at me, confused, then exchanged shrugs. As we continued on in an awkward silence, I blurted out, "Well, if I'm being honest, I would prefer another roll."

Katz looked at me and said, "You seem like one picky bastard. Kay's is, bar none, the best sandwich shop in the area, and you still find fault with it? Must have been all the good cooking in the Army!"

"No, not at all," I said. "I'm just a tad picky about food."

The car radio was on low volume, but when "Billie Jean" started playing, Lima said, "Change this please."

Katz apparently did not move quickly enough, so Lima turned the radio off.

"Okay," said Katz.

"Sorry, that song was my sister's favorite," Lima said. "Jean loved that song since it came out in early 1980s. She would always say it was her song. Whenever I heard that song, it used to bring happy thoughts, but now, they are always sad ones."

He said he could still see his sweet, innocent sister singing and dancing to "Billie Jean." He looked over at Katz and said, "That's why I named my daughter Billie Jean."

That was pretty heavy for all of us, and the mood was solemn as we pulled into Kay's parking lot. Inside, we got a table near the back, and Katz started into the case. He asked Lima, "Was there anyone else in her life that we haven't talked about?"

Lima shook his head. "You ask me this every week."

Katz was unapologetic. "I know. I'm hoping something will spark a memory of someone we haven't questioned prior. I know this is repetitive, too, but if she was going to confide in someone, who would that be?"

"Just her small circle of friends, and you've spoken to all of them."

"Was there anything she didn't share about? Anything she was ashamed of?"

"No, like I've told you many times, she mostly worked and hung out with her best friend, Cara, who you've already talked to several times."

"Where would they go?"

"Well, we talked about his before. They would go to a club in Providence, I can't remember the name, but it was a dance club."

"Yes, Cara said it was called the Living Room and they went there several times weeks prior, but they didn't meet anyone in particular. What about the night she was murdered?"

Sitting there, watching this unfold, I was waiting to hear something that would give me certainty that it was or wasn't Scott, hoping to find something to confirm it was not Scott behind this horrific tragedy. *Say it was mid-August, so we were not in Rhode Island*, I thought to myself. *Let it be June or July or any time when we were not in RI.*

"Let's recap," Katz said, opening his notebook.

I swallowed, my muscles tightening.

"...The night of her murder was the fourth of August. She was working till ten at the Lincoln Mall..."

Fuck, I thought to myself, *Scott was in Rhode Island, but I was back at Bragg.*

"...She went to work at three p.m...."

Come on, this can't be the same girl, I quietly hoped.

"...The night was uneventful other than her closing by herself, which she did not do that often. She had broken up with her boyfriend a few weeks before then."

I suddenly remembered: The 4th was the night Scott went out when I drove to Fort Bragg. I jumped up. "Where is the bathroom?"

All my conversations with Scott upon his return raced through my mind, how he said he had met some girl who was in college. I couldn't keep listening to these things, they only brought me pain.

I returned a good eight or nine minutes later.

"Shit yourself?" asked Katz.

"No, I'm good," I said. "Had to go really bad, though."

Katz shook his head. "Well, I hope you left the fan on."

Then he turned back to Lima and said, "Did anyone at her work say she met a customer?"

Lima shook his head.

"We went over the security video, and there was only one lead," said Katz. "But he had a firm alibi."

"Nothing else?"

"Nothing," said Katz. He went into a long story about another murder he had solved after the mother gave him the slightest piece of information that led to another piece of information, and so on and so on. He looked at me and said, "You were an MP. Did you ever investigate a murder?"

"No sir, I was a desk sergeant. The only death I ever investigated was a young soldier who fell off a cliff into a lake in Germany. Her dad went down to see if he could help, and he fell in as well. The poor wife was left to travel home with two dead bodies. It was a terrible thing."

"Most deaths are, but as a soldier, I'm sure I don't need to tell you that," said Katz in an uncaring manner.

"Yeah, I agree," I said, my mind flashing to Scott dying in front of my eyes.

"The good news is, in Rhode Island we don't see many murders, so we're able to spend lots of time looking into them."

I was quiet the rest of lunch, but Katz and Lima didn't seem to notice. I decided to go see Scott again that night, in the hope of learning something that might dispel any notion that it could have been him who murdered Jean. I continued to act like I was not paying attention while trying to take it all in, to remember as much as possible, in case any of it would be helpful in exonerating Scott. Maybe she was seen with a guy with blond hair or maybe a tall guy, a fat guy. Anything that pointed away from Scott.

We finished our sandwiches rather slowly, over multiple stories from Detective Katz, who never had a moment of silence. I later learned that Katz was regarded as good at his job, but that some had joked that he talked so much to the perps, they confessed rather than listen to any more of his stories.

Finally, I said, "We're going to be late, and I don't want to hear from TD Yale, as we may get some extra-duty things." Plus, being on time was my new motto, given how many years I was late.

Katz said, "Let me call there to give you guys some extra time. I own Yale!"

I looked at him. "You do?"

Katz nodded, but Lima said, "No, we better get back."

Katz looked at me and said, "Well, it was very nice meeting you, Anthony. Lima told me about you and your Army buddy. I read about you guys in the paper."

"Oh, yeah?"

"Your pal seems like quite the guy. Did he really save your life two times? And you saved his, too?"

Now uncomfortable again, I replied, "For sure, but you know how it is. We don't talk much about that time in our lives."

"Understood, but that guy is a hero," Katz said. "No doubt there are lots of guys who come home and tell everyone they're heroes. You and your buddy are way too humble!"

Lima said, "What's his name again?"

"Um, it's Christopher Scott," I said. I felt sweat dripping down my back saying Scott's name out loud in front of them.

Katz stared directly at me, as if trying to see if I knew something.

Does he suspect Scott? Did they bring me here to see if I would let some details out? Did he say something to Lima?

I knew I couldn't keep talking with him. Fortunately, Katz's beeper went off, and he left rather quickly—but not quick enough for me.

As he was leaving, he looked back at Lima and said, "I'm on it and will not give up." Then he stared at me and said, "Give my best to your friend Scott. I'd love to take him out to lunch some time." Then he got in his car and drove off.

This can't be happening. Does Katz know I know something? Why did he bring up Scott?

This was getting way too close. I needed to stop hanging with Lima, and definitely stop having lunch with him and Katz. I felt like I had aged six months over lunch.

Lima and I were both quiet as we walked back for our next class, probably both of us thinking about the fateful night our lives changed forever, although he probably didn't realize how it might have linked our lives. I still wasn't sure Scott had killed her, but the dates were starting to line up.

***

That night, my family got together at the Village Haven for family-style chicken, where the group shared large portions of chicken and pasta, something we all loved to do. We had been doing it for years, since back before I joined the Army, and I ate an entire chicken pretty much every time. All five of my sisters were there—they were always there to show their support for everything I did. They were all excited to see Scott, as well, fawning all over him. My mom and grandmother talked about how proud they were of his attendance, and how proud Grampa was, too, even though he wasn't able to attend the dinner.

As soon we arrived, the sisters all asked Scott how he was doing.

Molly asked rather directly, "How are you getting around now without your legs?"

Scott said, "Well, I'm not running, that's for sure."

The group laughed, a bit uncomfortably, but seemed to enjoy the humor.

"Hardest thing is waking up to go pee in the middle of the night," he said.

Lisa said, "Well, your buddy misses the bowl and dam near pisses all over the floor, but I'm sure you have much better aim."

That got more laughs. Everyone seemed at ease as Scott and Lisa looked over with smiles of affirmation that this was a good time right now.

The meal finally arrived. The best thing about Village Haven was that it had been and always would be a family restaurant. The chicken was always fresh and hot, never dry like some other nearby chicken joints, and the sides were so much better as well. I could have eaten their chicken seven days a week.

The meal turned into a two-hour affair, with lots of laughs, lots of chicken, and the world's best cinnamon buns. My sisters were giving it hard to Scott—something he needed to hear for sure, given most people had kid gloves around him those days. Scott said he might consider becoming a comedian given how well he dealt with this family.

Linda blurted out, "Well, we can't call you a stand-up comedian. What would you be?"

"Nubby-knee comedian?" he quickly replied.

Scott might not have been aware, but my sisters all had crushes on him from the first time I brought him home.

When we finally wrapped up and were getting ready to leave, Scott leaned over to my grandmother and said, "I'll be by to pick up Walter at 11:30 tomorrow."

I said, "Wait, what?"

"Oh, I'm getting lunch with your Grampa again."

"Again?"

"Oh, yeah, we have gone a FEW times already," he said. "He's very proud that his grandson is joining the police force, rather than going to jail like some of his other descendants."

"But you never told me you even met with him once!"

"Why do I need to tell you? Are we married?"

Everybody else laughed, and my sister Linda yelled, "Mind ya business!"

My sister Karen said, "If Grampa or Scott wanted you to know, they would have told you!"

***

The following week was uneventful, with more specific training on the legal and skills side, but the week after that brought more stress.

That Monday, we were doing a role-playing exercise on how to reduce stressful situations. TD stood up in front of the class, looked around, and said, "Okay, give me Lima and Anthony!"

As we stood up in front of the class, TD continued, "Listen up! Let's hope you never find yourself in this situation, but today we have two cops, and one knows something about an extreme breach of the law on the part of the other, who has not come forward. Lima, you know something Anthony did wrong relating to the job, and you want him to come clean on his own without you having to report him up the chain of command. The secret you're aware of is Anthony beat up some guy at a bar and put him in the hospital. You want him to come clean rather than have an investigator find this out."

I literally wanted to shrink and leave the building via a small hole somewhere in the wall.

The role-playing went well initially. Lima danced around the subject of fighting and people getting messed up in bar fights. I remained evasive, not wanting to give an inch.

"Dude, we need to talk about some stuff going on," Lima said. "I heard this guy got beat up at a strip joint in Providence."

"Yeah, I heard that, too," I said.

"Someone said the guy looked like he was in the military, or maybe even a cop."

"Hmm, did not know that."

"Well, what did you hear then?"

"Just heard some guy got his ass kicked."

"Nothing else?"

"What the hell, are you interrogating me?" I said, playing the role but also becoming very uncomfortable. "Are you accusing me of something?" I could hear the agitation in my voice, sounding like more than just the role.

"No," Lima said. "I just heard about some guy getting his ass kicked at the Over the Rainbow Bar, and they are looking for the guy."

"You don't know anything about it?"

"I know in the Army you broke up several bar fights, so I thought you might have insight on that topic."

I was struggling with the exercise because it was hitting way too close to home.

Yale was clearly frustrated. "You guys aren't getting anywhere," he said. "This is about the struggle to do the right thing even in the face of adversity. I promise, everyone in here will have the challenge of knowing something that a fellow officer has done. When it happens, you're going to be extremely uncomfortable with it, but you need to learn how to address these issues. Failing to do so will only expand the problem."

He waved us away and said, "Okay, give me two more cadets. Let's try another example."

I was beyond relieved to be done with it, but my mind was racing. *Was all of this a setup, too?* Like lunch with Katz. He knew Yale, maybe they were onto something, maybe they were feeling me out. Or maybe it was just a coincidence.

I decided it was time for another visit with Scott.

I gave him a call and we decided to meet at Chelo's, another Rhode Island favorite. Back then, there was only one Chelo's, on Mendon Road close to the Boys Club in Lincoln. They had the best fish and chips anywhere.

"The fish portions are huge," I told Scott when we got to our table, trying to convince him that was what he should order. "And the fries are always hot. You've got to order it, and if you don't like it, I'll pay."

He laughed. "Shit, you're paying anyway. I'm a handicapped veteran."

We bantered back and forth about the academy. I said legal training was much more detailed than what we had experienced in the

Army. However, Scott convinced me that CID was harder and more law enforcement-heavy training than Basic.

The waitress came and took our order, then Scott said, "How's your buddy Lima doing?"

"He's doing great," I said. "We don't play around anything like you and I did."

"Really." He shook his head. "You are such a rule-follower now."

"I guess I'm more mature than I thought I was."

The waitress brought our drinks, and Scott said, "Why did he decide to become a police officer?"

I paused for a moment. "Kind of sad. His sister was murdered. I see the investigator all the time when he visits with Lima."

I looked away, but from the corner of my eye, I could see Scott was showing absolutely no reaction. He simply said, "That's terrible. Please, give him my condolences. Do they have any leads?" He said it in a passive tone, still no expression, almost like he knew I was looking for some kind of reaction.

"Yeah," I went on, "it's a sad story. Poor girl died late summer, when Lisa and I first moved here. They still haven't found her killer."

"I hope they do. That's gotta be hard for him."

"Yes, it's what inspired him. He says he won't ever stop looking."

One thing about cop friends was that each knew when the other was trying to elicit information. The waitress brought our fish and chips, and as we dug in, Scott blurted out, "This fish is amazing! And the portions are huge. No wonder you're getting so fat here."

"Ha, ha, asshole, I can at least run mine off."

But for the rest of lunch, I was wondering if Scott and I were engaged in some kind of game of wits, or if he was just innocent and oblivious. By the time we said our goodbyes and headed out, I still didn't know.

The training rolled on, and when we had about five weeks remaining, Lincoln Police Officer Phil Gold showed up at the academy and said, "Hey, Ant, let's grab some lunch."

"Sure," I said.

I invited Lima to come along, but he declined. I tried to hide my relief, as I had no desire to repeat the stressful lunch we'd had with Katz a few weeks prior.

We hit Cumberland House of Pizza and I ordered my usual: "Small roast beef, extra pickles, lettuce, tomato, and mayo. I'd like provolone cheese, lightly toasted, but could you put the mayo on after it's cooked?"

"Okay, bud," Phil said after he had ordered. "I wanted to tell you a couple things. Looks like they decided where you are going: my buddy Smith's squad."

"Wow, after all these years, I have my path forward. Ah shit, that's awesome. I know you certainly helped me there, and I am extremely grateful."

"You will arrive at our station shortly after Memorial Day, so get ready."

"No way, man."

"You are sought after. SGT Smith and the other squad leader were having battles over who should get you. Speaking of Memorial Day, I also have a request, totally unrelated to this. You know we always have a veteran as grand marshal in the Memorial Day parade. I wanted to ask: Would your buddy Scott be okay if we asked him to be the grand marshal this year?"

For a moment, I was silent. "Hmm, let me think about it."

"And would you sit with him on the back of the convertible? We want to do a big write-up about the both of you saving each other's lives and so on. I've talked with the *Woonsocket Call, Providence Journal,* and even Doug White from Channel Ten to do some stories on you and Scott. They all loved the idea."

"So, I don't want to make it seem like I'm a hero, and I know Scott doesn't want that either."

"Gotcha, but this is about soldiers. It's Memorial Day. Lincoln boy comes home a hero, and now a hometown hero is on the police force in the town he grew up in."

"Wow, that's an extreme honor. I'm not sure I'm worthy, brother."

"Of course, you are. Stop acting all humble, that's not you!"

In the back of my mind, I was thinking: *What if Scott really did kill Jean, and what if they found out just before the parade?*

I said, "Well, I'm sure he'd be okay with it, but he is way more private than I am. I'll ask if you want me to."

"No, no, I'll ask. I just wanted to know your thoughts before I put him in an uncomfortable situation."

"Okay. I'm sure he'll say yes." Secretly, I wished I could convince Scott not to do it, but sometimes you had to let the chips fall where they will.

The grinders or hoagies—or subs, as the people outside of RI called them—arrived and, Gold didn't even look at his, he just started eating it. I lifted up the bread and put my finger on the mayo to make sure it was cool, not warmed up from the oven. Gold rolled his eyes.

We talked some more about life after the academy and what to expect. Gold had been an MP in the Gulf War as well, so he knew full well about the transition.

Halfway through his sandwich, Gold paused and said, "Dude, don't forget, I can't be in your chain of command, given the level of our friendship. I hope you understand."

"Not an issue. I am used to that from my Army days. I had friends that I made sure were not under my supervision, as well."

"Perfect. I'll swing past Scott's house today. Do you know if he's home?"

"He should be. He doesn't get out much. I should be on his case more about doing stuff, but I'm all consumed with the academy stuff."

"How is he? I know it must be hard, given this was a dream for the both of you and now you're riding solo."

"Well, he has his ups and downs. He's not the kind of guy who shares that stuff with me. When I visit him and talk about the academy, I know in part he likes it, but, in some ways, he is disappointed not being with me. Truth be told, Lisa takes all my free time, so I don't see him as often as I could."

Gold looked at me funny, then he said, "Well, I'd choose to spend my free time with Lisa, too."

After Gold left, I felt somewhat guilty, so I called Lisa and said, "Let's take Scott out to dinner tonight."

"Let me guess," she said. "Village Haven?"

"Yes, exactly. How did you know that?"

"You would eat chicken eight days a week, and you love that place."

"Who doesn't love family-style chicken, pasta, fries, and cinnamon buns?"

I got off the phone and called Scott, who acted like he was busy but, in the end, agreed to go.

When I finally got home, Scott was already in the kitchen, chatting up a storm with Lisa. Lisa believed—incorrectly—that she didn't talk much, but she was in rare form. I paused outside the kitchen door, listening to their laughter. It was refreshing to hear them both finding such joy in each other's company, something that did not happen with our girlfriends in the past.

I went in and said hi, then quickly got changed, and the three of us headed out to Village Haven. The ride there was all talk about the academy, then Scott mentioned he'd had a visitor today—Phil Gold.

"Really?" I said, feigning surprise.

"Why are you playing dumb? You know what he was going to ask me."

"Well, what did you say? "

"I only had one issue with it: Why do you have to sit next to me?"

Lisa was not tracking the conversation, so I explained what Scott was talking about.

"Oh, that's wonderful," she said. "Congratulations to both of you."

We arrived at the Haven, and I was surprised to find my brother Michael and all five of my sisters there. Lisa had called them.

I ordered family-style chicken for all.

"What if I wanted something else?" Scott said.

"You love it, so just eat it," I said. "I know you've come here with me at least ten times."

The food arrived quickly, as it always did, and as always it was cooked to perfection. My sisters were delighted to hear about the big news.

Molly, still holding onto her teenage crush, said, "I think I should sit next to Chris in the car, kind of like Ken and Barbie."

"Why?" I asked. "Is that because you think you're Barbie?"

They all laughed, and Linda said, "Sounds like a big party for us all at your house afterward. Plus it's Memorial Day right after."

Lisa grinned. "Sounds good to me! We were going to try and surprise you, but you're too damn nosy!"

Brother Michael said, "I'll get it set up, Lisa. You know your husband will leave it till the last minute."

We spent most of the meal talking about the parade and what it all meant. And Scott did love the chicken again.

As Memorial Day approached, Scott was super excited about everything, but I was getting more and more anxious by the day.

I checked back on the dates of deployment and confirmed that Scott had been in town the day of the murder. After our last lunch at Kay's, I knew that he had, in fact, still been in Rhode Island and had left the day after her murder. Coincidence?

Katz kept asking me to join them for lunch to discuss the case. It made me wonder again if it was possible he knew who did it, and if he suspected I had information about it. The stress was almost too much to handle, and I started getting short with Lisa and others. She thought it was the training that had me worked up. Keeping all this information to myself was overwhelming. I needed to find a way forward.

I kept thinking about the news stories that would come out about how great Scott and I were, what heroes we were, and then what would happen if it came out that Scott was the killer. Those stories would put me over the top. The situation kept escalating on a crazy, bizarre scale.

I decided one night to give Scott a call and check in the next morning.

"Hey, dipshit," I said. "What are you doing?"

"Still plotting the future. I'm definitely going back to school."

"Cool, I will too, but it will be based on my work schedule. Hey, I'm near your house. Want to get a coffee?"

"You don't drink coffee, and we don't need alcohol, so let's hit Dunkin' Donuts."

"Sure thing."

I pulled up to his house, and he walked out on his protheses, looking pretty good but still a tad awkward.

He got in my car and had to manually move his legs in. It reminded me of my grampa again.

As soon as we were on our way, he asked me, "Do you miss me?"

"Yeah, I miss you," I said. "Like when a hemorrhoid heals."

Scott laughed and said, "Perfect, cause normally you're the pain in the ass."

Then he asked how my friend Lima was doing.

I answered, very measured, "He is doing great."

Time at the academy continued to move rather quickly. There were only two weeks of training left when Detective Katz showed up again and asked me to join Lima and him for lunch.

"No, thanks," I said. "Trying to get my uniform ready and do some studying."

"Come on, you could have taken the final the first day you were here."

"Ah, thanks. I appreciate that, but I'm gonna pass for today."

"Are you avoiding me?" He was smiling as he said it, but I didn't know him well enough to tell how serious he was.

"Why would I do that?"

"I don't know," he said. "Why would you?"

I didn't reply right away, trying to read the guy. Luckily, Lima walked up. "Hey, Katz. Anthony." He looked at me and said, "We're getting lunch. You coming?"

I shook my head. "Got some stuff I need to catch up on."

Lima nodded. "Alright. Catch you later."

Katz shrugged. "Suit yourself."

After Katz and Lima headed out for chow, I went over to my locker. Looking over my uniform, I realized Katz was right—I didn't need to do a thing. I was just getting emotionally drained processing all the details and correlating them against details only I was aware of.

The course continued to move forward, and I was more anxious about graduation than excited. The last aspect of the academy was the skills portion of training, and I was the most experienced cadet in the class. So, yeah, Katz was correct— I could have passed it on Day One. But cooling my heels in front of my locker for no reason was the better option than going to lunch and dealing with all that anxiety.

After class, I stopped off again at Scott's.

Memorial Day was still over a week away, but he had his uniform ready, complete with all his combat awards and other decorations—including his Purple Heart and Bronze Star with a V for Valor, as well as his MP crossed pistols, all of them polished to perfection. Not many E-4s had been awarded a Bronze Star with a V for Valor. His spit-shined boots shined like glass again, and he had decided he wanted to wear his prostheses. His uniform was crisply pressed, and he seemed excited to be looking like the soldier of the year. I was more impressed with how he was walking with his prostheses. He had made great strides in less than a week.

"I haven't seen you this excited since we were running around Chicago chasing the ladies," I told him.

"Dude, this is an extreme honor," he said. "At first, I was reluctant, you know, I don't think of us as heroes."

"Yeah, well your head is getting so big you might tip the convertible over."

"Ha, ha! Fuck you. You're just as excited."

"Not a chance, Dog Jaw. This is your day, not mine."

I was happy to see Scott in good spirits, but I secretly hoped the parade would get rained out, although that rarely ever happened. I was still worried, wondering how I had been caught up in this mess. But I asked myself, how hard could it be? All we had to do was sit there and wave at the people along the parade route, then go drink at the VFW. But I couldn't ignore my deep concerns that people would be looking at Scott and me like we were special. In my heart, I couldn't get past the thought that at some point, the truth was going to come out and I would feel ashamed. I decided to call Grampa Walter for counsel.

"Hey, Gramps," I said when he answered. "It's Philip."

"How's my boy? Getting close to graduation."

"Yes, sir. I'd love to have lunch with you this week, if you can."

"Your buddy Scott and I are having lunch on Wednesday. You want to join?"

"No, actually I need my own time with you."

"How about Friday? But I'll have to check with my secretary."

"Your secretary?"

"Your grandmother. She's a taskmaster, always has me doing stuff on Fridays. That's payday for her."

"Okay, let's set it for Thursday then."

Thursday's lunch got pushed to an early dinner as Granma was called into work.

I pulled up at Granma and Grampa's at 4:52 and hurried up to the door, seeing as I was not 10 minutes early.

Grampa smiled at me in a way I'd never seen before, then he shook my hand.

"Let's go to Pawtucket House of Pizza," he said. "I went to Wiener Genie with Chris yesterday."

"Sounds good," I said. "I didn't know Scott loved wieners."

"He does now," Grampa said as we walked out to the car. "I have him addicted to them. After all, Wiener Genie is the go-to place for wieners. And congratulations. Your grandmother told me you and Scott are going to be the grand marshals in the parade."

I opened his door for him. "Yes, sir. Truly an honor."

When I got in and started up the car, he said, "How is the academy going?"

"Very well, but I've been struggling with a personal issue lately and wanted to ask your opinion."

"Okay, ask away."

"What if someone confessed a secret to you, something big, but you weren't sure he was in his right mind when he said it. What would you do?"

"Well, it depends on the secret. Was it serious?"

"Yes, very. I am afraid to ask him any more about it. You know my mom's theory, 'Don't go looking for pain.'" We both laughed and shook our heads in tacit agreement.

"Well, if you ask it, can you ignore the answer?"

"No. If I ask it and I hear the answer, it'll tear me up, and I'll have a responsibility to deal with it."

"If you don't ask, will it change anything? Or more precisely, will it make things better or worse?"

"Way worse."

"Will it improve anything for anybody?"

"No…not really, just closure for some people. But it won't change anything, really."

He paused. "Is it about Scott?"

This caught me off guard. "Did he say something?"

"Not really. He said he was dealing with some demons." Gramps took a deep breath, then said, "Philip, war exposes you to the ugliness of mankind. If it happened in combat, things are different than if it happened stateside. We all have our wartime demons. Talking to a priest is how I dealt with mine."

I nodded. I could see pain in his eyes—I wasn't sure if it was his or Scott's. What had Scott told him? He looked at me and paused, looking for the right words. You could see the heaviness he was holding onto, it was an odd position he was put into. Then he finally spoke to me.

"Philip, I can see this weighs heavily on you. The realism of what you and Scott have experienced is witnessed by so few, trust me on this: All who have seen war carry the emotional burdens that life placed on them. Most suffer in silence, as did I for so many years, but I found God again. Seek out God and talk with a priest for more answers, but I think you know what you need to do."

"I will, Grampa. Sorry to burden you."

"Philip, there will never be a time you are a burden to me. You're my pride and joy. Your grandmother likes to take all the credit, but I am damn proud of you. You know she thinks she's royalty."

"I know, Gramps."

"A royal pain in the ass, is more like it."

Pawtucket House of Pizza was established in the late 70s and still served pizza and grinders that were unmatched in the area. The meat they put on the sandwiches was 40 to 50% more than other locations. Although the building was not very impressive, the old pizza oven and grill were busy all the time. We ordered a steak sandwich and a roast beef and split them both.

"Well, I'm excited to attend your graduation," he said as we were finishing up. "I'm going to wear my Navy white uniform. I want to have a photo in my uniform with you."

"Ah, Gramps, that means a lot to me."

"Now, if I can only get your grandmother to get it to the cleaners in time. That's the struggle."

I laughed. "She will, and if not, call me. I'll come over and take it."

When we got back to Grampa's, I walked him to the door, and he did something he had never done. He leaned in, gave me a firm hug, and whispered in my ear, "I will always be here for you, Philip."

I drove home thinking, *No matter how you feel, you always feel better when you see Grampa or Granma..*

On graduation day, my entire family was in the audience with Lisa: Mom and Dad, Granma and Grampa, my seven brothers and sisters, and even a few aunts, as well as a few close buddies, Bob Wall, Gold, Cheryl and Tom, Paul Zen, Marty G, and Rob Turner. My family was always there for me, and even though I loved to give them grief, I truly appreciated their unwavering support over the years both in and out of the Army.

Grampa Walter made it in with his prosthesis. Most folks were unaware that my grandfather lost his leg in WWII. He'd been a Navy enlisted member who fought on the USS South Dakota, the most decorated battleship in the war. Like the rest of that generation, he spoke very little about the war or the effects it had on him.

Lima's family was sitting close to mine. This was the first time I had seen Lima's parents. Just before the ceremony, they walked over to me. His dad extended his hand and said, "Thank you for helping our son get through this course. He said you helped him immensely."

"No, sir, I think he helped me even more."

"That is very nice of you to say," he said with a big smile, "but we know better."

I shook his hand, wanting to get away from them as fast as possible, when I saw Scott walking a bit clumsily up to the seating area.

"Hey, bud, I am so glad you're here," I said. "I was worried you weren't going to show up."

"Well, Jerry Springer is on break this week," he said, "so this is the next best thing."

Scott and Grampa found some seats down low in front that said, "Reserved for distinguished guests." Scott turned to Grampa and said, "That's us, right?" He smiled, and each took a seat.

Graduation was the normal, run-of-the-mill graduation, more for the families than the officers being pinned. The town administrator, a former police officer named Joe Almond, gave the speech, but I don't recall anything he said. I was consumed with thoughts about Scott and Lima.

After graduation, there was a large group photo. My seating assignment was right next to Lima, just like I'd been next to Scott in Basic Training. The memory of standing next to Scott, six years ago, seemed like a lifetime ago.

Then it was over, and just like that, I was a graduate. My dream job was secured, but it did not feel like it would have if Scott had been graduating next to me. My whole family posed for a family photo with Scott standing by my side. It should have been joyous, and it was not, but I did my best to mask the sadness. My focus now shifted in my mind. I had one week off before I started duty with the Lincoln Police.

I was relieved that Scott didn't even talk with Lima—too busy talking with Gold and TD Yale about real police duty from his undercover drug days in Alaska. But as I started to leave the building, Detective Katz appeared, and he walked right up to Gold and started talking with TD and Scott. *Holy shit, I'm going to die right now.*

I made my way over to the group, hoping to provide a distraction, saying, "Hello. How is it going, great to see you."

Nodding, Katz said, "Congratulations." He looked over at Scott and said, "You must be his buddy, Scott."

"Yes, sir," Scott said. "Nice to meet you."

"I hear great things about you," he said, "but not from Anthony, as you might expect."

Scott laughed. "Yeah, I'm shocked he was able to graduate without me."

"Yeah, right," I said sarcastically. "Because you always carried me before."

Scott threw up his arms. "Finally, he admits it!"

The interaction was very limited, but my anxiety was not, and it mounted quickly as I noticed Katz watching me. I have a tell when I'm anxious, I start talking fast, and Scott screwed up his face at me. "Dude, you nervous?"

"Not at all," I said quickly.

Katz started to walk away, but he stopped and looked at the two of us. "You two stay out of trouble."

We laughed out loud, but my laughter clearly sounded nervous, at least to me.

Scott said he had some errands to run, and I said, "Like what?"

He said he had to get his uniform ready and drop off some film to be developed.

"Come on," I said. "You're sitting around the house all day just hanging out. You can spend some time with us."

Scott laughed. "No, I really want to get this film developed. It's from back in Iraq. I can't wait to see what's on it!"

CHAPTER 9

A HERO'S DAY

Music has an ability to take you back in time, to make you emotional. But things can change, and the music that once brought happy memories can bring negative ones, replacing tears of joy with tears of sadness. That's how it was for me and the song "Billie Jean" by Michael Jackson, which came on the radio just as the parade vehicles were being moved into place.

I smiled briefly, but then cringed at the song. My mind immediately flashed to Lima on the way to lunch with Katz, telling how he felt when this song came on.

As Scott and I stood there in our Class A uniforms, he barked out, "Remember that song?"

"Yeah, I do, obviously," I said somberly.

"Man, it would be great to dance like that again!"

"I bet."

"I was so much better of a dancer than you ever were, Anthony," he said, grinning.

But my smile had long disappeared as my thoughts turned to Lima's sister, Jean, who had inspired her brother to become a police officer. My mind swirled with emotions. How was it possible that a song associated with such amazingly happy memories could cause me so much anguish now? The thoughts were almost overwhelming. Sure, I was not the one who did anything, but I couldn't help but feel some of the guilt, knowing Scott said he killed someone. Even if it was not Jean, I was fast becoming aware that I had to deal with this soon or it would destroy me.

I knew Lima was going to be at the parade with his whole family, including Billie Jean. Two hours and this would be over, I told myself. It couldn't come quick enough. I continued to struggle in silence, all these thoughts filling my mind as I waited for the parade to start, next to my best friend, battle buddy, and lifesaver, Scott. How was I going to smile and wave at all the parade viewers? I was tired of thinking about all that shit. Fortunately, we would be the first ones moving down the road, a slight joy at that moment, but I would take it.

The Lincoln Memorial Day Parade was now a major event, thanks to its organizer, the newly promoted Lieutenant Phil Gold. He had transformed the parade from a small event into a statewide, must-see spectacle with an emphasis on the military and its members' sacrifices. Residents from all over town, surrounding communities, and across the state came to honor veterans and those who had made the ultimate sacrifice.

Festivities started off, as usual, with a small ceremony outside the Saylersville Fire Department, where local members of the VFW post gathered to place a wreath at the World War II monument at Dow Circle. A handful of men in VFW caps and American Legion garb

DYING CONFESSION

stood in front of the monument as the Lincoln Police Honor Guard marched into the middle of the traffic circle. The LPD sergeant called for the presentation of arms as Scott and I saluted. It reminded me of our days doing flag call while assigned to Fort Sheridan.

I thought about Grampa, and how proud he was going to be seeing me in the grand marshal vehicle. Then I thought about Scott, and I hoped the talks with Grampa were helping him deal with having to live his life with no legs. Although Scott acted like he was okay with losing his legs, I knew better, and I believed Grampa would find the right words to help him get past much of the emotional trauma. I had never talked to Grampa about losing his leg, and it occurred to me that their conversations might have impacted Grampa as much as Scott. Neither Grampa nor Scott had said anything about the meetings.

From where Scott and I were sitting, we could see a high school student in an LHS band shirt standing off on the side holding his trumpet. The sergeant called for the presentation of arms, and one of the older members of the VFW announced that the LPD Honor Guard would honor the fallen with a twenty-one-gun salute. The sergeant barked out orders, and the honor guard members raised their patrol rifles to the sky and began their volley of fire.

The patrol rifles, now a regular tool carried by Lincoln police officers, looked remarkably similar to Army-issued M-16s.

As the sound of gunfire echoed off the surrounding buildings, Scott leaned over to me and said, "Look at how sharp the officers are in their dress uniforms, how well polished the whole group is."

The smell of burnt gunpowder from the blanks filled the air, a scent so distinct and remarkably familiar, something Scott probably had not smelled since the day he died on the battlefield. Scott seemed consumed by the firing, as if transported by the smoke and the smell of the gunpowder. The group followed a couple more commands from the sergeant, then stood stoically as a Lincoln High School bugler gave an almost flawless rendition of "Taps." As he finished, Scott remarked how a couple of the old timers were visibly moved by "Taps."

"Do you think we'll ever get that emotional?"

"I hope so," I said.

"Yeah, me too."

The master of ceremonies was Kenny Shorten, who had been one of the grand marshals the previous year, along with his battle buddy. They had risked their lives for each other on patrol in the jungles of Vietnam, and both were surprised to find out the other was still alive. It had been a very emotional event for all who learned of the story, and this year was expected to be the same. Kenny had later become a police officer and was a town favorite.

LT Gold always got it right, finding amazing veterans and showcasing them in the Memorial Day parade.

Kenny cleared his throat and began his speech.

"There have been many sacrifices by the men of Lincoln, Rhode Island, and our little town has sacrificed many a man over the years…"

After his speech, the ceremony was over, and one of the town representatives walked over and told us the ride for the parade would be there shortly to take us to the rally point. "You should both feel extremely proud to be the grand marshals," he said. "I've met the last twenty-five grand marshals, and they're all great men, just like the two of you."

A few minutes later, a yellow '86 Corvette convertible pulled up.

The previous year, the organizers had started a new program called "Vettes for Vets" with a local Corvette Club that offered to provide rides for all veterans participating in the parade.

The driver of the Corvette came over and introduced himself as Peter D. He explained that he would be driving us.

"Do I get to keep the car after the parade?" Scott said, earning a chuckle.

Peter loaded Scott's wheelchair into the trunk, then Scott got himself situated in the back of the vehicle in the center left. I sat close to him, on the passenger's side.

"Just my luck," Scott said, as he moved his prosthetic legs onto the back seat. "I don't have any legs and there is no room on this side. Imagine if I had legs."

We began the journey sitting side by side, battle buddies home safe but scarred for life and grateful to be riding on the back of the convertible. We made our way down Smithfield Avenue to Higginson Avenue, where several people were starting to gather. A few bands and floats were forming up in the large parking lot in front of the Dragon Villa and CVS.

Another group formed up with a whole row of Corvettes behind the marshal vehicle. A few Boy Scouts stood on the sidewalk holding a big banner. Even more impressive were the veterans standing around talking, killing some time until the 11 a.m. kickoff for their trip, reliving their moments of service, enjoying it all. Amongst them were some parade regulars. Jim Battle, who served in the Korean War, still fit into his Class As, which were pressed and polished. Rick Folls, who served in WWII, was in a blazer and tie, still fairly fit and looking impressive with all of his military pins affixed to his jacket and American Legion hat. Bennie Lacombe, another Korean vet, proudly displayed his woolen Army dress blues, even though it was forecast to be close to 90 degrees and very sunny, a welcome alternative to the previously forecast heavy showers. The parade seemed to always dodge the rain, which was good because the parade had always been advertised as rain or shine.

I spotted another veteran who never missed the parade: Glenn Laupher, wearing his Vietnam War patches on his faded fatigue jacket and his Air Cav Stetson. He was a humble man who had seen his fair share of the horrors of war but shared very little about those days.

Other veterans were milling about, shaking hands and catching up, sharing an unspoken bond that was clear to see by most, but clearly understood only by those who served. The Memorial Day parade was the annual event that brought everyone out, especially the Lincoln veterans. Many of them were getting on in years, making the event even more precious for them as they made fewer and fewer public appearances. It was their day to shine, their day to bond, their day to remember wearing the uniform.

A few of them made their way over to Scott to shake hands and introduce themselves, thanking him for saving one of our "Lincoln Boys," telling him it was an honor to meet him.

Peter affixed the grand marshal magnets to the vehicle, making it even easier to identify Scott as the grand marshal. As the parade's commencement time approached, the area grew even busier, as people were directed this way and that to their appropriate division. The Lincoln High School band started forming up and tuning their instruments in the adjacent lot. The LHS band was a staple for the parade and had always been revered as a crowd favorite for its enthusiastic performances and snappy song selections. The staging area was on the brink of controlled chaos as the Shriners showed up with their floats and mini-cars. Even though most were getting up there in age, they seemed to fall back into being teenagers, flying around the parking lot in their little cars—another highlight of the event.

The gathering crowd was directed to move from the roadway as two National Guard Humvees pulled up to join the veterans contingent.

Scott pointed and said, "These new Humvees are a lot different than the soft skin we rode in."

I looked over and saw that the upper turrets were now reinforced with armor plating. "Yeah, that's great. A lot more protection."

Scott shook his head. "Perfect. They fix them up *after* my legs are blown off."

Several politicians started working the crowd, using the event to press the flesh. A few of them worked their way over to Scott and me and the other veterans to show their respect and thank us all for our service.

The honor guard, the police officers in charge of posting and protecting the colors, the flag, took positions at the beginning of the parade formation, and the parade officials began pointing and directing people to form up. Our town parade was about to begin.

Town Administrator Lincoln Almond said a few words, thanking all the participants, and concluding with, "Today will be a great event!"

Peter moved the Corvette to the front of the Dragon Villa, directly across the street from Brookside's bar. I leaned over to Scott and pointed across at the Dragon Villa. "That's where I had my first date."

Scott snorted. "Is this the one when you went on a date with some girl and gave her a nuggie rather than put your arm around her?"

"Exactly," I said.

The car moved out, and I felt proud but a little ridiculous sitting up on the back of the vehicle. As we moved down the road, I spotted Granma and Grampa, my mom, a couple of aunts and several cousins, all at the corner just before the Wiener Genie. Scott smiled and waved to the crowd. Granma blew me a kiss, and Mom seemed to be tearing up.

Grampa stood from his wheelchair and saluted us, We quickly raised our hands, saluting back. I tried to hide it, but to say I was getting emotional would have been quite an understatement.

Trying to lighten the mood, I pointed at Wiener Genie and said, "That's where I had my first wiener. They're amazing."

"That's where your grandfather and I go to have our heart-to-hearts. What an amazing guy. You never told me about any of his wartime experiences."

"He hasn't shared any of that with me. He must feel a bond with you." I laughed. "Shit, I guess I gotta lose a leg to get him to tell me that shit."

"No, he told me it's because he trusts me more. I can keep a secret!"

In a very sarcastic tone, I said, "Yeah, I'm sure you can, asshole," not realizing what I was saying until after I had said it.

Scott looked away from me and started waving, so I waved and smiled at the larger-than-normal crowd that had gathered to see the historic parade, one of the longest-running Memorial Day parades in the state. There were all kinds of vehicles behind us: fire trucks from Lincoln and nearby towns, mini-cars, and older police cars.

Toward the middle of the parade, I spotted Lima and his daughter, Billie Jean, waving at us. I was a bit nervous at first and looked away like I did not notice them.

But Scott spotted them and waved and smiled and said, "There's your buddy Lima." I waved, too.

People on some of the vehicles were handing out balloons and throwing candy to the small children gathered on the parade route. Every firetruck in the state seemed to be going down the parade route, lights and horns blasting. Too bad we were so close to them, I thought to myself, as it was extremely loud. There were people on foot as well, including several school bands and the Little League champions from Lincoln. But most of all, it was veterans.

We all made our way down Smithfield Avenue, then off to the right past the fire station. After thirty-eight minutes, the parade was over—much faster than I expected. But most of the folks knew that this was when the real celebration would begin.

Scott breathed a huge sigh of relief.

Gold yelled over at us. "You boys headed over to the VFW?"

"In Cumberland? Near the Boys Club?" I replied.

"Yeah, exactly."

"I'll follow you," Scott told me. "I'm not sure how to get there."

When the parade ended, there was always a celebration of all the hard work put in by the parade staff at the VFW, also known as The Dugout, where my dad used to go after work every day. I would meet him there after Boys Club and hustle all the old folks on the pool tables waiting for Dad to have "just one more," which was just one more after one more. Unlike current times, in the eighties there was very little focus on drunk driving. Today, the VFW patrons would have certainly lost their licenses or even gone to jail.

Scott and I arrived at the VFW relatively early, since we were at the front of the parade. As was the custom when current or former military members were involved, there was plenty of alcohol to celebrate. After a few minutes, people started arriving in groups of four to six at a time. Many had left their cars near the parade route and carpooled over.

Wheeling up to the bar, Scott yelled, "Let's do a shot!" He quickly grabbed his shot and held it up. "To friendship, loyalty, and the MP Corps!" Then he drank it down.

Skully, the bartender, shook his head, like he knew what kind of night he was in for. Skully was not his real name, but one night he overcharged my dad, who referred to it as a "skull job," and ever since everyone called the bartender "Skully."

The VFW filled up fast, as more and more parade attendees passed through the doors. Scott convinced the parade support staff to join him in another shot, but I just shook my head, knowing this was going to be a long night.

Scott asked me to get his wheelchair. "I'm not going to last too long drinking and trying to walk in the pegs!" Pegs was the term he used for his prostheses.

In the back lot, while getting Scott's wheelchair out of my car, I was surprised to see LT Gold walking up to me, followed by Lima and his daughter, Billie Jean, who said, "Thanks for waving at us!"

Lima, his wife and daughter waited patiently to talk with us. I could feel my face flush for a moment until I gathered myself, still holding onto a small degree of hope that it was all a terrible dream, and told myself, *Somebody else must have killed Jean, not Scott, no way.*

Lima and I briefly hugged, then Lima said, "You need to officially meet my daughter: Billie Jean, Officer Anthony!"

"Hello, Billie Jean!" I said, trying to make my voice bright.

"Hi, Mr. Anthony," she said. "I saw you in the convertible today and at graduation. My dad says you and your friend are real Army heroes."

"Well, thank you," I said. "I wouldn't say we're heroes, just a couple guys who went to war a long time ago."

"My dad likes you a lot. He talks about you all the time to my mom."

Lima laughed awkwardly. "Well, let's not go that far."

"Aw, thank you, young lady," I said.

We all made our way into the club, laughing and enjoying the celebration that the parade provided year after year.

I brought Scott his wheelchair and said, "Here you go, bud."

Scott slid out of his seat and into the wheelchair without pausing the war stories he was sharing with the other parade volunteers.

Gold called me over, and I joined him and Lima, talking about pending assignments. Lima was going to North Providence, which bordered Lincoln's jurisdiction.

"Hey, you guys may have some overlap," said Gold.

"Yeah," I said, "we can link up at Pawtucket House of Pizza for lunch."

Lima laughed. "Dude, is everything in your life related to food?"

"You just figuring that out?" said Gold.

We all laughed, then I went suddenly tense, as Scott wheeled over and yelled, "Hey, boys!"

Lima extended his hand and said, "It's an honor to meet you again.

And thanks for keeping Anthony around—he's a pain in the butt, but a great academy buddy."

Scott laughed. "Oh, yeah, I know what a pain he is. Just be happy you never had to make MRE meals with him in Iraq."

The rest of the group laughed, so I joined in.

"Yeah," Lima said, "we were just talking about food."

"No kidding," said Scott.

I stood there staring intently at the two of them, still praying there was no connection between Jean and Scott, just a coincidence. As the others made small talk, I stayed silent, consumed by anxiety and trepidation that some sort of link would come out.

Clearly, Scott had no clue that Billie Jean was the niece of Jean. He turned his attention to her. "Hello, and who is this young lady?"

"My name is Billie Jean."

"What? No way! That can't be your name, that's my favorite song of all time."

"Yes, sir, it is," she said with a big smile.

"I used to dance to it in the Army before I lost my legs," he said, pointing to his missing limbs, "I would be on the dance floor all the time to that song."

"It was my aunt's favorite song too. She used to dance to it all the time…well, that's what my daddy says." Her smile was replaced with a frown.

I was frozen in place, watching the interaction. Scott seemed to still have no clue whatsoever that her aunt could be the woman he "forgot" he told me he murdered. My mouth was dry, and I had no idea how to react, no idea what to say—something I had never experienced before. *Please, God, don't let this be the girl. And end this please, get me out of this nightmare.*

Lima was all smiles, from ear to ear, clueless to my anguish.

Gold said, "Hey, Anthony, what's going on? You seem a bit off, brother, everything okay?"

"No, I'm good," I said. This was the most common phrase soldiers used when they were dealing with over-the-top emotional issues. "No, I'm good" really translated to "I have nothing to say at this point, nor do I wish to keep talking about these issues."

"Dude, you're acting like you saw a ghost," he said with a chuckle. "Maybe sitting up on the back of that car was too much for your sensitive tummy?"

I forced a laugh, too. "No, just lots on my mind and I don't feel great."

At that moment, the door swung open, my dad holding it for Grampa Walter.

"Philip!" Grampa yelled, and I hurried over to them.

Dad put his hand on my shoulder. "Son, I was damn proud to see you up there today."

"Thanks, Dad."

"Philip," Grampa said, "I don't think I have ever been prouder of my grandchildren than I was seeing you back in your uniform today."

"Thanks Grampa. I was so excited to see you there."

"I went to that spot because that's where Scott and I meet for our talks."

"Yeah, he mentioned that in the car."

"I like to go there," Grampa said. "They have the best wieners in the state. I know the owner surprisingly well."

"Michael knows his son Steve."

"The food is great, and the prices are even better, although Scott always pays. Says it's cheaper than talking with a therapist."

Dad and I laughed.

As more of the parade team arrived, Scott finished talking to Lima and Billie Jean. He was now in full-blown, war story-telling mode, in all his glory, talking to any and all who would listen. His ability to hold a crowd was unsurpassed—except by me, of course. There were now half a dozen people hanging on his every word as he mixed praise and sarcasm about me into all his stories.

I was tired of it, the same stories over and over, but I said nothing. I knew Lisa had to deal with the same thing from me, but she said my stories were way funnier.

I got another drink and made my way back over to Lima and Billie Jean. Almost immediately, the conversation turned to her Aunt Jean again and all Billie Jean had learned about her. Lima was all smiles, but I was dying inside, and I quickly extricated myself from the conversation and walked away again to get some space.

Looking back, I saw Billie Jean whispering to her dad, who was smiling even wider. He walked over to the jukebox and selected a song.

I drifted over to the group surrounding Scott, all talking police stories or parade issues that they had resolved. Scott was feeling no pain, and I was finally relaxing a bit, knowing the situation was resolving itself peacefully.

Grampa came up to me and said, "We set for another appointment at Wiener Genie next week? My therapy schedule is wide open."

"Sure thing, Grampa," I said. "I love their food, too."

A song came on the jukebox, and from the beat I immediately recognized it. "Billie Jean." Lima nodded to his daughter, who quickly walked over to Scott and asked, "Would you dance with me, please?"

Scott grinned. "Well, by golly, I will give it a shot—it's our song—but only if you don't mind doing all the work." He pointed down to his legs.

I was stunned, wide-eyed at the gravity of the situation. When Lima started filming his daughter dancing with the hero of the parade, I could no longer contain myself. I ran to the bathroom—pushing past Gold, who was washing his hands—and burst into a stall and threw up in the toilet.

"Can't handle the after-party, I see," Gold said with a laugh. "You okay there, bud?"

"Yeah," I mumbled. "I'm good."

"Doesn't sound like it."

I threw up a little more.

"You should cut off the drinking from here," Gold said.

"Yeah, I guess so, but I'm just not feeling well. I'll be okay. I really haven't had that much to drink."

"Okay, man, just chill out a bit. You don't need to be drinking and driving so fresh out of the academy."

"Yes, sir. I understand."

As we walked out of the bathroom, the entire VFW was cheering on Scott and Billie Jean as the song was ending.

Scott was beaming. "Wow, that's the best dance I've had in years, young lady. I hope we can dance again together soon."

"Me, too!" said Billie Jean.

Shortly after that, Lima announced that it was time for him and Billie Jean to head home. It couldn't come quickly enough for me. They said their goodbyes, and mercifully there was very little interaction with Scott, who was back to telling his war stories.

I walked the Lima family out to their car, and his wife thanked me once again for helping her husband get though the academy. She said she was proud to know me, then she said she wanted to have me over for dinner. "Maybe you can bring your buddy Scott, as well," she said. "Billlie Jean seems to like him."

I was shaking my head as I walked back into the bar, where Scott was raising holy hell, clearly drunk now.

I went up to him and said, "Dude, you gotta stop drinking now." He was wasted and for sure not driving anywhere that night.

"You aren't my daddy, or even Sergeant Hankel," he said, his voice slurring. "So chill the hell out. I'm good!"

"You're not good, and you're not driving." He made a show of ignoring me, so I got Lieutenant Gold to come over and remind him he was for sure not driving.

We had been at the hall for almost four hours, and I kept trying to get Scott to eat some more, but with no success.

My dad had been sitting quietly at the bar. "Let me help him out," he said. We walked up to Scott and said, "What do you want? Beef or chicken?" My brother Michael and I knew Dad's joke that he was about to say.

Without pausing to think about it, Scott said, "Chicken,"

Dad turned to Skully, the bartender, "Can you hook him up with a pickled egg?"

Scott said, "Wait! What are you, crazy? I hate pickled eggs. I changed my mind—I want beef."

Dad said, "Okay, sure thing. Skully, give him a Slim Jim."

Skully tossed Scott one, and he quickly opened and ate it.

I grabbed a slice of pizza and tried to push one on Scott, with no luck.

"Shots for everyone!" Scott yelled.

After another round of shots, the crowd was thinning fast. I was sitting off to the side, frustrated, trying to cope with a range of emotions—anger, frustration, sadness, and confusion.

Dad walked over. A recovering alcoholic, he said, "Son, you can't help him right now, he is in party mode."

"I know, Dad, but I hate seeing him use booze when he is down and out."

"It was a great day for both of you," Dad said. "I'm proud of you. I don't think he is an alcoholic, Son. Trust me, I know what they look like. But for sure, take his keys and drive him home and leave your car here."

I shook my dad's hand as he headed out the door. Sitting by myself, I couldn't get the image of Scott dancing with Billie Jean out of my head. It was in this moment that I knew I had to confront Scott, but not tonight. I had to deal with it once and for all, although I knew it wouldn't be easy for either of us.

I yelled over at Scott, "Time to get out of here!"

Scott shook his head. "Nah, I'm good. Skully will call me a taxi. You can head out."

"No, I'll drop you off."

"Okay, one more shot."

Skully brought us each a shot, tequila for Scott and water for me—something I had arranged with Skully before.

Scott shouted, "We toast the boys we left behind! To our brother MPs who stood the watch, made it home alive, and especially the ones we left behind!" We downed our shots, which Scott followed up with a simple, "HUAAAA." He started to wheel himself outside, stopping again to talk to a few more people, like he always does.

He rolled outside toward my Jeep, and when he got to the door, he looked over and said, "Hey, you going to help me up?"

I got him into the Jeep, put his chair in the backseat area, and drove off, waving at Skully, who was standing at the door, shaking his head.

"Dude, you remember how much fun we had being MPs?" Scott said. "Man, I miss the days of beating you in the PT test. I think if I train and get me some of those new metal rod-like legs, I could still beat your ass again."

"Yeah, okay," I said. "Quit living in the past. Those days are over for you."

"What the hell is bothering you? All night at the Dugout, you were acting funny, like you're fucking pissed or something."

I was not planning on saying anything that night as he was too drunk to have this talk, but I knew I needed to get to it and see if it was Jean who he had murdered.

Scott snorted. "I know you, man, and you are not okay."

"No, I'm fine."

"Bullshit. Spill it."

"No, not tonight!"

"Why not?"

It was like he knew what I wanted to ask him and he was pushing me, but I didn't think we needed to do it that night. "It's too long to get into tonight. Let's just celebrate our day."

"Our day?"

"Okay, your day!"

He sat there quietly for a couple minutes and said, "I think tonight is just fine. What's on your mind, Ant?"

"I'm not sure I want to get into it, because if I do, I can't turn back the clock and un-talk about it."

"I got some more tequila at the house. We can talk there." Again, like he was trying to push me into it, knowing I didn't want to have that discussion that night. Fucker knew how to push my buttons.

"Man, you don't want to have this tonight!"

"Why not?"

"Not sure you're capable of handling it!"

"Spit it out, bitch."

That pissed me off, knowing he knew I didn't want to talk about it but kept pushing me to start a conversation I didn't want to have. *Asshole!*

"If I put it out there, then we have to deal with it, and I'm not sure I'm ready either." I think he knew he had pushed me too far, and that maybe I would ask the question neither of us wanted to address.

Then, out of left field, he hit me with a new tone, like he was playing mind games with me, trying to fuck with my head.

"Okay, listen to me, Anthony. I've got to tell you something, this one time and one time only: You are the best friend I've ever had. I don't think I would keep myself on earth anymore if you were not here. I've thought about killing myself so many times since we got back, and the only reason I don't is because you're here, and you'd be pissed. You are now a police officer, a fucking cop!"

"Yeah, I get it!" I screamed back.

"No, you don't fucking get it. Who the hell is going to save your ass now when you're back on patrol?"

"Someone will have my back."

"Not even close, dude. In my heart, I wish I could be right there, riding side by side on patrol again."

The last couple of shots must have still been taking effect, because he was getting louder and less clear.

I started crying as we pulled into the driveway of Scott's house.

"Great," he said, "now you're going to cry like a little bitch. Why?"

"No, man. We shouldn't be talking about it." I opened my door and got out.

"We got all night, don't we?"

I got his chair out, wiping the tears away. Normally, Scott never wanted help getting inside, but I stood close, knowing he was so drunk he might fall out of the Jeep. He got out and sort of fell into his chair. Although I was sober, I tripped twice over the uneven pavers and rocks as I wheeled him up the ramp and quickly got him into the house.

I wheeled him into the kitchen and sat at the table. It was the old metal type with chrome legs, extremely sturdy, and chairs built the same way. Built to last.

Scott had gotten it from his mother a few years earlier, and he took great pride in it.

He ran a finger along the edge of the table. "There have been a lot of long talks at this table over the years," he said.

"Well," I said, "this one may be the most difficult one you're ever going to have."

"One more shot," he said.

"Absolutely not," I said, letting out a sigh. "I'm gonna head home."

Not wanting the night to end, or maybe he was fucking with me again, I didn't know why, he said, "Wait, I thought you had something important to talk with me about."

"It's not the right time to have this talk," I said. "You're loaded, and today was a great day for you. Let's put it off."

"Well, you said it was so important that once you opened this Pandora's box, you wouldn't be able to close it. So, spit it out."

My hands were sweating and my breathing labored as I pondered how I could get this out. I let out a heavy sigh. "No man, I can't do this tonight."

"Sure, you can. You know you want to, so spit it out."

"I can't."

"Don't be a pussy. Let it fly."

Maybe it helped that he was making me angry. "Do you remember right after the vehicle blew up in Iraq?" I asked in a stern voice.

"Nope, I've told you a bunch of times. I only remember looking over at you in the Humvee and laughing about saving your ass so many times, then an explosion."

"Well, I do remember."

"And?"

"I've got to tell you, this has haunted me ever since it happened."

He stared intently at me with a puzzled look. "What the hell are you talking about?" he said, his voice soft, then louder, "Get it out already! Spit it out, pus bag!"

I opened my mouth, but all that came out was another deep sigh.

"Say it!" he yelled.

"Fuck it!" I said. "After we blew up, I came over to your side and dragged you away from the vehicle and started dressing your wounds." Another long pause.

"Well, then what? Spit it out!"

"You told me you weren't going to make it and there was something you had to tell me."

"Okay, what did I tell you?" he said again, almost like he was daring me to get it out. We were quiet for a moment, then he sort of barked out the word, *"And?"*

"You told me you killed some girl when you were home on leave," I said, just blurting it out.

Scott was silent for a minute, maybe, a look of surprise slowly assembling on his face. "I did?"

Military friends had a keen sense of when the complete truth was not being shared, and MPs had extra insight into when people were lying, their mannerisms or the motions people made when they lied.

I was poised for my next words, focusing on Scott for any of the things people did when they lied, waiting for some kind of clue or sign, knowing he was not going to admit it.

Scott sat in silence, like he was searching for the right words. I knew that he knew he couldn't lie to me. I'd know it if he did. There was a mental game of chess going on as we stared at each other, neither uttering a word until I said, "Well?"

Scott was very quiet, his forehead creased, like he was trying to remember.

Then two simple words came from his mouth. "I did."

"Wait, what?" I said. "Was that a question or a statement?"

After another silence, he said, "Yeah, I did it. I don't know how exactly it happened, but I did it."

"Oh, no," I said. "Shit, it can't be. Fuck, this is so fucked up!" God, I wished it was a bad dream.

He looked up at me. "Now what?"

"I don't know, man. Fuck, my mother was so right, 'Don't go looking for pain.' I didn't want to hear this shit, and now that I did, oh shit!"

"Now you know the truth, what's next?"

"Well, you've got to come clean and confess," I said. "It's the only thing you can do."

"Still happy we had this talk tonight?"

I just shook my head in disbelief.

"You're right about one thing," he said. "Can't just put this back in the box and ignore it."

"You have to turn yourself in, Scott. It's the only solution. I'll go with you. We'll find you a great attorney. I even have one lined up."

"What?" He looked at me, confused. "How would you..." Then he turned angry, his voice getting louder. "You think it's that easy? My life is shit! I lost my legs! I have nobody, and now you want me to go to jail for an accident with some girl I hardly knew. Why would you fucking do this to me? Especially today?"

"I don't know, man. Told you it wasn't right to bring it up."

"You just sat by my side as the grand marshal, then you hit me with this shit now?" His voice was growing louder and angrier.

"I've been dealing with this since Iraq," I explained.

"She was just some young girl. We met up a few times, and on top of this her family hated the military."

"I know who she was," I said. "Her name was Jean, right?"

Scott's face went completely white, and in that moment, I knew for sure, for the first time, it was Scott who killed Jean.

Confused and puzzled, he grew even angrier. "What the fuck, have you been looking into this and investigating me all the while acting like you are my best friend?"

"No, man."

"You fucking asshole!"

"No, I was just trying to make sense of it all."

"I can't believe you would do this shit to me after I saved your ass so many times. Fuck this, you just need to let it go, let me suffer in silence. Coming forward will only cause more and more pain, to me and many others."

"No, you know we can't go back to ignoring."

"Shit, why the hell would you do this? Today?" he screamed. "Right here, right fucking now?! He slammed his hand on the kitchen table.

Almost trying to justify bringing it up, I reminded him, "Remember your little dance tonight, with Billie Jean?"

"Yeah, what about it?"

"Billie Jean and Jean. That's why I thought I had to bring this shit up tonight. They're related."

"What? No fucking way."

"Lima is Jean's brother. Billie Jean is her niece."

"Holy shit." Scott slumped down in his chair, anger and sadness flickering across his face before ultimately settling on sadness, a solemnity and acceptance that this was not going to end well. Then he snapped his fingers and sat up. Grasping at straws, he said, "Wait, it can't be her, her last name was Cruz, not Lima, different fathers!"

He kind of collapsed back into his chair. "What the fuck? This can't be happening. It was an accident! I was drunk, I thought I would die with this."

We were both quiet for a moment, then he started talking, his voice flat and even. "I was so into this girl, Jean. She was amazing. We dated the entire time I was here. She had just broken up with her boyfriend a few weeks earlier, and we started going out every night. I would meet her out at the club, since her parents were so anti-military. She told me over and over, they would never let her date me."

He paused and stared off for a few seconds. "I think I loved her. There was no way I wanted that to happen. I even bought her a promise ring, not an engagement ring, just a promise ring. I asked her to wait for me to become a policeman. She was into me, too. We had this crazy, once in a lifetime connection, or so I thought.

"We went to the Last Chance Resort; it was kind of chilly for summer, and we sat outside on the picnic tables away from everyone. I had some tequila. I was drinking a lot before I got there, and I had a bottle of champagne for us to celebrate."

I sat quietly, wondering if I really needed to hear all of this tonight, seeing how painful it was for Scott reliving that night. But he seemed like he wanted to continue, so I let him.

"I asked her to take this simple promise ring, but she just stared at me. I just wanted her to promise to wait for me to come back from the academy. You know, I don't have a close family, they're spread out all over the place, and I thought she could be the one. She gave me this 'Oh, you poor fool' look and said, 'I will never be able to be with you. I've told you, my family would never accept it. I'm going back to the University of Rhode Island. I won't make you a promise I can't keep.'"

He took a deep breath and let it out, then continued. "Kind of almost feeling sorry for me, she asked, 'Do you remember what you told me when we first met? You clearly said after you got out you weren't interested in commitments, but you wanted to get to know me.' With a bit of a tone, she said, 'I never expected to like you this much either, but it can't happen, Chris. You're leaving in the morning, and I'm headed to school soon.' She said, 'Listen, let's just drink the champagne and celebrate the fun we've had. Who knows, when you get back, I may feel different.'"

I wanted to ask how she ended up dying, but instead blurted out, "Actually, don't tell me any more details." I was struggling with wanting to know, but also not wanting to know for legal reasons, as anything he said now I would more than likely share given I was now a police officer.

But he didn't stop. He poured himself another shot, I guess assuming the answer tonight was to get through this. I asked to limit the details, please, told him I would have no choice this time but to share any information I knew.

He quickly said, "Back to that night."

He told me he had finished the bottle of liquor he'd brought, and he was feeling tipsy, maybe even hammered. "I tried for one last flirt, to convince her to reconsider. She paused for a moment, which made me think she was okay with my advances again. She pushed me to stop, but I was hammered and pushed her back, maybe too hard. I was trying to be convincing, then from out of nowhere she starting yelling at me, 'Stop, stop, just stop!' I asked, 'What the hell is wrong?' It's sorta blurry from there for sure. But we fought, and I guess I must have passed out. When I woke up, she was dead. The back of my head was bleeding a bit, from when I fell."

"Oh, man."

"That's all I remember. I was so drunk, at first I thought she was asleep and I tried to wake her. Then I realized she was dead. She was dead. I needed to figure shit out."

I looked at him, confused. "Figure what out?"

"I was hoping she was drunk like me and passed out." He paused, clearly not positive of what the events were. "Fuck! It's not completely clear to me besides her pushing me backward. I saw her on the ground, motionless. I went over, shook her, and thought she was out cold. But blood was dripping from the back of her head. She wasn't breathing. I tried to give her CPR, but nothing. Her lips were cold, so cold, that's when I knew she was dead. I'll never get that memory out of my head: I loved her, and there I was, kissing her cold, dead lips." His eyes were pained and his breathing heavy. "I can't... I just can't face this."

After almost a minute, he rubbed his hands together, clearly trying to remember that night, that dreadful night, and then he said, "No breathing, no nothing. I have no idea how long we had been lying there. I panicked. I ran to my car and left."

"You left her there?" I asked, unable to keep the disappointment out of my voice.

"I just left!" he yelled, and his words shook me to the core.

How the hell do you just leave a young woman on the ground to die? I wondered, staring at Scott in disbelief.

As if he could hear my thoughts, he said emphatically, "She was dead. There was no pulse. After a few minutes of CPR, I panicked and just got the hell out of there."

I was quiet for a moment, trying to find the right words. "I am so sorry, Scott. I know you would never do this intentionally. It sounds like it was an accident, but you must come forward."

"That's what we tell suspects all the time, isn't it?!" he blurted out.

Uncomfortable silence filled the room for a few minutes, neither of us making eye contact. Then I looked him in the eye and said, "I have been wracked with guilt since you told me on the side of the road. I think about it every day."

Scott squinted and quietly said, "Really?"

"Yes!" I yelled. "Every single day and every fucking night. You realize how hard it was for me to confront you?"

"Yeah, I get it."

"Chris," I said, and he looked over, surprised— I never used his first name. "You are the best friend I have ever had. You were my best man. The overwhelming grief I feel tells me you must be feeling even worse. Everyone knows you would never do something like this intentionally."

"That doesn't change anything. To me, this has never been clearer: It's true, the cover-up is worse than the crime. I think God punished me and took my legs, then brought me back to life so I would suffer."

"Shut up," I said. "That's fucking stupid."

"I'm serious. It's my daily reminder. All I need to do is look down at my nubs."

"No, man, you know that's bullshit. He kept you here to make it right, and I'm right here with you, we can do this."

"God took my legs to remind me that I took her life, and I will have to live with this shit forever. I think about her every day, Anthony. She was so special, and I killed her. What the fuck is wrong with me?"

"It was an accident. We all have them, man. But then we move forward."

"Remember when you refused to tell on me when I got in the accident at Fort Sheridan? You are a better friend than I could ever be. You refused to give in to the pressure, even when they threatened your career."

"Chris, for your own well-being, it must be you that comes forward."

"I don't know, man."

"You have to step up. It's the only way past this."

"I can't. I just can't. I can't spend the rest of my life in jail."

"You won't. We'll get the best representation we can find."

His face looked pained as he shook his head. "No way," he said, angry now. "I won't do it."

"You have to!"

"No. I don't."

I felt terrible for him, but I was starting to get angry, too. "Okay, well, if you won't then I will!"

"What?!"

"You're giving me no choice, asshole."

"No way, you would do that to me? After all we've been through? You would rat me out? This is worse than losing my legs."

I took a deep breath and calmed my voice. "Chris, I know what guilt feels like and can't imagine how bad you feel about it."

He stayed silent, so I continued. "I saw it in your face, heard it in your voice. I feel every ounce of pain you're dealing with right now."

"I don't know, man." He shook his head. "I can't do this."

"You can. It's simple."

For a long moment, I looked over at him and he refused to look up at me. Then he shrugged. "Okay," he said with resignation. "I'll do it."

I paused for a few seconds to see his reaction, which was certainly not as excited as mine was to hear him say it out loud. I was beyond relieved to hear he was going to turn himself in; the biggest weight in my life had been lifted off me. "How are we going to do this?"

Scott slumped back, looking absolutely drained. "I don't know, but shit, it's late. Let's get some sleep. Let me clean up in the morning, maybe go in around ten or eleven."

"Are you sure? Bad news doesn't get better overnight," I said, echoing Sergeant Hankel's famous quote. We exchanged pained smirks then shared a look of resignation.

I nodded. "Okay, it's almost one-thirty. Do I go home, or should I spend the night?"

"Why would you need to spend the night?"

"I need to know you're okay. You admitted to me you thought about killing yourself. How do I know you're good with this?"

"Come on, I'm okay. Really, I am."

"I'll call Lisa and let her know I'm sleeping here."

"No, man, for sure I'm good."

I stared at him to make sure he was sincere. "I have things that I need you here for. Don't fuck that up."

In an almost relieved tone, Scott said, "Thank you for helping get me to this point. You are so right, man, I need to do this for me, too. And just so you know, I really did forget I told you anything on the side of the road. I truly don't remember anything after the explosion."

I nodded. "I know."

I was relieved we had arrived at this decision, but still felt uneasy about leaving him for the rest of the evening. He assured me he would be ready in the morning. A simple good night's sleep before the next drama in his life, before he dealt with his demons.

I leaned into his chair and we hugged, one of the longest embraces of our friendship. We both knew these demons would not be easy.

"You're my best friend," Scott said. "And you're right, we need to do this. Know that I couldn't do this without you. So, what I'm trying to say is thank you. It's a relief."

It was a relief for me, too, in a way. But as I walked to my car, I paused. An uncomfortable feeling washed over me as wondered again if leaving him was the right call. Scott had never lied to me before, and I hoped he would follow through on coming forward.

Driving home, I thought of Jean, of Billie Jean, and Lima, and how this would affect their family, but I pushed those thoughts aside. I needed to sleep. I walked ever so slowly into my home and undressed quietly, but secretly hoped that Lisa would wake up and talk to me. I knew she would be shocked to hear this, but it wasn't until I climbed into bed next to her that I realized I had never given a thought to what she would think of my not telling her. My mind wandered into all the areas she was going to question me about, which totally distracted me from thoughts of Scott.

I set my alarm for eight a.m., so I'd have enough time to get over to Scott's to pick him up and take him to the station. I climbed into bed, then immediately climbed back out and knelt at the side of the bed. I said a simple prayer asking to comfort Scott, Lima's family, and my own family, as well. I asked for the Lord's strength and wisdom to help me the next day. I very rarely prayed for anything for myself personally. I knew I was lucky, that I had all I ever needed, so I usually just gave thanks and asked for the Lord's blessing for others who were struggling more. But this time, I knew I needed help.

I climbed back into bed, exhausted but unable to fall asleep at first, unable to stop thinking about what lay ahead and the impact it would have on so many. But eventually, I drifted off to an uneasy sleep.

CHAPTER 10

SURRENDERING

Just before 5 a.m., the phone rang, and I jolted upright, waking Lisa.

"What's wrong?" she said.

"Relax, it's only the phone."

I grabbed the handset. It was Gold. "Hey, bud," he said, "we're at Scott's. It's not good. Can you get over here quick?"

"Is he dead?"

"What?" Gold said. "No, but he's barricaded himself in the house and says he needs to talk with you."

"Roger that, I'm on my way."

Springing out of bed, I started pulling on the clothes I had worn the previous evening after the parade.

"What's going on?" Lisa asked.

"It's Scott," I said, rushing one leg into my jeans and stumbling a bit. "I promise I'll tell you everything when I get back, but it's not good. He messed up, and I don't know what is going to happen but, it's not good."

She looked at me in disbelief. "Scott? No way, he's a saint."

"I can't go into it now, but I promise when I get back, I'll tell you everything—everything I can, that is."

Usually, you couldn't tell Lisa you'd have to tell her something later, because she would badger you relentlessly until you told her. Maybe she saw the panic in my eyes, because this time, she did not press it. Nobody understood the support of a great woman more than a soldier did.

I jumped in my car and sped off to Scott's house, just a few miles down the road.

When I got there, I saw three Lincoln police cruisers and newly promoted Lieutenant Gold standing a slight distance back from the home. There were generally only two officers on the road, so I assumed they must have brought in the person on call, as well. The only light in the house was the living room, but the shades were down and you could not see inside at all.

"What the hell is he doing?" I asked as I walked up to Gold, who was talking with SGT Wyman.

"The station got a call of screaming and things breaking in the house. When the patrol pulled up to the house, a single gunshot was fired at the officer. Scott started yelling out the window, 'Stay the hell away from the house and don't try coming in.' Then he asked for you."

"What did he say?"

"He would only talk with you. We explained you were not even completely on the job yet. He also appears to be drinking."

"I don't think he stopped after the parade," I said. "He had a few drinks before I left his house last night."

"We're hoping you can talk him into coming out."

"Okay," I said. "Let me go inside."

"Absolutely not," said Sergeant Wyman, the scene commander. He was a bit portly in the waist area and was already sweating. "He has already discharged a weapon. We can't let you go in there."

Gold looked at me and asked, point-blank, "Is it safe?"

"Yes," I told him.

Always the voice of reason, Gold explained to Wyman, "There's a bond you cannot understand between these two. They served together. You need to trust him."

Wyman reluctantly agreed, but he insisted I put on a protective vest. As I put on the vest and pulled my shirt over it, Gold said, "I know you guys go way back, but he's not thinking right. If we come in and he points a gun at us, then we have no choice."

"Understood."

"Convince him to give up, then get him to walk out with you and end this shit." Gold paused, and I looked up at him. "What happened between you two after the parade? I saw you at the end of the night, and it looked pretty heated."

"I can't talk about that right now. It does affect this situation, for sure. I promise to tell you after I get him to come out."

Gold wasn't happy about not being informed, but he trusted me enough to let me, a freshly minted police officer, go inside the house.

As I approached the door, I called out, "Scott! It's me, I'm coming in."

"No, just come to the side door," he called back.

"I'm not carrying."

"Well, you can't shoot for shit, so what does it matter?" He laughed, then said, "Stop on the ramp."

But instead, I kept walking in. The squad cars had their spotlights fixed on the door area, lighting it up.

"Man, shut your stupid ass up," I said. "You know I'm coming in. You need to man up with me, face to face, you big pussy."

Scott yelled forcefully, "Stop right there!"

"No, ass bag, I'm not talking from a distance." If I didn't get close to him, I wouldn't be able to stop him from killing himself.

I stepped inside just as he was rolling up to the kitchen table—the same spot where we'd been sitting just a few hours earlier. He had a gun in his hand.

I sat across from him. "Okay, what's going on, man?"

"Not easy to talk about." He looked away. "I can't deal with this reality." He looked down at the table and snorted. "It's hard to believe I used to eat oatmeal at this table thirty years ago, and now I'm sitting here trying to get you to understand …something."

"Understand what? We already talked this out."

A short pause. "I can't do it. I simply can't do it."

"What the fuck, Scott? We went over this last night. You have to."

"Listen to me, Anthony, I need to end it all, right here. It's not your fault."

"Wait, what? No shit it's not my fault, and it's not yours either. I'm sure you were right, it had to be an accident. Your service to the country will be considered."

"I need you to know, it's not your fault what I am about to do."

"Dude, put the fucking gun down. You know you won't shoot me."

"I know, but those idiots outside don't know it." He seemed to notice for the first time that I was wearing a vest. "Wait, is that what I think it is? Man, you put a vest on, you big pussy!"

"Yeah, I had to."

Scott laughed out loud. "Oh, my God, after all these years, now you're a rule follower?"

"No, goddamn it! But they wouldn't let me in here if I didn't put it on."

"Maybe we should call Sergeant Hankel or Top," he said. "What the hell, bring 'em all in here. They won't believe you're finally following rules."

We both chuckled.

"Listen, man," I said. "You're going to leave the gun on the table and roll out with me. All you have to do is put your hands up."

"Sorry, Ant, that's not going to happen. I don't think there is any way that I can do that. I told you—I need it to end here."

"I'm not letting that happen."

"Haven't you heard of suicide by cop?"

"Yeah, that isn't happening today, either. Besides, I told them to shoot you in the legs." I tried to get him thinking about my silly response more than doing this. Strange that even in life-and-death situations, our bond of stupidity rose to the surface, at least on my part, as I tried to bring down the tension.

"Listen, Ant, people will never understand the gravity of your situation because it's not theirs, it's all yours. That phrase, walk a mile in someone's shoes? Shit, I can't walk—if I could, I wouldn't want to walk ten feet in your shoes. These boots have seen some shit you wouldn't recognize."

"Listen to me," I said. "I don't give a rat's ass what people think, 'cause their thoughts don't change my situation. I care what my wife thinks, my mom and dad and grandmother and obviously my grandfather. And you, asshole."

"Oh, man, Gramps." Scott shook his head. "That is not going to be easy. He's going to hate me for this. Shit, I don't blame him, but I know he expects you to do the right thing all the time. I think he will have questions for you, Ant!"

"Yeah, not going to be easy," I said. "And I am not looking forward to having to explain it to him. Gramps has always thought I would do the right thing all the time. Often mentioning that he was proud of who I was and how I'm on the right side of the law."

"I'm sorry, man. I really am. But let me end this my way."

"No, come on, man, let's do what we said. I'll swing by McDonald's and get us a couple sausage, egg, and cheese McMuffins."

"With the undercooked egg? So the yolk is soft?" Scott said, eyes half-closed like he was picturing it.

"Yeah, nice and soft—just like your gut these days." We snickered for a moment. "Listen to me, I take the gun and toss it outside, then we roll out with me pushing you, and you put your hands up, it's very simple. Even a soup sandwich like you can do this. Once we get outside, I'll wave Gold over. Maybe tubby Wyman will want to come arrest you—don't give him shit, he'll only make it way worse for you if you do."

I told him what to expect out there, then I said, "There is something that I haven't told you. Something important."

"What's that?"

"Lisa is pregnant."

"What?"

"Yep. Twelve weeks!"

He paused for a moment. "Who's the father?"

"I'm still not sure, asshole!"

We both laughed a bit.

"Maybe I'll be out of jail in time to teach him to fish, certainly how to shoot a weapon."

"I hope so."

"Why are you telling me this now?"

"Scott, here's the deal: I want to name him Chris, but I can't name my son after someone who has killed himself."

"Slick, Ant, playing the guilt card."

"No, it's true. Only twelve weeks' pregnant, but that's our plan."

Scott looked at me and shook his head in disbelief. "If Top or Hankel could see you now," he said, staring at me like a grandfather looking at his grandson, thinking, "Wow, my boy is all grown up." Then his face appeared to be bitter, and he said, "When the hell did you grow up, man?"

The tone was almost sarcastic, and it hit a nerve. After a long pause, I said, "In Iraq, on the side of the road. Right after I fucking watched you take your last breath, look up at me, and die!" I shook my head. "You know, I don't pray often, but I did that day on the side of the road. I sat back in disbelief, then, right there, I made a promise to God that from that point on I would do the right thing."

He was quiet for a moment, then he figured to change the topic some, saying, "You know what I need right now? A cigarette."

"You won't get an extra five-minute smoke break in prison, so no need to start that shit back up again."

"I need to explain more on how it happened, and why I reacted the way I did."

"You probably shouldn't," I said. "Once you get your lawyer in the station, you can tell it all to him."

"No, I have to explain it to you. I have to tell you myself."

I stayed quiet, and after a brief moment, he continued.

"It was that July, 1990, when we came to Rhode Island for the physical training test and were moving more of your stuff into the new house. I was at the Living Room, the bar in Providence, and she bumped into me, spilled my drink. Her friend had just left the bar, and she was making her way to the exit as well.

"I joked with her, 'You spilled my drink. The least you could do is stay and have one more with me.' I was surprised when she said, 'I guess it couldn't hurt to have one more!' We just talked for a few minutes, had our drink. She told me her name was Jean. Then she said she needed to go, and I said, 'I'd love to grab something to eat.'"

Breakfast at one or two in the morning after a night of drinking was a very Rhode Island thing to do.

Scott smiled at the memory, then continued. "There weren't a lot of late-night options, back then, but we found one, a food truck called Haven Brothers that mainly served wieners. They called them 'gaggers.'"

I nodded. "Yeah, I knew that truck."

"Anyway, we grabbed breakfast and talked for an hour. She was captivating. She had this light in her dark eyes, they sparkled, and her whole face lit up when she talked about things she cared deeply about. I'd never met a girl like that."

"She sounds special," I said.

He nodded, his eyes damp. "That first night, I kissed her good night. It may have been the most awkward feeling I had experienced. But we started seeing each other, meeting up at different places, but she asked me not to mention her to anyone, or that we were an item. Her family hated absolutely anything everything to do with the military. Her real father had been in the military and used to beat her mom. If they found out, she would never see me again. She had also just broken up with some guy she had been dating, and he took it pretty hard and got a little crazy. That may have also been part of why she didn't want people to know about us. I didn't like any of that, you know? But I'd already fallen, hard. She was smart and funny and sweet and caring. A joy to be around. 'Sure,' I said. 'I get it.' She had a way of lifting my spirits. Whenever I was with her, I felt amazing."

A smile had spread across his face as he spoke, but now it faded. "Well, except for the last time."

He took a deep breath and continued. "She was working full time at Thom McAn's shoe store in Lincoln Mall, but she was starting her second year at University of Rhode Island in oceanic studies at the end of August. She loved school and dreamed of saving all the creatures in the ocean. She said, 'I can't believe I am going to be getting paid to do it.' I couldn't believe she was leaving, fast forward to our last night. I bought her a promise ring. I knew what she had said, but I really wanted to keep dating her, especially seeing as I'd be coming back to RI to attend the police academy. And I guess…I was so into her, I figured deep down she had to be just as much into me."

He sighed and shook his head, sorrow and regret radiating off him like heat. "It was the third of August, the night the Iraqis invaded Kuwait, and we were supposed to be meeting at the picnic table at the Last Resort. I was going to give her the ring. She was supposed to get off work at twenty-two hundred hours—I mean ten p.m.—but she was late getting out of work. She liked vodka and orange juice—screwdrivers—so I had brought some, as well as some Miller Lite for me. I was nervous, and had started drinking around eight-thirty. By the time she got there at ten-forty, I was pretty hammered. We talked for a while, about school and stuff. She had a few drinks and I had a few more, trying to work up my courage. It was all going well, but I was plastered by the time I decided to ask her if she would take a promise ring from me. I mean, it wasn't an engagement ring, just a simple ring to say she'd wait till I got out of the Army and came back to RI in May for the academy."

He shook his head and let out a sad laugh.

"She kind of snapped. 'I told you my family hates anything and anyone who is in the military. I can't take a ring from you.' And 'I don't want anyone knowing we even dated, you told me this was just two people having fun.' I'll admit, I was pissed at first and started giving her shit, that she needed to stand up for herself. She cooled off a bit, backed off some."

He shook his head. "I figured, what the hell, one for the road, at least. I kissed her. She stopped me at first, but I can be pretty persistent, and I was drunk, so I kept trying to convince her. I was kissing her, and she let me undo her top buttons on her blouse. I was hoping to get her back to the motel, but then it was like a buzzer went off, an alarm clock. She just stopped and yelled, 'No, I said, no! This is it!' It was like she was looking past me, not even at me. But I tried a little bit more, sliding my hand into her unbuttoned shirt, saying, 'Come on.' She yelled 'No!' And then *boom*, she whacked me in the head, harder than I've ever been hit. I...It's kind of a blur, man. I shoved her after that, after she whacked me, then I passed out. I woke up a bit later, and my head was throbbing, like I had hit it when I fell. I looked over at her and she was passed out, too, or so I thought. I grabbed her face and said, 'What the hell? Why did you hit me like that?' But she didn't answer. Wouldn't say a word. I said, 'Jean, Jean, are you okay?'"

Scott shook his head, tears streaming down his face. "Fuck, there is no way I pushed her that hard. I don't even remember hitting her back other than a push. But when I leaned in, I saw she was not breathing. I tried CPR, for like, five minutes, at least. Then saw blood coming from the back of her head. A lot of it."

Then, in a whisper: "She had no pulse." Touching his own mouth in a bit of a shock: "Her lips were so cold. I can't get that out of my head!"

He went quiet for close to a minute. "She was gone, and I was drunk, and I just panicked. There was nobody around us, so I gathered up the beer bottles and screwdriver mix and ran over to the car, got in, and drove off." Another moment of silence. "I know I should have called an ambulance, she might have made it, but I was so drunk I wasn't thinking straight at all. Now, nothing I do or say can change things."

"Fuck, man, it was an accident," I said, my voice shaking as I tried to comfort him.

He waved my words away. "I was going to tell you the next morning, was going to turn myself in. But then I woke up to a call from Hankel telling me we were going to war, that we were rolling out in forty-eight hours. I felt an obligation."

I clapped a hand on his shoulder. "I'm sorry, buddy. I know this must be hard."

He nodded, quiet for a moment, then he startled me with a sharp snort of a laugh. "I wish it was Hankel we were surrendering to."

"We? Who the hell is 'we', kemosabe?" We both laughed at that, a reference to the old *Lone Ranger* TV show. "But, yeah, that would have been funny if he was the guy."

"Actually, his big ass would have kicked the door down and rushed us already."

Scott got dressed, and when he was done, I yelled out the window, "We're coming out. I'm going to toss the gun out first. It's empty. Then I'll bring him out."

Scott handed me the .357. I emptied the rounds from the chamber, walked over to the door, and tossed the gun outside.

I took a big, deep breath, then leaned in for another firm embrace. "I will always have your back," I said. "You can do this."

I wheeled him out the side door and down the ramp.

Wyman yelled, "Hands up! The both of you."

I looked over at Gold, both of us shaking our heads ever so slightly. I stopped pushing as the officers rushed over to us. They immediately reached down into the chair, searching for other weapons, and as they did, Scott whispered, "Let's make a run for it."

I knew this was an uncomfortable attempt at humor to calm his nerves. I thought it was funny, but it startled one of the officers, a guy named Hodge. A few seconds later, he got the joke, but he didn't quite appreciate it. "You think this shit is funny?" he said angrily. "Sitting here for hours while you play angry, pissed-at-the-world Army dude?"

Scott said, "Yeah, don't you?"

Gold said, "Okay, Officer Hodge, step back, I got this."

But Wyman seemed to get even more angry, taking over instead. "You have the right to remain silent—"

"That's not possible," Scott said, interrupting.

"—Anything you say or do can be held against you. You have the right to an attorney; in the event you cannot afford one, counsel will be provided."

"I want a lawyer," Scott said. "Can you reach out to him? His name is Robert Fischbach."

"Once you arrive at the station, you can call."

"I'll call him," I said.

"He needs basic toilet items?" Wyman asked, and Gold motioned to let me go in and retrieve them.

Scott looked up at me. "Yeah, I need some undies, a couple T-shirts, and some socks."

I went inside the house as Gold wheeled Scott over to the squad car.

Before anything, I called Rob Fishman and explained the situation. He said he would get to the station as soon as he could. Next, I called Steve Zabatta, a lawyer who I knew through my old friend Tom, to represent me. Zabatta said he was on his way as well and instructed me to say nothing until he arrived.

The simple task of not talking might be easy for most people, but it wasn't exactly a specialty of mine. Saying nothing would be way harder than saying everything. My biggest concern now that Scott had come forward was how to help him without negatively affecting my future job as a police officer. Not talking would certainly come at a cost to me, hopefully not my job.

In Scott's bedroom, there was a picture on his dresser, the two of us on a weekend pass from Basic or maybe AIT, and another one from Sheridan in our tuxedo shirts, probably soul night at the NCO club. There were other photos from Iraq off to the side, some of them triggering memories, immediately bringing them back into focus.

It disturbed me to think that from now on, when anybody who didn't know Scott heard this story, they were not going to know the content of his character. The entire narrative would be the fact that he killed some young girl and left her to die alone in the woods. Scott was a man of high character, but he would never be seen that way again.

I found a small gym bag and began to pile the clothes in there. I found plenty of shirts but no pants, only shorts. For a moment, I thought it was strange, but then I realized that, of course, he only needed shorts. It was quick work gathering the items, and then I headed to the Lincoln police station, a short drive from Scott's home.

When I arrived, it hit me that I was supposed to start working here the next week. I wondered if that was still going to happen.

Gold was waiting outside for me. "He's been processed," he told me. "Being cooperative. Declined a phone call. Said you were calling his lawyer?"

"He's on his way."

"Well, he better get here fast. Scott already waived his rights. He's in there talking to Detective Heath, alone."

There was no way Scott should be talking without his lawyer. Shit, did he think he was smarter than the detective? In my head, I yelled, *Fuck, just shut up, Scott!*

Gold said, "Listen, bud, I've got to step back, and we need you to talk with the detectives. I'm removing myself from this situation, given my personal conflicts. I hope you understand that we can't have outsiders looking at this situation and thinking there was anything but professionalism and proper protocol."

"Yeah, I get it." But the detectives wanting to talk to me made my insides squirm.

The station was small, and as soon as I went inside, I could faintly hear Scott talking to detectives. I secretly hoped he wasn't saying anything, given the magnitude of what he was facing, but from what Gold had said, he was probably singing.

As for me, I was trying to determine the "good" in my internal "good-versus-evil" debate, a struggle as real as any I had ever experienced. The situation seemed impossible. I had signed up to be a police officer and committed to the creed, "Serve and Protect." There was no struggle on the serving-the-public side, I knew what I had to do there. The protect aspect, however, was more challenging. Who was I protecting? Obviously not my battle buddy—I had just convinced him to turn himself in. And I certainly couldn't protect Jean, she was already gone. *How does this serve justice?* I asked myself. Scott had suffered terribly since he made that one horrible mistake.

As I sat in a plastic chair in the waiting area, stewing in my thoughts, a guy walked up and introduced himself as Detective Peters. He said he wanted to ask me a few questions. Cursing internally, I politely told him that I wanted to wait until my attorney arrived.

He screwed up his face at me. "Really?" He seemed more confused than irritated as he walked away, but a few minutes later, I heard the chief, and those proportions were reversed.

The Chief of Police was William Stripe. I had gone to high school with his son Matt and daughters Nora and Susan.

"That's not what police officers do when they know a crime has been committed," Stripe said. "Clearly, Anthony has known about this for a while and simply blew off his responsibilities!"

Shit, I thought, wondering if he was saying that so I would talk.

Luckily, before I could dwell too long on Stripe's words, Steve Zabatta arrived. He wore a very expensive gray pinstriped suit and immediately started talking extremely fast. "What have you said? Have you said anything? For the love of God, please tell me you've kept your mouth closed."

"Nothing."

He squinted at me. "Really?"

"Yes. I told them I wanted to wait for you to arrive before I said anything. Sounds like the chief is already pissed about it."

"Let's review a few things," Zabatta said. "You cannot talk to them. At all. It's not just your job on the line. You could be charged with obstructing justice or as an accessory after the fact."

"Not sure I thought of that, I thought it would be something minor, but accessory after the fact? Okay, I understand."

Zabatta told me that no matter what, when I talked to the police I had to tell the truth. "If you lie, you won't ever wear a police uniform, especially lying about a murder. For the time being, we limit what you say until there can be an agreement in writing."

"Why would I need an agreement? He did not tell me until this evening that it was true that he killed some girl."

"When did he first tell you he 'killed some girl'?"

"In Iraq. On the side of the road just before he died, he made a dying confession."

"Did he say who he killed?"

"No, just some girl when he was on leave."

"Did he say where?"

"No."

"Did he say how?"

"No. All he said was that when he was on leave, he accidentally killed some girl."

We had been talking for an hour when Fishman arrived wearing a much less expensive suit, which I attributed to his years working on a government prosecutor's salary.

The two lawyers discussed the case and agreed that Scott and I couldn't talk to each other going forward. Fishman emphasized that the two cases would run exclusive of each other, two separate proceedings, and that it might be in Scott's or my best interest to retain a different law firm due to potential conflicts in the case.

I jumped in. "There's no conflict with me. I don't care much about what they do to me. I just want you to make sure my battle buddy isn't railroaded. From what he told me, it was an accident."

Zabatta said, "It is essential that you understand, my job is to protect your interests, and if that means rolling over on Scott, then that's what you will need to do."

"Holy shit," I said. "Is that where I'm headed? After I pushed him to come forward, now I am going to be prosecuted as well? Then they want me to help drag Scott down?"

"Not sure," Zabatta said, "but you need to think about *you*."

My thoughts raced, and once again my mother's words came back to me: "Don't go looking for pain."

If you really don't want the answer to a question, simply don't ask it. I called Lisa to explain that I would be a few more hours.

"Is Scott okay?" she asked.

"He's as good as can be expected, but this is about to be national news and we are going to be right in the middle of it all."

"In the middle of what? National news?" Her tone sounded confused and angry, although maybe I was reading into it too much.

"Lisa, it's too much to explain on the phone. I'll come right after I am released from the station and tell you what I can."

"'What you can?' 'Released from the station?' Philip, what's going on?"

"Sorry. To say it's complicated would be a gross understatement, but I'll tell you more when I get home, I promise."

"Okay. Tell Scott to stay strong. Tell him we love him, and we'll help him get past whatever it is."

I was paired with a detective who seemed decidedly more curmudgeonly than the officers I had met with on the scene at Scott's house, even more than Wyman.

"Hello," he said, "I am Investigator Parker. I've been assigned to this case. As you understand, you have the right to remain silent, and anything you say or do can be held against you in a court of law."

Zabatta waited until Parker was finished, and then told him that I had retained counsel and would only answer written questions that he had reviewed.

I looked over, thinking, *I did?*

Parker cocked an eyebrow. "Well, I'm not sure how this will be viewed from the leadership here at the station, especially seeing Mr. Anthony was supposed to start work next Monday."

"My client has not had sufficient time to speak with his legal team regarding these issues," Zabatta said. "So, the best way to move this along is prepare a block of questions you would like my client to answer. I assure you he is most interested in getting to the truth as to what happened and ensuring it is clear he has no culpability relating to Mr. Scott's tragic events. And, to be very clear, we wouldn't all be here today if not for my client encouraging Mr. Scott to surrender and confess to his involvement in the tragedy involving Ms. Cruz."

Parker turned to me. "Mr. Anthony, is there anything you would like to say relating to the events before and after Jean Cruz's death?"

I took a deep breath. "On the advice of my counsel, I will refrain from talking at this time."

Parker snorted and shook his head. "Well, I'm sure the chief is not going to be happy that a newly minted police officer is refusing to assist in a murder investigation."

"On the advice of counsel, I am only refusing to answer questions at this time," I said.

Zabatta jumped in and said, "If you will submit your questions to me in writing, my client may be willing to answer some of them."

"We can do that."

In an almost annoyed manner, Zabatta stood up and said, "If that will be all, my client and I would like to depart the station. It's been a very long night for everyone."

As we were leaving, Zabatta saw Fishman.

"Wait here," he said. "I'll just be a minute."

281

I stopped and waited as he hurried after Fishman The two of them spoke for a minute or two, their heads bent close together.

When he came back, Zabatta led me outside. When we got to the sidewalk, he turned to me and said, "Fishman said Scott seems to be holding up okay. Joking around some, maybe too much."

I smiled. "Yeah, that definitely sounds like him."

"But it's good that he's not that freaked out, people joke when they're nervous as well. Maybe since he's a former MP, he's already familiar with the process. Anyway, he recounted the events, and there were a few fuzzy spots."

I nodded. "Yeah, it sounded like it from what he told me when we were holed up at his place."

"So, that's good news. And there doesn't seem to be any physical evidence connecting him to the murder. Plus, apparently Ms. Cruz did have a belligerent ex-boyfriend."

"Really?" I said.

He nodded. "But one potential problem is that Scott keeps talking like a guilty man."

"How do you mean?"

"Saying things like, 'I didn't mean to kill her,' or making suppositions like, 'I must have pushed her, and she hit her head on rock.' If he doesn't stop, he'll be doing the prosecutors' jobs for them."

We stood there in silence for a moment.

"Maybe I could talk to him," I said.

Zabatta immediately raised a hand to cut me off. "No, you two are to have no contact. I shouldn't have told you what I just did, but I figured you'd want to know. You can't talk to anyone about this, okay? Only me."

"I have to tell my wife," I said. "I'm protected with her, right?"

He screwed up his face. "Somewhat. It's called 'spousal privilege,' but definitely the less you say the better."

When I pushed it, he reluctantly agreed that I could explain the situation to my wife, but her alone. "Stay away from heavy details," he said. "If this stuff comes back on you, it could impact your employment at a minimum and potentially your liberty if you're prosecuted."

CHAPTER 11

EVERYONE KNOWS NOW

Driving home from the station, I was consumed with how Lisa was going to respond when I told her what was going on. She was the best person I had ever known, but what would she make of Scott's plight? And mine? She would certainly have issues with my not saying anything after knowing for so long. When I pulled up at home, I saw her through the window, drinking her coffee, watching the *Today* show, part of her morning routine. I sat there for a few minutes in the car, putting off the inevitable, coming to grips with what was happening. Lisa saw the car and came over to the window. We made eye contact and she nodded, beckoning with her non-coffee hand, like, *You coming in or not?* I bowed my head and started to bawl, crying ugly, like I had never cried before. Lisa raced outside in her old blue robe, not worried about what people thought of her outfit, something she would normally never do.

She opened the car door and said, "It's okay, come on inside, don't do this here."

I was speechless.

She grabbed my hand and helped me out of the car. Halfway up the steps, I stopped, realizing I had left the keys in the ignition. "The keys," I said.

"Don't worry," she said. "Nobody is stealing that car anyway."

We went inside and sat on the couch. I put my head on her lap, continuing to sob.

"It's okay," she said, rubbing my back. "We'll get through this. You've been through much worse, I'm sure." I tilted my head up toward her and said, "No, never worse than this."

I got myself under control, then sat up and tried to explain.

Lisa looked me straight in the eye, calm at first, then growing more emotional, then shocked and incredulous.

Shaking her head rapidly. "Scott?! No way! That can't be true!" she said. "How? When did this all come out? Oh, my God, how is he? Who is the girl?"

I bit my bottom lip a bit, something I did when I was looking for the exact words to use.

Taking a few deep breaths, I explained in great detail what I knew and when I knew it, what I suspected, how I had tried to tease it out of him again. And finally, how last night it had all come to a head. But I left out Jean's identity, just not wanting to discuss Lima at this point.

"I knew you were weird at the VFW," she said. "That's normally your place, and I could tell something was bothering you, but you never said a word." She thought for a moment, then asked again, "Who is the girl?"

Biting my lip again, I paused, and in a soft tone I said, "Lima's sister, Jean."

She looked at me almost disoriented and softly stated, "Lima's sister was murdered by Scott?" Her face dropped, and she covered her mouth in disbelief. "Oh, my God!"

I couldn't tell if she was shocked or if she was disgusted with me. She was not looking upon me favorably, for sure. I began to talk in more detail at a rapid pace, hoping to change that look of disgust.

"It's a crazy coincidence. I didn't know for sure, but I suspected more and more as the dates aligned. The final straw for me was seeing him dance with Lima's daughter to 'Billie Jean'."

With a long pause between each word, "Oh, my God!" she said again, shaking her head, looking at me. I still couldn't tell if her expression was one of shock or disgust.

"She told me her Aunt Jean used to love that song," I said. "I ran and threw up when she told me that."

"Wait, wasn't 'Billie Jean' the song you and Scott used to dance to in Basic?"

"Yes, that's part of what made it all so fucked up. Scott didn't know it until last night. Jean's last name was Cruz. Different father I guess."

She took that in, then asked me point-blank—put her hands on top of mine and in the most direct manner she has ever spoken to me asked, "When did *you* know this?"

"It's complicated."

"Complicated?" In a very stern tone, she said, "Don't play word games with me, Mr. Anthony. I'm your wife, and this is not something you can just blow past. A girl has died, and I want to know what you knew and when."

Oh shit, this was hard. I tried to explain in some detail how I only knew it was "some girl" when Scott was on leave, and how I wasn't even sure about that, really. How I wasn't sure who she was until yesterday, but I had suspected since the first day at the academy, when Lima told me his sister had been killed. "Maybe my mom was right all those years."

"What does that mean?" she asked. "Right about what?"

"She always used to say, 'Don't go looking for pain.'"

I started to cry again, but this time more from relief, from being freed from the emotional burden I'd been carrying for so long.

"Has anyone called Scott's family?" she asked.

I nodded. "I'm sure his lawyers did. I'm not sure he has the money to pay for this defense."

"I know you're going to try and help pay for his legal bills, and I understand. But you do remember what is happening here in a few months, right?"

I nodded. "That was the only way I got him to drop the gun. I told him. Oh, and I may have put it out there that the baby is going to be named Chris."

Lisa shook her head, but I'm pretty sure she knew this was a possibility even before I told her.

"You need to get to sleep," she said. "There's a lot to deal with, and you know you don't do well without sleep."

I nodded, and we both stood. She put her arms around me and held me firmly. "You're a good person, Mr. Anthony. Don't let this change you. People know you're both good people, and the ones who know you will never abandon either of you. Now, get some sleep. I love you."

I went to our bedroom and lay on the bed thinking there was no way I was going to fall asleep, but within minutes I was snoring.

I woke up close to five p.m. and found a note from Lisa on the kitchen table saying she had run out to Almac's supermarket to pick up something for dinner.

She had left some folded sweatshirts on the dresser, and with summer around the corner, I decided to move them to the top of the closet. While putting them away, I noticed a package up there wrapped in brown paper with a bunch of postage and addressed to me, with a return address from SFC David L. Hankel at Fort Bragg. I wondered what it was, then realized it was probably all my stuff from Iraq. Hankel must have boxed it up and sent it home when I left for Germany. I paused for several moments, reflecting on the box in my hands, wondering what in the world was inside. I had filled it myself, but quickly and carelessly and more than a year ago.

My mind drifted to the fact that I was supposed to have sent Scott's box to his family and had completely forgotten about it after quickly shipping out of Iraq to Landstuhl. I wondered what happened with Scott's box, what they had put in there.

With great trepidation, I walked into the kitchen and unpacked my box, studying each item I found. It was a literal time capsule, transporting me back to Iraq, overwhelming me with emotions once again, somehow making me inexplicably anxious.

First, I found a few T-shirts, PT shorts, and underwear. I shook my head, thinking, *Why the fuck would I need to send this home?* Next, I found socks and running shoes—which I had not missed using—then a couple of framed photos I had kept near my cot, one of my mom and grandmother and me when I first graduated Basic and AIT, and one of Scott and me in tux shirts partying at the NCO Club on Fort Ritchie.

I dug through it all, looking for Scott's disc camera, which should have some interesting stuff on it. Scott was always taking happy snaps while we were deployed. He said he wanted to have proof of our time over there so, when we were old farts, we would have the photos to back up the stories. My mind flashed back to Scott coming up from behind and saying, "Smile! You're on Candid Camera!"

I found some other small personal items, like some letters from my sisters that I got just before my accident and never opened. There were also two nice pens, and my dad's old watch. It had stopped running from not being wound, something today's watches didn't need.

Looking back on the tragic events that had changed both of our lives forever, I nonetheless smiled, remembering how Scott had saved my ass more than once, remembering the fun times we had in Iraq.

Ask any soldier in Basic Training what they think of it, and to a man they will say it sucks, pure fucking misery. Ask them when they're getting ready to retire, and they'll say it was one the best times in their lives. Shared misery built bonds that others outside that misery would never be able to understand. I was hoping maybe Scott's photos might cheer him up, and me as well, but sadly there was no sign of his camera.

Lisa walked into the kitchen with two bags of groceries. She seemed surprised to see me with the box on the table and all the contents spread out on top of it. "What is that?" she asked, her tone sharp as she eyed the mess I had made.

"It's my personal items box from Iraq. They must have mailed it after I was injured. Didn't you see that a while ago and open one of those boxes?"

"Nope. It came in when you were in Germany, I told you that on the phone when you were at the hospital."

"I don't remember that," I said, my face clearly showing concern.

"Well, it's nothing, really. No big deal."

"It's been there for months."

"Wow! Look at that!" she said, distracted by the photo of Scott and me in our bow ties.

"I know, that was a different time in our lives, for sure."

"Yeah, you were both whores back then," she said sarcastically.

"Look how young we look! That was only a few years ago. Holy crap, I look like I've aged ten years since then." I slumped in my chair, looking sadly at his photo.

Lisa reached across the table and held my hand, not saying a word for a couple minutes. She started with, "It's gonna be okay."

"No, it's not," I said, starting to feel sorry for myself.

"In the end, it will."

"I don't think so."

In her unique way of getting me to see it her way, she started talking very deliberately, clear and concise. "Well, let's recap: Your best friend gets blown up and dies, but before he dies, he tells you he killed some girl. Then, if that's not enough stress, he comes back to life and tells you he doesn't remember telling you he killed a girl." She shook her head. "Then you leave the Army and move back to your hometown to attend the police academy, and now you find out you are about to be a father and it's a boy. You and your buddy are selected to be the grand marshals for the town's parade, a great honor. But after the parade, you find out the girl your best friend killed is the sister of your best friend from the police academy! You confront your best friend, get him to turn himself in, talk him out of killing himself, then find out that you might be prosecuted, too. Does that summarize your life over the last two years? I've aged two years just recapping this freaking nightmare. On top of that, you were dealing with it on your own, because you didn't tell your wife, which we are going to talk about at some point." She shook her head again. "Yeah, no wonder you look so much older. That's a lifetime of tragedies in such a short time. Quite frankly, I think it's more than most people could deal with."

Lisa had a special way of making you understand that your moods, emotions, reactions were understandable, and, in this case, she summarized things perfectly.

"Thanks, honey, I needed that."

"I can't tell you how much I feel for you right now, Mr. Anthony. But listen closely: Don't let all this change you. Our child needs the dad I know you are meant to be."

She was clearly avoiding calling the baby Chris, in the hope that his name would be off the table once the baby arrived. Her not-so-secret plan was to name the baby John, after her dad, which would make sense given that was my dad's name, as well.

"Well, I figured you needed some chicken to cheer you up, so I picked up some cutlets. I'll make some chicken parmesan." That was one of the few meals she still cooked. She liked to emphasize that she didn't cook because I was "so picky and always changing things," but we both knew that was pure crap—she didn't like cooking and used this as an excuse to get out of it. I didn't mind most times, because I could always put my special spin on whatever was on the stove.

"Thanks," I said.

She leaned forward, studying my face. "What is it?"

"Nothing, really. Just, Scott used to go around doing silly stuff and taking photos all the time in Iraq with his disc camera, pissing off Hankel to no end. He had a bunch of discs. I was hoping maybe the camera or some of those photos would be in here." I forced a smile. "Anyway, no biggie."

Lisa left to get dinner started, and a few minutes later the phone rang. I picked it up and was shocked to hear Hankel's voice.

"So? How are you doing?" he asked.

"I'm good," I said.

"Yeah, right."

"Hey, Hankel, I am looking at my box you mailed me. Did you find Scott's camera?"

"Not sure. Maybe I sent that in Scott's box when I mailed back his care pack. That was a long time ago."

"When did you send it? Did he ever get it?"

"I don't know. He never mentioned it. I sent it when he was in the hospital, around the same time I sent your package."

"Well, did you send the discs as well?"

"I don't remember what I sent. Why? What's the big deal?"

"Nothing," I said, smiling as I thought back on simpler times.

"Really, though," Hankel said. "How are you? I heard about this shit with Scott from one of the guys who saw it on CNN. Why the fuck didn't you talk with me?"

"Hankel, you have no idea. All this shit, it was way too complicated to talk about on the phone."

"Yeah, I know, I called your house this morning to say goodbye.

Anyway, I changed my flight. I'm at the hotel near the airport in Providence."

"Really?"

"Roger that. This place is like some of the shit holes outside the back gate at Bragg." The epitome of what a leader should be, SFC Hankel had known instinctively the right thing to do, then he did it. "I assumed you would be with lawyers and your wife. Listen, I'm coming to visit you tomorrow. Are you available?"

"Yeah, what else am I doing?"

"Okay, let's lock it down."

"You know, I'm not sure when or even if I'm going to be a police officer now. Is it too late to come back into the Army?"

I felt eyes on me and turned to see Lisa, stopped in her tracks, staring at me.

"Okay, dipshit," Hankel said. "Enough of that. We need to sit down and talk soon. How about breakfast?"

"Why don't you come over for dinner tonight? I'm sure Lisa won't mind."

"I think you need a private dinner with your wife tonight. You and I can talk in the morning. Is there a place around there to get a good breakfast?"

"Yeah, Frank's in Lincoln. We all go there. But I might have to see my lawyer first."

I got the number of his hotel and told him I'd call back to confirm the time, then we both hung up. Lisa and I had a quiet dinner

"I'm meeting Hankel for breakfast tomorrow," I told her.

"I know. That's good. I'm glad he had sense enough not to come over for dinner. The last thing you need to do is talk about this anymore."

What an amazingly smart lady, I thought, for the millionth time. Over time, I had learned that she had more common sense than anyone else I had ever met. She had met generals, ambassadors, and heads of state during my military career, and she was still one of the most grounded, smartest people I had ever known.

"Dinner is great, but I am not very hungry," I said, putting down my knife and fork. I was too distracted to eat. Plus, the chicken needed more cheese, but this time I said nothing.

Lisa put her hand on mine. "Are we going to talk about finances?"

"I guess, but I need a few days."

"I was planning on quitting my job at the dental office in the last month of my pregnancy, but we may need to hold onto that, given the bills we are about to have coming in, combined with not knowing what is going to happen with your job. Oh, wait," she said with a sarcastic tone, "you could go back in the Army."

I laughed. "Nope, that is not happening ever again. That door is closed forever."

I needed something to take my mind off things and decided to watch my adopted team, the Chicago Bulls, in the NBA playoffs. Ever since my time at Fort Sheridan, I liked the Bears and the Bulls, although I still loved my Celtics best, no matter how much I loved watching Michael Jordan play. I knew full well Lisa would not be joining me, and minutes after I plopped onto the couch and began watching, she went off to bed.

For a brief moment, I was distracted enough watching the Bulls win to forget about my troubles. Halfway through the game, the phone rang, and it was the mother of another of my Army buddies, Mark Ellington. She had served as a missionary in Africa most of her life. She said she was just calling to see how I was doing. I told her I was fine, but then she asked if she could pray for me.

"Sure," I said, thinking she would say a prayer for me on her own time. Instead, she broke into a long, heartfelt prayer right then.

"Lord, one of your devoted followers is in need of your care and concern now more than he has ever needed it before. We ask you to watch over Anthony and Scott and keep them safe from harm and further pain as they deal with this personal tragedy. We ask that you shelter them from further pain, we ask that you give them both the strength to make it past their troubles and difficulties and provide them enough light to see it through to the other side."

I thanked her profusely and thought about her kindness for the rest of the game. I just cried my eyes out, I never experienced this before, it was both uplifting and comforting.

When it was over, I went to bed and lay on my back staring at the ceiling, thinking about Jordan's game-winning shot, knowing it would be hours before I'd fall asleep. Then the next thing I knew, I woke up with a start, not knowing where I was—something not uncommon among veterans returning from war, although few talked about it. I looked around at the empty bedroom and noticed the clock: 9:13 a.m. *Shit!* I was supposed to be meeting Hankel for breakfast. I leapt out of the bed and hurried into the bathroom for my morning pee.

"Lisa! Where is that number to call Hankel back on?"

She appeared in the doorway. "I called him at 8:30 and told him you were still sleeping. He said okay. I told him I'd wake you at 9:30, so he's expecting you at 10."

Fifteen minutes later, I was speeding down 146 in the Accord. I still liked to brag about how I'd saved thousands on it when I purchased in 1986, but I was thinking I might need a new car soon.

I merged onto I-95 thinking, *Shit, I need to make sure I have a job, I can't be buying a car just yet.*

As I pulled up at the hotel, I saw Hankel waiting in the lobby, reading his paper with his legs crossed, drinking free coffee. I parked out in front, next to a sign saying, "Check in only."

I sprang from my vehicle and ran into the lobby. Obviously, I was okay showing affection, but Hankel, as he put it, was "not much of a hugger."

He gave me a side hug, then grabbed me by the shoulders and said, "How the fuck are you?"

I laughed. "Man, can't tell you I'm okay, but we've obviously seen worse things in our life, right?"

He nodded. "I hear you. Okay, I didn't eat, so let's get on the road and get some chow."

We made small talk on our way to Frank's Diner in Lincoln, just down from my house. "They're known for their portions and their great home fries, but I'm not a fan of those, myself."

"Well, I'm used to chow hall food, so whatever works for me."

We arrived at Frank's, and true to small-town fashion, most people knew what was going on. As soon as we walked in, almost everyone looked over at me, stopping and staring.

My high school friend Nora was the hostess. "How are you doing?" she said with deep compassion on her face.

"I'm okay, but this has only just begun," I said. I pointed over her shoulder. "Can we sit in the back over there?"

"Sure," she said, leaning in. "I'll try to keep the tables near you open for some privacy."

When you were dealing with personal drama in life, sometimes the simplest gesture could mean the world, like the call from Mama Ellington the night before.

Hankel gave me a puzzled look. "Why are you crying?"

I told him about the call, how she had broken into a complete prayer. "It's hard to explain. I was at one of my lowest points of my life, feeling sorry for myself, when she called me and prayed for me."

"I understand. Trust me, I do."

Hankel had also grown up Catholic and knew the importance of prayer.

"It was so impactful," I told him. "I've never experienced an event so…so powerful and uplifting. It might be the single most surprising religious thing that has happened to me. It moved me to tears and gave me such a powerful feeling of comfort, I can't explain it, Hankel!"

"I get it, trust me. My mom used to do that for me on the phone. It would annoy me at first, but later, I looked forward to her calls, knowing I'd get a special prayer on the phone."

We found ourselves alone in the back, facing the housing area behind Frank's and the back parking lot. Nora brought menus and asked if we wanted coffee.

I ordered a coffee milk with ice, and one for Hankel, too.

"What the hell is coffee milk?" he said.

"Just try it. You'll like it."

The coffee milks arrived and, unlike most people, Hankel took one sip and said, "This is like a milk shake. It's way too sweet for me." He handed it over to me.

"You might be the first person that doesn't love coffee milk." I took it and turned to Nora. "I'll drink his."

Hankel ordered a black coffee, and Nora said, "You need a minute to order?"

"No," Hankel said, "but take his order first, I'll know before you can write all the crap he is going to ask you to do."

I ignored him. "Okay, three eggs crispy but over light…"

Hankel shook his head as he scanned the menu. "See? I told you."

"…Put some bacon grease on the grill and then fry the eggs in that till the bottoms are crispy, then flip them over for about ten seconds, then take them off the grill. I'd like the home fries extra crispy, and my bacon as well. Do you have the patties or links?"

"We only have links," Nora said. "Sorry."

"Okay, just bacon then. Also, can I get one French toast? And do you have cranberry juice?"

"Sure thing," she said, scribbling furiously.

When she was done, she looked at Hankel, who simply said, "Give me the special with bacon, over easy, with white toast."

Over Hankel's shoulder, I saw Nora's husband, Kevin, working in the kitchen. We had known each other in high school, as well. He came out through the swinging saloon doors and caught my eye, giving me a nod and a slight wave, not the joyous behavior he normally displayed with me. Clearly, he'd heard what happened, and I could see the sorrow on his face.

Normally, Hankel had some witty words of wisdom, but he was extremely quiet, so quiet it made me uncomfortable, made me wonder if he had issues with me as well.

I leaned across the table. "So, what, do you have an issue with me, too?"

Hankel screwed up his face. "What?"

"You're so quiet. Are you upset with how things went down? Or passing judgment on me?"

He went into full SFC Hankel mode. "Listen, shit stain, you know I'm not one of those touchy-feely guys, so I'm not going to hold your hand and tell you everything is going to be okay. You're in some serious shit right now, but not as much as Scott. You two idiots were my favorite soldiers that I've ever led, and when Scott died, I thought that was the worst thing you and I were ever going to deal with. But this is a whole new level of shit storm that I'm not sure either of you will ever get past. You see how these people looked at you when you walked in here?"

"Yeah, no biggie."

"Well, I wanted to go over and rip every one of their asses out of their seats and toss them out the door like I used to do on patrol in Korea. What kills me here is, I know what the two of you are all about and the content of your character. I don't know the story yet, but I'm sure it was somehow an accident. Doesn't matter. You will be looked at like that for the rest of your fucking lives, regardless of the outcome."

"How so?"

"I call it the 'judge, jury, and executioner' look. Every one of those civilian bastards passed judgment on you without knowing one thing about you personally. I know the both of you probably better than you know yourselves, and this shit is going to change you. That might be the hardest thing you're going to have to deal with. That's what the fuck is going through my mind, not one ounce of negativity regarding you and your idiot buddy."

I sat quietly wishing Scott could hear all the things that Hankel was saying about us.

Nora returned with our breakfast. I saw Kevin looking over the kitchen doors again, waiting to see my reaction to the special egg order. I gave him a thumbs up and a big smile. He smiled at me, almost like he felt sorry for me. But maybe that was just me, maybe I was reading into everything now.

Hankel said, "You must come here all the time. He made it exactly how you asked for it. Haven't seen that type of dedication since the chow hall in Iraq."

We both chuckled, and as it died out, I said, "Well, I'm not sure where to begin."

"So, here's the deal," he said, "only tell me what you want to tell me. I hold no judgment. If your lawyer says to say nothing, then do that, but when I fly out today, I want to know a couple things, and we can talk about them later."

I told him what Scott had told me about the night of the murder, and as I did, Hankel went into to full lawyer/friend/MP boss protection mode.

When I was done, he said, "So, you didn't know other than just a simple, 'I killed some girl when I was home on leave'?"

"Yes."

"And you never asked him?"

"I asked him if he remembered anything about the day of the explosion, and all he said was riding in the Humvee. Nothing but before the explosion, no recollection of talking with me on the side of the road. And he never again said anything about killing anybody."

Hankel said, "Well, you had a concussion too, so make sure your lawyer knows that you were not in your right mind as well."

"Okay, I will let him know."

Hankel went on. "They have this thing they are calling traumatic brain injuries now, TBI. That's the official term for getting blown up and fucked in the head."

"I never heard of that."

"Just like the Army to find a term for everything. I thought my names have always been the best," said Hankel

I replied, "I think I'd call it sausage brain, mixing all that shit in your head into one piece of meat."

We both laughed, and I said, "Maybe you could Order and Soup Sandwich and a sausage brain to go."

Hankel turned serious again. "What is your lawyer saying?"

"He said I may not be charged with anything, given I had no real idea until yesterday, and since I pushed Scott to turn himself in once I knew."

"What are folks at Lincoln police saying about your job?"

"Nothing yet, but I heard the chief say I must have known, and that any cop who knew that should have done something about it."

"Yeah, like I said, you'll carry this for the rest of your life. What did your lawyer say about Scott's situation?"

"Well, his service and condition will help his cause, but he killed some girl and, accident or not, he walked away from her. The optics of that are not going to help him one bit."

"Yeah, I know," he said, his voice low and gravelly.

"The kicker for me is that Scott told me the night he confessed that he knew he couldn't let me deploy alone. He was worried that I wouldn't come back alive if he turned himself in."

"Well, I kind of had the same thought. That's why I called him the morning prior. I told him get his ass back to Bragg, that we were headed out of country on a real-world mission, not a simple training rollout. He knew we were going to war."

"He never told me exactly why you called him, just getting his ass back to Bragg."

"Wait, that must be the reason he didn't turn himself in," said Hankel. He sat back in his seat and nodded slowly. "I knew there had to be something that made him not turn himself in. It's just not like him to do something like this."

"You're probably right," I told Hankel.

He sat back up and said, "I'm willing to write you both letters of support and even come testify on both your behalf. If you need me to meet with your attorneys, I can do that as well. Let's try and call after we eat."

The rest of the meal was mostly small talk. The check arrived, and Hankel grabbed it and said, "Don't even try to pay, alligator arms. You got a lot of legal bills coming, so save your pennies, high speed, you are gonna need'em."

There was a subtle silence as Hankel rubbed his chin. "Watching you drive away from Bragg was one of the saddest days I've had in the Army. I never thought I'd see you two knuckleheads again. I wish it were under different circumstances, but I'm glad I was able to come up for the parade and be here for the both of you. Now, I need you to drop me off at the police station so I can hopefully see Scott before I leave."

"I'm not sure they'll let you see him. He's in for murder, and they haven't arraigned him yet. I think they're doing that first thing tomorrow."

Hankel raised an eyebrow at me, like, *Are you really questioning my ability to get to see him?*

"Well, you can at least try," I said. "I can drop you off and then come back later. I have to run an errand and get some stuff Lisa asked me to pick up at the paint store. Did I tell you she's pregnant?"

"Wow, that's awesome! Who's the father?"

I laughed. "That's the same shit Scott said to me!"

"Give me a minimum of an hour, maybe two. Call the station before you come get me."

I dropped Hankel off at the station and watched as he walked up to the front door like he owned the place, a gentle giant going to check on one of his men. He turned back at the door and waved at me to drive away, which I did.

When I was done getting paint supplies for the baby's room, I called the station and told Hankel I was on my way.

He was waiting when I pulled up, and as soon as he got in, I said, "Did you see him?"

"Yeah, I saw him."

"How's he doing?"

"First, I talked to Fishman told him about Scott's character and military service and the reason he didn't turn himself in before yesterday, about you guys getting called up to go into battle. I told him you two were battle buddies and Scott knew that if he turned himself in then, he would never have deployed, wouldn't have been there to watch your back. And he was right; he saved your ass more than once. Maybe it's corny, but I told him Scott was Robin to your Batman. Batman for sure always needed Robin.

"Next, I talked my way into Chief Stripe's office, told him I was a United States Army military police officer with twenty years of dedicated service, and a little bit about what that entailed. I told him about your service, too, and Scott's, that you didn't know anything until recently, and that, as a military police officer with over one hundred interrogations under my belt, I knew you were telling the truth. I told him you were going to be a great cop, and that he'd regret it if, because he was prejudging you, that ended up happening somewhere else."

I laughed for some reason, picturing it all going down. Then I turned serious. "What about Scott? How was he?"

"You two shit stains have taken a lifetime worth of my time and energy. I'm glad you are not in the unit anymore. People would think I actually like you two ass clowns."

"You don't like us?"

"Nope, I love you two jackasses, it's what makes leading soldiers the most rewarding job in the world, CFB." CFB was a military phrase for Clear as a Fucking Bell.

"Well, how the fuck is he then?"

"He's in good spirits. I had him laughing on the way out, told him his legs weren't worth shit when he had them anyway, he could not beat this old fart even on his best day."

I was incredibly relieved to hear this. Although it had only been a couple of days since I had seen or spoken to Scott, it seemed more like weeks. I was happy to hear he was doing better.

"I told him I'd spoken to his lawyer and Chief Stripe, that I was willing to come back and testify for you two idiots to make sure neither of you spent the rest of your life in jail."

He took a deep breath. "I made him look me in the eye and promise he wasn't going to do anything stupid, like take his own life. I told him a shit ton of motherfuckers, including you and me, had risked life and limb to save his ass. That he couldn't just throw that away, and if he did, I would take it personal, and so would you, and so would every doctor in Iraq and Germany, the other patrols that came to save his ass after he blew up, and the countless translators who helped us roll up the Haji that fucked him up."

I was stunned. "Wait, you got the bastard that put the bomb in place?"

"Of course, we did. I made sure of it personally, just like I promised I would," he said, adding with a grim smile, "fortunately, some of them resisted and chose to go out in a blaze of glory, so they sealed their own fate. I worked with a few of my intel buddies who knew how personal this was for me and our team. I had to promise a few return favors when we got to Bragg, and they have been cashing those in for the last year now." He shook his head. "Intel wienies think they can speed around Bragg all the time now."

"Wow," I said, still stunned. "I had no clue."

"How could you? You and your buddy are the first people I've told that to. Anyway, lastly, I told him you were all fucked up over this, that I thought your job was safe now, but that he couldn't involve you in it any longer. He had to be on his own now." He grinned. "Batman needs to leave Robin alone."

305

"Wait," I said, "I'm Batman."

Hankel shrugged. "He thinks he's Batman. For the time being, I say let him."

I couldn't tell if he was playing Scott or playing me.

"Anyway," he continued, "I reminded him that he had done a shit ton for this nation, and that would be considered at sentencing. He's been through way worse shit than this and he made it, so whatever happened, he'd recover. I reminded him just how many people wanted to see him make it out the other side of this, so he could never give up again. He seemed to understand."

We were quiet for a moment, then Hankel put on his seatbelt. "Now, take my ass to the airport."

We were quiet at first, on the way to the TF Green Airport in Providence. Then we made small talk.

Hankel said, "Hey, question: If the airport is in Warwick, why do they call it Providence Airport?"

"Hmm, I never thought about it, but that's a good question."

As we were nearing the airport, Hankel said, "I shared a story with Scott, one my father told me about men in battle from WWI."

"Wait, your dad was in WWII."

"Can you close your pie hole? I said a story my dad *shared* with me, not one he was in."

"Oh, okay."

"As you may remember—actually, you were a shitty student, so I'd better explain. WWI was characterized by trench warfare, with both sides sitting as close as fifty or seventy-five yards away from each other. There are these two Army battle buddies, Johnson and Murphy, who were trench mates and the best of friends, fiercely loyal to each other. Murphy decides he needs to crawl forward and clear some debris that is affecting his field of fire in order to better defend the trench he and Johnson are in. As Murphy is forward, removing the debris, he is wounded. Johnson attempts to climb out to assist his battle buddy but is stopped by his lieutenant. 'No, Johnson, he's wounded. It's a set-up. They want you to crawl out there so they can shoot you.' Johnson says, 'I can't leave him, sir, he's my battle buddy.' Lieutenant says, 'Sorry, I forbid you to go forward. That's a lawful order.'

"As the hours pass, Murphy keeps crying out, 'Johnson! Johnson!' but they're growing fainter, with more and more time in between. As night falls, Murphy can barely be heard now, and eventually he calls out one last faint, 'Johnson.' But the lieutenant still won't allow him to go forward. However, Johnson can no longer restrain himself, he pushes the lieutenant backward and crawls out to Murphy, then quickly drags him back to the trench. The lieutenant is fuming, just waiting to lay into him. A single shot rings out from the enemy trench, striking Johnson in his shoulder, causing both Johnson and Murphy to fall into the trench. The other soldiers rush to the two battle buddies. As the medics begin dressing Johnson's shoulder wound, the lieutenant tells him that Murphy is dead.

"'You idiot, Johnson, I told you not to go. What a damn waste, now I've lost two soldiers.

"Johnson says, 'It wasn't a waste, sir.'

"The lieutenant says, 'He's dead, you're wounded and may die, how the hell was you going out there not a waste?'

"Johnson says, 'He was alive when I arrived, sir.' And the lieutenant says, 'Well, Soldier, two minutes is still a waste.' But Johnson says,

'Sir, you simply don't understand what the true meaning of loyalty is. When I finally got to him, he looked in my eyes and said, 'I knew you would come!'"

As we pulled up at the airport, Hankel went quiet, maybe trying to keep his emotions in check. I went quiet, too.

After a few moments, he said, "You see, Anthony, my dad told me this story as it was from one of his sergeant majors who knew Johnson firsthand. What my dad explained to me is, never question the commitment of soldiers in battle and what they will do for each other. It does not matter to me one bit that you two are not in the military any longer, I will always come for either one of you. Stay strong, stay away from Scott, and listen to your lawyer."

CHAPTER 12

IMPATIENTLY WAITING

With Hankel departed for Bragg, I met with Zabatta for several hours, like I would almost daily. And, like I would almost daily, I wondered how I was going to pay him if I were indicted. Zabatta had explained that it was extremely good for both Scott and me that I had not spoken to the police. Talking would have affected our position on negotiation, especially for capital offenses. The fact that Scott refused to talk and was processed meant he would end up staying the night and be transported to court in the morning. The detectives still hoped to get him to plead guilty outright and move the case along.

I asked Zabatta, "Can you to get with the chief and find out my job status, or how am I going to pay for your legal services?"

"Let's worry about that down the road a bit," he said. "I talked to him yesterday, and he told me there is no change and that he didn't see you starting until they finished their investigation. He said it could speed things up if you would sit with the detectives, but I reminded him we said you'd answer questions in writing, and he hasn't sent the questions. I imagine they're waiting for Scott and want to cross his story with what you know. After that, we'll meet for what they call a proffer. That is when you sit down before you are to testify to sort of prepare the prosecutor for presenting the case against Scott. The only thing you need to ensure you do is to tell the truth. If you lie, any agreement is null and void."

"Why do we go through all this shit if he is pleading guilty? The military is way simpler. If this happened on base, it would be a much more streamlined process."

"Not for murder," Zabatta said. "Scott would have been prosecuted on the federal level and could have gotten the death penalty, so be happy that is not the case here."

"Good point."

"I'm working with Scott's attorney to figure out how things will play out. As of our last conversation, he was still working out terms of Scott's plea agreement. Anything you say could affect Scott's situation, so he would appreciate us not testifying or being deposed until he gets the deal worked out."

"Did he say how Scott was doing?"

"He's doing okay. Unfortunately, the judge will deny bail. You know, at some point you'll have to worry about your situation. If I am being honest here, you really should be putting yourself and your family first."

I was pissed by this statement and barked back, "Scott is part of my family, so yeah, I agree with you."

Zabatta nodded and backed off a bit. "Well, I assume we will have to wait until Scott pleads and his case is clearer. What has the chief said to you about your job? I want to ensure they will not hold that against you down the road, so keep good notes on anything the station says to you regarding your employment."

"Nothing yet, but I'm ready to get to work. This is the first time since age fifteen I haven't had a job. How can people not work?"

"Some simple advice: You can't do anything about it, so enjoy this time. Once you're on the job and working twelve-hour shifts, you'll regret not enjoying this freedom. Let's push off our meeting until next week." He paused. "Now, this is the uncomfortable part. As we discussed, I'm going to need a retainer of some sort. The partners are certainly understanding given your status and the high-profile nature of this case, but we will need something, like $25,000. When do you think that is possible?"

"Well, I'll need to talk with my wife. I do have some money saved up. I assume we should be getting a discount on your services. Does your firm happen to offer a military discount?

Zabatta looked at me like, *How is that question even coming out of your mouth? Your buddy is on trial for murder, and you could be an accessory after the fact.*

"Well, not normally, but I will certainly ask the partners if that is possible."

At that moment, Zabatta took out this brand-new thing called a cell phone. It was huge, compared to today's standards, like a large walkie-talkie. I was surprised to see him talking into it. I quickly realized he was talking with his buddy Tom Leach, who asked how I was going to pay for this effort. He reminded Zabatta that I was like a brother to him, one of his best friends, and there was a personal request from him and his lead partner, Al Santoni, to control costs.

Zabatta said, "I got it, Tom. By the way, he already asked me for a military discount."

I could hear Leach laughing. "You know how many times I've had to listen to him ask for that discount? When he's in his eighties, if he lives that long, he will have saved over a million dollars, that cheap bastard!"

Zabatta finished the call and told me I should not attend the plea hearing before the grand jury, but he would attend to ensure nothing Scott said could or would incriminate me in any way.

He got another call he had to take, and he headed off.

I stayed where I was, thinking about everything he had just told me, worrying about Scott and about how either of us was going to afford our legal bills.

As I was about to go, I noticed a guy just sort of staring at me. He was about fifty years old, 6 foot tall, wearing a Red Sox hat and a Rolling Stones T-shirt. He looked away when I met his eye, but then he looked back at me and walked over to where I was sitting.

"You're Phil Anthony, right?"

"Yeah, why? Who are you?" I was a little leery. I knew I wasn't supposed to be talking about the case, and I had no idea who this guy was, if he was maybe trying to glean information.

"I saw you in the parade the other day." He came over and sat down next to me. "I'm so sorry you're in this mess. You and your buddy. I was his driver, taking him to court this morning. Seems like a good guy."

I was taken aback, hoping he was not bullshitting me, "Yeah, he is."

"I'm sure there is an explanation for why he is there."

"Yeah, but you know what, I'm not supposed to talk about this with anybody."

He waved his hand. "I understand. Not asking you to tell me anything. I just wanted to tell you that your buddy is doing okay."

"That's good to hear. Thank you. I just wonder how he's going to hold up in jail."

"He'll be alright. I'll tell you what I told him: You think it's going to be the end of the world, but it'll be okay, whatever happens."

I appreciated the guy saying it, but he didn't seem to have anything to back it up, so I asked him, "How would you know that?"

"'Cause I've been in his situation. Spent three years in the same place he's in right now, after I got out of Vietnam. I told him, 'It'll make you appreciate freedom and liberty.'"

"Vietnam?" I said. "You served?"

He nodded. "I was there for two years and a wake up."

I put my hand out. "Thank you for your service."

He shook my hand and said, "You, too.

"I didn't hear that too much when I came back," he said. "They hated us. Fortunately, soldiers today don't have to deal with that shit."

"Agree."

"Anyway, I told him to be strong, and I told him no matter what happened, I knew you appreciated him saving your ass."

"Yeah, we don't tell each other things like that."

He laughed. "That's exactly what he said."

"But I do," I said.

He nodded. "Your buddy knows it." He got to his feet. "Anyway, I just wanted to tell you that."

I stood up and put out my hand.

"My name's Jake," he said.

"My friends call me Anthony."

We shook, and as he turned to go, he said, "I'll be cheering for you. You'll both get past this!"

"Thanks, Jake. It was great to meet you."

Over the next several weeks, I kept replaying details about what Scott had told me, wondering if there was anything I should have picked up on sooner. This, coupled with Lisa's growing stomach, helped divert my attention from the calendar as we waited for July 17, the date for Scott's plea hearing. I had been completely left out of the loop, so I didn't know any of the details, but I would be going to court to support my battle buddy as he took responsibility for his actions. I'd had no contact with Lima or the Lincoln police, other than a call from the chief to tell me he would allow me to begin duty at Lincoln at the end of July, after the plea hearing.

Zabatta told me Scott had made a few friends inside the ACI, the Adult Correctional Institution, and seemed to realize he might be able to handle a short prison sentence, just like Jake had told him.

CHAPTER 13

PLEADING GUILTY

July 17 was a beautiful summer day, not too hot and humid, which was rare for July in Rhode Island. The past few days, the quiet little town of Lincoln had been abuzz with the pleading about to take place in Providence. After almost two years, the mystery of Jean Cruz's murder was about to be solved. Rhode Island was not known for national events, but Scott's storyline had been carried at the forefront of all the major media carriers. CNN had been in RI since the announcement that a suspect had been arrested in the murder of a young lady, blaring, "Gulf War Hero Allegedly Brutally Murders Beautiful Young College Student."

The simple fact was most people missed the word "allegedly," and just as Hankel had said, most of society would look at Scott with judge, jury, and executioner eyes. But not me.

I awoke very early that morning, not something I was known to do, but the smell of bacon filled the air as Lisa made breakfast—something she wasn't known to do often, either.

"Good morning, Mr. Anthony," she said when I walked into the kitchen. "I hope you're hungry. I made you a big breakfast."

"Thank you."

"This is going to be a difficult day for you, so I wanted you to have a full stomach."

"Can you make it—"

"Yes, I know," she cut me off. "Crispy on the bottom but don't overcook the yolk!"

We both laughed.

I said, "Am I that bad to want my food a certain way?"

"No," she said patiently, "but people hate hearing you tell them how to do something over and over."

"Okay, I'll eat it whatever way you make it." I looked over and noticed she was showing even more. I had been so caught up in my own world, somehow, I had missed it. She was tiny, so even the slightest bump was very noticeable. I walked up and grabbed her from behind, rubbing her stomach. "Well, little guy, today is a day we will not remember so fondly, but this little sight gave me a glimmer of happiness, so for that, I thank you."

Lisa smiled back at me and said, "Push the toast down."

"Oh, any English muffins?" I asked.

"Don't push it, but, yeah, there are some in the bread bin. Help yourself if that's what you want."

I put the muffins into the toaster and pushed them down, then got some American cheese from the fridge. Lisa smirked and said she knew I was going to make an Anthony McMuffin—spreading the yolk on the muffin, putting the cheese on top of that, and using the crispy egg to melt the cheese. This little distraction allowed me to not think about the events to come that day, but not for long.

Scott was finally about to plead out. Since he was pleading, I would not be required to testify and only had to answer the questions provided during the proffer, which they would cross with his confession.

I finished making the sandwich and took a bite. "Can you say amazing?" I said. "Thanks. I needed this today."

Lisa smiled. "You have a problem, you know. You're like an alcoholic when it comes to food. I think you love food more than me."

"No, but it's close," slipped out of my mouth. "Damn Tourette's humor."

"I know you say it without thinking, hoping it's funny," she said. "Lucky for you, most times it is!"

I finished eating and took a quick shower, then walked briskly back to the bedroom. I laid the towel on the bed then sat on it and rolled back to dry my butt and back.

"That might be the most unattractive thing you do," Lisa said, watching from the doorway.

"I do worse."

"You roll up and your taint is right there. I can't unsee that."

I put on the gray suit pants I'd had tailored in Germany. The waist was a bit snug, but not too bad. I went over to the dresser to get my deodorant and saw the photo of Scott and me from Basic Training, doing the Greedy Club sign. I sat on the bed holding the photo, flashing back to better days.

Lisa reappeared and said, "Hey, ADD boy! Stay focused. You can't do anything about it right now, so stay focused and get dressed."

"Right." But when she left, I put the photo back and knelt at my bedside.

"Dear Lord, the last time I asked you for help, it was to keep Scott alive. Now, I need your help one more time. Can you please make this as painless as possible for Scott and for Lima's family. They have all been through hell, and today is the day we all need a miracle, so if you can do anything to lessen the burden on all, please intervene. I know it sounds crazy to ask you to help someone who killed somebody, but you know the kind of man he is, and only you know for sure, but he says it was an accident."

My mind wandered off, thinking I hadn't even spoken with Lima since Scott was arrested. He must hate me.

"Oh," I said, resuming my prayer, "and can you please take care of my wife and future son? And more than anything, I want to thank you for helping me see this through. I'm not sure I could have made it this far without your guidance and support."

I got back up and finished getting dressed.

Lisa returned with a disapproving look on her face. "No, don't wear that." She found a different shirt and dark gray tie to match. "Wear these."

She finished her make-up and hair much more quickly than usual.

"How come you can't do it that quick more often?" I asked.

"There's usually no need to rush," she said, glancing at me, then looking back. "Wear your black shoes and your gray socks."

"Yes, mommy!"

"You're going to be all over the news. You should look your best. And on top of that, you're going to meet with the chief later this week. I'm sure he'll be watching this as well. So, how about you just listen for a change? You should look as sharp as you can, and you're not giving me a lot to work with here."

"Good point!" I said. "Now, off to court!"

I was driving around the courthouse trying to find street parking rather than pay the $3.00 fee to park in the garage when Lisa said, "Can you just pay to park already?"

"Okay, I will," I said. I was still looking but finally gave in.

I pulled into a different garage down the road from the courthouse, which was two bucks cheaper. We exited the vehicle, and she fixed my tie one more time, telling me, "You can handle this. I'm right here with you."

We walked toward the courthouse in silence holding hands, something I loved to do with her, given her hand fit perfectly into mine. Outside the courthouse, there were several news trucks and reporters standing around with microphones. When they saw me, two of them rushed over to ask for a comment. For once in my life, I did not want to comment at all, and I briskly walked the rest of the way to the court, up the steps, and inside. I went through security and asked which courtroom Christopher Scott was being tried in.

"Courtroom Three, up the stairs to the left," said the guard, pointing over his shoulder.

"Slow down," said Lisa. "I have heels on. You still have twenty minutes, you'll be fine."

"I want to get in there early," I said, which might have been the first time those words came out of my mouth.

But when we started up the steps, I saw a familiar-looking face coming down.

"Jake!" I said, putting out my hand.

Jake nodded. "Anthony," he said, shaking my hand.

"Did you drive him here?"

"I made sure of it."

"I appreciate that. I'm sure it meant a lot to him." I introduced Jake to Lisa, then asked, "How's he doing?"

"He's doing okay. Lots of lame jokes about making a run for it or running away."

"That sounds like Scott."

"I told him, nobody understands what he's going though unless they have been there before, but a lot of people have been there. And I'm one of them."

"You?" Lisa said. "You were in jail too?"

"When I first got back from Nam. Liberal bastards, protesting me all the time. I couldn't stand it. One guy called me a baby killer, and I snapped and beat the living shit out of him." He paused and apologized to Lisa.

"No problem," she said. "I'm used to hearing Army guys talk."

"I still feel bad about it to this day," Jake said. "He had it coming, but maybe not as bad as I gave it to him. When I was sentenced to three years, I took my punishment like a man but only had to serve eighteen months. I told him, 'You have to atone for your bad deeds, and this is the first big step to getting past all of it.' I told him I've got some friends inside the ACI, and I'd make sure they took care of him."

"Thanks, Jake." I felt bad not being there for Scott, but I was glad he had Jake.

"He fought in battle for this country. It's my honor. And I told him, I'll be right here waiting for him when he gets out of the courthouse.

He just needs to man up and do what he needs to do. And he will. I can tell he's a strong man."

We said goodbye and headed up the stairs.

When we got to the top, I was blown away. There were so many green Army uniforms waiting outside the courtroom, and familiar faces, too. First Sergeant Carl Krieger—Top—was talking with Lieutenant-now-Captain Roger Clifford, who was standing next to Captain Mitch Pateirno. To their left were Specialist Tony Jones, Sergeant John Richter, Specialist Rob Bouford, Specialist Gary Grand, Specialist Ann Trainee, Specialist Tami Kaan, Bob Walters, and a bunch I didn't even recognize. Standing above all of them was Hankel, talking to none other than DJ Ross. All these soldiers were dressed in their Class A uniforms to demonstrate to the court the kind of man that Scott was. Some of my Rhode Island buddies were there, too: Marty and Dave Long, Rob Turner, Joe Yankee, Paul Zen, and Tom and Cheryl Leach. I was almost moved to tears. Lisa stood back as I embraced each one, even two MPs from Alaska whom I had never met before. I thanked them all for showing up to court that day.

Then I looked at Top, teary eyed, and said, "I'm sorry we let you down, Top."

"You guys never let me down," he said. "It was an accident. I knew as soon as I heard, it was not intentional."

We shook hands, and as Lisa and I moved past, I saw my mom, grandmother, all my sisters, my dad, and my brother Michael, who was always late but was on time today. I hurried over to thank them all, as well. It was starting to look more like a celebration than a hearing.

The courtroom doors opened, and all the soldiers lined up behind

Top and made their way inside. Lisa and I sat in the first row, just behind where Scott would be seated, and the rest of my family moved into the second row, with Michael and Mom sitting directly behind me.

Scott's father and his brother Tony arrived shortly after, and we moved down a bit to make room for them. I had never met them, but I recognized them both from old photos as soon as they walked into the courtroom.

The soldiers attempted to move into the second row, but the bailiff, a stocky, balding man with a beer gut pushing his stomach past his waistline, raised an arm to block them. "Sorry. This row is for family."

Top and Hankel, at the exact moment, in perfect unison, said, "We are all family here."

The bailiff paused for a moment, then lowered his arm and let them sit.

Once most of the courtroom was seated, the bailiff moved to the front and said, in a booming voice, "Good morning. Welcome to the State of Rhode Island and Providence Plantations courthouse. Today's case involves the State of Rhode Island and Christopher Neil Scott. If you have a pager, turn it off. If I catch you using one, I will remove you immediately. There is no talking in the courtroom. This is a very high-profile case, and our judge today does not take any of this lightly." His eyes moved over all the green uniforms seated behind the defendant's chair. "He will not tolerate any disruption. Are we clear?"

"Crystal clear," said one of the soldiers. A few other soldiers laughed as the bailiff walked off toward a door in the side of the courtroom, which opened ever so slowly. I had not seen Scott in almost two months, and I was staring intently at the door when they brought him into the courtroom. He was wearing his gray suit, the pant legs tacked up under his knees. I stared intently at him, waiting to make eye contact with my battle buddy. He looked like he was in a fog, like he couldn't believe this was happening. Scott could hide his emotions from others, but I could see he was scared, maybe even embarrassed, for the problems he had caused.

It took a few moments more than I expected for us to make eye contact, but finally, he located me. He stopped rolling his chair, just for an instant, no words, just eye contact, as if nobody else was in the courtroom, just a mutual display of respect and concern. He gave me a simple nod, and I responded awkwardly with our Greedy Club finger-shaking move and mouthed, "Better you than me!"

Scott gave me a pained smile, and for a brief moment he seemed content, almost relaxed, as if he had been transported back to a time when life was so much easier. Then that brief moment was gone, and he continued rolling toward his spot at the defendant's table.

When he got there, he didn't seem to notice at first all the soldiers in Class A green uniforms, there to provide him support that only a soldier would understand.

Scott made eye contact with Top and tilted his head down in what appeared to be shame. Top tapped his chin, motioning for him to pick his head up, then mouthing the words, "Chin up, Soldier," tapping his chin again.

That was when Scott seemed to notice the overwhelming turnout of support from his fellow soldiers. He lowered his head some, and his eyes started tearing up.

Then from the back, a commanding voice said, "Stand tall."

Scott looked around for the source of it and spotted Hankel off to the far left in the front row. It seemed like the exact encouragement

Scott needed in that moment. He nodded his head in affirmation and sat up straight. Yes, he would stand tall, even without legs.

Fishman was seated to the right of Scott's wheelchair, directly in front of me. I looked over to the prosecution table. Behind it, in the first row, sat the family of Jean Cruz: her mom and dad; her brother, José Lima from the Police Academy; José's wife and their daughter, Billie Jean.

I was actually happy to see them, but that happiness was quickly tempered by guilt and remorse as I made direct eye contact with José, and he just shook his head. It was clear there would never again be any friendship between us. Time would never heal these wounds.

Lima turned away as the judge entered the courtroom.

The bailiff boomed, "All rise for the Honorable Judge John J. Rogers."

Everyone in the courtroom rose, with the obvious exception of Scott, who sat up in his wheelchair.

"Welcome to my courtroom," Rogers began. "I'd like to remind you all of the rules the bailiff mentioned earlier today. We will follow those rules to the T, and my hope is that all of you will be allowed to remain in the courtroom today, but most times someone tests these rules and is asked to leave the courtroom and is not allowed to return. Don't let this be you."

He took a moment to scan the documents in front of him through his bifocals.

Scott was staring across the court at Lima and his family, his face stricken. I knew he wanted to say he was sorry, that it was an accident. But he couldn't, and it wouldn't have made it better, even if he could.

The judge put down his documents and cleared his throat. "The court is now in session. Prosecution, present your case."

The prosecutor stood and said, "The State of Rhode Island and Providence Plantations has charged Christopher N. Scott with second-degree murder for the killing of Jean Cruz."

The judge turned to the defense table. "How does your client plead?"

Fishman stood. "Your honor, I am Robert Fishman, attorney for the defendant." Just as he was uttering the words, "My client," Scott turned and met my eyes with a look of resignation and acceptance, and we nodded to each other.

Before Fishman could say another word, the doors to the courtroom loudly swung open. The portly bailiff quickly reached toward his weapon as a young woman rushed into the courtroom, closely followed by two law enforcement officials, who grabbed her by the arms.

The judge slammed the gavel down three times. "Order in the court! Order in the court!" he thundered. "Young lady, I'm not sure what you think you are doing in my courtroom, but you'd best have a good reason for disturbing this trial."

"Yes, your honor, I do." She raised her arm and pointed at Scott. "That man, Mr. Scott, is not the murderer of Jean Cruz."

"*What!*" a woman screeched.

The courtroom erupted in chaos, with everyone talking or gasping or moaning, all utterly shocked.

The judge slammed the gavel again and again, at an even more aggressive rate than before. "Order! Order! I have told you I will not tolerate disorder in my courtroom! Silence, everyone!" As the courtroom subsided, he focused on the mystery woman. "Young lady, how is it that you can be so sure this is the case? There is a process we follow. Why are you just coming forward now?"

"Well, I have this letter, Your Honor. Do you want me to read it?"

"No! Absolutely not!" the judge yelled. Then he motioned to the bailiff, who walked over to her and took the paper, which appeared to be a handwritten letter, and brought it over to the judge.

The judge quickly scanned the letter, then pointed to both attorneys. "You two, and you as well, young lady, into my chambers. This court will have a one-hour recess and resume at 11:30. I suggest you all remain in the area. Bailiff, secure the prisoner."

Fishman, the prosecutor, and the young lady were whisked off to the judge's chambers by another court officer.

Scott turned to look at me, and I said, "What the hell is that?"

He shook his head. "I have no idea. Never saw that lady in my life." Then he was taken away to the other side of the courtroom.

Scott's dad looked confused. His brother asked, "What was on the note?"

"I couldn't see," I said, "but it definitely got the judge's attention. Let's hope whatever the hell it is can help Chris some."

Hankel and Top came over and knelt next to me.

"What the hell was that?" Hankel asked. "Did you see anything?"

I shook my head. "No."

Lisa leaned over and said, "It was some kind of handwritten letter, but I couldn't make out who it was to or who wrote it."

Scott looked back at his dad and brother just before being wheeled out of the room, his face a mask of amazement and disbelief.

Michael came over and said, "I knew it. I knew there was no fucking way Chris could have killed that girl. He's a warrior; he wouldn't have killed some girl."

As the courtroom buzzed with dozens of conversations, Lima's family did not look happy. They were clearly uneasy about things. I made eye contact with Lima, whose face blazed with anger and disgust. I held my hands out, palms up, and shrugged, as if to say, "I don't know what's going on." But Lima just looked away.

His daughter, Billie Jean, however, saw me and gave me a little wave and an awkward smile, which was clearly not approved by her daddy. Her mom, sensing the girl's discomfort, reached over and rubbed Billie Jean's shoulders.

A few minutes later, the bailiff came out and whispered to the Lima family. They exchanged confused glances and then followed him into the judge's chambers.

Several minutes later, an anguished scream rang out from the judge's chambers. Everyone in the courtroom was looking around, alarmed and confused, then they wheeled Scott back in. The bailiff walked in and said, "All rise," and everyone but Scott anxiously got to their feet.

The judge emerged from his chambers, without the Lima family, and seated himself behind the bench. "In consideration of the new evidence, the charge of Murder Two has been dropped." Several people gasped. "Mr. Scott, your attorney will be working out a plea agreement. You are being released on bail of one hundred dollars." He then banged the gavel and said, "This court is adjourned."

As the judge returned to his chambers, the courtroom erupted, mostly with cheers from the soldiers who had come to court to stand by their brother. Hankel and Top seemed to be the happiest of all.

Lisa and I hugged, then I vaulted the railing and hurried over to Scott. "Are you fucking kidding me?"

Fishman quickly explained to all of us what had happened.

The young lady's name was Mary Barnes, and a couple of days earlier, she had found a note written by her old boyfriend almost two years ago. Fishman summarized, but I later got to see the note itself:

My name is Peter Stone. I have decided to end my life because of a horrible mistake I made. On August 4, 1990, I was sleeping at my girlfriend Mary's house, when I woke up in the middle of the night and realized I had left my work keys at my home. Rather than fight the morning traffic, I got up and went home to get my keys. On my way, I noticed my old girlfriend Jean's car sitting all alone in the parking lot, so I turned in to see why her car was there. She was not in the car, so I assumed she must have hooked up with some dude at the club. She broke up with me for no reason and I was still angry about it, so this pissed me off even more. I spotted her sitting at a picnic table playing kissy face with some guy. She sounded drunk and her shirt was open, like she was going to have sex with him. This infuriated me. I grabbed a rock and whacked the guy in the head, then I started choking her. I lost my mind, I'm so sorry I completely lost it. I could not take my hands off of her until I came out of my fit of rage and realized I had killed her. I ran off, back to Mary's, and got back in bed. She had no idea any of this happened. I can never bring Jean back or say or do anything to make up for this horrific mistake. I'm really, really sorry. My only hope is that her family and God can forgive me for what I did, and for being a coward and taking my own life.

It was signed on the bottom, *Peter Stone*.

Barnes said Stone was a violent drunk, and on two different

occasions, he had drunkenly threatened that she would end up like his last girlfriend.

They had broken up a few months ago, and a few days earlier she had finally started cleaning out the dresser drawers he had used at her place and found the note, which had fallen into the back of the dresser, behind the drawers. Initially, she had been so scared of him she wasn't going to say anything, but then she saw on the news that a soldier was being charged with Jean's murder.

Detective Katz had suspected Stone, but he had an alibi, one that Barnes had backed up, not knowing it wasn't true.

Scott and I were both first extremely excited, but then Scott's face turned serious, and mine probably did, too. Jean Cruz was still dead, and nothing was going to change that.

Scott looked over at me and said, "She was wonderful." He gulped, like he was swallowing back tears, overwhelmed by the emotions he had been holding at bay for two years. "Man, I am I so glad I didn't kill her."

Top stood, towering over the other soldiers, and said, "Well, boys, looks like we have a reason to celebrate tonight for sure. First round is on me!"

"No way, Top," I called out. "Scott is buying!"

"Well, we know for sure you're not digging in your damn pockets, alligator arms!" Hankel said.

The entire courtroom laughed at that, including Lisa.

"Okay, how about we head to Lou's Café tonight to celebrate. The food's not too good, but the beer is cheap."

"No, we should head to the VFW," said Scott. "The Dugout."

Scott's dad and his brother came over. His dad had tears in his eyes as he knelt next to Scott, their heads touching as he spoke to him.

After a brief hug from his brother, the group crowded around him, wanting to firm up plans.

We all agreed we'd meet at six p.m.

In the meantime, I suggested Stanley's in Central Falls for lunch. Hankel said the boys would meet us there, after they changed out of their uniforms. Then, one by one, every soldier walked up and shook Scott's hand, then mine.

Hankel stood off in the back, letting each of them give a few words of encouragement to Scott.

Scott's dad and brother Tony stood back with Lisa and Michael, waiting to wheel Scott out of the courtroom.

Hankel came up to Scott and said, "I never doubted you, Scott, and I would never leave you behind. God has given you a second chance. Make the most of it."

This went on for over 30 minutes, with person after person.

Hankel said his goodbyes to Michael and Lisa as well.

After hugging my brother, Scott asked Lisa and me to stand pat, he wanted to talk with us alone. At that exact moment, in the opposite corner, I saw my grandfather in his full Navy white dress uniform. He came over to Scott and Lisa and me and extended his arm to Scott. My grandfather then opened his arms and hugged me, rather firmly I might add. This was a rarity, as he was just not a touchy-feely kind of guy.

Looking back at Scott, he said, "Congratulations. Never underestimate the power of prayer. Do you know how many people were praying for you?"

"No, sir," Scott said. "I mean, Grampa."

Grampa said, "I even went to see my priest on this."

"Thank you, Grampa," Scott and I both said.

Lisa made eye contact with Grampa and simply smiled in affirmation. Grampa then rubbed her belly, shaking his head with a smile. "And here's more good news. I'm happy for the both of you. However, Scott, you can still buy me lunch every couple weeks. I've gotten used to our talks."

As Grampa left the courtroom, Scott said. "Now, I see where you get it. Still working me for a free lunch."

Lisa and I laughed, then Scott, looking uncomfortably emotional, said, "I want you both to know how sorry I am for all that I put you through. I sure would not be here today if you two had not stuck by me." Not wanting to give me credit, he looked up at Lisa and said, "I know he wouldn't be if you weren't by his side."

"It's okay," said Lisa.

His voice quivered as he tried his best not to be overly emotional. "I know this has been horrible for you guys, and I hope one day you can understand that I would have never hurt her."

"Well, I certainly hope not," Lisa said, rubbing her belly. "We're about to name this little guy Scott, so I'm glad you will be around to help him become a great man."

Scott looked stunned. "Wait, you're still naming him after me?"

Lisa leaned in and wrapped him in one of her patented firm hugs, holding on for a few seconds more than most people do. "That never changed," she said, then she turned to leave the courtroom to wait outside the doors for her husband.

I got down on my knees next to Scott, my throat tight and my eyes filling with tears. Neither of us said a word for a few minutes, as both of us started crying hard, overwhelmed with joy knowing this nightmare was over.

Scott regained control first, and said, "Wait, we don't do this, do we?"

I shook my head from side to side. "No, we don't, and I am glad I hate all the mushy shit." (Actually, I don't but I try and deny it.)

His voice raspy and cracking with emotion, Scott said, "I'm going to say this once, and I will never admit it if you ever try and tell anyone." He held up a finger for emphasis. "I can't thank you enough for your unwavering loyalty, support, and friendship."

"Never have to question that."

"I'm not sure I would be here today—heck, I know for a fact I wouldn't—without you in my corner."

"Yeah, I've always known it. Glad you finally admitted it. And for the record, now we're even. I saved your ass twice now, as well."

He laughed. Then his dad, who had walked up behind us, said, "Do you two ever stop?"

We both smiled and at the same time said, "Nope."

I left to give Scott, his brother Tony, and his dad some space for a few private moments together, joining Lisa, Michael, and Hankel in the hallway. Everyone else was already heading out of the building. Then Tony came out of the courtroom, pushing Scott and followed by their dad, and together we all made our way to the elevator.

Just as we arrived, Lima and his family came around a bend in the corridor from the judge's chamber. There could not have been a more uncomfortable chance meeting than of these two families and former friends. Silence consumed everyone. The elevator seemed to take the longest time.

I kept looking over at Lima, hoping to catch his eye, but he never looked at me. The elevator arrived, and I held the door open with my arm and turned to Lima. "I'm sorry that your family is dealing with this. I know she was amazing. I am so sorry for your loss."

Lima did not utter a word or even look over at Scott or me as his family filed into the elevator.

We stayed out in the hallway, and as the elevator door began to close, Scott said, "I am beyond sorry for your loss. I can't tell you how much I cared for her."

Lima kicked his leg out to stop the door from closing. He looked directly at Scott and said, "Nothing that ever comes out of your mouth is worthy of my attention. Please do not talk to me ever, ever in your life. What you did to my sister will never be forgiven, nor forgotten."

All of the joy and excitement from the courtroom was ripped from Scott and me, the mood now the exact opposite of how we had felt moments earlier.

"I'm sorry," said Scott.

"I'm sorry, too," I said, echoing Scott.

As the doors closed again, Lima looked at me and said, "The same goes for you, too!"

Then they were gone.

We all waited in silence, not looking at each other even as the next elevator arrived and we got on, took it down, and stepped out into the lobby.

Halfway across the lobby, Scott stopped wheeling and smiled. I followed his eyes and saw Jake, the driver from the ACI. Scott turned the wheelchair and rolled toward him, saying, "You won't believe this."

Jake cut him off with raised hands. "I know! That's why I came in, to congratulate you."

Jake and I shook hands and said hello again. Scott looked confused until I explained how we had met after Jake dropped him off at the ACI.

Scott shook his head at me. "Still spying on me, huh?"

Scott introduced Jake to Hankel, Lisa, and his father and brother, then said, "Come to the VFW tonight for a drink to celebrate my friends and family, Soldier."

Jake grinned. "Well, I'll be happy to join you, but I'm seven years' sober, so only ginger ale for me."

Scott looked thoughtful for a moment. "Maybe I should stop drinking." To which we all quickly responded, "Hell, yes!"

Scott looked around and said, "Maybe next month. It's time to celebrate now!"

"See you tonight," said Jake.

"Great!" Scott said. "You and Anthony can be the designated drivers!"

Lisa said, "He's always my designated driver," then she put a hand on her belly. "Well, not right now that is."

We all headed off to our vehicles to head to Stanley's for lunch.

CHAPTER 14

FOOD, FRIENDS, AND ALCOHOL

Stanley's on Dexter Street in Central Falls, Rhode Island, was an amazing place to eat that was famous for cheeseburgers. They grilled the burgers with fried onions underneath as they cooked. The grease from the patties dripped onto the onions and gave them a great flavor. I picked that location as it was a favorite of mine growing up, and it was just down the road from my grandparents' home. The restaurant only sat about 50 people, and there were close to that coming from court. When Lisa and I got there with Scott and his family, most of the group was already there, and many had ordered already when they rolled Scott through the door.

Back in the 1950s, when they built Stanley's, there were fewer folks in wheelchairs. I used to come here with my grandfather and didn't remember him having trouble coming in a wheelchair—maybe he wore his prosthesis, I don't remember for sure. These memories crossed through my mind as Scott attempted to get up the ramp and off to the booth just to the right.

Hankel caught my eye and held up a double with cheese and mushrooms. "I see why you like this place! This burger is amazing."

Top, sitting across from Hankel, held up a lobsta roll and said, "This is pretty damn good, too, Anthony."

Scott said, "I need to say something." It was like the old EF Hutton commercial—everyone stopped talking immediately.

"Listen, I have to tell you, from the bottom of my heart, seeing you all in the courtroom was perhaps the most powerful show of support I have ever experienced. I want to thank every one of you who made the trip here to show me the love and support you all did today." His eyes were filling up with tears. "I was touched to the core of my being and will never forget this for the rest of my life. Thank you."

"Okay, okay," I said. "Can we order already? I'm starving!"

The room erupted in laughter.

Scott said, "Okay, everybody, eat up. Anthony is right for once—the food here is amazing. But I need to tell you, even though he asks every time he comes in here, they *do not* give a military discount."

That set everyone laughing again, then even more when Hankel yelled out, "Well, it *must* be amazing if he comes here without getting a military discount."

I stood up and said, "I'm not that cheap!" which caused even more laughter.

"Yeah, right, cuz!" yelled Tony Jones.

I shook my head at Lisa. "Am I really that cheap?"

"Yes, you are, but I love you anyway, Mr. Anthony. Hopefully you can teach our children how to be frugal with money as well."

After most had finished eating, Grampa Walter walked in, still in his dress whites, and the room went quiet, even though most were unaware who he was.

In his loud naval voice, he boomed, "Why the hell are you all so quiet? You worried this sailor is gonna throw you all out the door?"

Huge laughter. I walked over and gave Grampa another hug.

Grampa looked at Scott and said, "I'm going to order mine to go. If I hang around all these Army guys, at some point I'm gonna have to fight one of them."

Jones yelled, "I hope you fight better than your grandson."

Grampa yelled, "Don't let me come there and embarrass you, young man."

"Yes, sir!" yelled Jones.

When the room settled down, I said, "Guys, like Scott said, we were touched to see all of you here today. It means a ton to me, as well. I've been living this nightmare for some time now, and I have always believed the best would come out by doing the right thing. Maybe when I was an E-4, I didn't understand this as much, but I get it now, more than ever. I want to invite you all to the VFW tonight for a pre-party and then to my house tomorrow afternoon for the big celebration."

Lisa looked up at me and said, "What?" She then shook her head. I'd been known to do that kind of thing without consulting her first.

"See everybody at 1800 tonight," I said. "Check with me before you leave for the address for both of these events. And by the way, Captain Clifford is buying tonight, so don't be late."

Clifford gave me that look he used to give me when I was a private, shaking his head and saying, "Anthony, Anthony, Anthony."

Then everyone started telling stories, or everyone but me. For once, instead of running my mouth, I was happy just relishing the moment. And eating, of course.

Lisa leaned close after a while and said, "I'm not sure I've ever seen you so quiet."

"If people can carry the conversation, then there is no need for me to talk," I said. "I'm with my peeps today, so yeah, no need for me to do all the talking."

Eventually, we left Stanley's and headed for home. Now exhausted, I knew I needed a nap before going out again to the VFW. As soon as I got home, I headed to bed, but just as I lay down, the phone rang.

"Hello, Officer Anthony. It's Chief Stripe."

I sat up. "Yes, sir."

"Congratulations on the news today," he said. "Based on all I heard about you two, I did not really think he was this stone-cold killer."

"No sir, neither did I."

"Plan to come in on Monday, so we can start the process of getting you on duty."

"Yes, sir."

Lisa looked on as I hung up the phone, obviously excited. "Well? What did he say?"

"I start on Monday."

We hugged and held each other for a moment, then lay back onto the bed. Her stomach was now poking out higher than mine. I rubbed it for a few minutes, talking softly to her belly, then we both fell asleep.

When we arrived at the VFW just prior to 1800, just behind Scott and his family, the parking lot was already pretty full. You had to drive down a small hill to get to the gravel parking lot in the back of the bar. Lisa had decided to drive separately, as she knew it could be a late night for everybody and, thanks to me, she had to prepare for seventy-five people showing up at her house the next day.

As we approached the entrance, she said, "Philip," using my first name to get my full attention, "don't go overboard tonight. You have a lot to do tomorrow, and you don't have a lot of time to get it all done."

"I got it for sure," I replied quickly, just as my brother Michael pulled into the parking lot.

"Yo, Dragon Balls!" Michael called out. "What's up, fellas?"

Lisa shook her head, now knowing for sure the night was not going to end well.

"Hey, Michael!" Scott called out. "Let's hope tonight ends better than the last time we were here!"—a reference to the night after the Memorial Day parade.

With a halfhearted laugh, Lisa said, "Yeah, it better!"

Scott and I laughed and waited for Michael to park his old yellow Bronco up the hillside in a spot not meant for parking but good enough for him, then we all walked into the club.

"Listen," I said, just before we stepped inside. "Without sounding too corny, the four most important people in my life are right here, and everything is now back in order. Life can't be better."

We stepped into the VFW, and the place had never been packed with so many people. My entire family was there, including my dad, who drank here for years before getting sober several years ago.

Lieutenant Gold was the first to walk over. "Man, I heard the good news today! Could not be happier for you both." He turned to me. "How'd the call with the chief go?"

"He said to just come in Monday and we'd figure things out then."

Hankel came over and thanked Gold for taking care of his boys after the parade. "I'm comfortable handing Anthony off to you, going forward."

Gold said, "Well, I'm not, I don't want that responsibility!"

They both laughed.

Scott saw his dad off to the side and brought him over to meet Top. "Dad, this was my first sergeant when Anthony and I were at Fort Sheridan. Top, my dad served in Vietnam, as well."

Scott's dad's eyes showed recognition. "Oh, yes, I remember you talking about him. Thank you, First Sergeant, for taking care of my son and shaping him into a good soldier."

"You're welcome," said Top. "But he and his buddy were some of the best young soldiers I ever led. A bit crazy with the young ladies, but you could always count on them."

I waved my dad over so we could pose for a photo with our dads and Top. "Dad," I said, "this is my first sergeant when I first went to Chicago. He helped make me a better soldier. Top, my dad served during Vietnam, as well."

My dad said, "Well, I was in the Army, but only as a meat cutter in Georgia, I never went over to Vietnam." He shook Top's hand. "Thank you. My son has always spoken highly of you. I appreciate you getting him squared away. I damn sure couldn't do it when he was a young boy."

They all laughed at my dad's dry sense of humor.

Soldiers were all crowding around Scott and trading war stories about how he saved my ass so many times. Scott said I must be Morris the Cat due to my nine lives.

"Bullshit, Scott," I said. "I had to save yours as well, and count today as another. If I'm Morris the Cat, you're Garfield."

I walked over to the bar with Hankel and Michael. Hankel leaned over and said, "Stanley's was a great place for chow, but I'm hungry again."

My dad was just passing by and said, "You like chicken or beef?"

Hankel said, "Well, I do love me some chicken."

Dad yelled to the bartender, "Hey, Skully! Give him a pickled egg."

"What the hell is that?" said Hankel.

"Just eat it," said Michael. "You may want some salt and pepper on it."

Hankel grinned and said, "Do I look like your damn brother?" The three of us laughed out loud, then Hankel swallowed the whole egg!

"Hey, that was not too bad," Hankel said. "What if I had said beef?"

Dad called out, "Skully, throw him a Slim Jim."

As Hankel graciously accepted the snack, my dad pulled me aside and said, "How are you doing, son?"

"Well, much better than I was twenty-four hours ago," I said. "But Dad, this has been the hardest thing I've ever had to deal with."

"Son, let me tell you, worrying about a friend will never compare to worrying about your child. And for the first time in my life, I was worried about you."

"Wait, you never worried about me prior to this?"

He shook his head slowly. "Not one time. I knew you would always figure things out. But when I heard about this? I know your buddy is a great guy, but a murderer?"

"Crazy, right?"

"Murder is not something that just goes away. Count your blessings, son, and pray you never have to deal with anything like this again. I know I couldn't handle it again. I'll tell you, I was close to going back to the bottle a couple times because of this."

"What? Why didn't you say something?"

"You had enough shit you were dealing with, Son."

"Dad, that's serious. Do you want me to go to a meeting with you?"

"If you came to a meeting, I might start drinking right then and there!"

The group all laughed, but I was not taking what he said lightly. "I know, Dad, this was quite the ride of emotions over the last couple months. I'm so grateful it's finally over."

"I know, Son. Are you good, for real? Don't just say, 'I'm good.'"

"I am, Dad."

Hankel was just behind my dad, and Scott wheeled over to him and, said, very seriously, "So, how do I get back into the Army?"

Hankel didn't miss a beat. "Not a shot, dipshit. We were going to run you out of the Army, but your bad driving did it for us."

The guys roared at that, and I had a little chuckle myself.

"Hey Dad," I said, "how about a game of pool?"

Dad laughed and shook his head. "Nope. You and your brother are forbidden from playing here ever again after taking everyone's money when you would come here from the Boys Club."

"Come on, Dad, we didn't hustle," I said. "We won 'cause all your buddies were always hammered."

He looked around, smiling, but wistful. "I'm going to head out soon. Being in a bar is never good for a recovering alcoholic, especially seeing as how this is where I did most of my drinking."

Dad was never a big hugger, but he did teach me how to shake hands firmly. Every time I shook someone's hand, I remembered my dad's advice. "Look them in the eye when you shake hands. Make sure to say, 'Yes, sir/No, sir.' Even if you're telling someone to go fuck themselves, shake their hand firmly and maintain eye contact."

"I love you, Dad," I said. "Thanks for always supporting me."

It was a poignant moment, one that ended when Gary Grand stood up on the pool table and yelled, "Why is there no country music on this jukebox? We need to drop a few shots here, fellas."

Dad shook his head and left, smiling, as Hankel told Grand, "Don't ruin this place. This is a home for our war veterans, so get your ass off that table."

Grand immediately jumped down.

Hankel decided to make the first toast. "First off, I want to share with you all my appreciation for all you soldiers coming out today to support Scott and Anthony."

Every glass in the house went up high.

"You see, it was to support the both of them, as their names are forever linked. I can't recall ever saying one of their names without the other. As far back as my time in Vietnam, soldiers have always been there to support each other in times of crisis. If there was ever a case to demonstrate standing by your battle buddy, this is it. No matter the situation, you never give up on a soldier, and it goes to show you that standing by your fellow soldier, even during the most difficult times, is the right thing to do. So now, I want you all to raise your glasses. Soldiers and friends, today we celebrate the vindication of one of our family members with his acquittal. Here's to Scott!"

A loud cheer ensued, and then Grand yelled, "One more!"

One more was never one more, so the shots were flying off the shelf.

Lisa looked at me and said, "Okay, Big Boy, you best not go too far. We have lots of people showing up tomorrow to a party we have done zero preparation for, so yeah, I'm leaving."

Michael looked over and said, "Lisa, Hankel and I got this, the barbecue set-up will be taken care of. Just make sure Big Boy buys enough beer and food. And make sure he doesn't just buy whatever shit's on sale."

"I'll get it set up," I said.

Michael shook his head and yelled, "Stay in your lane!"

Lisa gave Michael a hug, then turned to me and said, "Walk me out, please."

I listened, like I did most times when Lisa spoke, and walked her to her car.

"Don't be too late," she said. "You know you can't handle the drinks like your buddies can, especially seeing we have to get the tables set up and coolers and ice and all the food and beer."

"I got this," I said, even though I got the strong sense Lisa did not believe I did. "I love you, Mrs. Anthony. Maybe when I get home, I can wake you up to reward you for all your support."

She laughed. "Yeah, don't bother, Soldier!"

"Love you, too." We got to her car, and I said, "I need to tell you something."

"Make it quick."

"It won't be. I've wanted to tell you for weeks."

"Okay, tell me."

I took her hand and held it. I was a bit nervous and started to rub her wrist until I figured out exactly what I wanted to say. She looked at me with a slight smirk, maybe thinking I was setting up a joke. I touched her right cheek, finally finding my words. "There's a darkness in everyone. Some people fight to escape their darkness. Sometimes, the light for many is too bright, and people choose to stay in the dark. Some people only need a little light to escape the darkness, and many times there is very little light. You are the light for me during my darkness. I knew I could always escape it when you shined your light on me. And it's not just me, you're the light for so many of your friends and your mom and family. I want you to know I needed your light more than ever in my life recently, and for this I am grateful beyond words. I love you."

"Oh, my God," she said, her eyes glistening, "that was beautiful, the nicest thing anyone has ever said to me, Mr. Anthony." She stood on her tiptoes to kiss me and hug me. "Maybe I *will* wake up when you get home." We both laughed, knowing she wouldn't. I hugged her once more and opened her car door.

I watched her drive off, then walked back to the post, where Grand was now standing on a bar stool yelling, "Shot, shot, shot!" then slamming down another tequila shot.

This went on for another hour-plus. Scott was drunk again, as were most of the younger soldiers. But the old warriors, like Top, Patierno, Richter, Jones, Bob Walters, Rob Turner, and Marty Gaughan, they were all pacing themselves and appeared to be under control.

DJ Ross, standing at the jukebox, yelled, "What the hell? There's no damn black music on the box."

I laughed. "Yeah, not that popular in the VFW in Rhode Island."

Ross did find an old song, and said, "Oh, man, could not have a more perfect song."

He looked up, listening and waiting, and a moment later the song "White Horse" by Laid Back started and the whole bar went crazy, everybody flashing back to the days at Fort Sheridan.

Koon and Trainee sandwiched Scott like the old days at the club, and DJ Ross yelled out, "Yeah, baby! Talking about my main men, Anthony and Scott."

The celebration continued almost to midnight, when the VFW closed, but most of the crowd was heading out anyway.

"What a great celebration," Scott said, clearly plastered.

"Looks like I'm driving your ass home again," I said laughing. "You're such a pussy now, you can't even hold your booze."

Scott laughed and said, "Yeah, right. You hardly even drink anymore."

"No, we got him," said Scott's dad.

I was only joking and had forgotten his dad and brother were still there.

As we all headed out of the VFW, the air held a palpable sense of relief. Our misery had finally ended.

"Last time we were here, I thought the world was going to end," Scott said to me. "I'm not sure I can ever repay you for all of this, but know I will always have your back." He snorted. "Too bad I'm not going to be there to save your ass when you're out on patrol in Lincoln, but thank God, nothing ever happens in this little town."

"The next party starts at two tomorrow, so get some sleep," I said. "I'm headed home to see if I can close the deal with Lisa. And I think she might be hard to convince."

We both laughed, then got in our cars. As we drove off, Scott leaned out the window and yelled, "Let's go, Dog Jaw!"

On my way home, I drove past the police station without even thinking about my pending employment. That would wait for another day.

When I got home, I quickly undressed and got into bed. I nudged Lisa, but there was no movement. Probably just as well. I had tons of stuff to do in the morning. Thank God, Hankel and Michael would be there. They could take care of the physical things while I focused on the food, which was, of course, my specialty.

I fell asleep quickly and awoke at nine a.m. to voices in my kitchen.

"Wake your ass up, fuck face!"

Apparently, Michael was already there.

Next, I heard, "Let's go, dick weed! You're burning daylight!" which meant Hankel had also arrived.

I found them both in the kitchen with Lisa making breakfast. She looked over her shoulder and said, "I'll make you breakfast, as well, if you can just keep your mouth shut during the process."

Hankel shook his head. "No way in hell he won't advise you on how to cook. He is not capable of keeping his mouth shut."

Hankel, Michael, and Lisa all laughed. I ended up making my own breakfast, but I did it just the way I liked.

The next few hours were a buzz of activity. Like a well-oiled machine, Hankel and Michael set up the backyard. Lisa gave me a list of things she needed from the market, and after a quick shop, I made a big batch of my baked beans and an even bigger tub of macaroni salad.

At a quarter to two, as I was firing up the grill and lining up the burgers, dogs, and chicken, I felt a warm contentment come over me. Life was good.

Scott was out of danger and relieved of guilt, or at least the worst of it. The love of my life was pregnant with our first child. I would soon embark on the career I had been preparing for my entire life. And my best buddies—including the best buddy I'd ever had—were about to show up at my house to celebrate.

Lisa came outside and said, "You always buy too much food. We end up with so many leftovers."

This was not the first time we'd had this conversation.

"Better to have too much than not have enough," I said, like I always did. But this time, I added, with a smile, "Besides, today we are literally feeding an Army."

CHAPTER 15

At ten minutes to two, Scott was ready to go, waiting for his dad, whom he had asked to drive. He had taken his time getting ready for the party, and didn't want to get there early, but he didn't want to miss a moment of it, either. As he was waiting, Scott noticed a photo—him and the gang back in Iraq. It brought a big smile to his face. Everyone looked so young. It reminded him that he had still had some other photos to pick up at the Kodak hut, from the film discs Hankel had sent him. He had dropped them off to be developed back before he was arrested. He hoped they still had them.

When his dad arrived to pick him up, Scott asked if they could get the pictures on the way.

Dad said, "Of course," but he also looked at his watch.

Scott didn't mind being a few minutes late—it would be worth it to share the photos with the boys before they all headed out of town. It would be a great way to cap off their visit.

They pulled up to the Kodak hut, and Scott explained that he had dropped the photos off months earlier. The clerk found them, four sets, and Scott promptly paid for them, tearing into the first envelope and flipping through the photos as his dad drove off toward

Anthony's house. He was immediately transported back in time—to a time when he had all his limbs, when life was so different. In some, he was driving a regular car.

Dad looked over, glancing at the photos, and at Scott's reaction as he tore into the second envelope. There were pictures of the whole gang—posing, playing soccer, drinking. It was sad, in a way, but happy, as well. His mind flooded with memories and his heart with emotion. Scott could feel himself smiling even as his eyes clouded with tears. It seemed like so long ago, so much had happened since then.

He opened up the third pack and frowned. They were similar to the photos in the first two envelopes, but he wasn't in any of them, and he felt sure he hadn't taken them, either. Somebody else at the base must have.

As they parked in front of Anthony's house, Dad put a hand on Scott's shoulder. "You okay, Son?"

Scott nodded as he stuffed photos back into the third envelope.

"Are you ready for this?" Dad asked.

Scott nodded again, as he tore open the fourth packet of photos. "Yeah, just want to get a look at these before we go in."

Dad nodded. "Okay, Son. I'll get the wheelchair out."

Dad still hadn't quite gotten the hang of the wheelchair, but Scott wanted time to go through the last photos, and besides, it would be good for Dad to get the practice.

As Dad got out, Scott sensed motion outside and looked up, seeing so many of the faces from the photos arriving for the party, parking and getting out, walking up to the house.

He smiled, thinking he might have lost his legs, but he still had his friends. Part of him wanted to get out immediately and join them, get the celebration started, but first, as Dad opened the trunk, Scott slid the photos out of that last pack.

He froze, his blood going cold. *What the hell was this?*

He had no recollection or understanding of what he was looking at. He held up the first photo to get a better look at it—an Iraqi woman with a knife in her chest was slumped against a wall pockmarked with bullet holes, under a broken window. He flicked to the next one, a close-up of the same woman, clearly dead, her glassy eyes staring back at him.

What the fuck?

He was nauseated and confused. His first thought was to toss those fucking photos away, to get them away from him as quickly as he could, forget he had ever seen them. Instead, his heart racing, he flicked to the next one, a picture of Specialist Scalici, his eyes open, but oddly blank. He remembered Scalici, a reservist from the New Jersey area who was an MP dog handler with a different unit. The next photo seemed to be from the same angle, but farther back, showing Scalici's chest drenched in blood. Showing that he was dead.

Scott had learned while in the hospital that Scalici had died a few weeks after his roadside event. But why was Scalici, an MP dog handler, entangled in these horrifying images? And what the hell was this photo doing on his camera? *Who the fuck killed these people? And why?*

As he stared at the photos, feeling dizzy and sick, he heard his name and looked up to see all of his friends gathered on the lawn—Anthony, Hankel, Jones, Brother Mike, Grand, Burford, Walters, Richter, Clifford, Gold, Houlihan, Trainee, even Top Kreiger, with other Rhode Island friends quickly arriving. All calling out to him, waving, telling him to come join the party.

He swallowed, then looked down quickly, wanting to get through the rest of the photos, hoping to find some logical explanation for all of this. But the last photo may have been the worst of all. Scalici's dog Peete, a beagle mix, his loyal companion, lying on his side, dead—impaled by the same knife that had taken the Iraqi woman's life. *What the hell is happening here? Who the hell stabs a dog?*

Scott's hands trembled as he gazed at the grisly photographs, his world unraveling, along with the fragile semblance of normalcy he had clung to since his court hearing the day before.

The images were a grotesque fusion of past and present, turning the camaraderie of his military service into a nightmarish riddle.

The cheerful laughter and familiar voices from outside felt like taunting echoes from another lifetime, as happiness and normalcy slipped through his grasp.

Dad grunted and cursed as he wrestled with the wheelchair. The calls from outside grew louder, more insistent, his friends beckoning him to join the celebration. But the joyous sounds only served as a stark contrast to the nightmare playing out in the photographs.

Scott sat in the vehicle, struggling to make sense of this unfolding horror. He would need time to come to terms with the sinister mystery that had emerged, to grapple with the potential darkness within his own military family, and to determine how to balance the loyalty he felt for his friends with the duty to seek the truth.

Memories and hopes, what-ifs and what's happening—a thousand thoughts raced through Scott's mind as he tried to understand, to fully grasp what he was looking at. But the pieces refused to fit together.

Something made him go back to the photo of the dead woman, and he now noticed a face reflected in one of the shards of glass in the broken window. Then everything clicked together, even as Scott's life shattered into a million pieces.

He knew that face; he knew it well. And when he looked up from the photo, when he looked outside, he saw it in real life—smiling and laughing with the rest of his friends, calling to Scott to join them.

It was a face he loved, but Scott knew there could only be one explanation. It was the face of a murderer.

ACKNOWLEDGMENTS

Although my main focus in this book is the unwavering friendships I have made in the Army, I also need to express my gratitude to those who prepared me for that journey, my friends and family, who supported me over the years during my most difficult times. Writing this book gave me insights and reflections on the joyous life I live and the challenges many in uniform face.

I will start by saying thank you to the ones who helped me from the beginning. To my Mother Sandra and Grandmother Phyliss, who were the first role models I had in life, teaching me how to interact with people and inspiring me to be the best version of me. To my grandfather who instilled the military spirit and to live your life without accepting your limitations. I attempted to show that he was a man of character and did not let losing his leg slow him down. To my brothers and sisters—Kevin, Mary Ann, Michael, Linda, Karen, Molly, and Kathy—we have had quite the life, given our start. I hope you find the book funny and know we can still laugh at the stupid things we—well, mostly me and Michael—have done over the years. The next book should be our childhood, holy shit that rival the TV show Shameless. Other inspirational people during my youth were Barbara and Joe Yankee and my amazing baseball coach Charlie Darling. Charlie showed me that hard work and preparation will lead to success on the ballfields. I am reminded of a Winston Churchill quote: "The battlefields in Europe were won on the ballfields in America." To my dad, a.k.a. stepdad to others, John Gariepy. He took a family with 8 kids that were almost all fathered by someone else but if you asked him, he'd a just said, "that we were all his!" To Mr. Dickie Barr who stopped my high school from tossing, you changed my life. To Ray Killduff from CCRI, thanks for telling me I was wasting your time in college and to get my shit together.

After joining the Army in 1983, I had amazing friends and mentors in uniform. My best friend was my battle buddy Chris S. Nolan, known in this book as Chris Scott. The funny stories are all true, but the dying confession was not. We are a lot older now and a lot heavier—unfortunately me more than him—but just as stupid. Thank you, Chris, AKA Scott for making me laugh more than any other uniformed friend. You are clearly disturbed my friend don't ever grow up.

As far as mentors go, the most notable had to be my first—Sergeant Carl Krieger, while stationed at Fort Sheridan, Ill. He pushed me to think about the Army as a career, something I never bought into until I retired after 22 years. His favorite quote was, "You never know, you might want to make the Army a career." TO my Drill Sergeants SSG Scott aka SSG Scruggs in this book you worked me hard I almost gave up, thank you. The three LTs in my career who were all prior service that pushed me to become an officer Roger Radcliff, Alan Mahan and Bob Alexander, thank you. Although it would be hard to list all of military, here is a snapshot of some military friends: John Custer, Mike Flynn, Tony Jones, John Richter, Gary Grant, Rob Burford, John Ewbank, Bob Wall, Phil Gould, Dave Hankel, Bill

PHILIP OAKLEY

Leitsch, Roberto Villahermosa, , John Janiszewski, Gus Taveras, Jimi Holt, Andy Kalamaras, Lance Swankee, Roberto Villahermosa, Brian Feser, Steve Houlihan, Mike Patierno, Roger Radcliff, Tami Koon, Ann Trainee, Kathy Allen Korus, Laura and Nestor Rodriguez, Suzy and Courtney Vares-Lum, Mark Ulitowski, Brian Lesieur, Terrance O'Sullivan, James Peeples, John Ray, George Peters, Stephen and Kim Mercer, Dan Miller, Greg Meyers, Lance Swanke, Linda Dunn, Chris Sorrell, Karen Keith, Annie Redmond, Philip Parrott, Michael Hankel, Ken Rivers, DJ Ross, Mike Greenwood, Laura Leins, Bill Fillman, Allie Hollister, Colin Agee, Philip Powell, Charles Rucker, Jerry DeMoney, Bob Noonan, Freddie Bryant, Shane Coker, and LTG Ray Palumbo.

To friends who helped add content to the book who include but not limited to Christopher Nolan, Dave Hankel, Bob Wall, Phil Gould, Erik Katz, Kimberly & Steven Mercer, Gary Grant, Bill Lietsch, Philip Parrott, and Veronika Knoll. And a special thanks to my friend LTG (R) Ray Palumbo, who wrote the foreword for this book.

I also want to thank my lifelong friends in Rhode Island: Joe Yankee Jr, Rob Turner, Tom Lisi, Paul Zienowicz, Bob Wall, Dave Long and Marty Gaughan. To the girls I call my other sisters, Cheryl Lisi and Cara Fuscellaro, thank you for forcing me to talk on the phone all night with you both routinely and your unwavering love and friendship.

My children Alyssa, Matthew and Caroline have lived a crazy life filled with extreme highs and terrible lows. The lows have made you stronger and you are my legacy—don't screw it up! I hope you can appreciate the joys in life. Now, after hearing these army stories all your lives, I am forcing you to read them, too. But there are some in the book that you have not heard, I promise. Chase your dreams and never let anyone tell you, "You can't." I know I can be hard on you, but I always want the best for all of you in life. Enjoy it to the fullest. One day you will be 60 reflecting on your mistakes as a parent. I love you all.

To my wife, my last one that is, Lisa. She is the Lisa in the book. Thank you for taking a leap and changing your life to be with me. These last thirteen years have been fast-paced and crazy, with so many laughs. We have seen the world and you have showed me things in people I once would have missed. You are the smartest woman I have ever been with, but not smart enough to tell me no. You have made the best version of me that is possible. Your compassion for others has no peer, your wit keeps me laughing all the time. Everyone says you never forget your first love. Well, you are my last love. I look forward to our 60s, 70s, 80s, and 90s, unless you take me out before then. With all my love and appreciation for your unwavering love, thank you. You make me better every day. I love you.

Command Photo CPT Oakley

Military Police Motto

Old Photo From Fort McClelland

World War II Barracks like the ones at Fort Sheridan

Meals the food was delivered in the field AKA Mermite Cans

K Car MPs Drove in 80s

Gas Chamber Fort McClelland

Major Oakley Retirement Photo

SSG Phil Anthony

Drill Sergeant Borrell

Phil Anthony, Rob Woliver and Christopher Scott

Basic Training

Boys Club days that shaped Phil (Second row far right)

On Post Bar for Trainee's called the Pistol Palace

Trooper Bob Wall　　　　*Front Gate Fort McClelland*

Private Christopher Scott

PFC Phil Anthony

Christopher Scott and Phil Anthony

Some of the 3rd Heard Fort McClelland

MP Color Guard Duties Fort Sheridan Phil Anthony

Delta 10 Demons Logo

Patrolman Christopher, Fairbanks Police Department

Military Police School Headquarters

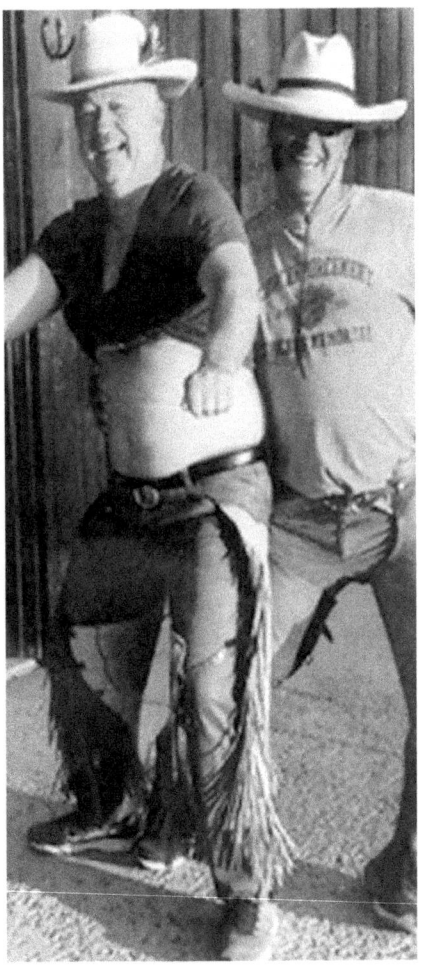

Retired Life for Anthony and Scott

Delta 10 Photo Fort McClelland

CSM Robert Wall

CSM Karl Kreiger

Tony Jones in military police uniform (basic training)

John Richter in military police uniform (basic training)

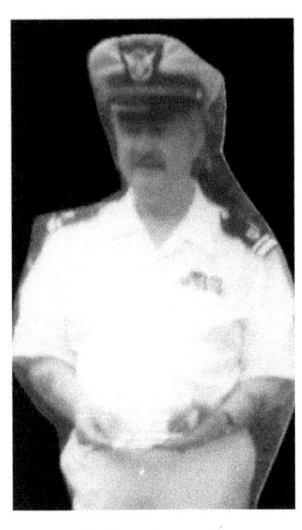

Walter B. Oakley    Anthony Jones    Phil Gould

Entrance to Fort Bragg

Cattle Car Transport Vehicle    Eric Katz

Drill sergeant Leach

Sergeant First Class Hankle

John Ricther and Tony Jones

Lisa and Phil at a country concert "save a horse ride a cowboy"

Lisa and Phils Wedding Surprise visit from Elvis

Milton Keynes UK
Ingram Content Group UK Ltd.
UKHW021103040724
444896UK00002B/28